SILENT FACES

C000240681

Kathy Shuker was born in
working as a physiotherapist, she studied design and went on to
work as a freelance artist in oils and watercolours. Now writing
full-time, she lives in Devon with her husband.
Silent Faces, Painted Ghosts is her second novel.

To find out more about Kathy and her other novels, please visit:

www.kathyshuker.co.uk

Also by Kathy Shuker

Deep Water, Thin Ice

SILENT FACES, PAINTED GHOSTS

Kathy Shuker

Published by Shuker Publishing

Copyright © Kathy Shuker 2014

All enquiries to kathyshuker@kathyshuker.co.uk

ISBN: 978-0-9928327-5-9

In memory of Pete
~ who loved Provence

Prologue

Le Chant du Mistral, Provence, 1976

She paused half way along the landing, pressed her hand to the wall to steady herself, and took a couple of long, slow breaths. The air had been heavy all day, the stones of the house and pathways dazzling in the unrelenting sunshine, a haze hovering just above ground level. Even now, with darkness long fallen, the old farmhouse was sticky and oppressive: too hot; airless. The nausea faded and she eased silently forward again, opened a door and slipped through.

The shutters were still closed and it was too dark to see. Switching on the small table lamp by the side of her bed, she blinked at the sudden light. The sickness built again and her skin prickled with sweat. It was hard to know which emotion was making her feel so bad: anger, guilt, grief and fear were all twisting and churning the acid in her stomach. This had once been a house of light but now it was a place of shadow; it was tainted and so was she. But she had done what she needed to do; let that be an end to it. There was nothing left for her here. Nothing.

She crossed to the washbasin, drank a little cold water then splashed some over her face and patted it dry with a towel, wincing as she caught the cut under her left eye. In the mirror the damage was obvious: her cheek was swollen and puffy, her eye socket stained dusky purple and blue.

A few minutes later she let herself out of the front door. The sky had now clouded over though, if anything, the atmosphere was more humid than ever. The tiny beam of her torch barely cut a trace before her but she would have known the way blindfold and she turned left to skirt round the east wing of the house.

A flash of lightning split the sky, followed by a slow rumble of thunder which echoed back off the pine trees behind then rolled down and along the valley. Someone called her name and she looked round in alarm as the tall figure of a man appeared at the edge of the terrace, illuminated suddenly by another flash of lightning. Fear had her rooted to the spot and she felt rather than saw him moving towards her as more thunder crashed overhead. Why was he not in bed and asleep like everyone else, safely shut away? The first sluicing drops of rain began to pelt the earth and hammered on the stones around her. Feeling her hair flatten and the cold water quickly soak through it and stream down her face, she began to run, away towards the woods, and kept running, not daring to stop to see if she was being followed.

Chapter 1

The letter was waiting in the post box for her when she got home from work. Terri saw the unfamiliar stamp and the almost illegible postmark but barely registered them, holding it in her mouth as she climbed the stairs to the first floor, fumbling for the key in her bag. She was distracted, her thoughts too full of Oliver. He'd been waiting across the street again, standing half-hidden behind the buddleia which arched over the pavement from the garden opposite. It was more than two months since she'd finished with him and still he was stalking her. Sometimes he followed her from work; more usually he was waiting here outside her flat, watching, jealously checking to see that she was alone. Occasionally he didn't turn up till later in the evening, a still, menacing presence. He rarely spoke; it was a war of attrition.

It was nearly seven o'clock on a dull Friday in March. Rain had threatened all afternoon and it had recently started to drizzle. The streetlights were on, casting a queasy orange glow through the windows. There was the distant pervasive throb of traffic from the London streets and the occasional blare of a car horn. Terri drew the curtains across and banged the lights on, claiming her space, dispelling the gloom. She walked into the kitchenette, filled the kettle and put it to boil, kicked her

3

shoes off and picked them up to take into the bedroom. Only then did she remember the letter, abandoned on the cupboard by the door. She dropped the shoes and picked it up, running a finger quickly under the flap, ripping it open. It contained a single printed sheet:

Dear Ms Challoner,

Following your recent enquiry I am prepared to offer you the post of curator for my Retrospective, a six-month appointment commencing April 4th. The advertised salary includes accommodation. I reserve the right to give two weeks' notice if you prove unsuitable. I will expect you to arrive the preceding Saturday, 2nd April.

Yours,

Peter Stedding.

The letter had been dated four days previously with an address at the top and two phone numbers at the bottom, one labelled 'office', the other 'home'. The signature was hand-written, a bold flourish of slanting letters and loops. Terri stared at it, automatically turned the sheet over to check there was nothing on the back, then reread it, frowning.

She had seen Peter Stedding's advertisement for a curator at Ferfylde's, the commercial gallery where she worked, where an A4 sheet of paper had been pinned on the noticeboard with the bare details of the post and a request for email enquiries accompanied by a CV. It had been a source of much amusement among the staff at the gallery. Peter Stedding was a famous artist and portraitist but he was also notorious for his short temper and petulant behaviour and had long since fallen foul of the art establishment. It was generally considered to be the job from hell. Even so, in a moment's desperation and without telling anyone at the gallery, Terri had sent off her CV, not expecting to hear any more about it. And now this letter had come with its arrogant phrasing and casual assumption that she would take the job.

The kettle boiled and she dropped the letter, made a mug of tea and went to shower and change. By the time she left the flat an hour later, heading up the road to meet up with her friend Sophie, Oliver had gone. She kept looking for him but he was nowhere to be seen and she tried to put him out of her mind.

Sophie, always talkative, had a new man in her life and all evening she glowed with the pent-up anticipation and excitement of a fresh romance. Her entire conversation revolved around Stuart: how much they had in common; how easy he was to be with and how they shared the same sense of humour. Terri was happy for her friend but cynically hoped that Stuart might live up to at least half of Sophie's expectations. In her experience, men rarely did.

Sophie didn't stop talking until they'd finished eating and sat cradling drinks. Taking a mouthful of white wine, she stared across at Terri as if noticing her properly for the first time.

'You're quiet,' she remarked accusingly.

'Couldn't get a word in.' Terri ran a finger through the condensation on her glass of soda.

'Yeah, I know. I've been talking too much.' Frowning, Sophie studied Terri's face. 'Still...what's up?'

'Nothing.'

'Oh come on Terri. Don't do that inscrutable thing with me. I've known you too long.'

Terri shrugged. 'I've got something on my mind. A decision.'

'Sounds intriguing.'

'Not really. You remember that job I told you about?'

'The one in Provence?'

'He's offered it to me.'

'But that's good isn't it? Why do you look as though you've lost a winning lottery ticket? I thought you were bored stiff at Ferfylde's, sick of selling 'drawing room art'? And this guy paints portraits, right?'

'Yes, brilliant portraits: very traditional and yet oddly modern too. But he'll be really difficult to work with.'

'You can't be serious. You can stand up for yourself. And with a summer in Provence thrown in? You'd be daft not to take it.' Sophie hesitated. 'Anyway it'd be a fresh start, wouldn't it, now you've finished with Oliver? And with your father, you know…' Her voice tailed off awkwardly.

Terri's mobile chirruped. She pulled it out of her bag, glanced at the screen and quickly dropped it back.

Sophie grinned, glancing towards the phone. 'Unless you've got a new bloke you're not telling me about.'

Back at the flat Terri reluctantly read Oliver's text: *Why r u ignoring me?* He sent her several messages a day, often repeats: *I need u* or *Theres someone else isnt there?* or *I wont let u leave me*. He didn't actually do anything but she couldn't escape him either. And his past violence was imprinted on her memory - she imagined it always would be - though she hadn't told anyone about it, not even Sophie. Humiliated and insidiously brainwashed by Oliver's insistence that it was all her own fault, she'd been left with a niggling, corrosive sense of guilt. She couldn't talk about it any more than she could admit to how much his stalking frightened her – she who always gave the impression of being so confident, so much in control.

She picked up the job offer again. Her contract at Ferfylde's was nearly finished and, though she'd been offered an extension, she had no desire to stay. Ironically twelve months previously she had turned down the offer of a job in Paris to work at the gallery and be near Oliver in London. On the scale of bad decisions that must rate as fifteen out of ten.

Chewing her lip, she read the letter through once more, unsure what to do. She couldn't afford to make another mistake or her professional life was going to go nowhere fast. Even with all the cutbacks, she might find something else if she stayed in London. But this post was only for six months and Peter Stedding, whatever his reputation, was a brilliant artist. If she could set up a good exhibition for him, it might restart her stagnating career. She frowned, staring at Peter Stedding's flamboyant signature. It struck her as odd that the self-styled 'grand master' of portraiture had offered her the job with no interview and without taking up her references. He could barely have had time to read her CV before sending the letter. And working for him directly rather than the gallery - well, it wasn't the usual way.

She threw the paper down and went to bed.

Still lying awake an hour later, her thoughts twisting in circles, she heard the phone start to ring in the sitting room. The luminous numbers on her bedside clock read 00:40. Oliver had done this countless times, waiting till she was in bed and the lights out before ringing her home line. She got up without putting the light on, walked through to the living room and stared at the phone still trilling in its socket on the wall. She didn't dare answer it. She had done that before, had tried to tell him to stop harassing her - had finally lost all control the one time and ended up screaming at him to leave her alone - but he never spoke; there was just a heavy silence. Besides, she had come to realise that even her negative responses only encouraged him. She lived in dread that the day would inevitably come when he would turn up at her door.

She crossed to the window and eased the curtain away a fraction, looking out across the road, feeling the familiar heavy beat of her heart in her chest. Not visible, still he was out there somewhere. Becoming aware that her hand was shaking on the curtain she pulled it away and clenched it into a ball, trying to control it, cross with herself for her weakness. She never used to be like this; she had allowed Oliver to get inside her head and destroy all rational thought. She turned away and, in the dim glow of orange light, saw the abandoned job offer tossed aside on the cupboard top.

It was a chance to get away and to get her life back on track. She would take it.

*

Le Chant du Mistral, Provence

Angela Stedding watched her husband struggle to cut the piece of beef with his fork but said nothing. If she offered to help, he'd tell her she was fussing. If she'd made a meal which he would have found easier to manage, he'd ask why she was giving him baby food. It was lunchtime on the first Saturday in April. Corinne, the *bonne*, cooked Peter's lunches in the week; Angela usually did it at weekends. It had seemed like a romantic thing to do when she had first started the routine all those years ago but now it was a tedious chore, a habit which seemed to bring neither of them any real pleasure. Would Peter care if she stopped doing it? She doubted it. He appeared to like Corinne for some reason – or at least he tolerated her - and the French woman would surely agree to take on the task; she regularly worked extra hours to earn a little more money.

Angela continued to eat her salad, ignoring her husband's grunts of exertion. He'd get frustrated eventually no doubt and lose his temper. For a little over four weeks now he'd had his left arm in plaster from his elbow to his knuckles, the result of a fall. Though the fingers and thumb were free, he was unable to use the hand in any practical way and was obliged to eat all his meals with either a fork or a spoon. Given his advancing years, there was something faintly admirable about his fierce independence, his determination not to let the accident slow him up, and he had complained little about the pain he must have felt, just the inconvenience. But it certainly hadn't improved his temper. Fortunately he generally reserved the worst of it for the studio.

'Oh, for God's sake. Damn and blast this bloody hand.' His patience finally snapping, Peter dropped the fork with a clatter onto the plate and swore again, more colourfully this time. 'I'll starve if I have to go on like this.'

'Peter, please.'

'What? Oh, mm. Sorry.' Tight-lipped, glaring at the plaster on his wrist, he appeared not remotely repentant.

'About this girl you've invited to stay with us.'

'Who? Oh her. What about her?' He picked up the salt cellar, sprinkled more salt over the remaining potatoes on his plate, grabbed the fork again and returned to fumbling about with his food.

'You didn't give me much warning,' she complained.

'Only just decided really. I nearly called it off. Then I thought I might as well take a look at her, see if she might be of any use.'

9

Angela ate another mouthful of food then laid her knife and fork down on the plate, pushing it away. She dabbed the corners of her mouth on her napkin, folded it and put it on the table. There was the distant ringing of the house phone. She wondered where she'd left it, thought of getting up to go and look but then the ringing stopped and she assumed her daughter had answered it.

'So who is she exactly?' she pressed.

'The curator? I've told you already: Terri Challoner. Odd name. Short for Theresa I suppose.'

Angela tutted impatiently. 'I know her name, Peter, but…' She shrugged. '…I don't know…how old is she?'

'Mid-thirties.' He forked the last piece of meat into his mouth, chewed and swallowed.

'And…?'

He puffed out his lips in that offhand French way she so disliked. 'She's got a good CV. Involved in some decent exhibitions. Specialises in portraiture mainly but she's done other work too, I believe, ranging…'

'Peter, please don't tell me her résumé. You know it means nothing to me. Is she English? Or perhaps American?' Angela had a soft spot for people from the States. If the girl was American it might make her more appealing.

'English I think.' He finished eating, put the fork down and pushed the plate away. 'Yes, English.'

'Do you want dessert? Tea then? No?' She sighed. Even after all this time, she couldn't get used to him drinking water with his meals. Another of his French habits. 'We're going to have this woman in the house for six months; I'd like to know something about her. You're usually so protective of your privacy, I'm surprised you've done this.'

He frowned at her as if that issue had not previously crossed his mind. She wondered if he was going senile; his sister certainly was and she was six years younger.

'She's here to do a job, Angela,' he said. 'That's all. Don't make a fuss about her. Anyway, you're putting her in the annexe aren't you?'

'Yes, but it's very small and it's still attached to the house. We can't expect her to stay in her room for six months like a monk or something.'

'A nun more like.' Peter unexpectedly grinned which suddenly made him look much younger. It occurred to her that he was still remarkably handsome in a craggy sort of way, a thought which obscurely made her more irritated.

'Well she can't do all her cooking with a microwave. I'm going to have to let her use the kitchen sometimes.'

'Are you? Well...' He waved a dismissive right hand. '...as you wish, my dear.'

As *I* wish, thought Angela. Hardly. She toyed with suggesting that Terri could eat with him each lunch-time but knew that would go down badly. In any case it seemed rather strange to have a member of staff regularly installed at the family table. She fixed him with a wary gaze.

'I'm still not sure it was wise to offer her accommodation.'

He hesitated, frowning, and began to look rattled as if the full implication of his decision had only just sunk in. 'I did think it through, Angela,' he said, irascibly. 'She'd be more likely to talk if she stayed in the village and you know I won't have that. It'll be easier to keep an eye on her here, you know, control her. Anyway, as I said: she's come to do a job. End of story.' He stabbed at the table with an emphatic index finger. 'Just make it clear to her where she can go and where she can't.

11

I'll leave that to you.' His tone softened; he almost smiled. 'The house is your domain after all, dear: your rules.'

That's only partly true, thought Angela, though she suspected that in the unfathomable workings of Peter's mind he might genuinely believe it. But Peter had his own rules, rules which were never even voiced, they just existed, as if they were part of the very fabric of the house and the air which they breathed.

'She's going to be late,' said a husky voice behind her.

Angela turned quickly in her chair. A white-haired woman wearing blue dungarees had appeared silently at the kitchen door. She was standing flicking an artist's brush back and forth across the gnarled index finger of her left hand. Her frizzy hair fell to shoulder length and a splodge of red paint was smeared across her left cheek.

'What *are* you talking about, Celia?' Angela demanded.

'Terri is going to be late. There's some problem with her flight.'

'How do you know?'

Celia wandered across to the island separating the long pine table from the kitchen proper and took an apple from the bowl of fruit. She bore a striking resemblance to her brother: tall and rangy with the same icy, pale blue-grey eyes. She could also be similarly evasive and irritating. Now she was polishing the apple on her less than clean dungarees. Angela's lip curled in disgust.

'She's just rung from Gatwick,' Celia replied, after closely examining the apple. 'She's not sure what time she'll arrive. Sometime this evening probably.'

'You answered the phone?'

'Someone had to.'

'I thought Lindsey had.'

12

'She's just left for work.'

'Oh? She didn't come to say goodbye.'

'Well she's a big girl now,' said Celia, and bit into the apple.

Angela's eyes narrowed and she glanced towards Peter who was staring out of the window as if the conversation were not taking place. 'I've asked you before not to answer the phone in the house,' she snapped at Celia. 'What did you say to her?'

Peter glanced shiftily between the two women, pushed his chair back and eased himself to his feet. 'I'm just going to rest for a few minutes,' he said, heading past Celia towards the door and pausing briefly as if he'd just remembered something. 'I've got something particular I need to finish Angela. I'll be working late tonight.'

Celia watched her brother out of the room and turned back towards Angela who was now on her feet, facing her. 'I wished her *bon voyage*, of course,' said Celia. She smiled blandly, took another bite of the apple and strolled out of the room.

Angela sighed, looked heavenwards and cleared the table. She had made plans for the evening and now she would have to shelve them to sort out this Challoner woman. So Peter would be working late. That was no surprise; he always was. No doubt he was now upstairs, stretched out on the bed for his routine siesta.

She loaded the dishes into the dishwasher, straightened up and leaned against the kitchen unit, her thoughts returning to Terri Challoner. Exactly what position was this woman going to have in their household for the next six months? Angela felt a growing unease. It wasn't that it was unusual for Peter not to tell her things, far from it – he was a secretive man - but still there was something odd about this whole situation.

13

Out of the window to the front she saw Celia pushing that ridiculous pram across the terrace, the apple now apparently finished. She'd probably thrown the core into one of the huge flower pots and Sammy would complain.

*

Night had long since fallen by the time Terri drove up the last winding track, shuttered on either side by the dark trunks of pine trees, drew the unfamiliar hire car into a gritty parking area and turned off the engine. She relaxed back in the seat and stretched her neck. It had been a tedious journey from Marseille airport. Peter Stedding's estate lay in an obscure spot, a little outside the village of Ste. Marguerite des Pins in the foothills of the Luberon mountains. Twice she had lost her way. The directions Peter's secretary had given her over the phone had been brief and of limited help.

She peered out into the darkness. A security light had triggered high up on the corner of the wall above a run of garages to her left. Ahead of her the scrubby ground rose steeply from behind a low retaining wall and to her right she could see a curving run of steps rise between bushes. The house was out of sight. It was called Le Chant du Mistral: The Song of the Wind. Just at the moment it sounded more romantic than it looked. She exhaled a slow, nerve-quelling breath, got out into the squally rain and walked round to open the boot. The sound of a footstep on gravel made her look round sharply. A man had materialised at her shoulder.

'*B'soir M'dame*,' he muttered in a low voice. He was olive-skinned and towered above her, lank and wiry, a neat, grizzled moustache on his upper lip and a large, thick cap pulled forward on his head. '*M'dame* Challoner?'

14

'Yes. *Oui*?' She hesitated; her French was rusty. '*Je…*'

But the man had gone. He'd pulled her suitcase out of the boot and was walking away with it. She grabbed the rest of her belongings and hurried after him up steps and along a path to a house which rose, dark and imposing against the blacker outline of the woods behind. There was a square of light in a window to her right, another somewhere upstairs then a lamp clicked on above the front door as they approached. Her mute companion opened the door and walked straight in, dropped her suitcase on the floor, touched a bony finger to his cap and walked out again, closing the door silently behind him.

Terri glanced round. She stood in a deep dark hallway with a terracotta tiled floor and a sweeping staircase to the left and rear. To her immediate left was a closed door. To her right an open door spilt a broad wedge of light across the floor. In the well of the staircase, its curved form picked out by the dim glow of a lamp from the upstairs landing, stood a life-size bronze of a kneeling naked woman, turning sideways and reaching out one suppliant hand. In the half-light it was an eerie, disconcerting piece.

'Hello-o?' she called out.

The house was still; no-one appeared. Terri dumped her flight bag and walked cautiously through the door to her right.

'Hello?' she said again.

Now she was in a cosy sitting room where three sofas circled a glass coffee table before a marble fireplace. Two large table lamps suffused the room with warm yellowy light. A handful of pictures hung on the walls and there were two bookcases filled with a mixture of old books. A sleek television and a DVD player stood in the corner of the room. There was no sign of life. Terri glanced curiously along the bookshelves. The titles were a mixture of French and English,

15

a few hardbacks but mostly yellowed paperbacks of varying ages.

Spotting a full length portrait hanging at the rear of the room, she forgot the books and moved towards it, instantly magnetised. A young, dark-haired woman stood in an olive grove. She had a clear, straight gaze, a teasing smile and wore a red check, halter-necked dress, fifties-style, her long hair tied back in a ponytail. It was an arresting image - a modern 'Mona Lisa' - and had been signed simply: P S. Of course: Peter Stedding always signed his work that way. Terri stood, open-mouthed.

'You must be Terri,' said a fluting voice behind her.

Terri perceptibly jumped and turned.

The woman standing in the doorway had strawberry-blonde hair and a slim, shapely figure. She was lightly made-up and wrapped in a shiny satin peignoir.

'I thought I heard a noise.' She came forward, smiling. 'I'm so sorry to have kept you waiting.'

'It's fine - I've only been here a minute.'

'I told Sammy to let me know when you'd arrived.'

'Was that the man who brought me in? He didn't say and he's just left.'

'Well, he's a man of few words and rather impatient, I'm afraid. He's Algerian. Does the gardening. He lives above the garages and when a car arrives a bell rings in his apartment.' The smile broadened and she offered a soft hand. 'I'm Angela, Peter's wife. It's a relief to see you here. I was starting to get worried, darling, imagining all sorts of horrors.' Two striking green eyes were fixed on Terri's face with a look of mild reproach.

'I'm sorry I'm late. The plane was delayed for hours and I'm afraid I drove rather slowly – I'm not used to driving on the right.'

Terri struggled not to stare. Angela was not what she had expected: Peter was seventy-seven; Angela could be little more than fifty. And the woman with the gravelly voice she had spoken to on the phone had sounded much older. Terri had assumed she was Mrs Stedding.

'I believe you rang and spoke to Celia earlier,' said Angela, as if reading her thoughts. 'She's Peter's sister. I hope she didn't say anything to trouble you?' She raised neat arched brows.

Terri remembered Celia's voice clearly, speaking in an overly familiar way: *Do you know anything about the family? No? Are you sure? Well maybe it's just as well.* It had been a strange conversation but this didn't feel like the right moment to say so.

'No,' she replied now to Angela's enquiring expression. 'Why do you ask?'

'Oh, sometimes she says odd things which can be unnerving if you don't know her. She lives in the old pigeon house and doesn't come into the main house very often.' Angela's tone suggested this was a good thing. 'But you're wet darling. Is it raining? Let's get your bags and take you to your room so you can get settled in.'

Carrying the flight bag from the hall, Angela led the way across the sitting room to the facing door, took a left along a dimly lit corridor, navigated another door and another passage, and then she was in a doorway, flicking a light switch on.

''Van Gogh'. This is your room.'

Terri paused, looking at the hand-painted nameplate on the door. Around the artist's name was a tiny pastiche of an olive orchard, cleverly cribbed from one of his paintings. Given the reputation of the man who owned the house, it seemed a surprising touch of whimsy. She followed Angela in and dragged the suitcase to a halt. To her immediate left was a bedroom and bathroom. Beyond was a tiny living room with an armchair and television and patio doors to the side. Against the back wall stood a cupboard with a kettle and the smallest microwave oven Terri had ever seen.

'The keys are in the doors,' said Angela. 'The second one on the main ring opens the back door.' She glanced round critically. 'I did ask Corinne to freshen it up. She's our *bonne*. You'll see her on Monday. I hope you've got everything you need. There's tea and coffee…and whitener I think.' She waved an elegant hand vaguely towards the cupboard and turned back to Terri with a warm smile. 'Do let me know if you're short of anything. Did you want something to eat?'

'No, I'm fine, thanks. But perhaps your husband was expecting to see me this evening…?'

Terri left the question hanging and Angela hesitated, then smiled a little too carefully.

'Peter's in the studio, working. He won't want to see you tonight. Now for your breakfast, go back to the hall and through the door opposite. That's the kitchen. I'll show you round in the morning and we can talk about how this is going to work.'

'Thank you.'

Angela turned to go and Terri followed her to the door.

'You know that portrait in the sitting room,' she said. 'It's a remarkable picture. Who is it?'

Angela gave a brief, tight laugh. 'Oh it's no good asking me about Peter's paintings, darling. I don't know anything about his work. Sleep well, won't you.'

18

She left. Terri locked the door and turned away, surprised. 'What an odd thing to say,' she muttered to herself.

She crossed to stand in front of the patio doors but all she could see was her own pale, pinched reflection in the glass. Flicking the curtains across, she heard a slow, muted howl well up from the rear of the house, drop pitch then climb again before finally dying away. After some rasping, creaking groans, it started again. 'It's the wind in the trees,' she said out loud, and almost laughed at the panic in her own voice. So that was the reason for the name: Le Chant du Mistral; it sounded more like a scream than a song.

She made herself a mug of tea, pulled a folder out of her flight bag and took them both across to the armchair. The folder contained a copy of the contract she'd signed and a sheaf of articles about Peter Stedding printed from the internet. They charted his training in the great art studios of Florence, his portraits of royalty, politicians and movie stars, and his admission to the Royal Academy at just twenty-eight. Then he'd become increasingly controversial, complaining abusively about the current state of art education, scuffling and rowing with photographers and journalists. One grainy photograph showed him in front of a major London gallery, setting fire to a pile of 'modern' paintings in protest, mouthing angrily towards the camera. The stories dried up after that and he'd become a virtual recluse, painting less celebrated personalities and teaching the few he thought worthy of his talents.

Terri stared at the chilling photograph, then let her gaze wander dejectedly round the clinically furnished room while the wind continued to howl outside. Every sense told her that this was a mistake. She was filled with a mixture of self-pity and self-loathing: she'd let Oliver drive her to this.

Chapter 2

The wind continued to howl intermittently throughout the night. Terri slept poorly, wakefulness interrupted by bizarre and unsettling dreams. In one of them, Oliver had turned up at the patio doors, staring in at her balefully, occasionally banging on the doors and trying to get in. When she drew back the patio curtains the next morning, she was irrationally relieved to find no-one there. Light flooded the room. The doors gave onto a small terrace with potted plants and a tiny wrought iron table and chairs. Beyond, bathed in thin sunshine, she could see paths and shrubberies, and trees which still danced in the breeze. It was a far more innocent scene than the one she had pictured in her mind's eye.

The night before, overtaken with weariness, she had abandoned her bags and fallen into bed. Now she stowed her clothes away in the neat painted furniture in her bedroom. Reaching the bottom of the case, she picked out a small hard-backed book on Indian art, carefully wrapped inside a cotton cardigan, and she stood, brows furrowed, flicking through its jewel-like illustrations.

It was a fine second-hand copy, unmarked, tracked down on the internet by her father the previous year: a birthday gift to replace one she had loved as a child, one he'd thrown on the fire one evening when he was drunk. Not that the book had offended him particularly, but it had been in his line of vision when he'd felt compelled to take his frustration out on something. It still amazed her that he'd remembered and had thought to replace it. But she couldn't understand why she'd bothered to bring it to France with her.

She put it to one side and finished unpacking.

It was nearly nine o'clock when she left the annexe but the house was still silent and she retraced her steps of the night before, crossed the hallway and opened the door to the kitchen. It was a large modern space with black marble worktops and a broad horseshoe of cream-painted units hugging the wall, separating the kitchen from a walkway through to another door beyond. At its centre was an island unit and to the right a wooden breakfast table where a young blonde woman now sat, eating toast and flicking through a celebrity magazine. She looked up, expressionless, as Terri walked in.

Caught off guard, Terri straightened defensively.

'Good morning,' she said. 'I'm Terri. Mrs Stedding told me to help myself to breakfast.'

'I know.' The girl sounded bored. 'You've come to work for my father. I'm Lindsey.' Her gaze raked Terri disdainfully before returning to her magazine. 'The bread's in the fridge.' She turned a page. 'Cereal's in the cupboard.'

'Thanks. And is there tea?'

Lindsey didn't reply.

A large, stainless steel toaster stood on the island unit. Terri crossed to the fridge, extracted a sliced loaf and put two pieces of bread to toast. She glanced round. At the back on one side of the worktop was a run of storage jars. She picked up the one labelled tea, pulled out a teabag and ran water into the kettle. Leaning against the island unit, she stared out of the front windows over the terrace, its stone and gravel surface

21

broken up with huge evergreens in terracotta pots. At its centre was a round stone basin with water trickling into it from a sculpted column and, at its furthest edge, a gap in a line of low walling gave onto a sunken parterre. Beyond, far in the distance, she could just make out the next line of hills. It was the first time she had realised what a stunning place this was.

'So what do you think?' said Lindsey.

Hearing the edge in her voice, Terri turned to find the girl's eyes on her again. They were hazel rather than green and her complexion was less fair, but the resemblance to Angela was certainly there. She had none of her mother's lambent charm however.

'I'm sorry, *what do I think?*'

'About our home?'

'It's beautiful. I've never been to Provence before.'

'What do you do exactly?'

'Do? I'm a curator.'

'Yes, I know. But what do you do?'

'Well, it depends on the job. I research an artist's work, organise paintings for exhibition, borrow work from other collections, write catalogues and labels, arrange publicity…' Terri stopped, aware that she probably sounded like something out of a job prospectus. She'd been asked the same question so many times that the answer now came out pat. Not that she'd done any of those things for a while now. She shrugged. '…all sorts of things like that.'

'And you're going to do all that for my father?'

'That's the plan, yes.'

Lindsey studied Terri for a moment, then sneered. 'He won't like that then. He doesn't like anyone else trying to organise him.'

22

'But that's what he's employed me to do.' Terri met Lindsey's gaze steadily, feeling increasingly annoyed. The kettle boiled and she turned away to pour water over the tea bag in a china mug. A few minutes later she carried the tea and toast across to the table.

Lindsey drank a mouthful of coffee, watching Terri over the rim of the mug.

'Mama tells me you're here for six months,' she remarked. 'It's going to be kind of weird having you in the house all that time.'

Terri forced a smile. 'Actually, it's kind of weird for me too.'

'Really? I'd have thought it was pretty cushy.' Lindsey looked at her with frank hostility.

Terri bit back a cutting reply and started on her toast, determinedly staring out of the window again. For some reason the girl was trying to get a rise out of her and she had no desire to get into an argument with her employer's daughter on her first morning.

There were light footsteps down the stairs and across the hall. A moment later, Angela, still in her dressing gown, appeared in the doorway. In the bright morning light she looked a little older than Terri had thought the night before, maybe mid-fifties.

'Terri,' she said. 'Good, I see Lindsey's sorted you out. Morning darling. Everything all right?'

'*Ah oui, tout baigne,*' said Lindsey ironically.

'Don't speak French darling,' responded Angela smoothly. 'You know how I hate it.' She turned her clear gaze on Terri, said, 'I'll show you round later, shall I?' and embraced them both in a smile before gliding back out of the room.

23

Terri waited till she'd gone and turned back to Lindsey. 'Can I ask what it was you said?'

'Sure. It means: everything's just peachy. Don't you speak French?'

'Some.'

There was a frosty silence.

'So what do *you* do?' asked Terri.

'I'm a receptionist at Le Vieux Manoir. It's a big hotel and restaurant a few kilometres from here. We get all sorts of celebrities there: Hollywood stars, sportspeople. It's rather chic and words gets around...you know?' Lindsey tossed her hair back in an affected way. She looked to be in her late twenties but appeared young for her age; there was something rebellious and adolescent in her manner. 'The worst thing about it is that I have to work shifts and they're a pain.' She returned to her magazine and they sat in silence while Terri finished her toast.

'Is your father about?' she asked. 'I haven't spoken to him yet.'

'He's down in the studio. Probably waiting for you. There's a note for you up there.'

Lindsey pointed to the other end of the table where a small piece of folded paper lay almost covered by another glossy magazine. Terri stood up and reached for it. On the top, her name had been written in a familiar sloping hand. Inside it read:

Miss Challoner,
I will expect you in the studio at 9 o'clock prompt.
Peter Stedding

Beneath his signature was a tiny line drawing of the route to the studio.

'Oh shit,' she said, and was aware of a smug smile on Lindsey's face as she quickly left the table, swallowed a mouthful of tea and threw the rest away. A few minutes later she had grabbed her bag and a notebook from her room and was running across the terrace.

*

Peter Stedding's studio occupied an old barn down the hill at least ten minutes' walk from the house. Built of the same stone as the *mas*, it sat in its ground with an air of belonging. Several windows had been let into its walls and four skylights into the northern pitch of the roof. A series of stone steps cut through a grassy bank created the final descent to a sturdy wooden door. Terri lifted her hand and rapped on it three times. After a minute's silence she knocked again and when still nothing happened, she tried the door handle and let herself in.

She could see no-one but there was music playing somewhere, something strong and lyrical; Beethoven perhaps. The space was immense but still looked cluttered. In the middle stood a huge studio easel with a table beside it covered in tubes of paint, bottles, brushes and rags. Nearby was a long, low platform with an oriental rug thrown across it and supporting a chaise longue. At the far end of the room to her left stood another easel and a series of trestle tables, all covered in equipment. And there were paintings everywhere, both on the walls and propped up on the floor below them, apparently several canvases deep.

She heard a string of expletives. It came from behind a half open door in a run of partition walling over to the right. She walked across but hesitated outside the door. A tall stand of shelves beyond housed a range of artefacts, pieces of fabric, porcelain and pottery, masks, wooden fertility symbols and assorted hats, all jostling for position. Terri wondered how he found anything.

She knocked twice and waited. The room went silent.

'Come in,' said a rich, baritone voice.

The room was larger than she had expected and furnished like a study: floor to ceiling bookshelves; a day bed with a throw and cushions; a leather wing-backed chair and side table. In the middle stood Peter Stedding, searching impatiently in the open drawer of a knee-hole desk. He straightened as Terri walked in. Despite a slight stoop at the shoulders, he was imposingly tall with a thick head of white hair and piercing grey-blue eyes. He immediately glanced at the clock on one of the shelves.

'Good morning,' she said. 'I'm…'

'You're late,' he remarked crisply, 'but I suppose you weren't sure where to come. I'll let it pass this time.'

Terri opened her mouth to speak and closed it again. She waited. He had resumed his search of the drawer with his right hand. The whole of his left forearm to his knuckles was encased in plaster of Paris.

'Blast it all,' he exclaimed and slammed the drawer closed. 'This bloody plaster's making it impossible to do anything.' He threw himself down in the chair behind the desk. 'A silly little stumble and I'm left like this.' He rapped the arm plaster with the back of his fingers. 'Apparently I'm old, Miss Challoner. I take longer to heal now.'

Terri struggled to think of a suitable response. She thought he looked remarkably, frighteningly, vital for his seventy-seven years.

'Sit, why don't you?' he barked.

She sat.

'Right...So-o Miss Challoner...Terri isn't it?...as you know, there's a gallery in Nice, the De Vilaney, who've offered me a retrospective. Starts thirtieth September. There's a lot to organise before then. I did start to do it but then this...' He raised the plaster and glared vindictively at it. '...and of course the gallery wanted to do it themselves but I've had trouble with galleries before. They start to think they own you. Now I see from your CV that you've had some experience before in this sort of work.'

'Yes, I have.'

'But never for a living artist.'

'Er...no.'

'Hm.' He studied Terri thoughtfully as if he was now having doubts about her suitability for the post.

'I believe I did make that clear in my application,' she said. 'But the procedures for organising an exhibition are the same whether the artists are alive or dead.'

'Except that the dead aren't in a position to express an opinion or complain.' He regarded her beadily.

'I did curate a very successful exhibition of portraiture not long ago.'

'Yes, I know. I saw it. Three years ago, wasn't it? Ye-es. Very...competent.' He looked back down at her details. 'Thirty-four. Good qualifications. But you're young to have done so much. You've moved around a lot I see. That's not necessarily good. Restless. And you've not done much of note recently. Ferfylde's: not the most adventurous gallery in the world to put it mildly.'

Terri said nothing. It was as if the whole job process had been reversed and she was having an interview after the job had been offered.

Peter sighed heavily. 'Well, time will tell no doubt...'

He pulled a piece of paper with a hand-written list towards him on the desk. On a cord round his neck hung a pair of half-glasses and he lifted them to place on the end of his long nose. Terri took out her pen and opened her notebook in readiness.

'Your working days will be Monday to Friday,' he began. 'Eight thirty with a break for lunch, one till two-thirty. Finish five thirty. I like punctuality. I will be here usually during the morning session. In the afternoon I generally start late and work into the evening. It varies. I often work at the weekend and insist on having the studio to myself then.' He paused to look over his glasses at her. 'I particularly want to impress on you that you don't speak to me when I'm painting. If you need to speak to me, you wait until I look at you. *Then* you speak.' He returned to his list. 'I hold life classes here once a week on a Tuesday. You'd better keep out of the way while they're on. God knows the students'll find any excuse to let their minds wander so the last thing we need is a pretty face getting in their eye line or any female chatter. They're morning sessions, nine till one.' He paused to glance up at her stony expression and returned to his list. 'When it comes to the retrospective, I shall decide which paintings are going into the exhibition and I will have the last say in how it is done. I don't want you making any arrangements without checking with me first. Is that clear?'

'But *not* when you're painting,' she remarked evenly.

He looked at her again over his glasses, eyes narrowing.

'Don't get cute with me, Terri. This is the way I run my studio. If you don't like the rules, you don't have to take the job.' He kept his gaze fixed on her and she reluctantly nodded. He returned again to the list.

'If Luc's not around – he's my studio assistant – I'll expect you to make my coffee. I have a couple during the

28

morning – black, one sugar. In the afternoon I drink tea, again black with one sugar. But the same rules apply: leave the drink on my table if I'm painting – somewhere sensible of course – but don't speak. In fact Luc won't be here till Tuesday this week so you can fill in on Monday.'

Terri's heart was rapidly sinking: she was going to be a highly qualified drinks monitor. She watched him root about under some letters. He produced a typewritten sheet of paper and pushed it towards her with a ball-point pen on top.

'I need you to sign that before we go any further.' Terri read it through. It was a statement declaring that she would not disclose any information to the press or publish anything without his agreement. 'I've had trouble with journalists in the past,' he muttered. 'Always want to know who you're painting, whether they're dressed or not. Bloody nonsense.'

'But I'm not a journalist,' she said coldly.

'No, but everyone seems to sell stories to the press these days. It's a disease.'

'But not one that I've caught.'

'Then signing it shouldn't be an issue for you.'

She met his gaze for a moment then signed the declaration, dropped the pen back on it and pushed it brusquely back across the table.

'Right,' he declared, 'so…about the paintings. I've made a list of pictures I definitely want in the exhibition.' He moved papers around on his desk again, then ferreted underneath a laptop. 'Ah, here it is.' He handed it to her. There were eleven paintings on it.

'Do you know where all of these paintings are?' she asked.

'Not all of them, no. That's what I'm paying you to do: track them down.'

'But I'll need something to go on. And what about the rest of the exhibition? Eleven paintings won't fill it. Has the gallery said how much space is available?'

'They might have. I can't remember off the top of my head.'

'I'll get in touch with them.'

'Do. But don't let them dictate. I haven't decided what else might be suitable.'

'Ideally we need a selection of works from the different phases of your career.' Terri glanced towards the studio. 'Perhaps there would be something suitable here. Mixing in some lesser known works is always a good idea.'

'Oh? I didn't know I'd had *phases*,' he said, scornfully. 'Still…there might be some worthwhile work here. You may look…as long as you don't get in my way.'

'Where do you keep the records of your paintings? On the computer?'

'Good grief, no. Computers are an abomination, designed to distract and confuse. I only use them under sufferance. I have notebooks. Every painting I do, I make a note and do a sketch of it.'

'The notebooks would be useful then. Do they have any other information in?'

'Sometimes, though I can't see how they would help.' He studied her critically. 'I suppose I *might* let you look at them. I'll think about it. Certainly there are some old exhibition catalogues you could have.'

'Good.' She glanced round. 'So where am I going to work? I'll need a desk and some storage space.'

'You can work in here. Nicole – my secretary - only uses this desk in the mornings, ten till one. You can work round her, unless I'm in here of course. Then you'll have to…' He waved a peremptory hand towards the door.

'I'm afraid that won't work. I need my own desk…and space to spread out.'

He swore vehemently. 'I will not have you taking over my studio, woman. What the hell do you need space for?'

'Because I have to chase up a lot of paintings. They'll need to be recorded and tracked and I need to make sure information doesn't become lost or mixed up. I'll also need to plan how the exhibition will look and hang…with your agreement, of course. It's not something that can be done working round someone else.'

Peter's pale eyes bored into her; he drummed the fingers of his right hand on the desk. Suddenly he slapped his hand down flat. 'All right…all right. I'll ask Sami to sort out the storeroom next door.'

'I'll need an internet connection.'

'Yes, well, we've got wi-fi. Right. So now, just go will you? I would like to get *some* work done today. I'll expect you here in the morning…eight-thirty prompt.'

He started collecting together the loose sheets of paper.

Terri stood up. 'Mr Stedding?'

'Oh, call me Peter, for God's sake. I can't stand all this Mister nonsense.' He thrust the paperwork in one of the drawers.

She stood as straight as she could; she wasn't tall. 'You clearly don't want me here. I'm not sure why you employed me.'

He took his glasses off and fixed his sharp raking gaze on her face again.

'I was talked into it,' he said, 'when I was still feeling groggy after my fall. I hit my head as well, you see. It seemed like a good idea at the time. Well, it would with a head injury I suppose. Still, you can be sure I'll give you the two weeks' notice if you're not up to the job.'

'I believe the contract provides for me to do the same if I don't think I can work here.'

Peter glared at her, a tic starting in his cheek. He pointed to the door.

Back out in the studio, Terri put her head back and blew out a slow breath. Why did she never know when to stop? When it came to her work, she always moved into another gear: too passionate, too keen to make her point or stand her ground; it had got her into trouble before. Here, of all places, she needed to control that mouth of hers.

Chapter 3

Oliver was an actor, classically trained, and it showed in the way he talked and in the way he moved. Sophie worked as a set designer and had invited Terri to a theatre party where she'd seen him across the room, telling a story to an attentive audience, gesticulating with an eloquent hand and putting on voices to embellish his tale. She had been drawn immediately by his lively, even features, the intensity of his delivery, the flash of his smile. He must have felt her watching him because he'd looked her way and levelly met her gaze, raising one amused eyebrow. In response to Terri's questioning, Sophie admitted that she hardly knew him though she had heard about him. He was very popular, she said, and probably a rising star; he was handsome; he was single. What are you waiting for? But it was Oliver who'd taken the initiative and had crossed the room to speak to Terri and before long they'd been inseparable. He'd been everything Terri was not: out-going, demonstrative and an easy conversationalist; he'd made friends without apparent effort. In introspective moments, Terri had come to the conclusion that his 'otherness' had probably been a big part of his attraction. It had happened before.

Now, sitting at her new desk, Terri checked the mail in her inbox. For someone so keen on his mobile phone and texting, Oliver was surprisingly disinterested in computers and emails. Even so, she was resigned to getting messages from him. Before leaving London she had acquired a new phone with a new number but changing her email address would have caused her far more trouble. She knew Oliver would quickly switch to email, however, when he realised his favourite avenue had been closed off. There were several new messages and, as she had expected, there were already two from Oliver Dent. The first had been sent on the Friday:

Is there something wrong with your phone Terri? Have you disconnected it? C'mon baby. You know you love me. I'm sorry. How many more times do I have to say it? It won't happen again. You need me. You're not as independent as you think. And I really need you. It's tearing me up. Call me.

The second was from the Sunday evening.

Where are you? I haven't seen you all weekend and there've been no lights on. Where are you? Who the hell are you with? I can't go on like this. Don't make me cross Terri. You know what'll happen and you won't like it.

It had been like this for ages now: one minute vulnerable and pleading, the next volatile and threatening. Terri quickly deleted them, feeling the familiar fast beat of her heart and the shaking of her hands.

It was Monday morning. Peter was already at his easel, engrossed in his work, and hadn't acknowledged her arrival. In the room next to his office she had arrived to find a trestle table and a wooden chair; the boxes, canvases, portfolios and assorted discarded frames and clutter which the room housed had been tidied back to one end. An old angle-poise lamp had been placed on the table, plugged into an extension lead and a revised list of the paintings Peter wanted included in the retrospective had been left nearby. It had grown by three and this time he'd added the potential locations of some of them scrawled alongside. Here also were a number of exhibition catalogues and a tumbling pile of Peter's sacred notebooks. She'd been relieved, having half expected nothing to have changed. Picking up a succession of the notebooks, she flicked through them to see what sort of information they held.

Each loosely covered one year and was dated on the front. Inside they contained sketches, sometimes filling whole pages, sometimes tiny thumbnails squeezed into a corner or sideways along a margin. Writing had been forced in around the drawings, often with cramped notes apparently added later. Which of them had gone on to be completed paintings and what had happened to them afterwards was not always clear. Some made a direct reference to a later work, others did not. The notebooks were out of sequence and she immediately put them in order. Unsurprisingly there was one missing: 1973. Given the state of the studio she thought it could be anywhere.

At the computer, she started to plan her work: a list of tasks that would need doing and goals to be achieved by approximate dates. She lived by lists – the only way she could keep her plans in order. Then she picked up the paper with Peter's choice of paintings. Any which were mentioned in the exhibition catalogues might be traced through the relevant gallery. After meticulous searching through every one, she found six of them. That left eight with no obvious history unless she found them in the notebooks. She would track them down though; it was the sort of challenge she liked.

Nicole had arrived promptly and installed herself in Peter's office. She was a forty-something French woman with impeccable English, long dark hair coiled up high on her head and sophisticated clothes. Terri introduced herself and took the opportunity to acquire the contact details of the De Vilaney gallery in Nice. She was in the middle of a telephone call to them when Peter opened the door of her office and walked straight in.

'I assume this is acceptable,' he enquired in his booming voice, gesturing at the room without waiting for her to finish the call.

Terri said, 'excuse me a second,' into the mouthpiece and covered it. It seemed the 'not disturbing' rule only applied to Peter. 'Yes.' She offered a polite smile. 'Thank you.'

'You can thank Sami. He spent all Sunday afternoon doing this for you.'

'Then I shall.'

'Don't take the notebooks out of this room,' he said sharply. 'You understand? Under no circumstances. I don't want you losing them. And I'm more than ready for my coffee by the way. No milk, remember, one sugar. The kitchen is at the other end of the studio.' He pointed a finger and walked out of the door, leaving it open.

She glanced at her watch; it was ten thirty-five. She finished the call and made her way across to the kitchen, a galley space with a run of wall and base units containing all that was necessary to make a range of drinks and light snacks. Next to it was a shower room and toilet. The studio was like a self-contained flat. She made coffee for Nicole as well as for Peter, getting a surprised thank you from Nicole and no reaction at all from her employer as she silently placed the drink on his work table.

She worked till one, planning and prioritising, creating documents on the computer, making notes of things to ask Peter, then went up to her room for her lunch break. Back in the studio at two thirty, she found herself alone and took the opportunity to glance through a stack of paintings stored against the wall. There were gallery stickers on occasional works – clearly exhibited but not sold - and Peter had written a year on a few others. Most were bare. When he returned, just after four o'clock, Terri was holding an exquisite small painting of a child's head and shoulders.

'This is lovely,' she remarked as he walked to his work station not far from where she stood.

He came closer and reached wordlessly for the painting. Like many of the other canvases propped up around the walls, it was unframed. He raised his glasses to his nose and studied it with a critical eye.

'Who is it?' she asked. 'Can you remember?'

'Certainly. It's Nicole's youngest daughter.' He turned the canvas over. It was dated 2002.

'I thought I could put 'possibles' for the retrospective on one side for us to choose from later. I think this would be perfect.'

She put out her hand to take the painting back but he held on to it and stared at her over the top of his glasses.

'You've been here five minutes,' he said in a mild, sarcastic voice, 'and you've already chosen another painting.' He glanced around the assembly of stored canvases. 'This could prove to be a *very* big exhibition. I think we should restrict ourselves to the more important works…' He held out the portrait for her to take. '…not these sketches.'

Terri frowned.

'But surely it's these 'sketches', as you put it, which bring an exhibition alive?' She gave an expansive gesture with her hand, taking in the canvas she now held and any as yet unseen ones stacked against the wall nearby. 'If you want the retrospective to capture your audience's imagination, it has to be surprising, it has to teach them something they don't already know about your work. Sometimes the sketches…'

'Miss Challoner,' said Peter, cutting across her. 'Are you familiar with the expression: teaching your grandmother to suck eggs?'

Terri was silent.

'Well, are you?' he prompted.

'Yes.'

'Then please bear that in mind next time *before* you try to tell me how my own retrospective should be.'

'But…'

'Is – that - understood?' His eyes bored into her.

She nodded. Peter turned away to his work station.

'I've spoken to the gallery,' Terri said to his retreating back. 'I'm going there next Monday to have a look round.'

'Then we'll be granted some much needed peace,' he replied without turning.

Terri's eyes narrowed in mute anger.

'Just get me a new jar of medium, will you?' Peter eased himself onto the tall stool in front of his easel. He pointed vaguely up the studio without looking at her. 'It'll be on the shelves beyond Luc's work station. Labelled Medium 3.'

Terri walked up the studio, past the assistant's easel and work table, and scanned the shelves for the jar. She found it and walked slowly back, glancing back at the painting on Luc's easel as she passed. It was a portrait of a young man and was remarkably good.

She put the jar on Peter's table and retreated into her office, keeping her lips firmly clamped together. The man was odious but she had to stick it out. She couldn't face going back to London. Not yet.

*

The estate the house sat in was extensive. 'Do make the most of the grounds,' Angela had told Terri. 'The woods are very large and our land extends into them – you can see a line of stakes in places, marking the boundary. They're rather dark but there are lots of footpaths; the main one goes through to the village.' She'd raised one amused eyebrow. 'Don't get lost though will you? We might never find you again.'

On the Monday, leaving the studio at the end of the afternoon, Terri detoured from the route leading directly back to the house and meandered on and up the hill, through a cherry orchard and past a *pétanque* pit, to the first line of whispering pine trees. When she stopped and turned to look down, the whole of Le Chant du Mistral was spread before her, a series of level terraces and sloping banks, basking in the spring sunshine. Below and to her right stood the huge U-shaped farmhouse with the old pigeon house – a tower-like building - behind to the west. In a dip on the other side lay a large rectangular swimming pool, still with its winter cover. To her left, separated from the pool by a line of shrubs was a large, incongruous area of lawn, bordered on two sides by flower beds, and in front, way below, was the unmistakeable red roof of Peter's barn. Beyond was the valley: a couple of distant farmsteads and countless fields of olives and vines stretching into the blue distance. It was a spectacular view and she stood, trying to soak in the peace and beauty of it.

Insidiously, she found herself thinking about Oliver instead: how well their first few months together had gone, how quickly she had agreed to go and live in his flat, sure that this was a relationship which would last. He used to make her laugh; he told her wonderful stories about life on stage and on television sets. He was waiting for 'that big break' which would get him into movies. He loved art and encouraged her to take him round galleries, explaining about the pictures he could see. She was beautiful, he said, fascinating, endlessly surprising. She wanted to think he meant it. Then, at the last minute, he lost a good part he had been promised and struggled to find any work. That was when it had all started to go wrong.

A brisk, cold breeze came up, setting the trees behind her humming and tugging at her hair. She hugged herself for warmth and made her way back down to the house.

The front door was unlocked and Terri let herself in. On the Sunday morning, during Angela's brisk tour of the ground floor of the *mas*, she had exhorted Terri to make herself comfortable – 'use the sitting room if you like; no-one goes in there much' - and to make use of the kitchen if she needed it. She had made it clear she expected Terri to fend for herself and to do it when she wouldn't be disturbing anyone else, but she'd done it with a great deal of charm.

'I must be in the way,' Terri had taken the opportunity to say, reluctant, despite Angela's courteous hospitality, to live the strange, skulking half-life she could see lay ahead. 'I could look for accommodation nearby. Could you suggest some local agencies?'

Angela had hesitated for the blink of an eye. 'Don't think of it darling. Peter insists that you stay with us. You'd never find anything for the summer anyway and I'm sure we can all rub along together. We all come and go so much anyway.' She'd produced one of her lovely smiles. 'I confess I was a bit taken aback when Peter first told me you were staying but now that we've met I can see that we're going to be great friends.'

Now, as Terri stepped into the cool, dark hall, the sound of piano music drifted through the half open kitchen door.

Curious, she pushed it back and looked in. The door opposite led into a smart *salon* where she knew a grand piano stood at the top of the room. It was slightly ajar and she walked closer. She was no expert but whoever was playing was good. Then a woman began to laugh and the music came to a halting stop.

'Useless,' said a man's voice with a discreet but distinct French accent. 'So come on, you didn't answer my question: why don't you tell her?'

Frowning, Terri bent her head forward, listening more closely. That voice was familiar... She shook her head. It wasn't possible.

'You know what mama's like. She'll overreact.' That was definitely Lindsey speaking.

'And your father?'

'Don't be ridiculous. I can't talk to him. Hey, I'll get us some more wine.'

Almost immediately, the door opened and Lindsey faced her.

'What are *you* doing here?' she demanded. 'Snooping?'

'Certainly not,' said Terri defensively. 'I've just come in and I heard the music. It was very good. Was that you playing?'

'Yes.'

'Liar.' A dark-haired man, dressed in black sweatshirt and jeans and with a day's stubble on his chin, moved to stand in the doorway. His gaze settled on Terri and their eyes met for a long, silent moment.

'I'm not a liar.' Lindsey glared at him. She turned back to Terri. 'We were both playing. It was a duet. This is Luc Daumier, my father's assistant. He helps me with my piano playing,' she added defiantly. 'And this is Terri,' she said to Luc, 'who's come to curate the exhibition for father.'

41

'Ah yes, the retrospective,' said Luc. '*Enchanté.*' He held out his hand. Terri took it and they exchanged a perfunctory shake. 'So you'll be joining us in the studio. Peter is...' He flicked a quick glance at Lindsey who was already at the fridge, refilling two glasses with white wine. '...excited about the exhibition.'

'How long have you worked for him?' Terri stared at him, frowning.

'Four months.'

Lindsey made a point of walking back between them and held out a glass of wine for Luc.

He shook his head. 'I should go.'

'You don't need to go on my account,' Terri said coldly. 'I was just passing through.'

'Even so, I must.' He stepped back, ramming his hands into the pockets of his jeans. 'I haven't long been back and there are things I need to do. You drink my wine,' he said to Terri. 'I don't think I have anything infectious.'

He nodded to her, exchanged a word with Lindsey, and walked away briskly. They heard the front door open and close.

'He lives in the *bergerie*,' said Lindsey. 'It's in a clearing near the edge of the woods.' She held the glass out grudgingly. 'Here, you'd better take this.'

'I'm not a great drinker, I'm afraid,' said Terri.

'It's one glass. It won't kill you. Here.' Her eyes narrowed. 'Do you and Luc know each other?'

'No. Why?'

'I just thought...oh it doesn't matter. Let's take the wine to the sitting room.'

The sitting room was gloomy. A vine, growing up and across a pergola on the terrace by the front window, starved the room of the late afternoon sunlight while the window to the rear gave onto a dark bank of rising ground. Lindsey put the table lamps on then threw herself down on one of the sofas next to the fireplace, stretching her legs the length of it. Terri sat on the sofa opposite.

'Mama doesn't like this room,' said Lindsey. 'She thinks it's too dark.'

'It is a bit...still it's cosy.' Terri could imagine the rest of the ground floor being featured in the smooth pages of a minimalist interior design magazine, but this room was more homely.

Lindsey fixed her with one of her flat, hard stares. 'So where do you live...normally?'

'I've got an apartment in London.'

'Have you got a boyfriend? I see you don't wear a wedding ring.'

'No, there's no-one special at the moment.'

'How did you get on with father today?'

'OK.'

'Did he give you a hard time?'

'Crikey, Lindsey, do you cross-question everyone like this? Am I under interrogation or something?'

'I was just trying to be friendly,' Lindsey said sullenly.

'Oh...well, OK. I'm sorry.' Terri felt wrong-footed, but then she never did this chatty getting-to-know-you thing well. She hesitated and tried again. 'I think your father is very sure what he wants.'

'And I suppose you want something different?'

'It's too early to say.'

Terri sipped her wine. It was dry and caught at the back of her throat. She looked up at the portrait of the woman in the halter-necked dress.

'That painting…it's unusual, isn't it? Really striking. Do you know anything about it?'

'Sure.' Lindsey glanced up at the picture. 'That's Madeleine. She was father's first wife.'

'Ah.' Terri nodded, surprised, and studied the image with fresh eyes. That possibility hadn't occurred to her and she immediately wondered why Angela hadn't told her when she'd asked about it. She considered asking Lindsey but then didn't. 'Do you paint at all?' she said instead.

'Me?' Lindsey forced a laugh. 'No, I didn't inherit the arty genes. I don't know one end of a paintbrush from the other.'

Terri sensed some intense personal disappointment behind the off-hand remark. Lindsey was hard to make out. One minute she was ignorant and rude, the next she seemed like a lost child.

'Maybe you're creative in other ways,' she said kindly, 'like your music.'

Lindsey stared at her warily. 'That's what Celia says. She's my aunt.'

'Yes, your mother mentioned her. I haven't met her yet.'

'Oh you will. She's barking by the way. And she and mama don't get on.' Lindsey laughed suddenly and the sullenness lifted from her face. 'That's a classic understatement. They can't stand each other.'

Terri grinned; the atmosphere had perceptibly thawed.

'Celia lives in the *pigeonnier*,' said Lindsey. 'She's got the top floor as a studio, daft old bat.'

'She paints too?'

Lindsey laughed. 'That's not what I'd call it. Very impressionist, *she* says. Really bad, I'd say. She doesn't paint like father anyway.'

Mention of Peter's painting had Terri automatically looking up at the portrait again.

Lindsey followed her gaze and regarded the picture dispassionately. 'She was supposed to be a bit of a free spirit or something. Hitched to Italy when she was a student and spent the whole trip looking at paintings. I mean, what a waste of a holiday…' She hesitated, looking across at Terri slyly. 'You'd probably have got on with her though - you know: another art geek.'

Terri ignored the pointed dig and studied the painting again, intrigued.

'She certainly had a very animated face,' she said. 'Expressive. So did they divorce?'

'No. She died…young. Why do you want to know?' The aggressive note had quickly returned.

Terri shrugged. 'Just curious.'

'It was a long time ago. And it's nothing to do with me. Anyway I'm not supposed to talk about her.' Lindsey's expression was shuttered again, her voice flat. She threw her legs round to put her feet to the floor and lifted her glass, tipping the remaining contents into her mouth before standing up.

'I'd better go,' she said curtly. 'I've got things to do.' She paused at the door. 'Mama doesn't like me playing the piano with Luc. I'd be grateful if you didn't tell her.'

Terri turned in her seat to look at her. 'Of course. I can't imagine why I would.'

Lindsey regarded her gravely, managed a weak smile, then disappeared. Terri heard her footsteps going up the stairs and looked back up at the portrait. Peter's first wife. She wondered when she had died, and how. Madeleine had looked so vital.

Her thoughts trailed away and her mind turned to Luc Daumier instead. Lies did not come easily to her but she hadn't hesitated to tell Lindsey that she didn't know him. So why was that? It was some years now since she had last seen him. And Luc had pointedly not acknowledged it either, though, given the way they'd parted, perhaps that wasn't surprising. It seemed that, in the four months he had been working for Peter, he had already established an easy familiarity with the man's daughter and was happy to visit the house behind her mother's back.

Of course it was none of her business, but Terri couldn't help but wonder why an arts journalist and critic, known for at least one major undercover exposé story and usually based in London and Paris, should be here in Provence, working for Peter Stedding as a lowly studio assistant.

*

Peter heard the door shut, heard the recognisable tap of Angela's shoes approaching across the studio floor, but didn't shift his gaze from the canvas. It was the Wednesday evening and already nearly half past seven. He was painting a portrait of Laurent Valdeau, a French businessman and philanthropist, and he wanted to finish the underpainting of the man's arm before the natural light became unusable. At the moment he was having difficulty getting one of the hands just right.

'Peter?'

He adjusted the lie of a finger and leaned back, looking over his glasses at the picture critically. He leaned forward again and put in another brushstroke.

'Peter? I need to talk to you.' Angela paused and glanced around. 'For heaven's sake, Peter, how can you work in this place? It's a mess.'

'Not now, Angela,' he said tersely, 'I'm busy.'

'You're always busy. You said you'd be over at seven and I've been waiting at the house for you. I was supposed to be going out twenty minutes ago.'

Peter sighed heavily, put his brush down on the table and turned to look at her over the top of his glasses.

'What is the emergency?'

'Sammy's dug up my roses. And a friend gave them to me. The man's driving me mad.'

'Not this again Angela. I don't suppose he did it intentionally.'

'Well, if he didn't do it intentionally, he's inept. He's supposed to be the gardener for heaven's sake.'

'Odd job man,' Peter corrected.

A late, low beam of sunlight caught the edge of Angela's head and made her hair glow a soft apricot. When he'd first met her she'd had deep auburn hair, coppery when it caught the light. Ever since then she'd dyed it - highlighting, she called it - but he'd been rather fond of its striking russet tones. Even so she had a good bone structure and was still a very beautiful woman with a fresh clear skin which belied her age. He toyed with how to say it but the words escaped him and the moment passed.

'Anyway he did do it intentionally,' Angela was saying. 'He argued with me about putting them in when I asked him to.'

'Sami *argued*?'

'I know he never argues with *you*, Peter. He's not so obliging with everyone else. Anyway, he made it clear he

47

thought it was a bad idea. You know the way he does: rolling his eyes away, getting all shifty and refusing to look at you.'

'So what do you want me to do about it? Perhaps it was a bad idea. Perhaps they didn't thrive and he got rid of them.'

'Oh nonsense. Why do you always take his side? There was nothing wrong with them. He just didn't water them enough. Look…' Angela dragged a wooden chair over to sit in front of him. '…it's time we talked about Sammy.' A bleeping noise sounded from the pocket of her jacket. She pulled out her phone, glancing at the screen.

'What now?' said Peter impatiently. He glanced towards the window. 'The daylight's going.'

Angela dropped the phone back in her pocket. 'I think he's getting too old for the job.'

'Sami?'

'Yes. I think we should retire him. There are plenty of people looking for work. We could get someone better.'

Peter slowly removed his glasses and stared into her face. He could feel that familiar tightness developing in the pit of his stomach and tension in the muscles of his jaw.

'Retire him?' he said guardedly. 'But he's only…' He thought for a moment. '…sixty-four.'

'Exactly. He's too old.'

'Thank you dear,' said Peter dryly. 'I hate to think what that makes me.'

Angela released a tut of frustration, as she so often did. 'Oh, you know what I mean: to do that job. You're just painting pictures all day. It's hardly the same.'

'Just painting pictures? No, hardly.' Peter turned his eyes back to the painting on the easel and tried to put the issue away from him. He could feel irritation and anger knot in the pit of his stomach but he choked it back; there was no point being sensitive to the way Angela described his work. She'd never made any pretence of the fact that she didn't understand all the fuss about what he did. And it wasn't the first time she'd tried to get rid of Sami, but he couldn't let the man go – for all sorts of reasons, some of which he could barely explain to himself, let alone Angela. 'We can't retire Sami yet,' he said firmly. 'He's fit enough for the job. Anyway we don't have any accommodation for another odd job man.'

'What do you mean? If we sack Sammy he could use the same rooms.'

'No. Sami's living there. I promised him he could stay there as long as he needed them.'

'Oh really Peter, how could you? You never told me.'

'I believe I did.'

Peter looked back at Angela and held her gaze. With some exceptions he left her to organise the house as she chose; he didn't like everything she did up there but he rarely quibbled. It was only fair since he was down in the studio so much and it was Angela's home. And though it was often a struggle, he tried not to argue with her, not seriously anyway; she was his wife and he thought he owed her that. But he wouldn't be swayed on this.

'Where would he go?' he said. 'In any case, I can't go back on a promise, now can I? Would you?'

'Oh really Peter, what a thing to say.' She stood up. 'Well, you should at least talk to him. There's no point in me trying to do it.'

She glared at him, then stalked out.

Peter wondered why she disliked Sami so much. Was it because she hadn't employed him herself, that he was one of the few relics of Peter's former life? Or was it because he was Algerian? Angela distrusted foreigners of every kind except –

for some reason she'd never explained - Americans. Sometimes it was funny; most of the time he just found it irritating, like the way she always had to anglicise Sami's name. She surrounded herself with ex-pats and disdained any kind of French culture. Her regular attempts to turn the estate into an English country garden mystified Sami and were in any case doomed to failure.

He returned his attention to the painting but Angela had disturbed his concentration and in the end he got up and walked across to his study. The door to Terri's office was open and he automatically glanced inside.

'We need to talk about your career and what got you started painting in the first place,' Terri had said to him that morning. 'Perhaps you could think through who your particular influences have been? We could incorporate reproductions of your favourites into the show. When would be convenient for a meeting?

'I don't know. I'll have to think about it,' he'd prevaricated.

'Shall we say Wednesday then?'

'For God's sake, woman, I said I don't know. I'll tell you when I'm ready.'

But before he could go, she'd started again.

'We need somewhere to keep the paintings which are going to be exhibited to keep them safe till they're shipped to the gallery. Some racks near the door over there would be ideal. Could I arrange to get some made?'

That, at least, was a good idea. He'd told her to ask Sami. Sami was good at things like that.

In the short time she'd been there he'd heard her speaking on the phone, had seen her talking to Nicole, nosing through pictures in the studio or flicking through his notebooks - he already regretted giving her those. Having been talked into accepting help - when he'd been too weak and muddled to judge what he was doing - it had occurred to him afterwards that perhaps it wasn't such a bad idea after all. He needed to paint and he didn't have the time or, honestly, the energy to sort out the exhibition too, and he certainly wasn't going to hand it back to the gallery. He liked the idea of having somebody in his own employ whom he could control.

But now she was here, Terri was not what he'd had in mind. She was smart but he didn't want smart, just efficient. And he could see wilfulness in her eyes: unusual large charcoal eyes, set each side of a small, straight nose. Her mouth turned up at the corners but looked remarkably stiff as if always holding something back. An insolent remark probably, to judge from their exchanges so far. Even so, she would be good to paint with her sleek dark hair and expressive eyebrows, though he doubted she would ever accept a pose; behind her crisp politeness he could sense obstinacy.

He turned away and walked into his study, crossed to the whisky decanter on the cupboard under the window and poured himself a measure, circling his long fingers firmly round the glass. The retrospective was the recognition he'd craved for his lifetime's work but all he'd had in mind was an exhibition of his paintings whereas clearly this Terri woman wanted much more: she wanted to examine him minutely and parcel his life up into neat little packages. He took a mouthful of whisky and enjoyed its searing warmth as it slid down his throat.

Well, he had no intention of letting her search and delve. The past was done and buried; he would not have her digging it up.

*

Luc finished the last of his pasta, laid the fork on the plate and leaned forward to put the tray on the scruffy wooden coffee table. He leaned back and stared towards the window. The daylight was nearly spent and he could see little of the woods outside, just washed out reflections of the room in which he sat. Still he was thinking about Terri. All evening she had intruded on his thoughts, odd images and scenes from the past dancing across his mind, though if he had hoped to analyse how he felt about seeing her again, he had failed. He still wasn't sure.

She looked older, of course, her features a little more prominent, her cheeks less rounded, but still she was pretty. He'd been stunned to walk into the kitchen and see her there. What chance had brought her to this place at this time? And what were her feelings about him now? Had they changed? It had been impossible to tell. There again, maybe it wasn't chance at all; maybe she had followed him there. He shook his head. After all this time, that was an absurd idea. In any case, she had looked too surprised to see him and he doubted she'd be able to fake it; she'd always been reserved but never devious. So perhaps it was Fate or some greater hand toying with him?

He got up brusquely, shaking his stupid superstitions away, and took his tray through to the kitchen. Whatever the reason, Terri's arrival didn't need to affect his plans - or at least, not in a bad way. Quite the contrary. He dumped his dishes in the sink, wondering which way he should play it, and almost smiled.

But hell, he'd kill for a cigarette.

Chapter 4

Terri got into the passenger seat of Luc's Peugeot hatchback, turned to put her bag on the back seat, and clipped the belt into place. She had expected a grander car – he had driven something sporty in London – but she supposed the more humble model fitted the part he was playing. Starting the engine, he set the car in motion down the track and out of the estate. He was driving her to Nice for her Monday morning appointment at the gallery. She had intended to drive herself but on the Friday afternoon Peter had informed her that Luc would be taking her and the subject had clearly not been open for negotiation.

Luc sat at the wheel, wordless. Terri ignored the silence and checked her phone. There was one brief text from Sophie; nothing else. Still she kept expecting to see something from Oliver and wondered how long it would be before he learned her new number. Her new phone was basic with no access to the internet. Not being especially technology minded, it had been no real sacrifice. If Oliver could only access her through her laptop, she felt she was keeping him at a distance. In a vain effort to feel more secure, she usually checked her mail in the office when there were other people around. This last week, his anger at her disappearance had been increasingly apparent. One message still haunted her: *I guess you've gone away but you know I'll find you, don't you? Just wait till I do. I can't forgive you for treating me this way.* Thinking about it again made her feel the familiar clutch of fear in her stomach and she quickly pushed him out of her mind.

She glanced across at Luc instead; he was staring at the road with an unreadable expression. In the studio she'd seen him at the other end of the room, preparing canvases or mixing mediums or doing any of the other monotonous tasks Peter required of him. And she'd seen him painting: putting the finishing touches to a portrait or laying in the underpainting of a landscape. They had crossed occasionally and Luc had even brought her coffee but, as if by tacit agreement, they had exchanged barely half a dozen words. Even so, they couldn't spend the entire day together without speaking.

'I didn't expect to see you here, in Provence,' she said eventually.

'No,' he said slowly, 'I was surprised to see you too.'

'But you didn't tell Lindsey that we knew each other. Why was that?'

'Did you?'

'No. I didn't think…' She stopped, unsure herself why. 'Why *are* you here?' she asked instead.

'I'm doing a job…and painting.'

'Yeah. I'm sure you are.' Terri studied his profile; it gave nothing away.

'Why are *you* here?' he countered.

'I'm curating an exhibition. As you know, that's what I do.'

He flicked her a glance. 'I saw you as more of a high flier. Buried away in rural France doesn't seem to fit.'

'I could say the same of you.'

He didn't answer and she looked away, watching the scenery flashing past. They were heading south to Aix-en-Provence to pick up the motorway east. Being in a car with him again felt odd. It was more than five years since she had met him for the first time. At the time she had been an assistant curator on an exhibition of work by Rembrandt at the National Gallery. As the art correspondent for one of the British broadsheets, Luc came to the preview night and started talking to her, asking questions, saying how good the show was. It was his way of speaking perhaps that she remembered best – perfect English delivered with a mild but distinctively throaty accent. She remembered the suddenness of the attraction. It had caught her off guard; Luc was more intense than the men she usually went for. But he moved off, talked to a number of other people, circulated, and she remembered trying to track his progress round the rooms while mingling and answering questions herself. To her surprise he'd sought her out again before he left and asked her out to dinner. They went out on four dates and she had been dangerously close to becoming serious about him when she realised he was not the person she had thought he was.

'Was this your idea?' she asked now.

'What?'

'That you drive me to Nice?'

He shook his head. 'Why would I do that?' he said coldly. 'I still remember the last thing you said to me.'

Terri said nothing. She remembered too. *You're just a bare-faced liar. I never want to see you again.*

'Peter wanted me to bring you,' said Luc.

'Why?'

'I'm not sure.' He glanced across at her again. 'I suspect he thinks you're a loose cannon. He likes to be in control.'

55

They began to loop round Aix and Luc concentrated on the road. She watched him surreptitiously out of the corner of her eye. He hadn't changed much. He wasn't classically handsome: his eyes were a little too deep set, his nose rather too long, but he had surprising pale brown eyes and a broad, warm smile on the rare occasions he chose to use it. His hair was still collar length and a little wavy; she remembered him regularly running a hand through it to push it off his face. Now a few grey hairs peppered his temples. His fingers kept fidgeting on the steering wheel and she frowned, trying to identify what was different about him.

'You're not smoking,' she said suddenly.

'No. I've given up.'

'About time.'

He turned his head briefly, looking at her sidelong. 'I remember you didn't like it.'

'No.' She wondered what else he recalled about her. In some ways she was surprised that he remembered her at all. 'How long since you've had a cigarette then?'

'Nearly six months.'

'But you're still craving them?'

He flicked her a surprised glance. 'Yes. Sometimes.'

'It'll get easier. A friend of mine said it took her two years.'

'Really? Some people say they never get over it.'

They picked up the road to Nice and Luc speeded up. Silence stretched between them again and Terri wondered at the misfortune that had brought them together again after all this time. For a while after they had split up she had followed his career, read his articles, second-guessed which shows he might attend. She told herself that she looked out for him as one does with a wasp in the room. Time passed; eventually she had been happy to let it go. She hadn't noticed his absence from London of late.

'What's it like, living in the house?' Luc asked, breaking into her thoughts.

'Why do you ask?'

'I imagine it's strange: living with your employer. At least I have my own space. In your place I think it would be difficult to switch off.'

'It's fine. Peter's rarely there. Lindsey's out more than she's in. Angela too. I often have the house to myself.'

She tried to sound more positive about it than she felt. She had cooked in the main kitchen a few times, had stored a couple of things in the fridge there and had even used the sitting room, but it was an uncomfortable situation. When she saw her, Lindsey was still guarded and largely uncommunicative and Peter barely acknowledged her presence. Corinne, the small, squat, black-eyed *bonne* – maybe a few years older than Terri - watched her warily and only spoke when she was spoken to. Terri felt like some sort of Jane Eyre, fitting in nowhere, living between stairs.

'Angela's charming,' she said now.

'Oh yes, Angela is charming,' he said, his inflection ambiguous.

'Don't you like her?'

'I didn't say that. And you?'

Terri hesitated. It was hard *not* to like Angela. She was consistently attentive whenever Terri met her, friendly and solicitous. And yet there was a distance between them as if they spoke through glass, at a slight remove from one another.

'We get on fine,' she told him. She flicked him a glance, lips pursed with amusement. 'But I gather she doesn't like you giving piano lessons to Lindsey.'

57

'Did she tell you that?'

'Lindsey did.'

Luc gave one wordless nod of the head.

'Are you becoming friendly with Lindsey?' he said after a pause.

'I hardly know her.'

'You need to be careful. She likes to play people off against each other.'

Terri frowned. 'Why?'

Luc shrugged and again didn't answer. 'I've heard Peter shouting at you,' he remarked a few minutes later. 'How are you managing?'

'You know…it's always difficult in a new job.'

'He's all right, you know. He's just passionate about his work and hates to be deflected from it. And the studio is his domain; what he says, goes. You need to learn to duck and dive.'

'Thanks. I'll bear that in mind.'

Terri couldn't see that it was that simple. Peter was frustrating her at every turn. Every time she tried to discuss the exhibition with him he put it off. Often he ignored her; sometimes he was offensive. The only real progress had been commissioning Sami to build the painting rack which she had done the previous week, explaining its details to his mask-like expression, giving him a drawing marked with dimensions. It was an absurd situation to be in. What was the point in employing someone when you wouldn't let them do their job?

Neither of them made any further effort at conversation and Terri turned back to look out of the window. It was just before eleven when they arrived in Nice and the hurly-burly of traffic swept them along the Promenade des Anglais.

'I'll meet you for lunch,' Luc said as he parked the car.

He suggested a restaurant and they fixed a time. She was amazed Peter hadn't given him instructions to accompany her to the meeting. Walking out onto the streets of Nice, it was a relief to be both alone and away from Le Chant.

The Galerie De Vilaney was on the Boulevard Victor Hugo, a broad, leafy street a short walk from the centre. A wealthy philanthropist and collector had set it up in the sixties. It was now run by a generously endowed trust and showed a permanent collection of fine art alongside its temporary exhibitions. The building – an elegant three-storeyed structure – was set back off the road behind a small, gated, parking area. Two palm trees flanked the entrance giving it an exotic air. She paused outside, gathering herself. From her telephone conversations with the gallery director, it was clear he was not happy with Peter's decision to employ his own curator. Caught in the middle, this visit was as much a diplomatic mission as a chance to view the exhibition space. She muttered the name Christophe Cahen to herself – the name of the gallery assistant with whom she would be dealing – and pushed the glazed door open.

*

The waiter put a glass and a bottle of Perrier by Terri and served Luc a glass of draught beer. He took their order for food and left.

'So how did you get on at De Vilaney's?' said Luc.

'Fine. Christophe was OK, helpful.' Relief made Terri smile. Unlike the gallery director the tanned gallery assistant was only too happy to have someone else to mediate; he had found Peter impossible to deal with. Christophe was also a merciless flirt but he did it lightly, almost as a matter of routine. She had found it amusing, even a little flattering, but not remotely threatening. 'Have you met him?' she asked.

Luc shook his head, downing a mouthful of beer. 'No. He came to the studio once but we didn't speak.'

She looked at him curiously. 'I'm surprised you weren't told to come to the gallery too, given that I'm supposed to be so out of control.'

Luc gave a typically Gallic shrug, disclaiming responsibility. 'He didn't specify. He just asked me to come with you.' He raised his eyebrows and held her gaze. 'I won't tell him if you don't.'

Terri looked away and drank some Perrier. They were on the terrace of a restaurant in the Cours Saleya where the flower market had been that morning. The stalls had all been cleared away and the ground hosed down. Water still pooled in places and odd flower heads and bits of stem lingered in the gutters. There was already warmth in the sun and all the restaurants lining the street were busy. She looked back at Luc to find his eyes still on her.

'So what did you do this morning?' she asked.

'I visited a couple of galleries and I bought some piano music. There's a good music shop here.'

'I hadn't realised you played the piano.'

'It never came up. Our relationship was short-lived.'

'We didn't have a relationship. You can't base one on a lie.'

Luc raised one eyebrow at her as the waiter arrived with his steak and *frites* and her mushroom omelette. They abandoned conversation and ate.

Luc finished first and cradled his beer. Terri felt herself being examined again.

'You haven't changed much,' he said after a couple of minutes.

'No? I'm surprised. I feel a very different person.'

'In what way?'

She was tempted to say, 'wiser,' but, given recent events with Oliver, wasn't sure she could claim that to be true. She finished eating and ignored the question, dropping her napkin on the table and picking up her glass.

'What are you really doing here, Luc?'

'I'm doing what you see I'm doing. I've had a career change.'

She looked at him scathingly. 'Really? What a remarkable coincidence.'

'It's true. And I could explain why but I suppose you wouldn't believe me whatever I said.'

'That's absolutely right.'

Luc finished his beer and thumped the glass down on the table, his lips pressed together in an angry line.

'Look,' he said. 'I told you: I didn't date you to get access to your father. I had already intended to see him. And then we met and I liked you. Just at the moment that might seem surprising, but I did. So I asked you out. I didn't say what I was doing because it was undercover work. And after all, you hardly ever mentioned your father.'

Terri rolled her eyes, shaking her head. 'I can't believe your arrogance. So now it's my fault? Can I just remind you that it was you who set out to single-handedly 'clean up' the art market? It was you who lied your way into my father's workshop, pretending to be a collector with a Pissarro which needed restoring. And you said you knew me, that it was I who had recommended him. It was a blatant lie. Just how many other innocent people had their reputations ruined by your exposé?'

Terri sat back, tight-lipped as the waiter came to clear. He asked if they wanted dessert. Terri declined and asked for tea; Luc ordered an espresso and the waiter left. Luc handled the remaining cutlery on the table with restless fingers.

'You don't condone forgery, I assume?' he said sharply.

'Of course not.'

'So where's your problem? I simply set out to find the crooks who were pushing fakes onto the market. I didn't target your father. I wanted to show how weak the whole system is. Paintings get passed through so many hands and nobody asks enough questions. The forger I revealed by my investigation – his paintings regularly got sent to a restorer. The guy he worked for used to 'age' them and then get them restored to give them more authenticity. The first time it was a gamble. Suppose the restorer said something? The guy would have claimed that he was duped. But the restorer said nothing, and was happy to do it again and again. He knew what he was doing but he was well paid. He didn't care.'

'I know all this. Spare me the preaching. But why drag my father into this? You tried him with one painting. He did the job he was paid to do. He didn't realise what was going on.'

Luc shook his head. 'I wanted to show how no-one says anything. There's a conspiracy of silence. Your father must have had some doubts about the fake. He was an experienced restorer, wasn't he?'

'That is completely unfair,' she responded hotly. 'Even the experts...'

Terri stopped as the tea and coffee arrived and the bill was left on the table. She dangled the teabag into her cup of hot water and left the sentence unfinished. She had wondered herself that her father hadn't noticed, had not voiced any concern, but she'd felt unable to ask him about it; they hadn't had that sort of relationship. Even so, she'd never doubted his honesty.

'You could have left him out of the article,' she said now, putting the teabag back on the saucer. 'But I suppose to you it was just a good story; to my father it was his reputation. Mud sticks in this business as you well know. And he had done nothing wrong.'

'I'm sorry, OK?' he shouted angrily, then dropped his voice as other diners turned to look. 'I didn't think it would upset you so much. You told me you didn't get on with your father. I got the impression you were largely estranged from him.'

'Well I wasn't...not estranged. But my relationship with him isn't the point, is it? You were deceitful. You lied. And you didn't even have the decency to tell me before it came out.'

'No, I know. I got a lot of things wrong.' Luc gave a brief shake of the head, drank a mouthful of espresso and drummed his fingers on the table. 'How is your father anyway?'

'He's dead. He had a heart attack in October.'

'*Ciel.* I'm sorry Terri. I had no idea. He can't have been very old.'

'Fifty-six,' she said. 'But he smoked like a chimney.' Terri bit her lip. A wave of emotion ran through her, hard to define and taking her by surprise. This kept happening. It choked her for a moment and she swallowed hard, suppressing it. 'So tell me,' she said, 'why I should believe that you're genuinely here to work as a studio assistant? An insider article about one of the most controversial characters in contemporary art would be a big story I imagine.'

Luc's eyes narrowed. He finished his coffee and sat back, regarding her dispassionately.

'If you expect to be disappointed in people, I guess you always will be. I can't win whatever I say. Have you finished? We'd better be on our way.'

Terri glared at him and put her share of the bill on the table. They left the restaurant and drove back to the estate, barely speaking. Drawing the car to a halt in the parking area, Luc left the engine running as Terri gathered her things together. Wordlessly, she opened the door to get out.

'Terri?'

'What?'

'I get on fine with Peter and he knows what I used to do. I told him. He won't believe you if you go to him with stories about me. It won't make your life here any easier.'

'That sounds like a threat.'

'It's advice.'

'Oh *advice*. Well it doesn't matter. You don't scare me. I'm not about to go telling tales and I know Peter wouldn't listen to me anyway. But don't even think about putting me in one of your sordid little articles.'

As soon as she'd shut the door, the car sped off, gravel spurting backwards as the wheels gripped. She watched it disappear down the track which wound round the bottom of the estate past the studio, and turned away, picking her way slowly up towards the house.

The conversation with Luc circulated in her head but her thoughts settled, reluctantly, on her father. She remembered his funeral all too clearly: the confusion, the anger even, the guilt and the sudden and acute sense of loss which had left her almost breathless with surprise. She had expected to feel nothing. Not that Edward Challoner had been a bad father;

there had been no physical neglect or abuse. But he had been preoccupied, disinterested and unable to show much affection. Left alone with him as a young child, Terri had felt herself a burden and had simply learnt not to need him. It was undoubtedly the biggest lesson he'd taught her: self-reliance. And then there had been the drinking: occasional benders when he tried to drown all his frustration and loneliness in alcohol, rendering him maudlin or volatile, often a mixture of the two. He had never hurt her but it had been unnerving all the same. They hadn't been 'estranged' though. As the years had gone on, they had just never had much to say to each other.

None of this excused Luc's behaviour however. He'd used her and now he was twisting her words to absolve himself of blame. She wondered if Peter, shut away in this secluded backwater, had any idea of the kind of man he was dealing with.

Chapter 5

As the second week of Terri's contract drew to a close, Peter continued to live up to the worst of his reputation. On the Thursday he had been due to have his plaster cast removed and his mood had noticeably brightened as the day approached. But he'd returned from the clinic in the afternoon with a face as black as thunder and with the plaster still in place. 'The bones aren't knitted enough,' he'd bellowed in the studio to no-one in particular. '*Monsieur n'est plus un jeune homme,*' he'd said, mimicking the doctor. 'As if I didn't know that I wasn't young any more.' He swore, violently, and thumped a fist against the door. 'Will I never get this thing off me?'

Terri had been using his regular absence from the studio in the afternoons to look through the stacks of paintings. Already she'd found some real possibilities for the exhibition but few of them had been dated and Peter refused to help, obliging her to make a laborious and time-consuming search through his notebooks in an effort to find the relevant entry. And he had rejected every request to sit down with her and talk through his early influences or the context of his work. Walking up through the olive grove on the Saturday afternoon, vainly trying to put the angst of the week behind her, Terri could feel the frustration bubbling up inside her again. Without

Peter's cooperation the job was a disaster; she was wasting her time.

She paused, running a hand along the gnarled, twisted branch of one of the olive trees. They were exactly as Van Gogh had painted them: dark, sinuous and faintly sinister, like the ones on the name plaque on her room door. The previous morning, trying out her French on Corinne, she had commented on the plaque and asked if the *bonne* knew who had painted it.

'*Non.*' Corinne, washing down the worktops, shrugged, her expression suggesting such questions were for idle minds. 'All the rooms upstairs have one. They were here when I came. I've never asked.'

'Oh, OK. So what names are on the rooms upstairs?'

Corinne stopped scrubbing and scowled. '*Voyons…*' she began, staring into mid-air. '…there is 'Vermeer', 'Turner', 'Giotto', 'Caillebotte', 'Rubens'…' She shook her head impatiently and went back to her rhythmic scrubbing. 'I can't remember them all now.'

'Do they all have a painting on them?'

'*Ah oui.*' She sounded unimpressed.

Terri had been mildly intrigued; sometime, when she had the house to herself, she'd maybe take a look.

Now she reached the terrace and made for the fountain. The previous evening she'd heard a bullfrog croaking loudly in the stone pool which surrounded it and she stared into its shallow depths hopefully. The basin contained a number of water plants but no fish and apparently no frog. The sweet aromatic scent of herbs from the parterre below drifted up to her on the breeze but she barely registered it and sat down gloomily on the rim of the basin.

'Now you don't look happy.'

Terri turned her head. A tall, thin woman wearing baggy blue trousers and a huge, striped cardigan was approaching across the terrace pushing an old-fashioned pram. Terri had seen her twice before but always in the distance, plodding purposefully through the estate. With that distinctive gravel voice this had to be Celia, Peter's 'barking' sister.

'What is it you're supposed to say…?' The woman stopped and put the brake on the pram, '…*Cheer up, it might never happen*? Such a silly thing, isn't it? Not helpful at all.'

She smiled cheerily to reveal uneven white teeth. The blue trousers belonged to a pair of dungarees and on her feet she wore worn yellow espadrilles stretched lumpily around bunions. Her frizzy white hair had been pinned up on one side with a red butterfly clip.

Terri stood up. A quick glance into the pram revealed an assortment of art materials and canvases. She was relieved to see no baby.

'You must be Celia,' she ventured.

'Yes dear. And you're Terri. I've seen you about.' The woman wiped her hand down her dungarees before offering it to shake. 'Paint gets everywhere,' she added genially.

Terri took the hand and felt her own shaken in a surprisingly strong grip.

'Thought I'd take advantage of the sunshine and get out painting.' Celia glanced round appreciatively. Her height and build brought Peter inevitably to mind; her manner was strikingly different.

'It's a nice morning,' remarked Terri.

'Isn't it? Do you paint?'

'No, I'm afraid not.'

'What a shame. It always makes me feel better. My brother driving you crazy, is he? Well, don't let him get you

68

down. He can be a complete bastard sometimes but you mustn't take it personally. Lindsey's the only person he doesn't shout at.' She shrugged. 'Probably because he hardly ever talks to her. Well, I suppose Angela usually manages to escape too – which is infinitely more surprising. I was hoping to see you but then you needed time to settle in. Angela doesn't like me in the house. Spoils the joy in the visit really but there you are. She denies it of course.'

Terri became aware of Celia scrutinising her face minutely, eyebrows raised, her left hand fingering one pendulous red ceramic earing.

Terri shifted uncomfortably. 'Is there a problem?'

'No, no problem.' Celia flashed a smile. 'I was right.'

'Right about what?'

'You said on the phone that you don't know about the family?'

'No.'

'No? I thought that was what you'd said.'

'I did. I meant no, I don't know anything about the family.'

'Really? You are sure?'

'Of course I'm sure,' said Terri coldly.

'I thought perhaps your mother might have said something.'

'My *mother*? Why on earth would she have done that?'

'Well...you know...' Celia appeared momentarily disconcerted, then produced another smile and shrugged. 'It was just a thought dear. So tell me all about her, your mother.'

'Tell you about my mother?' Terri shook her head, cross now. 'Look, I'm not going to discuss my mother with you. If you'll excuse me, I've got to go.'

69

Before she could move away, Celia reached out a hand and laid it on Terri's arm.

'Don't be offended dear. I meant no harm. I just like to know…things.' She grinned. 'Well, doesn't everyone? Still it *is* good to have you here. Do come and see me if you fancy it sometime. I live in the *pigeonnier* over there. No ceremony; none of Angela's airs and graces.'

Celia took the brake off the pram and walked away without looking back. Terri watched her go, frowning. As she turned away, she noticed a shadow at the window in the bedroom above the drawing room. Someone had been standing watching them and had just moved away.

*

On the Monday, Sami delivered the painting racks to the studio and they were surprisingly good, beautifully crafted. Peter was working and looked up, glaring, as Terri voiced her thanks and indicated where she wanted them put. When Sami left she followed him outside and asked if it was possible to have another trestle table in her room. She had decided to create a timeline for Peter's life: a physical, at-a-glance map of his career with paintings marked against one side of it and dates and important life experiences on the other; the relationship between the two would be immediately apparent. It would make the movement of his career easier to plot. Perhaps the physicality of it might even encourage Peter to focus on the task in hand.

Sami nodded and immediately turned to leave.

'Can I have it by tomorrow morning?' Terri asked him in her best French. Over the weekend, she'd overheard Angela complaining that Sami kept putting jobs off and that the swimming pool should have been cleaned and ready for use by now. There was a real risk she would never get the table if she didn't press the point now.

'*Demain matin*?' he grumbled. 'No, tomorrow is not good. No.'

'But it's important for *Monsieur* Stedding's retrospective,' she pleaded. 'I need the table to do the work. Please?'

Sami's dark eyes examined her face, then he touched his cap and walked away.

But Terri had forgotten about the Tuesday morning life class. Stuck in her office the next morning, having finally located the owner of one of the paintings on Peter's list, she was on the phone to an elderly lady when she heard Peter shouting in French and the less distinct sound of someone else's voice in reply.

'Yes, I'm sorry Mrs. Thripton-Brown, I didn't quite catch that…' She covered her free ear, trying to listen, '… yes, of course I'll put it in writing to you and I'll make all the arrangements… yes, Mr Stedding is very grateful to you, thank you for your help. I'll speak to you again soon.'

She finished the call just as the door was thrown open.

'What the hell is going on here?' bellowed Peter from the doorway. 'What do you mean by arranging to have this done on a Tuesday morning?'

Terri got to the door and looked past Peter to see Sami in the studio with the huge top of a trestle table balanced against his shoulder, waiting, gaze fixed on the floor. She eased her way past Peter into the studio and became aware of the eyes of all the life class students on her. Even the languid naked model on the chaise longue was glaring at her.

71

'Of course, the table. I am sorry. But it'll only take a minute to set it up.'

'Only a minute,' repeated Peter, eyes protruding in anger. 'I have to ask, do you actually understand English? Because if not I can't see how we're going to be able to do anything remotely useful here. I said I wouldn't have my classes disturbed so what do you call this?'

'Look, I'm sorry. But I didn't do it intentionally. I forgot about the class.'

'You forgot about the class. God Almighty, you're a complete liability.' He glared at her and then gestured at Sami to continue, muttered in French to him and turned away. He walked back to the class, saying something to the students about 'half-soaked women' which provoked a ripple of laughter.

Back in her office, showing Sami where she wanted the table put, Terri found she was shaking and folded her hands under her armpits in an effort to control them. A series of emotions vied for supremacy: anger, embarrassment, frustration. For the rest of the morning she stayed in her office. Struggling to concentrate, she made a note about the telephone conversation with Mrs Thripton-Brown and began laying out the timeline using sheets of card she'd bought at the weekend. Using separate blank cards she positioned the few paintings to which she could definitely apportion a year and tentatively marked in a couple of others. In an effort to make them immediately identifiable, she even did a quick line sketch on each one of the basic form of the painting. It was a start but there was precious little to fill in yet. Around half-past eleven, she was disturbed by a light knock on the door and Luc came in bearing a mug of coffee. He laid it on her desk.

'Thought you might need one,' he murmured. She thanked him but refused to meet his eye and he left without another word.

Ten minutes later she heard Peter's raised voice again, apparently describing some important approach to their naked subject. She tried to ignore him and carry on. Looking at the timeline it was obvious just how much there was to be done if this exhibition was going to be a success and, without Peter's input, the whole thing was going to be meaningless. Otherwise, he might as well just pick a few pictures at random and put them up as and where there was a space. Perhaps that was all he wanted: not a structured retrospective but an exhibition of his most famous work in no particular order.

But Peter didn't need her for that so why bother to put up with his temper and fight him all the way? He was making a fool of her. The laughter of the students still rang in her ears. She couldn't go back to London but surely she could find a job somewhere else? She had qualifications, experience; she had a few contacts. And being the supposed curator of a disorganised and meaningless retrospective was not going to help her career one jot.

These thoughts churned round in her head for the rest of the morning. She heard Peter dismiss the class just before one and was intending to escape up to the house when he thumped the door back and walked straight into her office.

'What on earth were you thinking of?' he said roundly. 'The one morning in the week when I will not have any disturbance - I thought I'd made that abundantly clear.' He looked round suspiciously. 'What do you need another table for, anyway?'

'But it's not the one morning in the week, is it?' Terri's eyes danced with anger and her cheeks flushed with heat. The

73

cork had come out and all her frustrations were starting to bubble out. 'You won't have any disturbance any morning or at any other time. I am kept completely side-lined. How can I do my job like that?'

'I made...'

'Let me finish. I can't discuss anything with you without making an appointment and I can't even make the appointment. But if you expect me to help you produce a good retrospective we have to work as a team. It requires mutual respect and it seems the respect is only going one way at the moment, from me to you. I made a mistake this morning and I'm sorry. But I apologised. And instead of letting it go you made fun of me in front of your class. That wasn't necessary, nor was it very professional. I'm open to constructive criticism when appropriate but it should be delivered in private. And if you can't co-operate enough with me to get the basics of this exhibition set out, there is little point in me continuing to waste my time here.'

Peter was glaring at her, that involuntary twitch developing again in his cheek. For a moment she thought he was going to hit her and she fought her fear and the desire to back away.

'I don't see...' he began.

'I'm giving you my notice,' she said. 'I shall leave in two weeks as stipulated. I'll do what little I usefully can till then and I'll put it in writing this afternoon.'

There was silence while they stared each other out then Terri walked as calmly as she could to the door.

'As you wish,' Peter said coldly to her back.

*

Peter raised his paintbrush to the canvas, tried to focus on what he'd been doing before but let his arm fall. He dropped the brush on his work-table and stared at it without seeing it. The nerve of the woman. Terri's words kept replaying through his head and he was stunned. All that anger and contempt directed at him. *It wasn't necessary, nor was it very professional.* He winced as the words paraded across his mind again, but when he thought of the way he'd behaved he wondered if he had indeed gone too far. It wouldn't have been the first time.

He got up from his stool, wandered across to Terri's office and stood in the doorway, taking in the open laptop on the desk, the notebook and pen, his own notebooks carefully stacked in separate piles and the newly installed table, already covered with her latest device. He went inside and approached the desk. On the pad he saw Terri's small, neat writing recording her conversation with a Mrs. Thripton-Brown. He flipped back through the pages and saw other notes of phone calls and a record of her visit to the gallery in Nice. There was a sheet with a number of questions, entitled: *Ask Peter.* There was a list of galleries to ring too, together with the titles of paintings they had handled. Many of them were already ticked and notes had been scribbled in alongside, sometimes with more names or numbers. Propped up against the wall by the door, he saw that she had put four paintings chosen from the studio. Each one had a label stuck to the back of the frame. She had achieved an impressive amount in a small space of time. He crossed to the new table and saw her carefully marked and annotated timeline with the painting cards placed in on one side. The sketchy line drawings of his work were comical in their simplicity but he saw nothing amusing today.

He turned away, lost in thought, left the studio and headed slowly back up the hill for lunch.

With work over for the day, Terri had a long shower, wrapped herself in her cotton dressing gown, threw herself on the bed and stared at the ceiling. She'd typed and printed out her letter of resignation and had left it on Peter's worktable when he wasn't there. Ever since, she had wondered if she'd done the right thing but kept reassuring herself that she had. Even so, she was surprised to feel so deflated. She ought to be pleased: the charade would soon come to an end and she could get a proper job somewhere else.

But she had the unpleasant feeling that though her unusually eloquent tirade might have won her the battle, Peter had in fact won the war. It was she who had blinked first. And then, of course, there was the prospect of returning to London and Oliver, and the thought sickened her stomach. She could pretend that she could go anywhere but the reality was not that easy. In London she did at least have a home and she would be sure to find some kind of work. It was a desperate feeling. Perhaps she'd been stupid.

'I don't have to go back to London,' she said defiantly to the ceiling. 'There might still be something in Paris. What about New York?' She'd had some good reviews in the American press for her portrait exhibition. They might open a few doors for her though, of course, that had been three years ago. She was being unrealistic, dancing on hope.

Her thoughts drifted back to Peter's retrospective. Frustratingly, having seen all his brilliant canvases round the studio and watched him working, it was clear that it could have been a truly great exhibition, a really fascinating project. It might even have got her work noticed…though only if he'd co-operated, she reminded herself. Cross with herself for

76

wallowing in her misery, she got up to find her laptop; she needed to start looking to see what jobs were available.

She'd just bent over to pick up the computer when two short knocks rapped the door and she looked round sharply; no-one ever came to her room except Corinne and her housework was done for the day.

'Yes?'

'Terri.' It was Peter's booming voice. 'Can I have a word?'

Terri tied her gown more firmly around her waist, smoothed down her wet hair, and walked to the door. She opened it just wide enough to look out.

'What is it?'

'Can I come in?'

'Yes...if you want.' She stepped back, pulling the door open.

He walked past her to stand in the middle of the floor. He was holding her letter in his hand and he fingered the paper, staring vaguely towards the patio doors. The room looked much smaller suddenly. He turned and fixed her with his pale eyes.

'I believe I owe you an apology,' he said gruffly. 'I...well, I have a temper. Sometimes it goes too far.' He hesitated as if he wanted to say something else. The silence lengthened. He cleared his throat. 'I'm sorry.'

Terri frowned, silent, unsure how to take him. She'd never heard him apologise before.

'And I don't want you to leave.' Peter gestured with the printed letter in his hand. 'I'm sure we can work something out.'

Terri's frown deepened.

'Do you mean that?'

'Of course I mean it. I want the exhibition to be good. It's…it's important.' He took a deep breath and let it out slowly. 'And I think you will do it very well.'

'But only if I can get your co-operation,' she said.

'And you shall have it,' he said grandly, raising his chin.

'Really?'

'Yes, yes,' he said impatiently. 'Didn't I just say that you would?'

Terri stared at him, still uncertain.

'So?' he pressed. 'What's the answer then: will you stay?'

Still she hesitated but knew she'd be crazy to refuse. 'Yes, all right, I'll stay,' she said eventually.

Peter tore the letter in two with a flourish and gave it back to her. He met her gaze for a second, nodded, and left. For a minute or two she felt elated, as if everything had changed. Then doubt slowly crept up on her again and she wondered if it had.

Chapter 6

Angela surveyed the long formal table in the dining room critically. It was laid with white linen, shining silver cutlery and sparkling crystal glasses. An elaborate floral arrangement stood in the middle and each setting had a rolled linen serviette in a napkin ring and a name holder. It was Easter Saturday and dinner was planned for eight-thirty. As usual, Corinne had come in to help with the cooking and it was she who had laid the table. While the French woman was almost obsessive about the way the food was prepared and presented, she was markedly less fastidious about the table. Angela eased round to the further side and straightened a knife here, a spoon there. The napkin in one of the rings looked badly rolled and she pulled it out and redid it. Her dinner parties were important to her; they had to be right.

When she was first married, young and flushed with her new position as the wife of a famous portrait painter, she had invited creative people to dine: artists and potters, sculptors and writers, designers and poets. She had expected them to be interesting, had played with the idea of sponsoring a Bohemian circle, but had quickly abandoned it. She'd been bored rigid. These people lived in a world she couldn't inhabit and sometimes she was sure they excluded her intentionally. They were unpredictable too, outlandish, wild and unconventional.

Angela found it threatening; she was conservative in almost every sense of the word. She stopped inviting them. These days, her guests were from the ex-pats society to which she belonged: stockbrokers and engineers, businessmen and property developers, sportspeople and entrepreneurs – all people who had escaped to the south of France for the sun. The most creative thing they did was indulge in a few theatricals. Angela had long harboured a desire to be an actress; she sang rather well too. Her dinner parties gave her the chance to indulge herself and her like-minded friends. While they drank pre-prandial cocktails they would all have a chance to perform.

She checked along the place-names, making sure Corinne had put them out correctly. The right mix and placing was important; she had learned that the hard way. Parties could be ruined if you got it wrong. It was like directing a play: setting the scene, choosing the best cast to play off each other, making sure everyone knew where they should be. At least Peter never attended any more. She suspected he used to come from some misguided sense of duty but then he would play up, hate being asked questions about his painting and more often than not slope away half way through the evening. It was much better for everyone if he stayed away.

One place-card leaned in its holder drunkenly and she fingered it back into position. Terri. Angela frowned. She had felt obliged to invite her but really, it was a difficult situation. And there was something about the girl which bothered her. She seemed pleasant enough but her eyes were dark and serious. And she was quiet, too quiet in fact. Angela liked company and she liked chatter; she preferred people with an open disposition. That's why she liked Americans: you knew where you were with them. With silent people you were never sure what they were thinking.

Angela sighed, gave one last sweeping look at her table and turned to leave. Then she noticed the wine cooler hadn't been put out on the side table, nor the dishes for dessert.

'Corinne?' she called. 'Oh really. Corinne, where are you?'

*

The guests drifted back into the *salon* in twos and threes, talking. Terri came too, alone. The after-dinner coffee was laid out on a table at the top of the room and was served by Corinne who'd been waiting on table all evening wearing a black dress, a small white apron and an expression of blank disinterest. Terri was relieved to have escaped the halting, awkward conversation with her neighbouring dinner guests. This wasn't her world. She was dressed in the most sophisticated of the three dresses she had brought with her but knew it didn't match the glamour of the occasion. With its exotic cocktails, recitations and Cole Porter songs, all interspersed with music on the piano by Berlin and Gershwin, the party had the feel of a Hollywood film set straight from the thirties.

She picked up a cup of coffee and wandered away down to the bottom of the room near the patio doors. One of them was open and she wondered how long it would be before she could politely slip away. Her grandmother would have liked this, she thought wryly. Janet Challoner had liked smart restaurants she could barely afford and dress shops where the assistant called you 'modom' and offered you a seat; she'd had a smart telephone voice, never left the house without make-up on and used to get her hair set once a week. Terri had been a disappointment to her: as a child, she'd been a tomboy and Janet had regularly chastised her son for allowing his daughter to 'grow up wild.' And what had her father thought about it? Terri mentally shrugged. She had no idea.

Lindsey came to join her. She had been seated at the other end of the table and they'd barely exchanged a word all evening.

'You survived then,' she said, cradling her coffee. 'Do you hate these things as much as I do?' She didn't wait for a reply. 'Mama has one of these dos every month. She loves them.'

'I see your father didn't come.'

Terri was relieved. Despite Peter's earnest promise of cooperation, she had managed to persuade him to only one discussion since their altercation, and his temper was as volatile as ever. Fortunately she rarely saw him round the house.

'Father never comes any more,' said Lindsey. 'Well, hardly ever. I can't say I blame him.'

'So why do you come if you hate them so much?'

Lindsey seemed surprised by the question. 'Because mama expects me to, I suppose. It's less hassle. Did you used to stand up to your mother?'

'I barely knew her so it never came up.'

Lindsey nodded slowly, apparently taking it in, unsure what to say. She glanced across at Terri furtively. 'I was thinking…maybe we could go shopping together sometime?'

'Yes,' Terri said carefully, 'we could do that. Where would you suggest?'

'Aix. I know some good boutiques there.'

'Fine.'

'Good.' Lindsey emptied the tiny coffee cup in one movement, glanced up the room and put a hand to her forehead, massaging it with her fingers. 'I've got one of my headaches coming on. I need some fresh air. Will you tell mama I've gone to lie down?'

'If you want. Are you OK?'

'Yes, of course, I'll be fine.' She dumped the coffee cup nearby and slipped out of the patio door into the night.

Back up the room, a wobbling contralto launched into a song. Left alone, Terri put her empty coffee cup beside Lindsey's and noticed a small bronze sculpture of a horse further along the console table. She reached out a finger to touch its patinated surface.

'Do you like my stallion? He is rather handsome, isn't he?' Angela moved smoothly to Terri's side. 'I know nothing about paintings but I do like sculptures. Are they part of your work?'

'I'm afraid not.'

Angela smiled. 'I saw you talking to Lindsey. I'm pleased. I'm afraid she gets a bit lonely here sometimes. And of course she's very shy. I worry that she doesn't mix more.' She turned her head, glancing round the room. 'Where is she, by the way?'

'She's got a headache; she's gone to lie down.'

'Oh?' Angela's eyes searched Terri's face suspiciously. 'That was very sudden. Did she say anything else?'

'No.'

'She shouldn't lie down after all that food. Perhaps I...' Angela's expression froze. 'Oh no,' she murmured. 'What now?' She abruptly walked away.

At the top of the room, Celia had walked in, wearing a calf length magenta dress and purple beads, a broad gold bangle pushed up into the soft, wrinkled flesh above her right elbow. Round her head stretched a half inch purple band holding a curling pink feather in place to one side.

'Hello Angela,' Celia announced loudly, 'Sorry I'm late; my favourite quiz programme was on the television. Do you know I've just seen an amazing advert for a gadget that uses an electric current to tighten up your buttocks?' She paused and looked round the now silent room, then fixed on Angela again. 'But maybe you already know about it dear? Keeps them taut and perky apparently.'

'Celia,' said Angela in a clear, icy voice. 'Don't apologise. We weren't expecting you anyway. But, since you're here, have some coffee.' She took Celia's arm and actively pulled her to the side. A few minutes later she was called away to a couple who were leaving and Celia bore down on Terri with an expectant expression. Terri watched her approach warily.

'Terri,' Celia said brightly, 'how nice to see you again.' She sipped her coffee, complained, 'I'd rather hoped for wine,' and surveyed the room as Angela came back to join them. 'Isn't Peter here? I was hoping to see him. Not that he's ever liked these affairs.'

'No, he's not here,' said Angela.

'And no Lindsey either. Have you fallen out again?'

'No, we have not fallen out,' Angela replied crisply. 'She has a headache and went to lie down.'

'Oh, well, if you say so.'

A taut silence fell between them. Terri cast about for something to say.

'Where did you go painting today Celia?' she asked.

'Me? I…' She stared into Terri's face, just as she had done on the terrace. 'Isn't that amazing? I thought there was something about you.'

'Sorry?'

'Your eyes.'

'Oh stop it Celia,' said Angela impatiently.

'Your eyes, they're ex*actly* like Madeleine's.' Celia gave Terri a knowing look. 'Madeleine was Peter's first wife.'

'Yes, I know,' said Terri.

Angela looked at her sharply.

'But you must see it too, Angela,' remarked Celia, sidelong. 'Are you related to Maddy, Terri dear?'

'Related?' said Terri, frowning. 'No. Why would I be?'

'Of course she's not related,' said Angela crossly. She checked herself and forced a tolerant smile. 'It's getting late and you do get muddled when you're tired, Celia. Let's get you a brandy and you can take it to bed with you.'

Celia shook off Angela's hand.

'I'm not remotely tired. And it can't be a coincidence. Go and look at the painting yourself if you don't believe me.' She turned back to Terri. 'You should go and look too, dear. The resemblance is striking. But it's a lovely portrait anyway. Have you seen it? It's in the sitting room.'

'Yes,' said Terri. 'It is a lovely painting.'

'Yes, we're all agreed it's a lovely painting, Celia.' Angela patted Celia on the arm. 'Now let's get you a brandy, shall we?' She looped a more determined hand through Celia's elbow and shepherded her up the room.

Celia turned her head as she moved away and winked at Terri. '*Ciao,*' she said, with a smile. '*Buonanotte.*'

Terri took the opportunity to slip back to her room. Brushing her teeth in the bathroom half an hour later, she found herself staring at her reflection in the mirror, trying to remember what Madeleine's eyes had looked like in the portrait. She resolved to take a look the next morning. But she failed to see why Celia had made such a point of the similarity and, coming so soon after that strange meeting on the terrace, she found it surprisingly unsettling. She finished in the bathroom, switched off the light and shook the thought away. Celia was batty; everyone said so.

*

Peter glared at the portrait of Laurent Valdeau. He still wasn't happy with the right hand but couldn't identify why. It was the Thursday morning and he'd been working at it for days already, building up the whole painting in layers but always coming back to that hand. He sighed and forced himself to concentrate on the area around the mouth instead, balancing the mahl stick on dry paint to the side of the head, steadying his right wrist on it as he touched in a little colour. But the stick began to slide and he felt powerless to stop it. Down it went, dragging slowly and inexorably into the wet paint in a long smudgy line before finally falling with a clack to the floor.

'Oh – my – God,' he bellowed, and cursed violently. 'It's useless. I mean, just look at it.' He flipped his left hand back in frustration and then slapped at it with his right. 'Useless. Absolutely – bloody - useless. I can't grip *anything.*'

In a fit of temper he bent over, picked up the mahl stick and threw it across the studio where it bounced off one of the windows – leaving an oily imprint on the glass – before falling to the floor. He sat down heavily on the stool, his temper already burning out, a feeling of impotence and desolation sweeping over him. His plaster had finally been removed the previous Thursday; he had been relieved and had expected so much. But his left hand simply would not work and now he felt more frustrated than ever. He rested it down on his thigh, looking at it forlornly. It was limp, swollen and pale grey, the skin dry and flaky. It was as if it belonged to someone else. It might as well do because it was no good to him. He raised his eyes to the painting again. It was a mess.

'What crap,' he declaimed.

He didn't notice Terri, who'd been crossing to the kitchen when he shouted, pick up the stick from the floor and walk back up the room with it. He only became aware of her as she put the stick down on the worktable and then stood looking at him. She had this way of sneaking up on him, saying nothing, making sure she was just within his eye line. If he didn't speak she would say something and wait and speak again until he finally answered. She was so irritatingly persistent.

'Your hand looks awful,' she said now with a look of frank exasperation, and he watched her reach out, pick it up and begin to rub it. 'Didn't they suggest you have treatment?' Peter raised surprised eyes to her face then watched her fingers massaging his.

'They might have done,' he said grudgingly. 'But I don't see why I should need it. Anyway I haven't got the time to be footling around in some clinic while...'

'My grandmother broke her arm once...' Terri interrupted, still rubbing his hand. '...and it was useless for a while afterwards. But she had treatment and it helped; it made her hand stronger and less swollen.' She turned the hand over and rubbed at the palm, then kneaded up Peter's normally wiry forearm, now quite puffy.

'Your *grandmother*? Is that supposed to make me feel better? What *are* you doing?' He did not pull his hand away however. Actually it felt quite good.

'I'm massaging the fluid out of it. This is what the physios did to my grandmother. And they gave her exercises to do. I went with her once and they showed me how to do it. She admitted it felt better afterwards. And believe me,' Terri said with feeling, 'she was the last person to say that if it wasn't true.' Peter looked up into her face again, frowning. 'And she got the movement back,' she added pointedly.

'Work is exercise,' he grumbled. 'I try to use it as much as I can. But it's got worse since the plaster came off. They probably didn't set it right.'

'Maybe. But apparently the muscles forget how to work when they're in plaster. They need retraining.' Terri stopped massaging and let go of his arm. 'If you want it to get better you should have treatment. And you should rest with your hand up to stop it swelling.' She shrugged. 'But it's your arm.'

'Exactly. It's my arm.' Peter cautiously tried to flex his fingers and straighten them; they moved a little better. 'Mm,' he muttered, surprised. The outline of his knuckles was just visible under the skin for the first time since the plaster had come off. He raised his eyes to the portrait. 'Wouldn't you know it,' he groaned. 'That infernal hand hasn't been damaged at all. What *is* wrong with it?'

'The right hand?' said Terri, who was already surveying the damage. 'I think it's a little too small.' She pointed at it and then at the face. 'You see, in comparison to…'

'I was *not* asking for your opinion,' barked Peter, glaring at her.

Terri stared at him a moment, expressionless, then resumed her route towards the kitchen.

Peter considered the hand, frowning. 'Too small indeed,' he grunted, and picked up a brush to start removing the smudged paint from his canvas. 'Damn cheek of the woman.'

*

Terri paused on her way through the sitting room and crossed to look at the portrait of Madeleine. It was a week since the Easter party but Celia's odd behaviour still stuck in her mind, like a riddle it was trying to solve, and it was not the first time she'd been back to look at the painting. She stared up at it now, flipping her car key between her fingers, then went in search of Lindsey. Peter's daughter had the weekend off and they were going on their shopping trip to Aix-en-Provence.

According to the guides Aix had elegant shops, beautiful architecture and a noble historical heritage; to Terri it was where Cézanne had kept his studio and painted some of his most famous works. When they arrived it simply felt like a modern town, its streets bustling with Saturday morning shoppers and tourists. Lindsey showed Terri where to park the car and proceeded to lead her on a tour of her favourite boutiques.

Late morning, they stopped for coffee high up in the old part of the town, sitting on the terrace of a café bar. It was the last day of April, a clear, sunny day with a fitful chill breeze. Lindsey had said little all morning. She had occasionally picked out a dress or a top, held it up for Terri's opinion, replaced it and moved on. Now she sat dunking a sugar cube in her coffee, her expression unreadable. Terri had tried a couple of opening gambits of conversation with little response. Now she had given up and wondered why Lindsey had invited her in the first place.

'Thanks for covering for me last Saturday,' Lindsey said suddenly, staring into her coffee.

'Hm? Oh you mean the headache thing? Why, what were you doing?'

Lindsey ignored the question. 'Mama didn't make a fuss about it so you must have been convincing.'

'She was probably distracted. Celia made a dramatic entrance just after you'd gone.'

'She has a way of doing that.' Lindsey spooned the sugar cube into her mouth and sucked on it, refusing to meet Terri's eyes.

'She really behaved quite oddly, announcing that my eyes were just like Madeleine's. Then your mother got cross and dragged her away.'

'Sounds like Celia.' Lindsey took a mouthful of coffee. 'Mama is convinced the old bat's determined to cause trouble and make her life a misery.'

'Why?'

Lindsey shrugged and dunked another sugar cube in her coffee. 'She thinks father should exert more control over her since he invited her here in the first place. But he thinks Celia's harmless. Of course she doesn't play up the same when he's around.'

'So she's done this sort of thing before?'

'Oh yes. Celia's compared all sorts of people to Madeleine in the past.'

'I see.' Somehow it didn't feel that simple. Maybe she was taking it too personally but Terri couldn't let it drop. 'Does your father know she does this?'

'He might do.'

'So why is Celia so obsessed with Madeleine?'

Again Lindsey shrugged, continuing to play with the sugar cube in her coffee.

'Have you ever gone out with a Frenchman?' she asked.

'Why do you ask?' said Terri warily.

'Do you know Thierry?'

'Your father's student? The one with the beard?'

'Yes.' Lindsey lifted her eyes to meet Terri's and produced a rare smile. 'I'm seeing him. Only mama doesn't know. So you mustn't say. She doesn't like me going out with French men. She thinks the culture's too different. She's got a thing about it.'

'Well, that's for you to decide, surely?'

Lindsey said nothing and finished her coffee.

'I thought you were dating Luc actually.' As soon as she'd said it Terri regretted the remark.

'Luc? No.' Lindsey fixed Terri with an enquiring gaze. 'Are you sure you haven't met him before? Only the way you looked at each other... And you went to Nice together the other day, didn't you?'

'That was work.' Terri hesitated, then offered a half-truth. 'But it turned out we did meet years ago - at the preview of an exhibition.'

'Is that right? I guess that is somewhere you'd meet people.'

Lindsey clearly didn't believe her and Terri changed the subject, returning to the issue uppermost in her mind.

'You told me Madeleine died young. So what happened to her exactly?'

'Oh God, Madeleine, Madeleine. Everyone's obsessed with Madeleine. Why do you want to know?'

'Because if I knew it might make it easier to deal with Celia.' Terri did an impression of Celia, staring fixedly into Lindsey's eyes. *'Your eyes, they're exactly like Madeleine's,'* she mimicked in a ghoulish voice. She sat back again and raised her eyebrows. 'She's scary, frankly.'

Lindsey assumed her more familiar mulish expression.

'Well…Madeleine died in childbirth, apparently. Had some poor little kid who didn't live long because there was something wrong with him.'

'Oh no, how awful. Poor Peter.' Terri felt a pang of guilt for some of the things she'd thought about him. 'Do you know anything else about her?'

'Yeah, of course: she liked paintings. Especially that Italian painter - what was his name: the one with a name like an angel…?'

'Raphael?'

'Yeah. Him. Maybe. Maybe not. But that's all I know and I don't want to talk about her,' Lindsey added fiercely. 'And I don't think you should either.' She got to her feet. 'You've finished, haven't you? Shall we go?'

Chapter 7

Peter started going for physiotherapy on a Thursday afternoon but omitted to tell Terri and it was Luc who informed her.

'Quite a coup for you,' he remarked dryly. 'What did you do to his hand that day? Whatever it was he must have liked it. Perhaps you'd like to hold my hand sometime...'

Terri refused to rise to the bait. But Luc was often missing from the studio too, either for a couple of hours or half a day.

'Collecting materials,' he'd responded one afternoon when her curiosity got the better of her. 'Peter is very particular. He has to have canvas from one place and paints or pigments from another; brushes from somewhere else. I could order it all but he likes me to check it for myself, make sure the quality's right.'

And so it was that, on the second Thursday of May, Terri found herself alone in the studio for the entire afternoon. Peter was at the clinic and Luc had gone to Avignon to collect a selection of pigments, a journey of at least an hour each way. With a mug of tea to hand, she took the opportunity to pick up where she'd left off the previous week, looking through the disordered stacks of paintings. Every few days she now managed to persuade Peter to glance through the pictures she thought might enhance the exhibition. 'Definites' – of which there had only been three so far - were put in the holding racks near the door and 'possibles' stayed in her increasingly crowded office, pending a final decision. Most of the work she had found up to now had been from the middle or later years of his career and she was still searching for examples of his early work. Peter had been unforthcoming on the issue. 'How the hell would I know?' he'd bellowed.

After an hour of bending over, sorting through dusty canvases, she pulled out a striking image of a nude: a large, unframed painting of a young woman standing at an open window, her arms raised to lean on the sill, her back to the artist. The face was largely in profile, *contre-jour* and lacking in detail. The model's chin length apricot-blonde hair, in big looping curls, gleamed in places where it caught the light. Terri turned it over. 1981 had been scrawled on the back. She put it to one side to show Peter.

Straightening up, easing her head back to stretch her neck, her gaze fell on a cloth-covered mound on the roof of the offices at the end of the barn. The rooms had been built with partition walling and flat roofs, leaving a tall, open triangle of loft space above them where something had evidently been stored. She retrieved an old wooden ladder from the end of the studio where a high window kept jamming, leaned it against the office wall and climbed its creaking steps. Finding the roof stronger than she'd expected, she made her way cautiously to the back, lifted the huge piece of hessian, thick with dust, and saw stacks of canvases buried beneath it, propped any which way. She dragged the cloth away, coughing as a cloud of dust motes rose into the air, and picked up the nearest picture. It had 1964 written on the back. Finally she had found the early work.

'Yes.' She punched the air. 'Why didn't Peter tell me these were up here?'

She immediately returned to the studio for her notebook and labels. There were portraits and nudes, landscapes and intimate interiors, though several were damaged with mildew or beetle infestation. Peter should be shot, she thought, for letting his paintings get into this state. Slowly and methodically she began to work through them, though it was clearly going to take several days.

It was engrossing, grimy work but, by the time she was ready to give up for the day, she had lined up nine 'possibles' at the edge of the roof. About to abandon the rest for another time, a small framed picture caught her eye, nestling against the back wall where she had cleared a way through. It had been carefully wrapped in a separate piece of cloth - the only painting which had been given this special treatment.

'So who are you?' she murmured, easing forward again, lifting it up and slowly pulling the cover off.

It was a small head and shoulders of a young boy, his lively, intelligent features full of mischief, his expression perfectly caught as if he was on the point of saying something. The familiar prickle of excitement ran down Terri's spine. This was something special, reminiscent of the painting of Madeleine, vibrant, intriguing. In fact... Terri frowned. The boy even looked like Madeleine. No, that was ridiculous. Celia had put that thought in her head, comparing everyone to the woman.

She looked at the reverse of the canvas where 1974 had been pencilled onto the top stretcher. She turned it back. How old would the child have been? Maybe seven or eight. His mouth was slightly lop-sided but there was definitely a resemblance to Peter's first wife, she would swear it.

'Now that *is* odd,' she muttered.

Lindsey had said that Madeleine had a '*poor little kid who didn't live long because there was something wrong with him*'. Terri had assumed this meant that he'd died in infancy. So was this a different son or had she misunderstood? If she knew when Madeleine had died it would help. Had Peter had another child? Or had Lindsey been misinformed? She propped up the picture to one side and took the selected paintings down the ladder. Returning to the loft she picked up the boy's portrait again. It was excellent but, if this was indeed the child who had died, hardly appropriate for the exhibition and quite impossible to ask Peter. Even so, on an impulse she wrapped it up in its swaddling again and took it down to her office where she hid it among the clutter at the back of the room.

Straightening up, she started, catching sight of Luc standing silently in the doorway.

'Is something the matter?' he said.

'Not at all. I wasn't sure you'd be back this afternoon.'

He looked at her with a quizzical expression and she held his gaze, wondering if he'd seen what she'd been doing.

'The ladder is propped up over Peter's door,' he remarked. 'Is there a reason for that?'

'I found some paintings stored up in the loft.'

'Really?' Luc automatically glanced upwards though he could see nothing from where he stood. 'Anything of note?'

'I've only just started looking. But I've found a couple of things.' She gestured towards the pictures she had put near the door. 'There are a lot up there. I'll have to go through the rest another day.'

'That looks good.' He'd noticed the nude with the tumbling apricot curls. It was a large picture and she'd propped it up against a box. Luc moved closer, his critical gaze running systematically over the canvas.

'Who is it?' he asked.

'I don't know…yet.'

'The use of light is powerful. It's hard to make out her features. It looks more instinctive than Peter's usual.' He leaned in closer. 'It's quite a sensual painting. The pose, the use of paint…' He nodded as if trying to memorise its techniques.

'I have to admit: you're good,' said Terri mildly, perching on the side of her desk.

He straightened up, looked round at her and frowned. 'What do you mean by that?'

'I mean you're really quite believable as the apprentice, desperate to learn from his master…almost anyway.'

Luc sighed, his mouth settling into a resigned expression. 'You're still convinced I'm writing a story, aren't you, that I'm only pretending to be a studio assistant?'

'Of course.' She eased herself off the table, closed down her computer and began to collect her things together.

'Have dinner with me,' he said.

She looked round sharply. 'What? You must be joking.'

'*Ciel, Thérèse chérie*. Don't be so stubborn. I've thought about you so often over the last five years. This is a chance for us to make up and be friends. A lot has changed in that time.' He took a step closer to her and looked as if he was about to reach out for her hand but then forced his fingers down into his pockets instead. 'Have you never thought of me?' he asked diffidently.

'Oh yes,' she said, moving away from him round to the other side of the desk. 'But not in a good way. And don't call me *chérie*.'

'Well at least let me explain how I came to be here.'

'Does it matter?'

'We're going to be working together for the next…what…four, five months. Wouldn't it be better to clear the air?'

'Fine,' she said crisply, zipping her laptop in to its bag. 'So tell me.'

'What, here?' He spread incredulous hands, taking in the dingy, cluttered space.

'Sure. There's no-one else here.' She piled her things at the end of the desk, ready to take back to her room, and sat down, looking up at him expectantly as if he was about to tell her a story.

Luc stared at her, his mouth a pinched, tight line of frustration. 'OK, if I must.' He closed the door and began to slowly pace up and down the floor between the two tables.

'*Alors*…the first thing is; I always wanted to paint. As a kid I was always sketching and painting. Awful stuff but I loved it. But my father didn't think it was a 'serious' career.' He looked across at her. 'You remember I told you about my father: old school diplomat, very authoritarian, the reason I lived in London as a kid?'

Terri nodded.

'So…I studied art history instead, then drifted into art journalism because I didn't know what else to do. And I enjoyed it – some of it. Can't pretend I didn't, but it wasn't fulfilling. It wasn't what I wanted to do for the rest of my life. Then about a year ago, I'd just had my thirty-sixth birthday, and it occurred to me that if I didn't do something about painting soon, it would be too late. I'd saved some money so…' He paused in his walking and shrugged. '…I took the chance.'

'So you had an early mid-life crisis?' Terri suggested, amused.

'You can put it like that if you want,' he said coldly. 'I gave up the day job and came down to Provence. It seemed the obvious place to try my hand at painting again. Then I heard that Peter Stedding taught a few days a month and I approached him to see if he'd take me on. I showed him some paintings and, amazingly, he agreed. Then, about three months later, his studio assistant left…after some big row. He offered me the job which came with the use of the cottage and it was too good an opportunity to turn down.' He smiled, a little ruefully. 'It was stormy at first but Peter gets easier when you you've worked with him for a while.'

'It's certainly a good story.'

Luc stopped pacing and turned to look directly at her. '*Merde,* Terri. Peter wouldn't have taken me on if I couldn't paint. And I've got a cottage full of paintings. You can come and see them if you don't believe me.'

'Thank you but no thanks. Whether you can paint or not isn't really the point, is it? In any case it doesn't matter what I think.'

Terri got to her feet and picked up her bags. She walked across to the door but Luc blocked her way. She raised her eyebrows expectantly. He didn't move.

'And why was it you came here again?' he said softly, leaning down to speak into her ear. She could feel the warmth of his breath on her skin, see his long eyelashes which she remembered so well. 'A career move? Didn't you tell me you wanted to specialise, become an expert in your field, write monographs on Holbein and Rembrandt? Though I suppose a book on Peter and all his painted ghosts would have a certain popular appeal.'

He straightened up and put his hand to the door handle.

'You never told me about your great desire to paint when we were dating,' said Terri.

He turned back. 'No, I didn't. We never got beyond the first stage did we: guarded conversations, both scared of embarrassment or rejection? I wasn't likely to tell an art curator that I had aspirations to paint until I was more certain of her. Especially when that woman is as reserved as you are.' He paused. 'Everyone has corners, Terri, places they're scared of shining a light into. So how many things do you keep to yourself, *hein*?'

He stared at her a moment then flung the door open and walked out. Terri watched him cross to his work station, dumped her bags on the floor, and quickly pushed the door to. She put two fingers from each hand up to massage her temples, trying to clear the tension. She hadn't expected Luc to affect her in this way. He was so plausible. And there was a small but worrying part of her which wanted to believe him.

She tried to push him out of her mind, remembered the little portrait of the boy and returned to her desk to root through Peter's notebooks. She found the one for 1974, slipped it into her bag and left the studio without looking in Luc's direction.

*

Peter looked up the ladder to where Sami was stretching one long, scrawny leg up into the loft space.

'Careful,' he said in French.

He now doubted the wisdom of doing this. Sami might be thirteen years younger than he was but he was no longer the lanky, gangling youth whom Madeleine had befriended all those years ago and for whom she had insisted they should find

100

a job. He too was grey and occasionally stiff; he stooped a little when he walked. Peter sometimes forgot how much time had passed. There were scuffling noises as Sami successfully negotiated his way onto the roof of the office and disappeared out of sight. Peter was relieved. It would have been difficult to have asked anyone else to do this with him and he had reluctantly accepted that he could not do it on his own. The fall had sapped his confidence and he had balked at trying to climb the ladder. Not that he would ever admit it to anyone.

'Which ones do you want?' came Sami's flat disembodied voice from the loft space.

'All of them,' said Peter firmly. 'Just pass them down to me two at a time.'

Peter saw nothing for a few minutes but could hear odd sounds and grunts, then Sami appeared at the top of the ladder, looking, from below, even longer and stringier than usual. He was dragging a large piece of hessian in his hands and he folded it over and over to make a pad and put it down by the edge of the roofing. He disappeared and returned a moment later with a painting in each hand, slowly knelt onto the pad and leaned down to place each picture in turn into Peter's outstretched hands. Without giving them a second glance, Peter propped the paintings up against the shelving nearby, then returned to receive the next two. He had no idea how many were up there. He couldn't even remember how long it was since he'd put them there. All he knew was that he wanted to look through them before Terri did and without her being anywhere around.

'I've found your early work,' she'd declared to him exultantly on the Friday. 'They were up in the loft space. But some of them are in a terrible state; they need attention.' She'd pointed a reproachful finger towards the loft. 'You'll lose a lot of your work if you store them that way. Anyway, I've brought a few down which look interesting. It'll take me a while to go through the rest of them. Why didn't you tell me they were there?'

He had dismissed her find as unimportant, remarked that there would be nothing of interest in the loft, but then insisted on retrieving the rest of the paintings himself when she refused to let the matter drop. 'I will not have you clambering about up there,' he'd said firmly, closing the subject. 'You'll probably fall and then sue me.'

So now it was Saturday morning and he and Sami had the studio to themselves. It took them more than an hour and a half to move all the stored paintings down to the studio floor. During a short break in the middle they sat on two wooden chairs in the studio, drinking coffee, saying nothing. We're just two old men now, Peter thought, glancing across at Sami whose dark eyes, sunken in his withered, tanned face, seemed fixed on some distant, imagined horizon. Their pasts felt inextricably linked – they had spent the larger part of their adult lives together - and yet it occurred to him that he barely knew the man. Madeleine had been the one who always made a connection with people. He cast about for something to say. Then he remembered Sami having a day off to go and visit an ailing friend a couple of weeks before. He could ask after him, or perhaps it was a 'her'.

In the end Peter asked nothing; he had never been good at the personal talk. He wondered if Sami missed not having a wife. Peter had formed the impression that Sami had had lady friends in the past but he'd never settled with anyone. Did he get lonely? If he did, he didn't show it. Sami kept his own counsel; he was the most silent person Peter had ever met. More than once he had thought that it was probably one of the things he liked most about the man. But did Sami regret anything? Had he made mistakes? Peter was curious to know but could not imagine asking him. In any case it would be unlikely to make him feel better. If their respective transgressions were put in a balance, Peter had no doubt that his own would weigh by far the heavier.

'What do you think of Terri?' he asked suddenly, unsure where the question had come from but dimly aware that she was often on his mind. Sami, he knew, saw everything. He never volunteered an opinion unless asked but could be a wise old bird at times.

Sami hesitated as if considering all the possible meanings of the question.

'Miss Terri takes her work very seriously,' he said, flicking Peter a glance before looking away again. He rubbed one spindly index finger at a mark on the knee of his trousers.

'Ye-es,' said Peter dryly. 'Don't I know it.' In the studio he was always aware of her presence; she seemed impossible to ignore. In the house she was more elusive. He occasionally saw her flitting through like some sort of sprite, reluctant to be pinned down. They rarely exchanged more than a few words. 'Does she go out? I mean, has she made any friends?'

Sami looked up to the distant rafters as if watching a film of Terri's movements.

'She sometimes goes out,' he said slowly. 'She went out with Miss Lindsey the other day.'

'Oh? Well that's good, I suppose.'

Sami tipped back the remains of his coffee and carefully placed the mug down. 'I've seen her talking to Corinne,' he added.

Peter frowned. 'What about?'

'I think she practises her French.'

Peter grunted and let it drop. What Terri did outside her working hours was no concern of his. He finished his coffee and got stiffly to his feet. When they had moved all the paintings, Sami eased himself back down the ladder again, the dusty hessian cloth balanced on one bony shoulder, and carried the ladder back to the wall where he had found it.

Alone again, Peter started to look through the paintings. There were pictures there which dated back to the fifties and his first professional offerings. He cringed at some of the canvases with their immature technique and predictable compositions. And it was draining too, working his way through them all. As he looked at them, images came back into his mind, of people long forgotten or even dead. He came across a landscape, a view across the valley from the top of the hill, with the house – still an L-shaped tumbledown farmhouse – partly showing in the foreground. It was not dated but he remembered it vividly. He and Madeleine had been married just a year or two. He recalled painting it, standing up on the hill with his easel, urged by Madeleine to do the whole thing outside 'with the wind in his face'. He smiled at the memory. She occasionally, silently, came to stand behind him, putting a hand on his shoulder and checking to see how it was going. She had loved this picture. Why? He could point out a million faults with it. But of course she had loved it for its association. And he supposed he'd kept it for the same reason: or perhaps because she'd loved it. Otherwise he would have destroyed it when he'd burnt the others.

He picked through the last of the paintings and then sat down, exhausted. He was relieved and yet a little disappointed. There was nothing there that he needed to keep from Terri's probing hand. With all the time that had passed, he could not now remember which paintings he had destroyed and which he had decided to keep. He had done it in a rush of emotion, desperate to put everything behind him. Perhaps he had been too rash and there were some which he should have kept, but nothing would bring them back now. It was a blessing that he'd never destroyed the portrait of Madeleine which hung in the sitting room. Even so he sometimes wondered that he kept it on the wall, a bittersweet and taunting memento, and yet he couldn't bring himself to take it down.

He got up and wearily stretched. It was lunchtime but he had no great hunger and Angela had said that she was going out for the day. If he was going to sit alone he would prefer to do it here than in the house. He walked into his office, stretched out on the day bed and was asleep within minutes, twitching occasionally and mouthing names in his dreams.

Chapter 8

Terri smoothed skin cream into her face, staring once more at her reflection in the bathroom mirror. Did she look like Madeleine? The almond shape of her eyes was definitely the same but little else. Madeleine's face had been heart-shaped and her eyes sepia brown; Terri's face was elfin, her narrow, straight nose making her dark grey eyes appear disproportionately larger and closer together. When serious, she thought it gave her an intense, almost puzzled look, odd. She had been teased about it at school. So who did she look like? Her father? No. Her mother? She couldn't remember. When she was six, her mother had disappeared out of her life like a conjuror's assistant evaporates from the magician's box. One day she had been there; the next she had gone. 'She won't be coming back, Terri. You must be strong,' her father had said, she wasn't sure how much later. Her mother was a shadowy figure and her memories of her early childhood had long since been stacked away, little more than wisps and snatches of conversations which danced away from her whenever she tried to bring them close.

She put the tub of cream to one side and began to apply mascara. Finding the portrait of the little boy had both intrigued and unsettled her. It still stood at the back of her office, wrapped up and out of sight. She had found its entry in the appropriate notebook but all it had provided was a name: Tom. And going through a notebook for 1975 a few days later, she had found one of the sheets torn out. Elsewhere in the books, when Peter had abandoned a painting or disliked its final appearance, he had scribbled it on the entry. So why had the record of a completed painting been removed? In a time-consuming and increasingly obsessive chase, she had searched through the other notebooks and found three other sheets similarly torn from the spines, all from the years up to 1976. Had they all been paintings of Tom? Had Peter's grief been such that he'd felt compelled to destroy every picture of the boy? But surely it would have been more normal to have cherished the pictures of his only son? And the missing notebook for 1973 had never turned up which began to seem suspicious. What had it contained? Perhaps the whole thing had been destroyed. Several times she had thought of trying to broach the subject with Peter; every time she had abandoned it. But all the secrecy and silence was unnatural. What had happened to Tom?

She finished with the mascara and put a brush through her hair. Her mind wouldn't leave the subject alone. And Celia's bizarre behaviour only added to the jumble of her thoughts: those questions about her mother and the astonishing suggestion that the Stedding family were known to her. Clearly, Celia wanted to believe that Terri was related to Madeleine in some way, presumably through her mother. But that was impossible. Well, unlikely for, in truth, Terri knew next to nothing about her mother's family. She felt a rush of anger and dropped the brush down roughly on the shelf. After all these years, she was not going to start thinking about her mother now. It was all nonsense and she didn't care anyway. Angela was right: Celia just delighted in stirring people up.

Even so, a few minutes later she was glancing at Madeleine's portrait again as she cut through the sitting room to the hall. Earlier that week, Angela had pointedly commented on how often she had seen Terri looking at the picture. 'Is it particularly special in some way?' she'd asked dryly. Terri had passed the question off, commented on the pose and the handling of the paint, but Angela had looked unconvinced, her easy charm evaporated. Studying Terri with shrewd, penetrating eyes, she'd smiled coolly and walked away. Terri guessed she had crossed some invisible line of acceptable behaviour, a demarcation of a house rule.

Now she shrugged it away from her. It was Saturday morning and she had to go into the village to collect her car from the garage.

*

There was a woman walking by the side of the tree-lined road and a car coming the other way. Even without a pedestrian, the winding road to Ste. Marguerite barely allowed two cars to pass. Luc slammed on the brake, tucking in behind the woman and crawling in second gear, tapping the steering wheel impatiently. He saw her glance back as the oncoming car went past and belatedly realised it was Terri. He'd been miles away. He drew the car to a halt a few yards beyond her, flinging open the passenger door. A couple of minutes later, she got in.

'Thank you,' she said in a pinched voice. Her face was abnormally pale and her hand shook as she pulled the door closed.

'Are you all right?' He put the car into first and they moved off.

'Yes, fine.'

'Going into Ste. Marguerite?'

'Yes. My car's in the garage. I'm going to pick it up.'

He glanced across at her. 'Are you sure you're all right? You look like you've seen a ghost.'

'Yes, yes, I'm absolutely fine.' She glanced across at him, almost nervously. 'It's just…some guy stopped his car and pestered me. He rattled me.'

'You should have gone through the wood.'

'I thought I might get lost.'

'You didn't need to worry. The main path's pretty obvious.'

Terri stayed unnaturally silent. A few minutes later Luc took the turning into the village. 'Shall I take you to the garage?'

'I'm going to do some shopping first. Wherever's convenient for you.'

'*D'accord.*'

Ste. Marguerite des Pins was a village of two parts. The original, old settlement stretched up the hill with, at its highest point, a small square dominated by a solid Romanesque church. Three winding streets, lined with houses and tiny boutique shops, led off the square and tumbled down the hillside. More houses and a range of modern retail and service units had been developed on the level ground below.

Luc parked the car at the side of one of the hillside streets and turned off the engine.

'Thanks for the lift.' Terri reached for the door handle.

'Let me buy you coffee,' Luc said, turning to face her.

'No, I don't th…'

'Just coffee,' he pressed. 'Don't always make such a big deal out of everything.'

She stared ahead of her for a silent moment then acquiesced with a brief smile. 'OK. Thanks.'

Luc led the way up the road to a café where they sat at a terrace table and ordered two *cafés crèmes*. For several minutes neither spoke. He noticed Terri glancing round then slowly relaxing back in the chair.

'Remember that nude which you admired so much?' she remarked.

'Of course. You were sarcastic about my appreciation of it as I recall.'

'I was sceptical.'

'It sounded like sarcasm from where I stood.'

'Oh dear, were you terribly wounded?'

'I'm used to you. I'll survive. So what about it?'

'It's a painting of Angela in her twenties.'

'Angela? Really?' He pulled a face. 'I'm surprised. I've hardly ever seen her come anywhere near the studio. She was very striking.'

'She still is.' The waiter brought the drinks and they waited until he'd gone.

'I imagine Peter won't put it in the exhibition then,' said Luc. 'Shame. It's really good.'

'He said it was up to Angela.'

'Have you asked her?'

'Yes. She said we could use it. She seemed quite proud of it, actually.'

'Interesting.' They drank for a moment in silence, then Luc saw Lindsey across the street and raised his hand to wave. Terri turned her head to see who it was and Lindsey waved a second time before moving on.

'Oh great,' she complained, 'now she'll be convinced that we're an item.'

'What, because we're having coffee together? Anyway, so what if she does?'

'You were the one who warned me about her. And she's already guessed we knew each other before; she's been asking about you.' Terri paused, studying him with suspicious eyes. 'Unless you've already told her about us?'

He shook his head. 'I've said nothing. Why? What did she say?'

'She just asked, that's all.'

'And what did you say?'

'That we met at a Preview. That's all.'

'Ah.'

Luc drank a slow mouthful of coffee and replaced the cup carefully on the saucer.

'Lindsey tells me that Celia caused a scene at Angela's last party,' he said, '…and it was all about you.'

'Did she, indeed? And how did she come to tell you that? Over a cosy piano lesson?'

Luc raised his eyebrows. '*Tiens,* that sounded suspiciously like jealousy.'

'Oh please.'

'So is it true?'

'What?'

'That your eyes are like Madeleine's and Celia thinks you're related.' He leaned closer, studying her eyes till she flushed. '*Are* you related?'

'No, of course not. Don't be ridiculous.' Terri sat back, purposefully looking away across the square.

'*Is* it ridiculous? Stranger things have happened. Some long lost relation of Madeleine's, perhaps? Do you have a French connection in the family?'

Terri shook her head firmly. 'No.'

'What did Peter say about it?'

'He wasn't there.'

'No, of course not. He doesn't like Angela's parties.' Luc looked thoughtful. 'It'd be interesting to know though, wouldn't it?'

'Oh for goodness sake Luc, drop it,' said Terri impatiently. 'Lindsey said Celia's always coming out with this sort of thing, but of course you think it would make a good story.'

Luc's lips compressed in annoyance.

'I thought you'd be interested yourself.'

'Well, I'm not. Celia gives me the creeps.' She let out a slow breath, shaking her head. 'I'm sorry Luc. That was unfair. I overreacted. I'm still a bit uptight after, you know…'

'Forget it.'

He finished his coffee, aware that Terri's eyes were on him.

'So how's the "not-smoking" going?' she asked lightly.

He frowned. 'OK.' He glanced towards a couple of young women who were both smoking at a table further along the terrace. 'Except when I can smell cigarette smoke.' His gaze lingered on them wistfully.

'I'm sure it'll get easier.'

Luc looked back at her and they both smiled. For a moment she looked as if she wanted to say something else, but then she looked away and drank the last of her coffee instead. A few minutes later they had gone their separate ways and he headed for the newsagent's, wondering what was bothering her and why she was so touchy about her family. But she had always been reticent and defensive; if he was going to draw her out, he would need to tread softly.

*

On the Monday morning, Terri's phone rang within minutes of her arrival in the office; the owner of one of Peter's portraits had finally returned her call. Logging onto the internet shortly after, she found an email from Sophie who wrote at length about Stuart and how well they were getting on. Apparently she'd been invited to his family home in Hampshire the following weekend to meet his parents. In panic, she'd written:

I don't know what to wear!!!

Then, almost as an afterthought, she'd added:

By the way, I saw Oliver the other day at a theatre party. He came straight over as if he'd been waiting for me to arrive and asked where you'd gone. I told him what you told me to say - that you were touring round Italy, visiting a few places you've always wanted to see. I'm not sure he believed me. Fortunately Stuart was with me and he soon gave up. He seemed quite distraught. I think he's missing you badly. I hope I did the right thing – you still don't want to see him?

Terri felt a chill settle on her. Coming so soon after the encounter with the man in the car on the road to Ste. Marguerite – at first glance he had looked strikingly, frighteningly, like Oliver - it was as if she'd conjured him up with her wild imagination. She quickly answered: no, she did not want to see Oliver again, thanking Sophie for the lie and apologising for putting her in such an awkward position. She toyed with finally explaining about Oliver's behaviour but wrote instead how pleased she was about Stuart; that work was going fine; that the weather was getting warm and how great

113

it was to be able to go for a swim in the pool after work. She pressed *send* and sat staring into space.

A few minutes later, in an effort to clear her mind, she got up and wandered across the studio to the kitchen, made four coffees, put them on a tray and took them back into the studio. She put one by Luc who was applying gesso to a succession of canvases and left one with Nicole. Then she approached Peter. The painting of Laurent Valdeau had been put on one side to dry and he had a portrait of a young woman on his easel. Terri watched him apply a couple of delicate brush strokes to the woman's lower lip. He dropped his arm and turned, fixing her with a hard, expectant look over the top of his shallow lenses. She put the coffee down at a safe distance from his paints and returned his gaze.

'I've tracked down 'The Boy with Olive Eyes' - the one you wanted for the exhibition,' she said.

'Yes, I know. And?'

'It's in Monaco and the owner, a Frenchman called Pierre Marineau, is prepared to loan it to the exhibition. He's thinking of selling it apparently and thinks the publicity will put the price up.'

'Oh does he?' Peter grunted. 'A true lover of art then, our *Monsieur* Marineau.'

He turned away and added more medium to the rosy colour on his palette until the pigment swam in an oily suspension.

'There's hardly any colour in that,' she remarked.

'No.' He flicked her a glance. 'It's a glaze for the cheeks. If it needs more, I'll put another layer on later. Building it up like that gives the picture more depth, makes the skin look more alive. We don't want her looking like a common tart with make-up plastered on.'

114

He picked up a fine flat paintbrush and Terri watched him dip the brush into the glaze. 'Was there something else?' he remarked acidly, squeezing the excess from the brush.

'Do you mind if I watch you put it on?'

He hesitated. 'If you must.' He leaned forward, carefully applying the oily mix. 'The oil will make it slow to dry. But the lower levels have less oil in them so they dry more quickly. Otherwise the painting might crack.'

'Fat on lean,' recited Terri.

'Exactly.' Peter lifted the brush from the canvas and regarded his work critically. 'So they teach you practical stuff like that in fancy art history degrees do they?'

'Some do. But I already knew it from my father.'

Peter turned and rested mildly curious eyes on her. 'Artist, was he?'

She shook her head. 'A conservator. He used to complain that some galleries like their old paintings cleaned up too much. He said they ended up stripping off the top oily glazes till they were nothing like the artist intended. And he was right: I've seen some like that.'

Peter grunted. 'I wonder what savagery people'll do to my pictures in a couple of hundred years.' He studied the painting again and waved an impatient arm at her. 'For Christ's sake, woman, just bugger off will you? You're putting me off.'

Terri took her coffee back to her office. It was strangely comforting having Peter grumble at her in that way: normal and reassuring. She deleted the message from Sophie, keen to have its contents removed from her inbox, then made out a card for 'The Boy with Olive Eyes', placing it down on the year 1978 of her timeline. Her gaze slid back to 1974 and then was drawn inevitably towards the hidden canvas at the back of the room, the mysterious Tom.

*

Peter eased himself back into Celia's armchair and watched his sister busy herself in the little kitchen at the back of the room. It was some time since he'd last visited the *pigeonnier*; he always dreaded that she would ask him to look at her paintings. He still remembered venturing to make a helpful suggestion – many years ago now – only to be told forcefully that he did not understand what she was trying to do. He hadn't expressed an opinion since. He thought they were beyond help anyway.

Celia approached him with a glass of red wine in each hand and leaned over to put one down on the small table to his right. She sat in the chair facing him and raised her glass.

'*Santé,*' she said.

Peter picked up his glass. '*Santé.*'

'Mm, good wine. Thank you.'

'You're welcome.'

'So-o, you come bearing gifts.' She raised her eyebrows, looking at him quizzically. 'To what do I owe the honour?'

'You say that as if I'd never done it before. We've often shared a bottle of wine.'

'Indeed, though not recently. Does Angela know you're here?'

'She's out. It's her yoga class tonight, I believe.'

'Yoga?' Celia snorted. 'It doesn't seem to have done much for her inner calm.'

'Please Celia.'

Celia grinned and sat back in the chair, taking another sip of wine. It was seven-thirty in the evening but still she wore her blue dungarees. There was cadmium red paint in her hair and the residue of a darker pigment under the nails of her right

116

hand. Angela kept insisting that Celia was 'losing it' and that she would need more attention before long than could be provided at Le Chant. But Peter thought Angela was dramatizing the situation. Celia showed no sign of being unable to manage or even of being disorientated. She behaved oddly, certainly, and had done so for a number of years. He was personally convinced that she took great pleasure in it. With him, she could be impressively sensible at times; it was Angela who brought out the worst in her. The feud between them was childish and infuriating but he had long since abandoned any attempt to encourage them to patch it up.

'How are you getting on with Terri then?' she enquired. 'Pretty little thing.'

Peter grunted. 'For Pete's sake, Celia, don't patronise her. You make her sound like a bit of a girl. She's a grown woman.'

'So she's good then?'

'Well, she certainly knows one side of a picture from the other,' he conceded. 'Her father was a picture restorer, you know. Probably explains her interest.'

'And her mother?'

'I've no idea.' He hesitated and sipped at his wine. 'Why are you so interested in Terri anyway? Angela tells me you've been pestering her.'

'I have not.'

Peter sighed. Why had he let Angela talk him into doing this? In some ways Celia was the only person he felt he could be himself with. Why could he not just have a quiet drink with her without always getting caught between them? He stared at his wine glass uncomfortably. 'Angela said that you caused a scene at one of her parties and embarrassed Terri. Apparently Terri didn't go to the party last Saturday. She said she had a headache but Angela is sure that it was because of you.'

'Well I'm sorry if I embarrassed her,' said Celia. 'I didn't mean to. Has Terri complained?'

'No.'

'Well, there you are then.'

Peter took another, larger, mouthful of wine, wondering if Terri would be likely to say anything to him if his sister had upset her. On the experience of the last few weeks, if it was something which affected her work, he thought she would complain promptly and loudly; if it was a personal issue, he rather suspected that she would let it go. 'Celia gets fixated on people,' Angela had said to him. 'You know she does, Peter. It's embarrassing sometimes and I imagine can even feel a bit threatening. And now she's doing it with Terri. She turned up at the last party, uninvited, and hounded the girl. You should have a word with her. You're the only one she listens to.' But Peter did not want to get involved in this enduring squabble. In any case, he was sure that Terri was quite capable of looking after herself.

'I see your hand's moving better,' Celia remarked, breaking into his thoughts.

Peter automatically flexed and straightened the fingers of his left hand, studying it with an intense expression. 'Should be with all the work that bossy physio's making me do,' he muttered.

'No pain, no gain,' said Celia blithely. She paused. 'And it was Terri who persuaded you to have some treatment, I think you said. A good thing too.'

Peter grunted a vague agreement, abandoning his exercises and drinking some wine.

'I suppose you, of all people, must have noticed,' Celia remarked casually and paused, an arch expression on her face.

'If you have something to say, Celia, say it will you? I'm too old for tantalising conversations.'

'Well, Terri…I mean it seems so obvious to me. She's the absolute spit of Madeleine, God rest her soul.'

'What? Oh don't be absurd Celia. She's nothing like.'

'You mean you really don't see it? Look at her eyes, Peter – *so* similar. And have you noticed the way she bites her lower lip when she's thinking about something? Do you remember?'

'Remember? Of course I remember.' He shook his head. 'I'm not listening. I don't want to hear any more of this nonsense.' His chest felt tight as if he couldn't breathe properly and his hand was shaking; he carefully steadied his glass on the arm of the chair. 'You've said all this before, Celia. Remember that student I had and…and…and the *bonne*? When is it going to stop? If it's some sort of game you're playing, it's in very poor taste.' He unsteadily tipped the remaining wine into his mouth.

'I'm sorry if it hurts, Peter. But of course it's not a game. I meant it, truly I did. Of course I've made mistakes. But Terri's different, I promise you. She is really. I have no desire to upset you. Let me get you some more wine. It's good, isn't it?' She stood up and crossed to where he sat but, instead of taking his glass she rested a hand on his shoulder. 'You shouldn't keep blaming yourself, dear,' she said softly. 'You were upset…beside yourself. It's time to let it go. It was long since.' She raised her hand and patted him playfully just once. 'Do you fancy some apple tart? I got it at the market on Saturday but there's too much for one.'

Peter stared into mid-air while Celia wandered back to the kitchen. A flood of painful images vied for position in his mind's eye. How could he let them go if she kept reminding him about them?

*

May was nearly over and the temperature had already risen to levels more common for the middle of summer in England. Yet still no-one used the pool. Terri was surprised. Once or twice she had seen Angela sunbathing by it, her face carefully shaded by a large-brimmed hat, her limbs anointed in oil, but she never saw her break the surface of the water. Sami checked it regularly - Terri had seen him staring into its depths – and he set a machine to clean it every morning, but it was as if the pool was there for show only: the obligatory accoutrement of a Provençal villa.

And Terri doubted if she should be disturbing it either. She had exaggerated to Sophie, keen, in the face of her friend's happiness, to give the impression that she was having a good time. Only once had she been for a swim, on a beautiful day the previous week, and had been disconcerted to notice Sami pause in the pushing of his wheelbarrow on the pathway above to watch her for a couple of minutes before moving on. She wondered if Angela's invitation to her to use the pool had been a polite perfunctory affair, proffered with no real expectation of it being taken up. Terri increasingly felt as if she were living on a film set, the house mostly composed of background scenery to occasional, carefully scripted conversations.

Even so, leaving the studio the following Wednesday, sticky and tired, she toyed with going for a swim again, and took the longer route round by way of the pool to see if anyone was in it already. She paused at the top of the olive grove, looking down to where the water glinted in the sunshine. Of course, there was no-one there. She hesitated, imagining the soothing sensation of the gently heated water against her skin. Did anyone really care what she did? Was it just her imagination that made her think people had begun to watch her? Her grandmother's voice waltzed into her head. *I saw you sneaking outside, young lady. What do you do out there? And don't say 'nothing'. I hate that. Why do you have to be so secretive?* Terri no longer saw the swimming pool. She was back in the kitchen of her father's crumbling house in Kent with his studio in the converted stables at the back and its rambling garden. Her grandmother had come to live with them permanently when Terri was twelve. *Really, you're just like your mother,* she had said once or twice, always when she was cross. *Why, what was she like?* Terri remembered answering, a question she often wanted to ask her father but never did. *Don't be cheeky,* was the immediate response.

'Going for a dip?'

Terri started and looked round. Celia had come up behind her. She had a surprisingly quiet step. Terri watched her draw level with mixed feelings. 'Maybe,' she equivocated. 'Are you?'

Celia offered a slow smile. 'I generally prefer it when the mercury approaches tropical levels, but somebody should, don't you think? It looks rather sad all abandoned like this.'

'Yes,' agreed Terri warily. What was it about Celia? She was the only person who appeared to talk unreservedly and yet clearly she always had a sub plot. So what was she up to now? 'Going painting?' Terri enquired, glancing at the pram Celia had brought with her as usual.

'No, I'm on my way back. Nothing very successful today. Are you going to the house?'

'Yes.'

'I'll walk with you then. I fancy a bit of toast and marmalade. Quite a craving. Now what's that all about, I wonder? I can't be pregnant. Anyway, Angela's bound to have

121

marmalade. Probably has it shipped in specially from England.' Celia linked her free hand through Terri's arm as they walked. 'Do you like marmalade?'

'No, not especially. I prefer jam.'

'Ooh, what flavour?'

Terri couldn't stop herself from smiling at the beguiling silliness of the conversation.

'Blackberry,' she said, after a moment's pause. 'Or black cherry.'

'Excellent. I must make some scones and we can have them with jam and cream.'

Terri glanced sidelong at her companion who gave her a broad smile and squeezed her arm. They crossed the terrace, the pram trundling behind. Then Celia suddenly pulled Terri to a standstill near the fountain and looked up at the house.

'Lovely old building isn't it?' she said. 'The east wing was a later addition. Of course the west wing is too – Angela had that put on. The original farmhouse was a much simpler affair. But the east wing's more interesting. It's got an attic and I always think houses with attics are more exciting, don't you?' She barely paused before adding, 'Madeleine wrote a history of the place, I think. Haven't seen it for years. But it's probably still in her studio – well it was more of a den really: her private place.'

Terri frowned, turning quickly to look at her companion. 'Her studio?'

'Yes…of course. 'Raphael'.'

''Raphael'? Where's that?'

'In-the-attic,' Celia enunciated slowly, as if talking to an imbecile, and glanced up to the top of the east wing where two low, wide windows had been set high up in the wall facing them. 'You know how the rooms have names? – well they do in the older part of the house anyway. Madeleine painted them. It's locked up, of course – 'Raphael', that is. Peter won't have anything in there touched.' Celia leaned across and dropped her voice. 'Touchy subject, you see.' She straightened up and smiled. 'Useful for research though I dare say.'

'Celia?' Terri hesitated, wondering at the wisdom of asking this strange woman anything.

'Yes, dear?'

'Was Tom Madeleine's son?'

Celia's expression changed subtly; for once she seemed reluctant to talk. 'Why do you ask?'

'I found a painting of a boy and his resemblance to Madeleine was striking. And Lindsey said that Madeleine had a son who died young.'

'I see. And what did Peter say about it?'

'Nothing. I didn't mention it to him.'

'Very wise.' Celia started to walk again and glanced sideways at Terri who hurried to catch up. 'So what made you think he was called Tom?'

'Peter had written it in his notebook entry.'

'That would be him then.'

Terri choked back her impatience. Celia was so hard to pin down; she talked in riddles. 'So he *was* her son?'

'Yes, dear. Very sad. Sweet boy.'

'But he died?'

'Yes dear,' she repeated with a broad toothy smile. 'We all do, you know.' She paused and tilted her head sideways. 'You know, I don't think I want marmalade after all. The craving's gone off. By the way, I belong to an art society and it's our summer show soon. If you get a moment, I'd love your help in choosing what to submit. Come up and see me. *Ciao, ciao.*'

She suddenly changed direction and Terri watched her walk off across the front of the house and turn out of sight.

*

Angela clicked on the light in the en-suite to her bedroom making the extractor fan whirr smoothly into action. *Her* bathroom: clean, sweet-smelling, tidy. The pleasure of claiming it as her own had still not left her though it was some years since she and Peter had regularly shared a bedroom. He now slept in the room next door, though in reality he often stayed in the studio all night, sleeping on the day bed in his study when weariness finally dragged him from his easel. It was his erratic nocturnal behaviour which had finally prompted her to suggest they had separate rooms; she had become tired of the uncertainty of his return and the consequent disturbance. To judge from his reaction, or rather the lack of it, she suspected that he had felt as much relief at the new arrangement as she had. It had never been discussed since.

She put a brush through her hair, watching in the mirror as it repeatedly fell neatly back into place. She understood why cats groomed themselves so often; it had a soothing, mesmeric effect on the senses. She frequently did it as much for the balm to her spirit as the need to tidy herself up. But noticing the line of her roots, she leaned forward suddenly, laid down the brush and pressed a finger to her parting: she needed to get them done. And with her head tipped forward like this, the flesh on each side of her mouth sagged alarmingly, drooping, she thought, like the exaggerated pout of a melancholic clown. Quickly straightening, she pushed her index fingers up across her cheeks, stretching the skin, and saw her jawlines reaffirm themselves. For months she had been trying to pluck up the courage to get a little cosmetic work done but the thought of needles, foreign substances and surgical knives terrified her and she kept putting it off.

She turned away brusquely, flicked the light off and returned to the bedroom. It felt stuffy and she crossed to the open window in search of fresher air. Hers was a bright, first-floor room at the front of the west wing with a commanding view over the terrace and garden, over the cherry orchards and out down the valley towards the distant blue mountains. She considered this spectacular vista one of the highlights of the house. Even so, good view or not, Corinne should have closed the shutters that morning; in the summer the atmosphere in these sun-drenched rooms could quickly become oppressive.

The sound of voices rose from the terrace below and Angela looked down, raising a hand to shield her eyes against the light. Celia and Terri were standing by the fountain, talking, glancing occasionally towards the house. It wasn't the first time she had seen them talking together like this and now it occurred to her that perhaps it was no coincidence so she watched them more closely. Celia leaned close to Terri, conspiratorially, said something, then straightened up in that smug way she had, as if she'd just pulled a rabbit out of a hat. Terri's face wasn't visible but she seemed to be asking a question. Frowning, Angela strained to hear what was being said but failed and a couple of minutes later saw the two women walk on again towards the front door.

She stood, unmoving, the significance or otherwise of the encounter below her still running through her mind. Her eyes refocused on a movement in the parterre where Sami was silently weeding one of the beds. He hadn't been visible before, she could have sworn, so where had he been hiding?

Tucked in behind one of the overhanging shrubs, listening in? He had always been like this, Sami. She thought of him as Peter's spy, watching, listening, skulking around. He was devoted to Peter, would do anything for him, it seemed - presumably because he had no life of his own.

She turned away from the window and went downstairs. Lindsey had arrived home some twenty minutes earlier and she found her in the kitchen, pouring chilled orange juice into a tall glass. The fridge door stood open.

'Hello, darling,' Angela said, walking across and giving her daughter an air kiss. 'Don't leave the fridge door open dear.' She pushed it to. 'Everything all right?'

'Yes, thanks,' said Lindsey listlessly. She replaced the juice in the door of the fridge and exaggeratedly closed it, glancing pointedly towards her mother.

'Have you seen Terri?' said Angela.

'She's just gone through to her room.'

'And Celia?'

Lindsey shrugged. 'No idea.'

Still frowning, Angela picked up the electric kettle and walked to the sink to fill it. She switched it on and turned, leaning her back against the unit.

'How well have you got to know Terri?' she asked.

'Not very. Why?'

'I have seen you together though.'

'We've talked a bit.'

'Do you think there's anything…odd about her?' asked Angela.

Lindsey frowned, drank some juice and shrugged again. 'In what way?'

'She's quite reticent usually isn't she? But I've just seen her chatting to Celia.'

'That'd be two odd people together then.'

'Mm. Have you ever seen them together?'

Lindsey pulled a face. 'Maybe. I'm not sure. Does it matter?'

'It might do. You've got to look after your own interests darling, I've told you before.'

'Uh?' Lindsey wrinkled her nose up, uncomprehending. She was worryingly naïve, Angela often thought.

'Look darling, just let me know if you do see them together again, will you?

'I do know she's going out with Luc,' Lindsey said moodily, wandering away to the door.

'Really? Since when?'

'Not sure. Maybe before she came here. But they're an item, you can tell. I've seen them in town. You watch them together sometime.' She left the kitchen.

The kettle boiled and Angela distractedly poured water into the teapot. She had forgotten to put the teabag in. The image of Terri talking to Celia kept running through her mind.

'So what are they up to?' she muttered to herself.

Chapter 9

The idea that Madeleine's attic studio still lay untouched somewhere in Angela's chic, contemporary home was laughable. Terri shrugged it off as a bit of gothic fantasy, yet another of Celia's bizarre flights of fancy. Even so, she caught herself glancing up to the top of the east wing each time she approached the house, unable to completely dismiss it from her mind. If such a studio did exist it might give an insight into the enigmatic woman behind the intriguing portrait. Her den, Celia had called it, so it would possibly also contain information which would throw a light on the mystery of Tom. But Terri repeatedly checked her curiosity. This was none of her business and, even if Celia were telling the truth, the studio was a forbidden place belonging to a woman no-one was prepared to discuss. Was that simply the result of a tragic bereavement? That seemed unlikely after all this time. So why the wall of silence?

It was pointless to brood over it; she was unlikely to ever learn more. The house keys, including the ones to the studio, were all kept on lines of hooks in a shallow cupboard under the stairs. Glancing along the tagged keys one day, she'd seen none labelled as 'Raphael'. Further proof, if any were needed, that Celia had made the whole thing up.

The following Sunday afternoon however, stretched out reading on one of the sofas in the sitting room, Terri found herself alone in the house: Peter was in the studio; Lindsey was working and Angela had gone out. For more than half an hour after the last sounds of Angela's shoes had faded on the terrace outside, Terri argued with herself about whether to take advantage of the opportunity or not. In the end the temptation proved too strong and she abandoned the book on the sofa and cautiously climbed the stairs to the first floor.

The staircase emerged in the middle of a long, straight landing with doors to left and right and windows looking out to the rear and the woods. Reminding herself that she was looking for an attic room, somewhere in the old part of the house, she paused to get her bearings, examined the illustrated nameplates on a couple of the doors - 'Vermeer' and 'El Greco'; they were impressively good - then walked the length of the passage and descended two steps down to the upper floor of the east wing.

It didn't look promising. To the front was a large bedroom - 'Rubens' - and behind it a walk-in linen store, but there was no obvious staircase to a loft. She glanced up at the ceiling; there was no trap door either. Still, something didn't feel right. She looked back in at the linen store and then in the bedroom again where the en-suite bathroom extended back behind the wall of the corridor. Terri was a fair judge of size and distance and it didn't look as if the two rooms between them were big enough to quite fill the space. So perhaps there was a passage between the two rooms after all? She examined the wall; it was smooth. She tapped it; it sounded solid. Clearly her imagination had been fed by too many films involving ancient houses and secret passages.

Even so she walked into the linen store and clicked the light on. The room was lined with slatted shelves, each covered with stacks of towels and assorted bed linen. To the right was a gap in the racking where a long-handled brush and a small folding stepladder were propped against the wall, a laundry trolley roughly pushed in front of them. The ladder made Terri look up, hoping to see the trap door, but again the ceiling was unbroken.

It wasn't until she turned to leave that she saw the small, low handle on the wall behind the stepladder. And there was the unmistakeable outline of a door too, neatly flush with the wall. She dragged the ladder and trolley out of the way, turned the handle and the door opened smoothly away from her, into darkness. Leaning in, she could just make out the bottom of a flight of steps which turned and rose away to the left. *Curiosity killed the cat*, her grandmother had said to her once, finding Terri nosing through the contents of the old sideboard in the dining room. The back of the drawers had been full of all sorts of odds and ends she had never seen before. *What does that mean?* the young Terri had asked. *It means people who go looking for things usually find out something they don't want to know,* had been the snapped response, and the drawers swiftly closed.

Now Terri straightened up and listened, but could hear nothing save the thumping of her own heart. The house was still empty. She stepped into the darkened passage, flicked a switch which made a lamp glow dully somewhere up above, and climbed the stairs, each step groaning at the unaccustomed tread.

At the top was yet another door and it had a nameplate – 'Raphael' - with a clever pastiche of one of the artist's paintings of the Madonna. So Madeleine's studio did exist after all. She tried the handle but it was locked, just as Celia had said it would be.

Excitement quickly gave way to apprehension and she softly retraced her steps down the stairs to the linen room. Among all the confused thoughts which ran through her mind as she put everything back the way she'd found it, the most disquieting one was the realisation that the eccentric Celia had to be taken seriously after all.

But more importantly, where would she find the key?

*

Having finished picking her way through the canvases, Terri now had an office full of 'possibles', waiting for Peter's final judgement. Pressed to engage in the decision – and bribed with coffee – she finally managed to persuade him to join her in her office the following Wednesday, where they worked their way methodically through each picture in turn for more than an hour. Terri made a second round of coffee to keep Peter sweet.

'These are the last two.'

She held up the final canvases, waited, then turned to look at him to find him staring at her face and not at the pictures.

'So what do you think?' she prompted, disconcerted.

He switched his gaze to the paintings, studying each one with a glazed expression.

'Put that one in.' He pointed at a brooding image of Ste. Marguerite des Pins viewed from the bottom of the village, looking up to a twilit sky. 'The other one can go in the bin as far as I'm concerned. I don't know why we picked it out in the first place.' He took a mouthful of coffee. 'Thank God that's over. So...have you tracked down all my choices?'

131

'No, not all. There are still two I haven't located yet.' She hesitated. 'Do you often bin pictures?'

'To judge from this studio, not enough of them. Are all the paintings coming here?'

Terri put the pictures to one side, sat down and picked up her coffee, but didn't reply.

'Terri? Pay attention. What's the matter with you?'

'Hm? Nothing. Er…yes, I'm going to get all the pictures collected here and check them over, then I'll ship them all to Nice nearer the time. That's why I suggested you fit a burglar alarm. Have you thought about it?'

'Yes, yes,' he muttered grudgingly. 'I suppose we should. You can arrange it…for what it's worth. It never stops the big galleries from being targeted.'

'And insurance?'

'Yes, if it'll shut you up. I'll speak to my insurer.' He glanced down through his spectacles at the calendar on his watch. 'First of June. No hurry. Lots of time still before the exhibition.'

'Yes, but lots of things to do too. Restoration, framing, photography, publicity. And there's the catalogue to write. I wanted to talk to you about that.'

'I don't want any personal mumbo jumbo in the catalogue.' He regarded her beadily over the top of his glasses. 'The exhibition is about the paintings, not me.'

'It's usual to have a biography though. People will expect it. They like it.'

'Maybe. Something simple. But, remember, I want to see the catalogue before you have it printed.'

'Of course. But I haven't started writing it yet. I need to ask you some more questions.'

'Questions, questions,' he grumbled, without malice, sipping his coffee.

'For example…' She cast about for something to draw him out. He was in a surprisingly genial mood; it was too good an opportunity to miss. '…was painting your first love?'

'Yes, definitely.' He paused. 'Of course there was cricket. When I was a boy I was quite good at cricket.' He formed his hand into a cradle for an imaginary ball and twisted it over his head. 'A fast bowler. I had the height you see. And I was pretty nippy in those days.' His lip curled with amusement. 'To judge from your blank expression, I guess you're not a cricket fan.'

'No, 'fraid not. But tell me: what about your family - what did they think about you painting?'

'They were pretty good about it. My father was a successful businessman. He'd assumed I'd follow him into the family business. Even so they were supportive when they realised I was serious. Fortunately I had a brother who wanted to work in the firm. Or at least he couldn't think of anything else to do.'

'Was there anyone else in the family who'd been artistic?'

'An older brother of my father; he died in the First World War.'

'And I believe Celia paints too?'

Peter looked at her pityingly. 'Have you seen her work?'

'Not really. Just odd bits when she's out with her easel. She seems very passionate about it.'

'Oh, I'd give her full marks for enthusiasm,' he said dryly.

They both fell silent. Terri cast about for another question. Her mind was full of Tom and Madeleine but neither were subjects she dared broach. It was hard to focus anyway because he was studying her face again with a strange intensity

133

as if she were a model whose planes or tints of colour he couldn't get quite right.

'What does your mother do?' he said suddenly. 'You said your father was a restorer. So is she artistic too?'

Terri hesitated, examining the remains of her coffee. 'She made hats.'

'Hats?' Peter looked surprised, or perhaps disappointed. 'Past tense, I see. Doesn't she make them any more then?'

'She died.' She looked up to find him frowning at her. 'Why do you want to know?'

He lifted the mug and tipped back the last of his coffee.

'You ask a lot of questions,' he said, putting the mug down with a flourish. 'I think I'm allowed to ask some too.' He drummed the table with his middle finger. 'What was her name?'

'Her name?'

'Yes, you know, her given name.'

'Susan. Why?'

'Just curious. Do you paint?'

'Not at all. I'm useless.' She finished her coffee too and hugged the empty mug, determined to regain control of the conversation. She didn't like the way it was going. 'So you studied in Italy. What made you settle in France?'

'The south of France had attracted so many artists. It seemed the obvious place for a young man to learn his craft.'

'And yet you stayed. It's a long way from all the big cities: London, Paris, Berlin, New York. Didn't you think it might be difficult to get noticed here?'

'No, not really. They're good places to visit but you can't work in that sort of environment; at least I can't.' He paused, studying the fingers of his left hand and flexing them. 'Besides,' he added slowly, 'I met someone.' He raised his

134

eyes to study her face again. 'You must have seen the portrait in the sitting room?'

'Yes.' She wondered what was coming, was almost holding her breath.

'Well, she was my first wife: Madeleine.' He said the name oddly, as if it felt strange to actually hear it said out loud.

'It's a stunning portrait; she was beautiful.'

'Yes.' Peter nodded. 'Yes, she was.'

'And…was she an artist too?'

'She was an art student when I first met her.' Peter's eyes developed a faraway look and he was silent so long that Terri began to wonder if he was all right. Then he started talking - in a soft, gentle voice she'd never heard him use before. 'She came to an exhibition I'd put on with some others. Told me what she thought of it…just like that. And it wasn't all good. Oh no.' He snorted and smiled indulgently. 'And yes, she painted. All sorts: people, still life, views, buildings. So many influences. She was really eclectic in her taste: she loved Turner, Caillebotte… Caravaggio…' His voice drifted away.

'And Raphael, of course,' said Terri, barely conscious of having vocalised the thought but becoming aware of a growing, deafening silence in the room and Peter, eyes now alert and angry, staring at her, brows furrowed.

'Who told you she liked Raphael?'

'Lindsey did.'

'Lindsey? *Lindsey?* What were you doing talking to Lindsey?'

'We were just talking.'

'About *Madeleine*?'

'I asked her about the portrait.'

'And have you been going round everyone asking questions?'

'No, of course not.'

'And I suppose you want all this for the catalogue, do you?' he demanded.

'No…' Terri hesitated, sure that whatever she said now would be wrong.

'I believe I made it clear to start with: I will not have my private life put on record. That is not what I employed you to do. Who else have you been talking to?'

'I'm living here. Who do you expect me to talk to?'

'I expect you to do the job I'm paying you to do…the way I want it done. Nothing more.'

He got up, glaring at her, and abruptly left her office, slamming the door. The door failed to catch and it bounced open again, just as Terri was doing a military salute to his departing back. So much for the good mood. She saw Luc looking across the studio and met his eyes briefly before stepping forward quickly to close the door.

*

On the first Saturday in June, Angela organised a barbecue and, for the first time, Luc was invited. Peter passed the message on when Luc was about to leave the studio one afternoon.

'I gather you're dating Terri,' Peter said. 'So Angela thinks it only makes sense to have you there too. Place'll be swarming with people anyway – biggest event on my wife's calendar.'

'Is Terri going then?'

'How should I know? I imagine so. *Everybody* goes. Anyway, why don't you ask her yourself? You do talk I assume?'

'I'd love to come. Should I let Angela know?'

Peter shook his head. 'I'll tell her.' He studied Luc morosely. 'Don't be too pleased: it'll be boring as hell. A load of people all trying to look wealthier and more fashionable than everyone else. Tsch. Idiots.' He studied Luc's face, expressionless. 'Brave chap, aren't you, dating Terri I mean.' He trudged away.

Peter was right: the party was enormous, spread the full width and depth of the terrace and spilling out beyond, with a team of outside caterers providing the food and waiters serving wine from long trestle tables. It was already in full swing by the time Luc made his way there, the babble of chatter reaching him as he cut through the olive grove. He could hear music too, the resonant tones of Sinatra, Nat King Cole, Bing Crosby and Rosemary Clooney ringing out in the smoky, fragrant evening air. There had been noise and activity round the house all day, vans grinding up and down the track from the road and sounds of hammering and voices from the terrace. Getting closer he could see lights had been strung across the front of the house and between posts erected at the edge of the terrace. It was still light and they twinkled insignificantly.

With a glass of red wine in his hand, he worked his way through the crowd to the edge of the terrace, checking out Angela's guests. There was hardly anyone he knew. Peter had come – surprisingly – and was holding court on the other side of the terrace, and he'd seen Angela up near the house, but there was no sign of Lindsey nor, yet, of Terri. He hadn't told her that he'd been invited and wasn't sure why. Did he think she wouldn't come if she knew he would be there? But maybe Peter had told her anyway. Though, given Peter's fit of temper the other day when he'd stormed out of Terri's office, that seemed unlikely; Luc had seen little interaction between them since. He mooched to one of the linen covered side tables, speared an olive with a cocktail stick and popped it in his mouth.

Then he saw Terri. She was standing near the drinks tables with a glass of something orange in her hand, looking across to where Peter's booming voice appeared to be holding his listeners in thrall. Luc saw her exchange a polite word with someone, then move on. He raised a hand but she failed to see him and for a moment was out of sight. When she reappeared she was just a couple of yards away and again he raised his hand. This time she noticed and crossed to join him at the edge of the terrace.

'I didn't know you were going to be here,' she said. She looked almost glad to see him.

'Angela thinks we're dating so she felt she had to invite me.'

'Oh great. Thanks to Lindsey no doubt.'

'Probably. Is it so bad?'

'Honestly? At the moment I'm just glad there's someone here I know.' There was a peal of laughter from the circle round Peter and she glanced back towards him. 'He seems to be on good form tonight,' she said bitterly. 'I believe he saves his worst moods for me.'

'I saw you had another fight the other day. I thought you were getting on better with him.'

'So did I.'

'What was it about?'

Terri eyed him warily. 'I was asking some questions. I need to write a biography for the exhibition catalogue. Peter mentioned his first wife and became upset when he found out that I'd already asked Lindsey a couple of questions about her. He overreacted.'

'Ah.' Luc took a sip of the wine from his glass, watching her over its rim. 'So perhaps you remind him of the delightful Madeleine too? It might make him oversensitive.'

'Nonsense,' she said, not altogether convincingly. 'I mean, do you really think I look like her?'

'I haven't looked at the painting recently.'

She grunted and sipped her drink.

'What do you know about her?' she asked.

'Madeleine?' He pulled a face. 'Not much. The same as you I imagine: died in childbirth; the baby was sickly and didn't live. *C'est tout.*' He met her gaze again. 'You seem to have taken a particular interest in her though.'

Terri studied him a moment as if she were considering telling him something. But Angela banged a large spoon on a table, drawing all eyes and announcing that the food was ready.

They collected plates of cooked meat and salad and a second glass of wine for Luc, and moved away from the already congested tables and chairs of the terrace, down into the sunken parterre where they found a bench looking out over the herb garden and the cherry orchard beyond. The night was warm and redolent. Sitting with the wall at their backs and buffered by a run of dangling shrubs, the chatter of the party above was dulled and irrelevant and for a while they ate in companionable silence. Luc finished first, picking up his wine glass. He wished he could get the conversation back to Madeleine - it intrigued him that Terri was apparently so rattled by Celia's remarks - but could think of no subtle way of doing it.

'You know,' he said instead, 'the last time I saw you was at the preview for an exhibition at Tate Britain: spring last year.'

'The Tate.' She finished eating and wiped her fingers on the napkin, frowning. 'I don't remember seeing you there.'

'You were with someone.'

She nodded slowly. 'That's right, I was.'

'Are you still with him?'

'No.' She hesitated. 'And you?'

'No, I'm not with anyone.'

'No?' She flicked him a glance, unreadable as usual. 'I'm sorry I didn't see you…at the exhibition, that is. There were a lot of people there.'

'There were.'

They sat looking out over the garden. It was a beautiful scene. The sun was already setting, the yellow light already dimming to blue-violet.

'I saw that portrait exhibition you curated,' said Luc. 'When was that…two years ago? It was really good.'

'Three. It was three years ago now. Thanks.' She offered him a quick smile. 'I have to admit I was pleased with it – eventually.'

'What else have you been doing with yourself?'

'Oh, you know, this and that. I was filling in for someone's maternity leave at Ferfylde's before coming here.'

'Ferfylde's? What, persuading the wealthy to buy something that'll both match the wallpaper and count as an investment? That's hardly your style, is it?'

'No, well, there aren't always the right jobs when you want them,' she said defensively. 'Especially if you want to work somewhere in particular. And I do have bills to pay.'

'You wanted to be in London?'

'Yep.' She finished the orange juice and leaned over to put the glass down on the floor. 'I was stupid enough,' she said, straightening up, 'to think that guy you saw me with was worth compromising my career over.'

'Ah. And now you've finished with him, you came here to forget? I've been trying to figure out what would make you take this job.'

'Something like that. But I'm not saying the challenge of creating a retrospective for one of the world's best living portrait painters didn't have some appeal too.'

'Really? Despite the man's appalling reputation?'

'His reputation didn't stop you wanting to work for him.'

'OK, true.' He finished his wine. 'Look, can I get you another drink? Join me in a glass of wine? I could do with another.'

She shook her head. 'I'm fine, thanks. I don't drink much.'

'I remember.'

'Do you?' She looked sceptical, or maybe hopeful. That surprised him: she looked as if she wanted to believe him.

'Sure I do. I remember you used to have one glass of wine; that was your max. You never explained why though.'

'I didn't think it was anyone else's business.'

Luc gave a wry laugh. 'You see, that's your problem, Terri. You think no-one should know anything about you. You keep it all locked up inside and then get hurt when people don't understand you. How can they if you don't give them a chance?'

Her dark eyes flicked to his face for a minute, then away again.

'Well if you must know, it's because my father drank,' she said. 'Not all the time. Sometimes he would go for weeks without touching alcohol. Then something...' She shrugged.

141

'...I don't know...something twisted inside him and he'd spend all night drinking. He'd get completely smashed.'

'But his work? How could he work if he was drinking? He must have needed such a steady hand.'

'He wasn't an alcoholic. Or maybe he was, I don't know. The next day he'd have a headache in the morning and that was it; he'd get on with it. But it wasn't that he needed a drink to get through; it was like something built up in him over time and every so often he had to release it.' She shook her head. 'I can't explain it. I just decided I wasn't going to get like that. It's the way people change when they've been drinking...' She stopped abruptly and he got the impression that still she was holding something back.

'But you could have one glass.' He grinned. 'I'm sure you wouldn't suddenly change into a monster.'

'Oh sure, joke about it,' she said gloomily. 'You never know what people will be like. Really ordinary, nice people can become...become...' She had that hunted expression again that she'd had when he'd picked her up in the car. And he saw her hand shake as she reached up to push a strand of hair behind her ear.

It all clicked into place - of course: she had come here to escape someone.

'Your ex-boyfriend?' he said softly. 'He drank too?'

Terri nodded, refusing to meet his eye.

'Tell me.'

'No...no. What's the point, Luc?'

'I dunno.' He gave a brief laugh. 'Didn't you ever take your angst out on something when you were a kid, when you'd been told off maybe for doing something and sent to your room? I did. Honestly...' He waited for her to look at him before continuing. '...I had a huge stuffed rabbit I used to

142

complain to loudly. That rabbit was the best confidant I ever had. He never judged, always listened.'

She was smiling now, shaking her head at him. 'What was his name, this wonderful rabbit?'

'Albert.'

'Albert? Why?'

'I have no idea. I liked the name I suppose.' He repeated the name with a French pronunciation. '*Alberrrt.* Very international.'

She laughed.

'That's better. So think of me as your own personal *Albert.*' He raised one hand. 'I promise not to judge...really.'

Terri stared down the garden, watching the leggy purple shadows gradually dissolve in the dying light.

'OK, well...Oliver's an actor, very talented, but he hit a rough patch and couldn't get work. He always liked a drink but, then, with each failed audition, the drinking just got worse. He started chasing bottles of wine with shorts. Then he began to resent that I was working when he wasn't. Nothing I said or did was right any more.' She paused, glancing at Luc sidelong. 'I always swore I'd never stay with someone who hit me. But the first time it happened, he was so out of it, I made excuses. All sorts of excuses. Then the next time, he was drunk when he tried to...' She shook her head and swallowed hard. 'He lost it when I pushed him away. I missed work for a couple of days, then had to use make-up to try to cover the bruises.'

She exhaled a long, shuddering sigh. 'That was it. I finally finished it and moved back to my own place. But almost straight away he began to stalk me. He was there...all the time, watching, waiting...so I had to get away.'

'*Quel salaud.*' Luc reached across and gave her hand a brief squeeze. 'I'm glad you had the sense to leave. And he'd never find you here.'

'Don't even go there. I certainly hope not. He keeps sending me messages but they haven't been quite so regular lately so…' She stretched her head forwards, peering down the garden. 'Who's that?' she said sharply.

Luc stared into the dark shadows. 'It's Peter. Heading for the studio I imagine.'

Terri nodded, relaxed back. 'Anyway, now you know: that's why I won't drink much. First dad, then Oliver. He changed, you know. He was OK before he started drinking.'

'Was he? I'm sorry if I can't agree. There's got to be something fundamentally wrong with a man who takes his disappointments out on his girlfriend. He's weak and inadequate. He must be. So he's had tough times. Everyone does. It's how you deal with them that shows what you really are.'

He got to his feet, stacked the plates and glasses together, left them on the seat and looked down at her expectantly. 'So…no more wine. What about tea? I could make you some at the cottage. I also remember how much you liked your tea.'

Terri smiled but already he could sense her guard had come up again.

'Yes, I know you always found it funny. But if you don't mind, I think I'll call it a night. I'm rather tired.'

She stood up, was tantalisingly close. He thought how easy it would be to put his arms round her and hold her.

'I'd forgotten how well we got on,' he said. 'You're safe with me, you know. I wouldn't hurt you for the world. We could…'

'No, Luc, please. Don't.' She stretched up a finger as if she was going to press it against his lips, but she let it fall and took a step away from him. 'We can't go there again. It wouldn't work. Why can't we just be friends?'

'Friends can still come round for tea though.'

'Maybe. But not tonight.' She stared at him, reached her hand to his arm and touched it lightly. 'Thanks.' He watched her walk away, up out of the parterre and out of sight.

Luc abandoned the party and wandered back to the *bergerie*. He poured himself a brandy and sat cradling it, still able to smell her perfume on his clothes.

*

Peter let himself into the studio and flicked on the pendent ceiling lamps. They were fitted with daylight simulation bulbs and a blue-white light filled the space. The smell of oil and turpentine rose to his nostrils and he welcomed it like an old friend. He walked across to his work station and stared critically at the painting on his easel, trying to work out what he should do next, but his mind was too restless to settle to paint. Why had he gone to the party? It had been tedious as usual and absurdly huge. Still he preferred these summer parties, outdoors. Angela's guests seemed less cloying out in the open air.

He walked into his study and closed the door, poured himself a large whisky, took a stiff draught of it and stood, cradling the glass. Terri had been at the party; he had seen her with Luc. For days their conversation of the previous week had echoed through his head. He rather regretted shouting at her in that way but he refused to have Lindsey drawn in to his past. And he was scared too of Terri's quick, probing mind. Where

145

once he had thought he had her under control, now he was not so sure, and then there was the way she had tricked him into talking about Madeleine...

After a moment's reflection, he put the glass down, retrieved a small key ring from the top drawer of his desk, and bent over stiffly to unlock the cupboard below the window. Pulling out a covered cardboard box, he took it and the whisky over to his chair, sat down and cautiously lifted the lid. In one corner was a small stack of photographs and on the top was a black and white photograph of Madeleine, sitting astride the carved zebra of a merry-go-round, the only adult on the ride. He pulled it out, tipped his head back and peered down through his glasses, tilting the photograph to catch the best of the light. She was laughing as she spun into view. They hadn't long met when he'd taken this; she had been just twenty and unlike anyone he'd ever known before. From the very first moment he had found her enchanting. He stared at the picture; it had been years since he'd looked at these photographs. An ache started to develop deep inside him but he ignored it and kept picking the photographs up, print after faded print.

He found a photograph of the two of them together, taken by a friend. Madeleine had been much shorter than he and his arm was looped loosely round her waist, his head bent sideways over her, a stupid expression on his face. He tried to place where it had been taken but failed. It was such a long time ago and it was hard to associate this tall, good-looking idiot with the man he was today. Where had the years gone and what had he become since then? Shrivelled, bitter, haunted? Peter picked up another photograph: a toddler sitting in a tiny model car, his pudgy hands gripping the steering wheel and an expression of rapt concentration on his face. He immediately put it down and quickly replaced the rest of the photographs on top of it.

He took another mouthful of whisky and was about to close the box up, then hesitated and pulled out a broad flat wooden jewellery box, tipping the lid back. He nearly smiled. On the top of a pile of necklaces was one of Madeleine's favourites: an assortment of pretty coloured shells intermingled with beads. How typical of her that she should favour something so worthless. But there was some good jewellery here too. He picked up a box containing a pair of gold drop earrings. She'd fallen for them in a shop window and he'd bought them for her just after she'd told him she was expecting another baby. Each one was set with a cascading fall of tiny deep blue sapphires intermingled with three little diamonds. 'They look like stars in a night sky,' she'd said. By a cruel twist of fate she'd not lived long enough to enjoy them.

Peter eased one off its cushioned bed and held it up to let it fall and catch the light. Beautiful. When Lindsey had reached eighteen he'd intended to give her Madeleine's jewellery. But then he'd thought better of it, unsure what she would make of being given personal things which had belonged to his first wife and concerned that it might upset Angela. He'd bought her a fancy gold necklace instead.

He put the earrings away and picked up the fairground photograph of Maddy again, his thoughts returning to Terri. Since Celia had mentioned it, he too thought he could see a slight resemblance in the eyes: not the colour of course, but the shape and the way she moved them. And of course she was direct, blunt even. Madeleine had been like that. If you asked her opinion, she gave it frankly. He remembered a painting he'd done of her mother. 'You haven't caught her intensity,' she told him, 'her devoutness.' She laughed and put her arms round him as he stood before the easel. 'You're too Anglo-Saxon Protestant,' she said teasingly. 'You don't understand how she thinks.' When he pressed her to explain, she added, 'Oh I don't know...think of a dark church smoky with incense and people on their knees, praying. Imagine what it would be like to spend your whole life feeling that you can't atone enough for your sins.' She had squeezed him hard, stretched up and kissed him, and left him to it.

In a brusque movement he put the photograph back in the box and slammed the lid on again. 'Bloody Celia,' he said, draining the whisky in his glass and dumping the box on the floor.

Chapter 10

Terri picked up a feather boa and draped it round her neck, flicking it back over her shoulder. There was a mirror hanging from a hook further along the shelves and she went to examine the effect, turning a little this way and that, gauging the effect from different angles. It was the Monday afternoon and she was alone again in the studio. Peter had not returned from lunch and Luc had gone to Marseille to visit a supplier. Walking back to her office, she was idling along Peter's jumbled collection of artefacts and props. She removed the boa and tried on a succession of hats, then pulled out a piece of exotic fabric to find that it was a long silk smoking jacket. 'Oh, very elegant,' she murmured. On a lower shelf she found a tumbling stack of Venetian masks and picked through them, holding a couple against her face, checking them in the mirror. Then, buried at the bottom of the pile, she found the missing notebook for 1973. So it hadn't been destroyed, just mislaid. She'd created an intrigue where there was none. Probably everything she'd thought was odd or suspicious could be just as easily explained.

She flicked through it and noticed that yet another page had been torn out. But it was the following sheet which really caught her attention. The reverse of the removed drawing must have been covered in soft pencil and some lines of the sketch and of Peter's annotation had been transferred, ghost-like, to the paper beneath. Through the smudging and confusion of marks, the drawing suggested the outlines of two people, one taller and female; the second smaller, little more than a child and, underneath, were two clear initials: J and T. Terri glanced towards the door, quickly replaced the masks as near to their original position as possible and took the book into her office, pulling the door to behind her.

She stared at the initials. J and T. T for Tom? It must be. From the drawing she thought she could see the similarity with the features of the boy. So who was J? She studied the shadow drawing till her eyes ached but it was too hazy to make out. Then she heard the unmistakeable sounds of Peter returning, quickly slipped the book into her bag and returned to her work. He'd been courteous to her that morning, almost cheerful, as if the quarrel of the previous week had been forgotten. But she wasn't going to be fooled again into thinking that they'd formed the kind of relationship where they could genuinely talk. It was going to be quite impossible to mention the notebook entry to Peter. In any case, he was intentionally hiding something and the clue to what that something was might be in these notebooks.

Collecting her things together at the end of the afternoon, Terri surreptitiously slipped the rest of the damaged notebooks into her bag and took them back to her room. After carefully checking through them for more ghostly imprints, she found two more pencil shadows which were just legible: one said Tom and the other Josie.

Josie. So who was Josie? The question distracted her all evening. An older sister perhaps? But if so, why had she been removed from the record? Did she die too? But that would be surprising, surely: two children from one family? Or maybe she hadn't died. Maybe… All Celia's hints about Terri being part of the family fell into place. She thought she'd been stupid not to realise before. Even Peter had started questioning her about her mother. Terri fought the implication, laughed at the absurdity of it, but found herself inevitably returning to the same conclusions. If Madeleine had indeed given birth to another child who lived - a daughter - that child if still alive would be about the age Terri's mother would have been. Terri snorted, shaking her head. Really it was too preposterous to take seriously. There was no way that her mother could have been Madeleine's daughter. Why would Celia even think it? And what had happened to that daughter that might make it remotely possible?

But the thought lodged in her brain, tenacious and insistent, and she began to dredge back through the memories from her childhood. What did she actually know about her mother? Bits and pieces that amounted to nothing really. So how could she be sure? There again, Terri had never really wanted to know anything about her mother, not after what she'd done. She simply didn't think about her.

But the issue would not be so conveniently dismissed. By the time she went to bed, having argued herself round in circles, she reluctantly accepted that the only way to settle her mind was to go and see the eccentric Celia. And it wasn't a visit she relished.

*

On the Sunday afternoon, Terri walked up to the *pigeonnier,* knocked three times firmly on the door and waited. She glanced round Celia's personal domain: a scrap of dusty garden, unkempt and bordered by a low stone wall. A wooden

151

seat, painted a vivid purple, stood against the wall and, to the side of the door, a couple of gaudy glazed pots contained sickly plants. The high afternoon sun glared off stone and wood and Terri shifted restlessly in the heat. There was no answer to her knock and the waiting ate into her resolve; this had been a stupid idea.

A head appeared through a window high above her.

'Oh it's you, Terri,' Celia called down. 'How nice to see you. Come in. It's not locked. Keep coming through and up to the top.'

Terri opened the door and stepped into a room which looked dark after the sunshine outside. She waited while her eyes adjusted and saw that she was in an open-plan living room: a large square space with a sitting area, a small table and two chairs, and a run of kitchen units along the far wall. To the right, at the back, was a staircase. She climbed to the first floor where a landing gave access to two doors and yet another staircase took her up to a large bright square room.

Celia's studio made her brother's look tidy. There were paintings propped up everywhere, put down wherever opportunity presented, and every surface was covered in artistic paraphernalia. On the table against the side wall an old laptop computer stood open, red paint smudged across its blank screen, both the table-top and keyboard swamped in odd fragments of paper and articles torn from art magazines; a colour-stained painting cloth hung over the back of the chair in front of it. At the far side of the room, at a huge wooden easel, Celia, brush in one hand, cigarette in the other, contemplated a broad canvas. She turned her head as Terri appeared and put her brush down.

'Welcome to my eyrie,' she declaimed. 'Coffee? Tea?' She made for a cupboard on which stood a tray with red wine, whisky, a bottle of mineral water and a selection of glasses. Another tray had an electric kettle on it, coffee, tea bags and a couple of mugs. She waved the hand with the cigarette in a circular motion. 'Or would you rather have wine?'

'No, tea would be fine, thanks.'

'Find a seat…if you can. Throw something on the floor.'

Terri glanced around.

'Black,' Celia said, dangling tea bags in each of two mugs. 'If you want milk I'm afraid you'll have to go down to the kitchen for it. Long-life stuff. Disgusting.'

'Black's fine. Thanks.'

Celia removed the teabags, took a final drag of her cigarette and stubbed it out in a dish. She handed one of the mugs to Terri. 'There's a chair under those sketches there.'

'I'm OK standing, thanks.'

'Really? Is there something the matter?'

'No.'

Celia raised enquiring eyebrows but said nothing, manoeuvred her way back to the high stool by her easel and perched herself on top of it. She sipped her tea, her eyes not leaving Terri.

'Enjoy the barbeque, did you?'

'Yes…thank you.'

'It sounded jolly. Though I'm not sure Angela does jolly exactly.' Despite a line of amusement to the set of her mouth, her gaze was intense, the resemblance to Peter unnerving.

'You didn't go,' said Terri.

'No, that's right, I didn't.'

There was an uncomfortable silence.

'You want me to look at your paintings,' said Terri. 'Any in particular?'

'Are you in a hurry?' Celia smiled but appeared to be disappointed. 'I'll have to find the ones I was thinking of putting into the exhibition. Though you could suggest anything really.' She dumped the mug on her table and got up, wandering round the room, peering at pictures. 'Except the ones I showed last year. Have a nose around, do. Five I can put in. I'd appreciate an opinion.' She bent over to look through a stack of paintings balanced against the leg of a table, pulling out a couple as she did so. 'I hope I sell a few this year. I'm running out of space to store them.'

Terri, cradling her mug, slowly worked her way round the room, glancing at paintings as she went. Any comparison with Peter's work would have been risible; Celia applied her paint quickly and thickly. There was none of Peter's nuance and delicate handling, nor apparently of his careful draughtsmanship and planning. These were broad, colourful statements: flowers and landscapes, farm buildings and town terraces, recognisable but loosely painted, crude even.

'Very expressive brushwork,' Terri observed politely.

Celia paused in her search, looked up and gave a beaming smile. 'Thank you. I don't like to take too long over a painting. Makes it more spontaneous I think…' She bent over again, rooting through a stack of pictures. 'Ah, good, here it is. I wondered where this picture had got to.' She picked up a number of canvases and moved them over to one side, lining them up. 'These were my suggestions. What do you think? You can be honest. Painting's a very subjective thing. Peter's paintings are wonderful of course, but I don't have his patience…or talent. I don't pretend I do.'

Terri ran her eyes from one picture to the next. 'Have you been painting long?'

'Donkey's years. I started when my husband walked out. It was therapy. Though I was better off without him; he was a bastard.'

Terri glanced up at the suddenly acerbic remark but Celia had wandered back to stand in front of her easel and was blandly studying the current painting.

'I think I've used too much raw sienna in this picture,' she said. She tipped the last of the tea into her mouth and turned to look at Terri. 'Can I get you some more dear?'

'No, I'm fine, thank you.'

Celia grunted, picked up a brush and began to lift some paint off her canvas, tongue protruding a little with the concentration. 'Did you ever look for that history of the house I told you about?' she said, still staring avidly at the tip of her brush.

'No.'

'No?' The word held the clear note of disbelief. Celia continued working however, dabbing the brush on an old cloth to remove the paint before reapplying it to the painting.

'Celia?'

'Mm?'

Terri waited for the woman to look at her. 'Who was Josie?'

Celia stared at her for the fraction of a second then turned back to the painting.

'Why dear?' she enquired, mildly. 'Have you found a painting of her?'

'I found…a reference to her.'

Celia turned and smiled knowingly. 'Now you're being coy.'

'I don't seem to have the monopoly on that.'

With a fleeting expression impossible to pin down, Celia returned to the picture and continued dabbing at it with her brush. Terri was increasingly convinced that the woman's apparent absence of mind was faked - a useful way of avoiding questions and being underestimated. It was becoming frankly irritating.

'There, that's better.' Celia wiped the brush and leaned back to regard her painting more objectively. 'I'll use a different green there...perhaps with a bit of lemon yellow though I'm afraid all this fiddling will make it look overworked.'

'So who was Josie, Celia?' Terri pressed. She abandoned her tea and the pictures she was supposed to be examining, and walked across to stand by the easel, obliging Celia to look at her.

'Why do you want to know?'

'Isn't it what this is all about: the comparisons with Madeleine? The suggestion that I look in her studio? The way you look at me...the way Peter looks at me now because of what I guess you've said to him. So who was Josie and what happened to her?'

'Have you asked Peter?'

'No. I'm asking you.' Terri threw her hands in the air and shook them in angry frustration. 'For God's sake, why will nobody talk around here?'

Celia paused and her eyes rolled towards Terri then away and around the room. Finally she got up and walked across to the cupboard, pulled the stopper out of the red wine bottle and poured some into each of two glasses. She came back and handed one to Terri who accepted it wordlessly.

'Josephine was Peter and Madeleine's daughter,' she said. 'Simple as that.'

'So what happened to her?'

'Nobody knows.' Celia drank from the glass, savouring it in her mouth before swallowing. 'After having her, Madeleine had a series of miscarriages. She became frail and I came to stay. My husband had walked out…I told you that, didn't I? Anyway Peter thought I might be able to help out.'

Celia turned and eased herself back onto the stool. 'Maddy finally managed to carry a little boy: Tom…remember? But there were problems in his delivery – took an absolute age. Not that I know anything about these things.' She took another large mouthful of wine. 'Drink up dear. It's not good but it's not plonk and it's keeps you hearty. Anyway Tom was damaged, poor little mite, and Maddy died soon after - complications. Peter was bereft. Josie too. She was only ten. She struggled to come to terms with it and she…became a handful, shall we say?' She smiled at Terri. 'So…have you chosen which paintings you think are best?'

'Yes I think so but, please go on, what happened to Josie?'

'Like I said. Nobody knows. When she was nineteen she had a row with Peter. A big row. She ran away.'

'Where to?'

Celia smiled again as if Terri were simple.

'That's the thing about running away,' she said, 'you don't want people to know where you are. She could have gone anywhere. She might have gone to England. She'd been to school in England. She spoke both English and French fluently.' Celia leaned forward and put a couple of fingers under Terri's chin as if examining her and then moved them up to lightly touch her cheek. Terri flinched. 'Josephine was pregnant when she left here,' said Celia. 'It was August, thirty-five years ago now. When is your birthday, by the way?'

'February,' said Terri slowly, counting the months back.

157

'Hm. Were you premature, just a couple of weeks maybe?'

'No.' Terri shook her head. 'I don't know. Look, you can't really believe that Josephine was my mother. It's absurd. What possible reason could you have for thinking it? My mother's name was Susan. She was English and...' Terri waved her hands about, searching vainly for other information. '...blonde.'

'My, how strongly you protest,' said Celia mildly. 'I'm not saying anything. She would probably have changed her name but of course you're right. How could she have been?' She paused, flashed her bright smile and stood up. 'Anyway which of these paintings do we favour?'

Forcing herself to concentrate, Terri pointed out the ones she preferred.

'Thank you, dear.' Celia picked up a palette knife and started mixing a new green.

'Are you sure about all this?'

'About Josie?' Celia flicked her a glance. 'Are you suggesting I made it up? Well, of course, Angela does that all the time.' She returned her attention to her palette. 'I believe Josie wrote a diary. A number of them in fact. I think they're in the attic too. You can read her story by her own hand if you're that interested. Of course it would probably be wiser if you didn't mention what you were doing to her ladyship. Believe me, it wouldn't go down well. Or Peter, come to that.' She paused. 'Just a suggestion.' She finished mixing, picked a fresh brush out of a jar, and dipped the tip into the paint. She turned suddenly and smiled at Terri who was staring at her blankly. 'Sorry, would you like another drink?'

'I should be going.' Terri deposited the barely touched glass of wine in a narrow gap on a nearby bureau. 'Thanks for the drink,' she added vaguely.

'Oh, well, thank you for coming. Would you mind seeing yourself out?'

Terri paused by the door. 'Supposing, just supposing, that there were any truth in this idea…isn't it an amazing coincidence that I should come to work here?'

'Only if you don't believe in fate,' replied Celia serenely. 'Things have a way of coming round, don't you think?'

Terri frowned but did not reply. 'Where's the key to 'Raphael'?' she asked.

'The key? Peter keeps it in his study…drawer of his desk. Or did anyway.'

Terri slipped out of the door and hurried downstairs, suddenly anxious to get away. Celia was manipulating her, she was sure. She felt like a character in a play except that no-one had shown her the script.

*

Angela had a headache and was resting in the garden room at the front of the east wing, her feet up on a stool, her eyes closed. The patio doors were open but she had latched the shutters across to stop the glare of the sun. Even so, the air was still and humid. She had consumed a little wine the night before but dismissed the idea that the headache was a hangover, blaming tension. She'd been under a lot of stress lately and she tried some breathing exercises learnt from her yoga classes. They didn't help and after a few minutes she gave up. Sleep was elusive. Then she heard Peter calling her name from the hall. A few minutes later, the door opened. She feigned sleep but could sense him there, staring at her, and eventually, reluctantly, opened her eyes.

'Did you want me?' she murmured.

'Ah, you are awake then. I wasn't sure.' Peter crossed to stand nearby, looking down on her. He didn't look cross exactly, more preoccupied. 'Are you all right?'

'I've been dozing a little.' She fluttered a hand up towards her forehead. 'Bit of a headache. I didn't sleep well last night.'

'Oh…yes…well, I didn't mean to disturb you.'

Angela lifted her head to see him better and noticed that he was holding some papers in his left hand. While wondering what was so important that he had brought them with him like this, it also occurred to her that his hand was much improved. He was using it in a more normal way.

'Don't stand over me like that Peter.' She put her hand to her head again. 'Please sit.'

'Mm, what? Oh, right.' He perched on the edge of a neighbouring chair. 'I've been going through the bank statements.'

'Ye-es. And?'

'I haven't looked at them for a while…got rather behind with things…' He hesitated. 'Anyway there are some entries I'm puzzled about. I wondered if you could shed some light on them.'

'Oh Peter, you aren't going to ask me what I spent money on six months ago, are you? I really won't remember.'

'But they're cash withdrawals. Large ones.' He tapped the papers impatiently with the fingers of his right hand. 'From our current account and one from a savings account. Here…' He held out the papers to her. '…look for yourself.'

Angela sighed. 'Do we have to do this now darling?'

'Well I'm worried. It could be serious. Did you really take all this money out?' He began to read a list of withdrawals.

Angela shrugged. 'Yes, probably.' She massaged her temples.

'But you must remember?' His voice had risen, developing a strident, insistent note. 'We're talking about several thousand euros over the course of six months…in cash. I'm concerned someone else has gained access to our money. Have you lost any of your cards? I'm thinking of putting a stop on the accounts.'

Angela was aware of the slow fuse burning on his temper. She pushed herself up, reaching to the side of the chair for her handbag. 'OK, I'll check now.' She pulled out her purse and began to flick through the card pouches. 'No…no…no…no…' She moved across to the other side. 'No…no. No, they're all here I think. There's no need to alert the banks Peter. I can't remember exactly but I'm sure it was me who took the money out.' She snapped the purse closed and dropped it back in her bag. 'But I can't believe we're having this conversation,' she added, sounding hurt. 'You've never checked up on my spending habits before. I didn't realise I had to account for every little thing I bought or did.' There was silence. Peter got to his feet, frowning. 'Just the other day you suggested we might have a trip to Paris,' she added. 'Now it seems we've got money problems. I really don't think it's fair to accuse me in this way.'

'No, we don't have money problems,' said Peter heavily. 'I thought you said you wanted to visit Paris.'

'Well not if you're going to check on all my spending.'

Peter looked on the point of saying something else but wandered out of the room instead.

Angela listened to his receding footsteps along the passage. A few minutes later she heard him padding across the terrace, heading back towards the studio. His behaviour bothered her. He had never challenged her use of money before. His early success had already made him a wealthy man by the time she'd married him and, though he'd never squandered money, he had never been mean with it. And it was not just this business with the accounts - for she had indeed withdrawn a lot of cash lately, had perhaps been incautious. But in all sorts of subtle ways he'd not been quite himself recently. He was alternately more talkative than usual, then more introspective; his temper had shown less frequently. And then there was the offer of a weekend in Paris. Or Rome, he had suggested. 'We don't get away enough, do we? You must get bored.' It had been years since he'd thought to take her away like that. She'd put it down to the head injury but now she was less sure. And she supposed she should be glad – she had struggled long enough with his temperament and his neglect.

Restless all of a sudden, Angela got up and walked through to the kitchen. She stared listlessly at the kettle; it was too warm for tea. The endless summer had started. Most of her friends thought the long hot days were a joy but she'd never really adjusted to the Mediterranean climate. When Peter had proposed to her all those years ago – handsome, wealthy, charming in a gruff sort of way - she'd thought his life in France was something exotic and exciting; she'd had no idea what the reality would be. And she'd vaguely assumed that they would split their time between France and England, taking the best of both, not hole up permanently in this forgotten corner of the mountains. True, Peter *had* suggested at the outset that he intended to live in France but she hadn't really thought he meant it, or maybe she'd expected him to change. She had been disappointed.

She shrugged the thought away, poured herself a glass of chilled cranberry juice and was putting the carton back in the fridge when she heard the front door open and close. She got to the hall doorway just in time to see Terri slipping through the sitting room towards the annexe and she stared after her pensively. When she'd asked Peter what Celia had said about hounding Terri, he'd been vague, evasive even. And she'd seen him watching Terri at the barbeque, a reflective expression on his face.

And now Terri was creeping about in a strangely furtive way. So where had Peter's little helper spent the afternoon, she wondered.

*

Terri fumbled in the back of her bedside cabinet and pulled out a small plastic wallet, flipping its two leaves open. It was an old, cheap affair - she couldn't remember now why or where she'd bought it – but years before she had put a photograph of her father in each of the two clear pockets. In the picture on one side he was standing alone in the garden, looking awkward, cigarette in hand. She had taken it herself with her first camera. How old had she been? Ten? No, the camera was her eleventh birthday present. It wasn't easy to see him in the weak bedroom light and she leaned across and flicked the bedside lamp on, moving closer. The photograph on the other side had been taken of him with his young daughter, his arm awkwardly round her shoulder. To judge from the way he looked, it had been taken around the same time, probably by her grandmother.

Her eyes glazed. The last time she'd seen her father had been six months before his death. They had lunched together in a pub near where he lived. A little over four years previously a woman called Lizzie had moved in with him and Terri had rarely visited the family home after. The two women had been mutually suspicious, wary, an uncomfortable atmosphere sitting between them. At her father's funeral at the crematorium, Lizzie told her that her father had wanted his ashes scattered on the downs where they often went walking and a week later they had gone to do it together, virtual strangers, a difficult and somewhat bizarre expedition. Lizzie had seemed genuinely distraught. Presumably her father had loved her and his love had been reciprocated. Ever since, Terri had felt a painful regret at her behaviour before he died; she thought she'd been childish, jealous perhaps of her father's new found happiness or feeling herself excluded.

She tried to put the thoughts away, felt two fingers down behind the second photograph and carefully pulled out two more pictures. These were snaps of her mother. The first was taken in a park somewhere, her mother standing in front of some iron railings. Behind her, ducks and moorhens paddled on a lake. Her eyes were puckered against the sunshine and she seemed to be saying something to the person taking the photograph. Terri peered more closely at it. It was small and the extreme brightness of the day had rendered her features flat and hard to distinguish. Her hair was shoulder length, pushed back behind her ears, and blonde. She was wearing a mini skirt, a short-sleeved, V-necked top and platform mules. She looked very young. Presumably it had been taken in the seventies.

Terri picked up the second photograph. In this one her mother was cradling a baby, her face turned down to look at

164

the child. Terri stared at it and felt the familiar pang somewhere deep inside. She hadn't looked at these pictures for years; they'd been left in a drawer, ignored. Only when her father had died had she taken them out again. Coming away she had slipped the wallet in her bag on an impulse, reluctant suddenly to leave it behind.

She always told people that her mother had died young from a short, aggressive illness. She'd told the story so many times, she almost believed it herself. But the truth was that Susie Challoner had simply walked out of the house one day and, nearly two years later, thrown herself from a bridge into the Thames. As a child, Terri had struggled to sleep. Creeping down the stairs one evening, long after bedtime, she'd heard her father and grandmother discussing the news and how it would be best to tell her. Confused and upset she'd crept back to her bedroom. On top of her certainty that she was to blame in some way for her mother leaving, it had been the final proof of what she had already known: her mother could not have loved her or she wouldn't have left her like that. Not a word; not a single word. And now she'd gone forever. It was a hurt that had burnt deep into her. Even after all these years, the pain had hardly diminished.

Terri pushed the photographs back roughly into the wallet. She was angry, really angry. She was not going to go searching for diaries and who knew what. Damn Celia and her stupid games, bringing it all back again. The whole story was foolish anyway and what difference did it make to her who her mother was? She never knew her and it was too late now.

Chapter 11

The next Wednesday Christophe was due to visit the studio to discuss progress and plans for the retrospective. On the Tuesday evening, Terri worked late, adding notes to her timeline, making sure everything was clear and well-presented, determined to make a good professional impression, though what preoccupied her most was how Peter would behave. When she'd told him about the visit he'd been rude about the gallery in general and Christophe in particular. But it would be impossible to keep the two men apart; without Peter's input - and approval - the meeting would be meaningless.

Christophe arrived soon after ten, studied Terri's presentation and looked through the final choice of paintings, making notes. Afterwards she made coffee and invited Peter to join them. He greeted Christophe perfunctorily and watched him suspiciously while, in a vain effort to ingratiate himself, the young man talked too much about the gallery, gushed about Peter's work and stressed how much they were all looking forward to the exhibition. He was trying too hard.

'I have discussed the publicity with our director, *Monsieur* Stedding,' he continued under Peter's baleful gaze. 'The gallery has a photographer we use always who will be good for the publicity shots. And I have approached some newspapers and magazines to make articles. They will contact you for the interviews.'

'Interviews? I never said I'd do interviews.' Peter glanced darkly at Terri.

'It might be better to just do one,' Terri suggested. The idea of Peter sounding off to half a dozen newspapers was alarming. 'Do an exclusive for one of the bigger publications. Make it more important.'

Peter grunted ambiguously.

'And this is a list of paintings I suggest we merchandise.' Christophe handed Peter a sheet of paper. 'Are you content with this?'

'Merchandising.' Peter glanced over the list with distaste. 'It's a tawdry thing to do with a work of art.'

Christophe frowned, clearly unsure on the vocabulary but picking up the negative tone. 'But it was agreed in the contract, was it not?' he said defensively.

'Yes, yes, I know.' Peter gave a resigned sigh. 'You have to make money. I understand.'

'Indeed. And we need to make the decisions quickly. Time is hurrying. Do you agree with my choices?' He pointed impatiently at the paper in Peter's hand.

Peter thrust the list at Terri. 'Depends what you're going to reproduce them on. I don't want any of those desperately awful tea towels or umbrellas or…what did I see once?...toilet roll holders. Nothing like that.' He turned abruptly to Terri. 'What do you think?'

'I'm not sure about the Earl,' she said, studying the list. 'In any case I think I might have difficulty getting permissions for it.' She turned to Christophe. 'I think the Durance landscape would be better. The light in that one is striking and it would add variety.'

167

'It is an unknown work though,' protested Christophe.

'Exactly,' said Terri. 'And it has instant appeal. Not all the paintings need to be famous. If they're popular at the exhibition, the goods will sell.'

'Oh for God's sake.' Peter put his empty mug down and got to his feet with an exasperated grunt. 'I've got work to do. You can argue it out between you.' He looked directly at Terri. 'I'll let you decide. But make sure he doesn't do anything embarrassing with my paintings. I'll trust you to keep him honest.'

They watched him pad out, closing the door behind him. Christophe turned to look at Terri, eyebrows raised, and nodded knowingly.

'You have made a conquest with this man,' he said admiringly. 'He lets you decide. I am amazed.'

'Ssh,' hissed Terri. 'There's nothing wrong with his hearing.'

But she was amazed at Peter's behaviour herself. And obscurely uncomfortable with it.

*

We can't go there again. It wouldn't work. Why can't we just be friends?

For the umpteenth time, Terri's clear rebuff ran through Luc's head. Friends. He supposed this at least was progress. A few weeks ago she would barely give him the time of day. He pulled his eyes away from the laptop screen and picked up the glass of wine sitting on the table nearby. He would have to watch this. Since he'd stopped smoking it was too tempting to subdue his cravings and tension by substituting with alcohol and he didn't want to end up like Oliver. The man sounded like

168

a complete pig. Just thinking about him made anger pulse through him again. And he remembered Terri, shaking, barely able to talk about it. Luc had never been a violent man but he thought someone like Oliver could change that.

He turned back to the screen, wrote another couple of sentences, then found himself thinking about Terri again. When they'd dated in London she'd been different: easier somehow and with more sparkle in her eyes, though it had always been difficult to get her to talk about anything personal. He had just been starting to know her when that article had come out and the whole relationship had come crashing down. Those dusky charcoal eyes of hers. Not exactly sparkling now but still they held fire and passion, a passion he guessed she found easier to give to her work than to another person.

But did her eyes resemble Madeleine's? He hadn't had a chance to look at the portrait since. The idea of a link was intriguing - how could that have come about? - but it was doubtful: Celia came out with all sorts of bizarre statements. Still, if it were true, there could be a good story behind it, a unique slant on an eccentric and infamous character. And what interesting titbits of information did Peter tell Terri when they were closeted together in her office – odd comments which seemed insignificant in the context of her work but might be truly revealing of the man?

He finished the last mouthful of wine and pushed the glass away. There was no doubt that Terri had been pleased to see him at the party. If he wanted to get close to her again, he needed to be patient. The attraction between them still lingered; he could feel it.

*

169

Terri parked the car and carefully unpacked the paintings from the back. It was the Friday and she had brought the damaged and dirty canvases to a restoration studio in Avignon which Christophe had recommended. It was the only one on his list which had promised to complete the work in the limited time available. The painting conservator, Stéphanie Lebrun, was a short, round ball of a woman with a glum expression and a sad offer of refreshment. Her workshop was at the back of an uneven stone courtyard, hidden away through an arch behind tall, wooden gates.

Stepping inside the low stone outbuilding, Terri was immediately reminded of her father. It was not so much the clutter of tools and equipment nor the procession of paintings in various stages of undress as the all-pervasive smell which conjured him up so vividly. No matter how often he opened the doors and the windows to ventilate the space, he never succeeded in removing the distinctive aroma of oils, spirits and adhesives which hung in the air. As a child Terri would feel her nostrils start to tingle as soon as she walked in; invariably she would sneeze. She did it in front of *Madame* Lebrun. Perhaps it was a Pavlovian reflex in the familiar surroundings; Peter's oils and mediums never had that effect on her.

Stéphanie assessed the paintings, complained plaintively that one of them, which had a small hole in the canvas, was in worse condition than she had expected, but said she saw no problem in completing the work in advance of the exhibition. Terri thanked her and took the road back to Le Chant, memories of her father continuing to parade through her mind. She remembered him playing Monopoly with her when she had measles – a special event because he never normally played games with her; she remembered watching him standing smoking a cigarette outside his studio, staring into

170

space, wondering what he was thinking about; she remembered him shouting at her when he found her in his bedroom, searching through the cupboards. It was an indistinct memory, more emotion than detail, and had something to do with her mother. What had she been looking for? She could not now recall.

Turning off the *Route Nationale* to loop into the foothills of the Luberon, Terri's thoughts moved reluctantly to her mother. It was so hard now to remember her, harder still to separate out the genuine memories from what she'd been told or heard from somewhere else, or even from her own imagination. Waking up slowly the previous morning, her thoughts had slipped seamlessly from a dream she barely remembered to a memory of being with her mother when she was a little girl. They had been on a day trip up to London and, somewhere in the centre of town, a group of boys had stopped them and asked the way somewhere. She remembered that the boys had funny accents and that her mother had replied using strange words. French? She had no idea. Schoolgirl French or the mother tongue of a French native? Perhaps neither and Terri had made the whole thing up.

Arriving back at Le Chant, she parked the car and wandered back up to the house. Angela was sitting on one of the chairs on the terrace, reading a magazine. She looked up at the sound of Terri's footsteps.

'Terri?' She tossed the magazine on the table under the pergola, rose to her feet and crossed to meet the younger woman half way across the terrace. 'I was hoping to see you.' She lifted her sunglasses to push them up into her hair.

'Hello Angela...Lovely day,' Terri added vaguely.

'Are you doing anything tomorrow evening?' Angela's green eyes studied Terri's expectantly.

'Er…no, I don't think so.'

'Good. Would you have dinner with me? Peter's going to see a friend who's ill and Lindsey's working late. I hate eating alone.' She smiled, like a politician. 'Anyway, it'll give us a chance to get to know each other. Say seven-thirty for cocktails?'

'Sure. Thanks.'

Terri continued into the house, frowning. Angela's manner had definitely cooled of late. So why the invitation?

*

They ate outside, sitting at the long iroko table under the pergola with two citronella candles lit to keep the flies away. The sun still bathed the terrace in a warm glow, dappled where they sat by the fronds of the vine climbing overhead. Across the background thrum of the cicadas, birdsong started up again as the air slowly cooled. Angela had gone to some trouble with the meal, serving melon and blackberries doused with limoncello, followed by grilled John Dory with French beans and tiny roast potatoes, all accompanied by generous amounts of red wine. But Terri had drunk little, despite much pressing, and the conversation had so far been polite but stilted. A succession of questions about herself, her travels and her family had produced only wary, guarded answers. Behind the apparently casual questions she was sure Angela had an agenda.

Now Angela returned from the kitchen with two dishes of *crème brûlée* and a chilled bottle of white wine. She poured the wine into fresh glasses.

'So the work's going well?' She picked up her spoon. 'All going to plan?'

'Yes, more or less. Though there's still a lot to sort out to make sure everything comes together.'

Angela took a spoonful of dessert. 'And Peter seems to have warmed to you. Honestly, I'm amazed. He's not the easiest person to work with and he was in such a bad mood after that fall. What *have* you done to make him so co-operative?'

'Me?' Terri gave a weak laugh. 'I don't think I've done anything. And we do still have...differences.'

'It's a brave person who argues with Peter,' said Angela lightly, '...or perhaps someone with, shall we say, particular qualities?'

Terri didn't reply, unsure what she was being drawn into. Angela abandoned her dessert and picked up her glass, looking at Terri speculatively.

'I see you and Lindsey seem to be hitting it off. I'm afraid she finds it quiet here. But she told me you went together to a concert in Ste. Marguerite the other night. Did you have a good time?'

Terri had not been anywhere with Lindsey since the shopping trip but she remembered seeing the posters in the village.

'Yes, the tribute band.' Terri spoke a little too quickly. 'They were very good, though not really my thing, honestly.' She frowned. 'But surely Lindsey could move away if she finds it too quiet here, go and live somewhere bigger? She doesn't have to stay.'

Angela didn't quite manage a smile.

'No, of course...she could. The thing is: she's quite nervous. I try to encourage her to get out and meet people but she likes to stay close. Perhaps it's just as well; she's always

173

had a tendency to fall in with the wrong sort. She's easily led. I suppose it makes me…protective.'

The barb was unmistakeable. Out of the corner of her eyes, Terri watched Angela down the last of her wine and reach for the bottle.

'Wine not to your taste?' enquired Angela, glancing at Terri's barely touched glass.

'It's very nice, thank you. I just don't drink a lot.'

'I see.' Angela refilled her own glass and picked it up, taking a generous draught.

Terri finished eating, laying the spoon down and folding the napkin onto the table. 'Delicious,' she said. 'Thank you.'

Angela was staring at her, an odd expression on her face.

'I suppose you've heard about all the sadness in Peter's life?' she said.

Terri hesitated. 'Yes, well…some.'

'Peter told you?'

'No. Lindsey. She told me his first wife died in childbirth - when I asked about the portrait.'

'Ah yes, the portrait…The one you admire so much.' Angela nodded, toying with her unused dessert fork. 'But then Lindsey doesn't know much of what happened before she was born. We thought it was wiser that way.'

'Why? What did happen?'

'You mean you don't know about the tragedy?'

'Do you mean about Madeleine's son?' said Terri uncertainly. 'Celia did mention that he'd died.'

'Celia…yes, I'm sure she did. Did she say how?'

'No.'

'Maybe that's just as well. Her version of events does tend to vary according to her mood.' Angela glanced across at Terri as if considering the wisdom of saying any more. 'The truth is

174

he drowned. Tom – that was his name, but I suppose you knew that already – loved to swim. Went swimming every day virtually. And one afternoon he drowned in the swimming pool. Everyone was out except Josie…' She shrugged. '…and the servants, I suppose. Josie was his older sister by the way.' Terri nodded. 'Oh, of course you knew that too. And you didn't know about the drowning?'

'No. How old was he?'

'He was nine. Anyway, by the time we all got back, well, nothing to be done, I'm afraid. It was a tragic accident, but then he *was* very disabled; it was a miracle he could swim at all really.'

'That's awful,' said Terri, automatically reaching for her glass and swallowing a mouthful of wine.

'So you're very pally with Celia then.' It was a statement, not a question.

'No, not at all. But she asked for advice about paintings for an exhibition so I went to look at them. Inevitably we got talking.'

'About Madeleine?'

'Yes, a little.'

'Really?' Angela looked at her sceptically. 'Madeleine's not the most obvious subject, is she? Tell me, did Celia approach you in London or wait till you came here?'

'In London? I'm sorry, I'm not sure what you mean.'

'Celia likes to go back to London once or twice a year to see exhibitions, she says. Maybe she approached you there, told you she could arrange something to your advantage? Or did she come to the studio when Peter wasn't there and produce her little plan?'

Terri straightened in the chair. 'I have no idea what you're talking about. Why are you so cross?'

175

'Cross? I think I have a right to be cross. I'm talking about inheritance, Terri, that's what I'm talking about.'

'What inheritance?'

'What did Celia tell you about Josephine?' Angela pressed. 'No, let me guess: she told you that Josephine had a terrible row with Peter and ran away and that you're probably the baby she was carrying at the time?'

'Yes, actually. That is what she said.'

'Of course. Because she's done it before. She's trying to create a fictitious granddaughter of Madeleine.'

'Why?'

'Oh come on, you can't be that naïve.' Angela smiled grimly. 'Peter is a wealthy man. In France, direct line children and their offspring cannot be disinherited.'

'So how would she benefit from that?'

Angela snorted softly. She had drunk a great deal now and had a wild-eyed, woolly air. 'Celia? She won't, I assure you. She just hates me and wants revenge. But you might benefit, quite a lot – *if* you got away with it.'

'Me? You think I'm after Peter's money?' Terri shook her head in amazement, felt anger bubble up inside her and briskly got to her feet. 'That's so…Jesus, words fail me. What do you think I am?'

Angela sat back and regarded her dispassionately, cradling the last of her wine. 'Don't get all offended and go off in a huff. Look at it from my point of view. You come here to stay with us. I don't know anything about you. Then you get all pally with Celia. What am I supposed to think?'

'I've come here to do a job.' Terri leaned forward onto the table and fixed Angela with a hotly indignant gaze. 'I am *not* pally with Celia and whatever plot she might have hatched, it's nothing to do with me. I am *not* after Peter's money. I don't even believe half she says.'

'Good.' Angela continued to study her shrewdly. 'Then there's no need to get upset,' she said, more calmly. 'Please sit down. It was just something that crossed my mind when I saw you talking with her. That's why I wanted to get to know you better…and get a few things clear between us.' She picked up her glass, held it towards Terri and smiled a little drunkenly. 'Let's drink a toast to our new friendship.' She waited, while Terri reluctantly sat down and did the same thing. 'Friendship,' said Angela and downed the last mouthful of wine. 'The thing is,' she said, putting the glass down, 'you can't *be* Peter's granddaughter, because Josephine didn't run away at all.'

'Why, what happened to her?'

Angela sat back. Despite the softness and slur of her speech, her eyes still held a steely purpose.

'Josephine had a row with Peter – that much is true. I hadn't been here long enough to know her well but apparently it wasn't the first – everyone said she had become very difficult after her mother died. And her brother had recently drowned so of course she was…distraught.' She paused. 'But I'm afraid Josephine went off and killed herself…out in the woods. She even left a suicide note, quite explicit, said she was sorry but she couldn't cope any more. The body wasn't found but the police thought that meant nothing. People had gone missing in the woods before. They're enormous and full of wild animals: boar, you know, that kind of thing. But you can see why we fudged the issue with Lindsey. These things can be very impressionable on a young mind.'

She leaned forward again, staring into Terri's face.

177

'So you won't tell her about this, will you? In fact I'd advise you don't tell anyone.' She raised her eyebrows and looked at Terri meaningfully. 'Peter would be absolutely furious if he found out we'd been talking about it.' She nodded once to emphasise the point, her eyes never leaving Terri's face.

*

Barely a quarter of an hour later, Angela retired to her room. She had insisted that Corinne would clear the dishes in the morning but Terri ignored her, and took everything back to the kitchen. Clearly Angela had forgotten that the following day was Sunday and Corinne wouldn't be working. In any case Terri was glad of the activity and loaded the dishwasher before wandering back outside.

The last of the light had faded to nothing and a velvet darkness had settled over the grounds. She blew out the candles on the table then found herself staring in the direction of the swimming pool, its eerie desolation and disuse now explained. But these were unnaturally long shadows that had been cast; Tom had drowned decades ago.

Her thoughts were muddled and contradictory. So everything Celia had told her was false. Or was it? Why had the old woman not told Terri that Tom had drowned? And what other information might she be holding back? Presumably Angela was the more credible witness. Of course she was – Celia was several cards short of a pack. And yet Celia could be remarkably lucid when she chose and Terri was convinced she was not as confused as she pretended. Madeleine's studio did, after all, exist, just as she'd said. But, feuds aside, why would either of them lie? Clearly Angela had

Lindsey's inheritance in mind. And Celia? Did she just like causing trouble? Angela's pointed intervention had somehow only served to make Terri suspect there was more truth in what Celia said than she'd thought.

But how and why had Tom drowned given that he swam every day? Terri turned and looked towards the top of the east wing, towering above her, an inky shape against the midnight blue of the sky. Her mother had committed suicide in London. But suppose she *had* been Peter's daughter, and Angela was wrong and Josephine had indeed run away? Her behaviour and her desperation might have had their roots here, in Provence, several years before. And Celia said the girl had kept a diary. If Terri could find those diaries, perhaps she could prove it one way or the other…and maybe even begin to understand why her mother had behaved the way she did. It occurred to her for the first time, with a feeling very akin to hunger, that she needed to understand why.

Chapter 12

Terri pulled into the car park at Le Chant, saw Lindsey get out of her car and drew her own alongside.

'Honestly, Lindsey,' she said tersely, getting out, 'if you expect me to cover for you, you should at least have the courtesy to warn me what the story is. You nearly landed us both in it.'

It was six-thirty and she'd just got back from a shopping trip to the village. She'd intended staying to eat in one of the restaurant bars but she always felt conspicuous, eating alone, and had changed her mind as she often did. Now she pulled a bag containing cheese, cooked meats, salad and bread from the car while Lindsey stood watching her.

'Sorry,' Lindsey mumbled. 'It was the first excuse I could think of.'

Terri grunted and locked her car. 'It's OK. I covered it.'

'So mama asked about it then? What did you say?'

'I lied. I said we'd gone to that tribute concert. I assume that is what I was supposed to say?'

'Yes,' said Lindsey sheepishly. 'Thanks.'

'That's OK. Are you just home?'

'Yes.'

They walked up the path together. Sami was raking the gravel on the terrace and touched his cap to their greeting as they passed. The previous evening, Terri had seen him mowing the stretch of lawn in careful stripes; that morning he'd been brushing the stone paths, something she'd never seen him do before.

'Sami seems very busy at the moment,' she remarked. 'Is there something happening?'

'Aunt Patricia is coming to stay,' replied Lindsey gloomily. 'Mama's sister. It's her annual visit. She's arriving tonight.'

Terri grinned. 'Is that not good?'

'She's all right.' Lindsey pulled a face. 'She interferes. And she talks too much, very fast, without really saying anything. Father teases her about it all the time but she never gets it. She takes him seriously.' Lindsey flicked Terri a glance and smiled suddenly. 'It *can* be very funny.'

There was a huge display of flowers in a jug on the hall stand and a strong smell of lavender in the air; the floor had recently been washed. Lindsey carried on through and up the stairs and Terri crossed into the kitchen where she found Corinne kneeling on the floor, a bowl beside her, cleaning the oven. They exchanged a greeting as Terri put some of the chilled goods in the fridge.

Corinne straightened up, stretching her back.

'You're working late,' said Terri, in French. Corinne had been remarkably patient with her attempts to improve her language skills, painstakingly correcting her more glaring errors. They had gradually formed a relationship of sorts though Terri would have hesitated to call it friendship; Corinne was too guarded for that.

'I have to stay; there is a lot to do,' Corinne said now. '*Excusez-moi.*' She walked into the utility room and emptied out the bowl before returning to the kitchen. '*Madame*'s sister

181

is coming to stay, and everything has to be absolutely perfect.' She rolled her eyes just as Angela marched in, looking at her suspiciously.

'I'm sorry to disturb you, girls,' she said pointedly. 'Corinne, you haven't made the bed yet.'

'No, *Madame*. I am doing it next. I have cleaned the bedroom though.'

'I know. I've just put some flowers up there. I'm hoping we'll eat at eight-thirty...assuming her flight's on time. Lay up in the dining room, will you?' Angela breezed out of the room again with a distracted air.

Corinne peeled her rubber gloves off and dropped them on the side of the sink, sighing wearily.

'Let me give you a hand with the room,' said Terri. 'No, really,' she insisted, as Corinne protested. 'It'll take half the time if we both do it. And I've nothing special to do.'

Corinne reluctantly agreed and led the way upstairs. She retrieved sheets and pillow cases from the linen room and took them into 'Rubens', the bedroom at the front of the east wing.

'Is this where she's staying?' asked Terri, dismayed.

'Yes, *Madame* Patterson always has this room.' Corinne tossed the sheet across the bed and Terri caught it, smoothing it out across the mattress.

'How long does she usually stay?'

'Three weeks,' said Corinne laconically. 'Sometimes longer.'

'Oh. Is she married or does she come alone?'

'*Seule*. She is widowed. She has two sons and three grandchildren.' Corinne gave a wry smile as they raised the mattress and tucked the sheet under. 'And she talks about them *all* the time.' They placed the mattress down and she raised a hand, mimicking a mouth talking, rocking her head side to

182

side. She glanced warily towards the door and they moved to tuck the other end of the sheet, working easily together. They each began drawing a case over a pillow.

'From the outside it looks like there's another floor above this side of the house,' Terri remarked casually. 'You can see a line of low windows.'

'Yes. There's an attic.'

'What's it like?'

'I don't know. I never go up there.'

'Oh. I thought you might have had to clean it.'

'Clean an attic?' said Corinne incredulously. 'Do you do this in England?'

Terri smiled and shook her head but she was disappointed. To judge from Corinne's expression and disinterest, she knew nothing of Madeleine's studio. Terri had hoped Corinne might have been able to tell her something about it, might even had access to another key.

They spread a light counterpane over the bed and smoothed it out.

'Corinne?' fluted Angela's voice from the hall.

'*Oui Madame*?' Corinne hurried from the room.

Terri stood and looked up at the ceiling, remembering the creaking steps up to the attic. 'Raphael' was immediately above her; with Aunt Patricia staying, exploring it was going to be out of the question.

*

The longest day had come and gone but the temperature continued to rise. The studio, with its skylights bleeding sunshine, became sticky and still. Peter, who was happy to paint to the sound of music but refused to have the intrusion of a fan whirring, took to leaving the door ajar and asked Luc to open all the windows. In the house Terri was politely introduced to Angela's sister, a small woman with a big voice and an inquisitive smile, but tried to keep out of the way and had little contact with her. The two women were sometimes to be seen by the pool – Patricia occasionally even swam – or sitting with drinks on the terrace. Sami hammered croquet hoops into the lawn and the sisters played an occasional lethargic game in the late afternoon.

Luc knocked at Terri's office door one afternoon and walked in to find her sitting at her computer, fanning herself with an art magazine.

'Too hot for you?' he remarked blandly. He came to stand behind her and bent over to look at the screen. 'What are you doing?'

'I'm *trying* to write the catalogue.'

'In your way am I?'

'Yes.'

He moved away and leaned against the trestle table where the timeline was laid out.

'Don't move anything on that table,' she ordered, and returned her eyes to the computer.

'There's a dinner party tomorrow night. Are you going?'

'I haven't been invited.'

'Oh? Why not?'

Terri shrugged, her gaze not leaving the screen. 'It's for Angela's sister. People she already knows I imagine.'

'Fine. In that case I was wondering if you would like a day trip to the sea tomorrow?'

Terri raised her eyes to look at him, frowning.

Luc raised his hands in a gesture of innocence. 'Just a trip to get some sea air. No strings.' When she hesitated, he added, 'Sea breezes - it'll be cooler.'

She hesitated, then nodded, smiling in spite of herself. It was too tempting to refuse. 'Sounds like a good idea. Where did you have in mind?'

'Wherever you like.'

*

Terri chose to visit St. Tropez though Luc had insisted that there were closer places they could go. In the early July traffic they got stuck in endless queues, all heading to the coast. Luc complained that they should have left earlier as he had suggested. Terri told him he was being impatient – which was typical of men when they were driving. He protested against the generalization. She abandoned the argument and looked out of the window. They had spent much of the journey either in petty dispute or in teasing, often absurd, exchanges; the cosy familiarity of it had a disconcertingly intimate feel at times.

They drank coffee on the quay facing the water, watched a procession of tanned and glamorous people walking past, then strolled around the old town and ate lunch at a backstreet restaurant, sitting on a terrace under a sweeping canopy.

In the afternoon, they explored the harbour, sight-seeing the enormous yachts with their uniformed crews and luxurious fittings. When they reached the end of the harbour wall, there were seats and a welcome breeze off the sea. Terri sat down, stretching her arms along the backrest and leaning her head back.

'That's the first time I've felt the air move since we've been here,' she said appreciatively. 'When I complained about the heat to one of the shopkeepers in Ste. Marguerite the other day, he said: *What do you expect? It's Provence.'*

'He had a point. You should wear a hat.'

'Probably.' She closed her eyes, enjoying the whisper of the wind on her skin, but was aware of Luc sitting down beside her and immediately drew her arms back to her side.

'Have you heard from Oliver recently?' said Luc.

Terri's eyes sprang open and she sat up straighter.

'No.' She frowned at him. 'Not for a few days now. Why? Have you seen him?'

'No. Hey, don't panic. I've seen no-one – no strange Englishmen anyway. Only you told me he'd been emailing you so I wondered how persistent he was.'

'Oh he's persistent.' In fact he had become increasingly abusive. His last message had been: *You're just a whore who'll go with anyone, aren't you?* And he'd gone on to describe what he'd do to her when he found her. It was sick and her skin crawled at the memory. Why she felt she had to read them was beyond her; she should just delete them as soon as they arrived. But it had been more than a week since that last email. 'He's been strangely quiet for a few days actually,' she added.

'Good. He's probably moved on to torture someone else.'

'Maybe. Poor girl then.'

Luc smiled and she tried a smile too but Oliver's silence felt ominous and made her irrationally uneasy. She pushed him out of her mind, reluctant to let him spoil her trip.

Luc leaned forward, elbows on knees, looking out between the boats to sea. His expression became reflective, preoccupied even, and they sat in silence. Terri glanced across at his thoughtful profile.

'What does your father think now…about you painting, I mean?'

He shrugged. 'He doesn't know. I haven't told him.'

'But surely he must know you're not writing? Or are you, on the side?'

Luc turned his head to look at her. 'You still don't trust me.'

'No, it's not that...' She paused as it occurred to her that she actually meant it, and noticed Luc raise one questioning eyebrow. '...I thought he'd make a point of reading your articles. I thought he'd notice if they stopped.'

'I do still do an occasional piece for a magazine. The money's useful. But my father wouldn't notice.' He looked out to sea again. 'We fell out some time ago.'

'I'm sorry.' She was tempted to ask why but didn't think she could. 'Maybe he'll come round when you become a successful painter.'

He laughed ruefully.

'Maybe. I doubt it. But there is a gallery in St. Rémy which might give me an exhibition. They want me to produce more work to show them. Then...' He shrugged again. 'Who knows?'

'That's wonderful. Congratulations.'

He turned to look at her and smiled. 'Thank you.'

'When do you think it might be?'

He shook his head and looked at her quizzically. 'Not sure. I'm a slow worker. But I'll let you know - if you'll come, that is.'

For a moment she let her gaze rest on his face. 'OK,' she said off-handedly, standing up. 'It's very hot here. Can we move on? I need a cup of tea.'

It was just after ten o'clock when Luc drove up the winding drive back to the mas. He paused in the main parking area with the engine still running. A number of unfamiliar cars were lined up in front of the garages. The dinner party was clearly still in full flow.

'I had a great day,' said Terri, putting her hand to the door handle. She turned her head. 'Thanks for inviting me.'

He smiled at her. 'Me too. Thanks for coming.' He quickly leaned across and kissed her: warm, gentle, chaste. It was over before she had time to react. He sat back, looking at her expectantly. 'Maybe we could do this again sometime? Explore somewhere else?'

'OK…yes, I'd like that.'

She watched the rear lights of his car disappear along the track, her thoughts confused, and made her way up the steps to the terrace. Light spilled out from the downstairs windows of the west wing and she paused, glancing across. There was no-one visible in the drawing room; the guests were apparently still dining.

She heard the crack of something trodden underfoot and looked quickly to her left where a narrow path led round the side of the house to the garages. The long, lean figure of Sami was moving away. He'd been silently watching her. That man could be unnerving.

*

On the Sunday morning, Peter went into Ste. Marguerite to get his newspaper. He could have had it delivered as they did with the weekday papers, but he liked the trip. He liked to consider the different titles, glance at the cover stories, before inevitably buying the same paper he always did. And he liked the feel of the village on a Sunday morning, with people going to buy bread and pastries or just out for a walk, and the background chime of the church bells calling the faithful to Mass. With his newspaper under his arm, he stopped afterwards at his favourite café on the Rue Victor Hugo. They served decent coffee there and a particularly delicious chocolate brioche. There were never enough sweet things in the house for Peter's taste. Angela refused to buy things like chocolate brioches or apple tarts unless she was entertaining. When he complained, she said they would make her fat; he told her not to eat them then, but she ignored him. 'You could buy them yourself,' she had said more than once. So he did.

That Sunday morning was dry but a bank of high cloud had made it cooler and sticky. Peter finished his pastry and sat reading, a light breeze occasionally flicking the pages of his newspaper. Turning a page of the broadsheet, his attention was caught by a familiar figure on the pavement on the other side of the street. Peter peered through the fronds of the adjacent potted fig tree. It was Lindsey – he'd thought so - and she was not alone. He stared more intently. She was with Thierry, his own student, and he watched, frowning, as they stopped and lingered over a kiss, the boy's hand roaming down her back. Then Lindsey looped her arm through the boy's and they walked on down the street.

Peter was stunned; he'd had no idea. He hadn't even realised they knew each other and he felt a reflex charge of anger build inside him: Thierry was taking advantage of his little girl. But the fire dissipated as quickly as it had come. Lindsey was no longer a little girl and Thierry was twenty-six or twenty-seven. It was he, Peter, who was old which was why they seemed so young. And he thought his daughter deserved some fun; she got precious little at home. Angela fussed over her and hedged her in. And with Patricia in the house poor Lindsey was being more hounded than ever.

But suppose the girl was falling for Thierry and then he dropped her? She would be broken hearted and Peter would feel responsible. He shook his head, resolutely picked up his coffee cup and took a mouthful. He was not responsible; Lindsey had to learn like everyone else. Angela might treat her like a child but she was all grown up now. Anyway, Thierry seemed like a good boy: he worked hard, he had talent, and he was able to use criticism. And Peter rather liked the idea of having another artist in the family.

Madeleine drifted into his mind. After years of keeping her at bay, she kept doing this lately as if she stood waiting for him to open a door and let her in. When he'd first started dating her, he remembered walking the streets with her, just the way the two youngsters were, hand in hand or with his arm around her shoulder. No-one else had existed for him when he was with Madeleine; he simply did not see them. And he remembered Madeleine's father calling to see him at his studio, a dump of a place, looking at him suspiciously because he was English and, worse still, an artist, and asking what his intentions were and if he thought he would be able to earn enough to support her. If not, he should do the decent thing and leave her alone – right now. *Comprenez?* Peter smiled sadly now at the thought. He had not remembered that conversation in donkey's years.

He finished his coffee, folded up the newspaper and threw some coins on the table. He was about to get up but then remembered that Patricia would be up at the house and his heart sank. His sister-in-law was a decent sort but her prattling conversation revolved entirely around her family and she was currently obsessed with the potty training of her youngest grandchild. Even Angela, who usually enjoyed her sister's visits, had started to become frayed at the endless bulletins provided courtesy of Patricia's new smartphone.

Perhaps he should suggest to her that she take her sister over to the Côte d'Azur for a few days? Any available accommodation would cost a fortune at this time of year but he would happily pay. Since that little unpleasantness over the accounts he had thought a few times that he should treat her, prove that it had not been about the money. His father had been mean. By the time he was an old man, it had shown on his face: he was pinched and shrivelled. Peter, whatever his other faults, had always been determined not to be like that.

He tapped a jaunty middle finger on the table and got to his feet, feeling better suddenly. He was certain Angela would love a trip to Cannes – she adored the place; surely Patricia would too? He knew people who would help; he would arrange it for them.

Chapter 13

At Terri's request, Gilles Arnaud, from the security firm, came to the studio the following Friday to upgrade the locks and fit an alarm. Before leaving, he explained how to programme whatever code she chose into the alarm, how it worked, and how to deactivate it. There was no-one else in the studio to hear. An old artist friend of Peter's had an exhibition preview that evening in Vence and Peter had invited Luc along. He'd asked Terri too, almost diffidently, and she might have been tempted but they had to leave mid-afternoon and she couldn't leave Gilles alone in the studio. 'Indeed not,' Peter had replied vehemently. 'Well...there we are then.'

Now she saw Gilles to the door and turned back into the room, glancing up at the huge clock on the wall. It was barely ten past six. She retrieved her things from her office, left the studio and locked the door behind her, feeling a buzz of nervous anticipation. Earlier that afternoon she had taken the key ring from the drawer in Peter's study. Her fingers automatically felt for it now in her pocket as she quickly climbed the hill to the house.

The two sisters had gone away and the old *mas* was quiet. According to Corinne, they were staying in a smart hotel in St. Raphaël near Cannes. 'A few refreshing days by the sea,' was the way Angela had described it. Lindsey had been working late all week; Corinne would have gone home. This was Terri's best, if not only, opportunity to gain access to Madeleine's studio. She deposited her things in her room, quickly changed into cropped trousers and a T-shirt, and made her way back through the house and up the stairs, on and up the hidden flight from the linen room, to the attic room door.

Once there, she fumbled with the lock. There had been two key rings in Peter's desk drawer – neither were labelled - but the one she'd left behind held cupboard or suitcase keys, too small for an old door. The ring she'd taken held three large old keys. The first entered the lock but wouldn't move; the second was simply too big. By the time she tried the third - sure that someone would come back any moment and find her there - her hands were damp with sweat. It fitted and turned with a clunk which seemed to echo through the whole house. A wild idea had thrust itself into her mind earlier that day and had refused to leave: suppose there was someone hidden up there, alive or maybe even dead? It was nonsense, of course, and anyway she'd come this far...She pushed the door back and took a cautious step inside.

It was a studio cum day room. Dust motes hung in the air along with a dry musty smell mingled with a tired hint of lavender. There was no body. She looked around. The windows she recognised: low and wide, two into each long wall and one at the front, open a crack at the top. At the back, facing north, was a large window which reached up into the apex of the roof. It hadn't been visible from the outside but there was a creeper growing across it, spreading its sticky tendrils across the glass. Below it, against the rear wall, stood an old roll top desk. Straight ahead of her was a cabinet with a record-player on the top and a small stack of vinyl records lying alongside. At the front of the room stood a chaise longue in faded linen, a small, low table and, nearby, a long cupboard with a tray and an old kettle on top. On the other side of the room a bookcase stretched the height of the wall.

Terri closed the door behind her and took a few hesitant steps inside. On the other side of the partitioning for the stairs was a door to an old-fashioned washroom. The centre-piece of the room, however, was a large wooden studio easel with a table alongside spread with tubes of oil paint, brushes and rags. A wooden palette was still covered in dried, crusted oil paint. On the easel a vivid painting of a flower shop, with buckets of brightly coloured flowers on the pavement outside, had been left unfinished. A yellowed reference sketch was pinned to the easel; others lay on the table. Getting closer, she could see the dust lying in the grooves of the congealed paint and fragments of colour which had flaked off.

On the walls and propped up on the floor were more canvases: still lives of flowers, pottery and fabrics; intimate interiors; people working; sweeping landscapes - cheerful, optimistic pictures, enthusiastically and efficiently executed. All had been signed: Madeleine. It was a room frozen in time, left as it was the day it had been abandoned. And there was a layer of dust over everything while gossamer thin cobwebs hung and looped from the ceiling. Surprisingly, despite the neglect and forlorn associations, it was a charming room: untidy and homely. Terri could almost imagine Madeleine walking back in, taking up where she'd left off. It was an odd feeling. She moved round, occasionally letting her fingers rest on something: the brushes on the table, the edge of a canvas, the high gloss glaze on a gaudy vase.

Down in the sitting area, at the front, an old mahogany writing slope on the cupboard top glowed in the flattening rays of the sun. In front of it the sunlight reflected off a couple of photograph frames containing black and white images. The first was a wedding photograph: Madeleine in a pale lace dress and Peter looking happy if bashful in a dark suit. The second was of Madeleine with a baby in her arms. Terri studied it then slid the photograph out. On the back someone had written: Madeleine with Josie 1957. So this was Josephine, but the child's tiny features told her nothing and she replaced it in the frame.

She stood, surveying the room. Where would Josephine's diaries be? She crossed back to the roll top desk near the door. The top was unlocked and it snaked back easily under the pressure of her hands. In its pigeon holes she found drawing pins, paperclips and stationery. There were receipts, odd lists, an open bag of brittle elastic bands and a wad of yellowed letters, written in French, signed with names Terri had never heard of. The drawers held nothing of interest either. She abandoned it and crossed to the bookcase.

The upper shelves were full of paperbacks, the lower shelves held folders, files and large, hardback art books. There were no diaries. On a lower shelf was a photograph album containing Madeleine and Peter's wedding photographs, a time-capsule of the nineteen fifties: fascinating but irrelevant.

Terri suddenly remembered asking her father if there was a photograph album for his wedding and he'd said no in that clipped way he had when he was reluctant to talk. They'd married in a registry office, on the spur of the moment, he'd said, and had immediately changed the subject. And then, as if the one memory had jostled another, she remembered doing a project on family trees at school and asking her father to help her fill in the names. But he didn't know the names on her mother's side apparently; she'd fallen out with her family and never talked about them. The more she remembered, the more

195

it all seemed to fit. She felt a bubble of excitement forming inside, or maybe it was apprehension.

After the heat of the day the attic air was warm and close. She rubbed a hand across her damp forehead and looked round, forcing herself to think. This was Madeleine's room, not Josephine's. Where would a grieving daughter be likely to put something in her mother's room? Her gaze fell on the work table by the easel – arguably the most important place in the room.

She heard a man cough outside and quickly moved to the window, peering down. She couldn't see anyone. It was probably Sami; he rarely came in the house but, perhaps, with Angela away... She needed to get on and finish here. She crossed briskly to the work table.

An old oilskin tablecloth disguised the fact that it was actually a big kneehole desk. Terri pulled out the upper right hand drawer. It was full of pencils, rubbers, sharpeners, a box of charcoal and some coloured crayons. The second drawer held a tray of watercolour pans and brushes. The bottom drawer was full of old sketch books. She checked through the top one: it was full of neat pencil studies.

About to put it back, she found the remaining sketch pads had tipped unevenly in the drawer and, pulling them out, she found three hard-backed lined notebooks underneath. The first contained clumps of writing in a childish, uneven hand. They were in French and the top entry was headed November 1967. Terri struggled to read it but grasped the gist.

Dear Diary,
Madame *Grancourt gave you to me because I need a friend. She is my favourite teacher and very kind. She thinks I should talk to you and it will make me feel*

better. I miss maman *so much that I don't know what to do. I don't want to do anything. My friends don't understand.* Madame *Grancourt said to write anything I want. But I don't know what to say. I'm so unhappy.*

Today I had stew for lunch. The tartines *I had after school were stale. I haven't seen* papa *all day.*

Terri closed her eyes, clutching the book hard between her two hands. 'Yes,' she hissed triumphantly. Glancing through them it was clear that the other two books held similar writing and were marked with later dates.

She slipped the diaries into the cotton shoulder bag she'd brought with her, carefully closed the drawer and stepped back softly across the room and out of the door, locking it silently behind her.

*

November

The baby came home from hospital today. His name is Tom. He hasn't been well and they say he's very weak. He was supposed to come home before but then he got an infection. There is a nurse to look after him. Her name is Denise. Tom is very small with tiny little fingers and nails. His eyes are very dark, like maman*'s, and he has a lock of dark hair on the top of his head. I'm not sure I want him here. It was because of him that* maman *died so now he's here and she isn't. Why did she have to have another baby?*

It had been Terri's habit, as a child, to read in bed – a safe, cocooned world - long after she was supposed to be asleep.

Now, having furtively returned the keys to the studio, she was in bed again, reading the earliest entries in the first diary. Josephine had been haphazard about dating her entries, usually just marking the month, sometimes forgetting to do it at all. The first entries were the woebegone jottings of a bright but unhappy child. Occasionally there was one line; other times a wordy, rambling paragraph. Terri turned the page.

December
School finishes for Christmas next week. All my friends are excited about it. Angeline is hoping for a pair of skating boots. I don't know what I want. Maman *always made a nativity scene but when I asked* papa *about it he said no. He said he didn't know where it was and he got cross when I offered to look for it. Yesterday we put the* santons *round the crib at school. It looks very nice. I brought one of the* santons *home and I've hidden it in my room. It's a lady with a basket of flowers and she reminds me of* maman.

Terri had seen the little painted clay figures which the Provençal people used in their nativity scenes each year. There was a shop in Aix-en-Provence which specialised in them. She yawned. It was a laborious process deciphering both the undisciplined handwriting and the French.

Isabelle found the santon *when she was cleaning my room.*

Isabelle had been mentioned before; she was the *bonne.*

She showed it to papa *and he got very cross. He says I must take it back to school in January and say I'm sorry. I told him I was going to take it back but he didn't listen. He never listens. Isabelle says he's just very sad and I have to behave. But she should not...*

There was a verb Terri didn't know. Too often she found she was guessing meanings. Maybe this was 'search or snoop'.

...in my room. She probably reads this diary too even though I hide it. Aunt Celia asked me what I wanted for Christmas today. She said she would take me shopping tomorrow. I wonder if she'll remember. She'll probably make me get something horrible. She likes strange things.

Terri put the notebook down again, rubbing her eyes. It was nearly midnight and she ought to go to sleep but first she'd read just another couple of pages...

A few minutes later she fell asleep with the light on and the notebook still on her lap.

*

With the two sisters away, the days appeared longer; time felt elastic and flexible, the routines temporarily adjusted or even abandoned. The old mas basked in the summer sun, its pale sandy stone changed, like a cygnet to a swan, into a dazzling white. The chorus of *cigales* rose each afternoon to a deafening pitch then slowly fell away again as the sun set. It was almost as if the house itself seemed watchful, waiting for something to happen.

Corinne fussed over Peter. When she got back to the house on the Tuesday afternoon, Terri found her arranging a *salade niçoise* on a plate.

'What's that?' she asked.

199

'It's for *Monsieur* Stedding. I leave him food for the evening.'

'You spoil him.'

'I have to or he won't eat.'

'Why not?' asked Terri.

'Because he is a man,' Corinne replied simply. 'And they are stupid. He will eat crisps. Or chocolate.' She shook her head. 'It's not good for an old man. He needs proper nourishment. And he drinks whisky,' she added sadly, as if that itself proved the point. She finished preparing the salad and wrapped it in cling film. 'He will probably leave it anyway.' She switched her gaze sharply back up at Terri who was smiling. 'You think this is funny?'

'I think you worry too much about him.'

'*I* think you should make sure he eats it.'

'Me?' Terri's eyebrows shot up. 'I don't think he'll listen to me.'

'Perhaps I should make one for you too? You probably don't eat properly either. You could eat together.'

'I don't think so,' said Terri, with a grin. 'You just fuss over Peter and leave me out of it. Anyway, he'll probably work till late and I'll be in bed.'

But Peter seemed to be spending more of his evenings around the house. Terri didn't want to spend all her spare time in her dark room but nor did she want to get in his way. It was like being in some kind of party game where she had to guess where he would be next and move on to avoid him.

On the Thursday evening, sure that she'd heard him go out, she walked into the kitchen to make something to eat only to find him sitting at the big wooden table. Not far from where he sat, clearly pushed to one side, sat Corinne's plated meal, still wrapped in cling film. There was a glass, half full of red wine, near his right hand and the open bottle further up the table. Lying close by, flat on its side, was a packet of salted nuts with the corner ripped open. A couple of peanuts had fallen out onto the table. Peter raised his eyes from a book at her approach and his expression noticeably brightened.

'Ah Terri,' he said, 'how are you?'

'Fine, thanks. Sorry, I didn't mean to disturb you. I was just going to get something to eat.'

'Carry on.' He waved a hand towards the kitchen. 'What are you going to have?'

'I haven't decided yet.'

Peter examined the wrapped salad.

'If you like tuna and…fried potato…and egg... and, let me see, French beans, you could eat this. You'd be doing me a favour.' He looked up at her again, eyebrows raised in a pleading, comical expression.

'But Corinne wouldn't approve,' Terri said. 'She told me to make sure you ate her meals.'

'Did she indeed? The madam. She makes too many salads; does she think I'm a rabbit? Anyway, I'm not going to eat this so it's up to you.' He pushed the plate towards her. 'No doubt she'll be cross with us both tomorrow morning when she finds it in the fridge.'

Terri moved closer to the table.

'What will you eat then? Do you want me to make you something?'

'Are you a good cook?'

'Terrible.'

'Then no. I had a meal at lunch-time in any case. There's a large tiramisu in the fridge which is beckoning. If you eat this thing, I'll let you share it with me.' He got up, grabbed another wine glass from the rack and poured red wine into it. He put it firmly down on the table by the salad.

Terri slid into the chair nearest the plate and put her things – including an old hardback book - on the chair alongside.

'What's that?' demanded Peter, looking at the book.

'It's the French dictionary from the sitting room. Do you mind if I borrow it?'

He shook his head. 'Of course not. In any case, it's ancient and out-of-date. Why, what are you reading?'

'Nothing special,' she said. 'Just a cheap paperback.'

She was embarrassed at the ease of the lie. She peeled the plastic off the salad, picked up the cutlery Peter had moved her way and started to eat. Peter returned to his book. He ignored her and she watched him out of the corner of her eye. Over the last three months she had spent a lot of time with him and yet really she barely knew him. In Josie's diaries there had been glimpses of him as both the withdrawn grieving widower and the clumsy father of a troubled child. But the night before she had read about a trip Peter had made with Josie into town where, after a ride on the roundabout, he'd bought her a huge ice-cream. It had been an exceptional outing, a rare moment of connection between them, and the girl had seemed briefly happy.

It had brought to mind a long-forgotten trip Terri had made with her own father. She had no idea how old she'd been – nine or ten perhaps – and they'd gone to the seaside. She remembered playing crazy golf with him – he'd let her win - and yes, there was ice-cream, melting too fast and running down the cone over her hand. Why had she never remembered that until now? It always seemed to be the dark, silent times which stuck in her mind.

'What are you reading?' she asked Peter suddenly.

He looked up, surprised, then picked up the book to show her the cover. She looked at it blankly.

'It's a thriller,' he said, 'American.'

'Good?'

'Not bad.'

'I wouldn't have expected it,' she said, without thinking.

Peter studied her face, his lip curling in amusement.

'Why? What would you have expected me to read?'

She shrugged, swallowed the last mouthful of Corinne's salad and laid the cutlery down on the plate.

'I don't know. Something more literary perhaps. I noticed that the bookshelves in the sitting room are full of classics – both English and French.'

Peter looked at her with a knowing smile.

'I do that just for show. A lot of them are very old. I have read them, mind you, but years ago. These days, I like books which move along. Time is shorter – or maybe I'm more impatient.' He looked at the empty plate. 'How was that?'

'Delicious. I'll have to tell Corinne.'

'Mm…you'd better not.' He fell silent, lips pursed up, studying her speculatively. 'So…what do you like to read?'

He topped up the wine glasses and they sat, surprisingly companionable, discussing books and then films. About the most recent films, Peter knew only what he'd read in newspaper reviews – he never got to the cinema these days, he said – but with old films he had an endless supply of stories and anecdotes.

'Have you tried the old fleapit in Ste. Marguerite?' he asked eventually.

'No, not yet.'

'Then Luc is slipping, isn't he?' said Peter, archly. 'Don't chaps do that with their best girls anymore? Back row of the cinema?' He winked. 'I'll have to have a word with him.'

She was about to protest that she was not Luc's girl when Peter pushed his chair back and got to his feet.

'Dessert?' he offered, and immediately walked away to fetch it.

*

Angela sat alone at the kitchen table and ate her grapefruit, breaking each segment in half and chewing carefully. It was just after ten o'clock on the Monday morning and her sister was still in bed. They'd got back the previous evening, a day earlier than intended because Patricia had gone down with a streaming summer cold. It looked like the few remaining days of her holiday were going to be blighted.

It was deadly quiet in the house. True, Corinne was in the utility room, bustling about, doing some job or other, but no-one else was around. Already St. Raphaël and the buzz of life in their sophisticated hotel felt like a world away. Angela desultorily finished the grapefruit and replaced the spoon in the dish, then poured herself a cup of tea and sipped it. At least that was one thing which was better at home: she knew how to make a decent cup of tea.

She got up, took the dish over to the sink, then pushed two slices of toast down in the toaster and idly looked round. It was all so boringly familiar, so dull. Except that there were three DVDs stacked together on the edge of the worktop nearest the passage. That was unusual. Puzzled, she moved closer and picked them up, glancing at each one in turn. *The Maltese Falcon*, *True Grit* and *Rear Window*. She frowned. They were each still labelled with the price on a sticker which named the shop where they'd been purchased; she'd never heard of it. She had certainly never seen these films in the house before. She turned, the DVDs still in her hand, as Corinne emerged from the utility room hauling a bin bag of rubbish and a plastic carrier bag with newspapers and flattened boxes protruding from the top.

'Do you know what these are?' enquired Angela, holding the films up.

Corinne hesitated. 'Yes,' she said cautiously. 'They are films that belong to Luc.'

'To Luc?' Angela frowned. 'So why are they here?'

'I don't know. Perhaps they haven't finished with them. Perhaps he comes to get them…later.'

'Who hasn't finished with them?' said Angela, the frown deepening. 'And why are they are here in the first place?'

'It is nothing to do with me,' said Corinne defensively. 'Excuse me, I must put these outside.'

She began to pass through the kitchen but was stopped by a hand on her upper arm. Angela pulled at a cardboard box poking out of the carrier bag.

'Popcorn,' she said in amazement. 'Who's been eating popcorn? Tell me what's been going on Corinne.'

Corinne rested the bag of rubbish down on the floor and paused, looking at Angela with a resigned expression.

'*Monsieur* Stedding had a film night.' She shrugged. 'He wanted to see some old films…and Luc knows a shop in Avignon where he can buy them…cheap. So they all watch films, eat popcorn and ice-cream.' She took the flat box back out of Angela's hand and replaced it in the bag. 'They did not make so much mess so I am happy.' She picked up the bin bag again and carried it out, muttering to herself.

The toast popped and Angela automatically walked across to take it out and put it on a plate. She took it back to the table but sat, doing nothing with the toast, just staring, unfocussed, into space. It was such a strange story; Peter hadn't watched a film in years. He'd not shown any interest. And to sit there eating popcorn? But then she remembered hearing him singing in the bath just before she went away. She couldn't remember when he'd last done that either.

Corinne returned, walked through to the utility room and could be heard washing her hands. Angela began to spread margarine on the toast then stopped half way through as something Corinne had said came back into her mind. She got up again and walked into the utility room.

'You said 'they all watched films',' she stated firmly. 'All who?'

Corinne was now drying her hands on the towel behind the door.

'Monsieur Stedding, Luc, Terri and Celia,' she replied.

'Where was Lindsey?'

'I don't know.'

'And when was this?'

'Saturday night.' Corinne smiled and raised her eyebrows. 'Movie night,' she said, rocking her head side to side. When she saw Angela's expression, the smile faded. 'It has nothing to do with me,' she repeated.

'No, I know. But you don't have to find it amusing either.'

Angela walked out, abandoning her breakfast. In the hall, she stood for a moment, thinking, uncertain what to do or say. Perhaps she should do nothing; perhaps any intervention on her part would only make things worse. Peter was being manipulated, she was sure of it, but confronting him might make him take sides. She felt out of her depth, scared even.

206

Then her phone rang and the sight of the name of the caller on the screen made her smile. She quickly answered it.

'You got my message then,' she said, walking through to the sitting room. 'Yes, we're home. Patricia's not well.' The caller's voice buzzed in her ear. 'No, it's nothing serious but she's not up to doing anything.' She listened then smiled again. 'That sounds good. Wait a minute.' She closed the door onto the hallway. 'No, I'd love to.' She laughed at the reply. 'No, just tell me what time and where.'

*

Tom is growing but is still very small. Everyone is worried about him. Denise thinks he's not normal and he's going to be backward. I asked papa *what that meant exactly but he didn't explain. Aunt Celia said the nurse didn't know what she was talking about but she often says things like that. I put a snail in Denise's bed yesterday. She told* papa. *He was very cross and said I was too old to be playing silly games. She said if I do it again she'll leave. Sami found me crying in the garden and gave me some sweets – a kind I hadn't seen before. I didn't like them much but it was nice of him. He's a strange man. He never speaks but I've noticed him watching. I know he adored* maman. *Maybe he misses her too.*

Terri sighed. Josie was a consistently unhappy but naughty child. She moved on to the next month.

Tom was taken to an expert in children's illnesses yesterday. The doctor said Tom had been damaged at birth. I overheard papa *talking to Aunt Celia about it.*

207

Tom won't ever be normal. This morning I saw papa standing in the nursery, looking down into the cot. I thought he looked miserable so I went in and tried to hold his hand but he told me to leave. He's more interested in the baby than he is in me. I told him that the baby should have died, like maman. I said it wasn't fair that she died and Tom lived. He was furious and shook me, said I must never say that again. He was frightening and I've got bruises on my arms. I hid in my room for ages afterwards.

Terri closed the diary and laid it on her bedside table. She was used to Josephine's handwriting now which, with the passing months, was already starting to mature, and the dictionary had often helped with the translations. But it was harrowing to read. Josephine showed a warm personality sprinkled with generous doses of impulsiveness, sullenness and outright rebellion. There had been a catalogue of minor attention-seeking pranks as well as the brooding – and more disturbing - resentment of Tom. Peter's famous temper had shown itself several times in the pages; he'd been an occasionally kind but more often insensitive or absent father.

Terri thought of him at the 'film night' which he had been so keen on organising. He'd been amusing and he'd been generous; they'd all had a good time. Then she thought of him when she had first arrived at Le Chant: cantankerous and sarcastic. It was hard to reconcile all the different sides of him. But what would it have been like for him, bereft after losing his wife, trying to bring up his little girl by himself? Her train of thought sidestepped. What had it been like for her father?

Too often the diaries made her think of her own childhood – sometimes Josephine's loneliness and confusion mirrored her own too closely - and Terri frequently questioned what she was doing. Why read it? Why live it all again? But she couldn't stop reading the diaries now; she had to follow the story through.

Chapter 14

So the film night had gone well; Luc was a little amazed at just how well. He hoped it had marked a turning point in his relationship with Terri and that she was beginning to trust him. Four days later, when the village celebrated its Saint's Day with its biggest festival of the year, he asked her if she'd like to go with him. Despite his optimism, he was a little surprised when she readily agreed. Apparently she'd seen posters for it pinned to every tree and notice board for weeks, and even the usually taciturn Corinne had been enthusing about it.

It fell on a Wednesday, starting mid-afternoon, and Luc managed to persuade Peter to let them leave early. Setting off on the woodland path through to the village, Luc felt a nervous excitement develop in the pit of his stomach. It almost made him laugh: he hadn't felt like this in years. He was reminded of afternoons skipped from school when he was a kid, sneaked trips to the cinema or football matches, or just to mess about; he'd had his pocket money withdrawn for an entire month once when his father had found out.

Terri flicked him a brief, bright glance, eyes shining. Maybe she thought it was a stolen moment too.

It was just after four when they emerged into Ste. Marguerite des Pins. The streets were already jammed with locals and tourists, all browsing the market stalls squeezed down the old medieval streets.

They idled the stalls, jostled by the crowd, pausing here and there before pushing their way on again. Every kind of local craft and produce was on show: lavender goods, pottery, hats, jewellery, linens, pictures and *santons*; olives, biscuits, pastries, bread, olive oil and wine. The hot air was heavy with perfume and the smell of food; it vibrated with noise and chatter. Somewhere a jazz band was playing and the music bounced and resonated down the narrow streets. Luc watched Terri with amusement and some frustration as she stopped at nearly every stall, treating herself to perfumed soaps and pot pourri, a beaded necklace and a silk scarf. It's a *fête*, she protested when he complained, and she wasn't spending his money. They could split up if he preferred. He didn't.

They ate ice-cream and drank home-pressed fruit juice, and ended up at the bottom of the village sitting on wooden benches in the gritty *boulodrome* watching a traditional *pétanque* competition. Later they pressed with everyone else to see the Saint's Day parade passing by: a woman, dressed in sackcloth with a large wooden cross hanging round her neck, led a huge purple dragon by a yellow ribbon. Behind her, brightly costumed children marched to the beat of a pipe and drum band.

'What's it all about?' Terri asked him.

'That's St. Margaret. She was thrown in a dungeon by a Roman governor for refusing to renounce her Christian faith. Then she was tortured but still refused to recant.'

'So what's the significance of the dragon?'

'I think it represents the devil and she overcame it with the sign of the cross - something like that anyway. She was still put to death though.' He nodded, his eyes flicking across

211

the scene. 'I must paint this sometime. It'd make a great image.'

When the procession had gone past, they eased their way back up to the square and dined early at a restaurant opposite the church. A stage had been built to one side of the square ready for music and dancing later in the evening and from their table on the terrace they watched the band setting up.

'I should've gone to the exhibition,' said Terri, glancing around the heaving terrace as the waitress walked away with their order. 'I forgot.'

Luc frowned. 'What exhibition?'

'The Art Society exhibition.'

'Why on earth would you want to see that? Don't you get enough of that every day?'

'I helped Celia choose which paintings she'd submit. She'll probably expect me to know all about it.'

'*Non*? *Vraiment*? How did that happen?'

'She asked me.'

'Why?

'Because I have impeccable taste?'

He smiled pityingly. 'She probably doesn't even remember you came to see her.'

'Of course she will. She's not as batty as she makes out.'

Luc looked at her curiously. 'What makes you say that?'

'Oh, I don't know...something about her,' Terri said vaguely.

Over the meal they discussed places they'd visited and where else they'd like to travel. Making conversation with her felt easy at last, comfortable, even one on one, like this. He talked about America and a cousin who lived there whom he'd not yet managed to visit, and of his brother, Jean-Pierre, who lived in Canada. His brother was coming over to Paris the

212

following week and Luc had arranged a few days off to go and see him. Terri kept asking him questions about Jean-Pierre: Were they similar? Did he miss not having him closer? Did they get on when they were growing up? He could sense her avid fascination with the idea of a sibling, what it would be like to have one.

'No, we're not remotely the same,' he told her. 'He's an economist, not arty at all. We get on but I couldn't say we're close exactly.' He shrugged. 'But he's my brother. He's...' Luc struggled to articulate it. '...he's always been there. He's a couple of years older than me and he's just...part of me too, in a way, part of my life.' He grinned. 'After all, we've shared so many arguments.'

Terri didn't smile. She was looking at him blankly, chewing her lip.

'And does your father get on with him?' she asked.

'With Jean-Pierre? Oh yes,' he said lightly. 'No problem there.'

She nodded, saying nothing, giving no clue to what she was thinking. They finished eating and Luc ordered coffee; Terri asked for tea.

'Tell me,' he said, stirring a sugar lump into his espresso. 'Why did you never talk about your father?'

'What was there to say?'

'I don't know...People usually talk more about their family. You seem very interested in mine.'

She was silent for a long moment. She appeared to be working up to an answer, and he waited. If he pushed too hard, he was sure she'd withdraw.

'I didn't see a lot of him, not latterly anyway.' She took a mouthful of black tea. 'My father had a new lady in his life.'

'And you didn't like her?'

213

'It wasn't that exactly. I didn't know her well enough to say. It just felt…awkward.'

'What was he like, your father?'

'You met him,' she said defensively.

'Only briefly.'

She sighed. 'He was patient. About some things anyway. I suppose you have to be to be a conservator. He would take days just to mend a tiny section of canvas. And he liked to read…biographies and travel books and art books.' She shrugged. 'He was very…self-contained.'

He gave an amused, indulgent smile. 'That's where you get it from then.'

'What do you mean?'

'You're very independent.'

'Why do men always say that like it's an insult?'

'I didn't mean it as an insult. It's just a fact. You are.' The smile faded and he nodded reflectively. 'I think it's a good thing. I'd much rather a girl was her own person. Why would I want to be with someone who always liked what I liked or did what I wanted to do?'

'Well I think you're unusual.'

'I'm guessing Oliver didn't like it?'

She shook her head. 'But he wasn't the first. Some men seem to feel threatened if you have a mind of your own.'

'More fool them,' said Luc. 'Are you happy to finish this?' He held up the bottle of wine. She hesitated, then nodded. 'I think you said once,' he remarked, dividing the wine between them, 'that your mother fell ill and died when you were very young. Do you remember much about her?'

'Not really.' Terri finished her tea and sat, fingering the glass of wine. 'She wasn't ill, you know. I just say that because…I dunno: it's easier. The truth is…she killed herself.'

She paused. 'She left home when I was six, but she killed herself two years later. I found out by mistake. I overheard dad and grandma talking.'

'*Mon dieu,* that must have been tough.'

'Yes, it was.' Still she wouldn't meet his eye. 'My father couldn't cope with being left with a daughter he barely understood. Yes, it was difficult.'

'But you said your grandmother helped out?'

'Well, *she* called it helping. She came to live with us eventually. It wasn't great but I guess we'd have struggled without her. Dad had no idea about the house. He lived for his work.' She glanced up at him. 'Anyway you know all about difficult families.'

'Yes, but nothing like that.' Luc took a mouthful of wine, put the glass down and casually rubbed a stain off its base. 'So has Celia been telling any more stories lately? I'm surprised you think she's sensible.'

'Not sensible exactly. Just not as foolish as she seems.'

'She stills seems cuckoo to me. Are you starting to think her comments about your eyes have some significance, that maybe one of your parents was related to Madeleine after all?'

'No.'

'What about your mother: do you know much about her?'

'Some…enough.' Terri's tone had definitely hardened. 'Why?'

'Just a thought. Peter is a changed man since you came to work here.'

'You think?'

'Definitely. That's what made me wonder. But it's a good change.' Luc lifted his wine glass towards her. 'I salute you. He can be almost human on a good day.'

Terri grinned, raising her glass too. 'It's my charm.' She promptly changed the subject.

The band struck up at a volume which precluded conversation, and a few minutes later they watched the first people brave the square and start to dance. More quickly followed and soon it was a heaving mass of jigging bodies. Though not yet fully dark, multi-coloured lights had come on, glowing dimly, strung between the trees and posts around the square. They left the restaurant and stood among the people watching at the side. There was a buzz of happiness in the air and Luc noticed Terri, smiling, tapping a foot along in time to the music. A moment later, he grabbed her hand and pulled her onto the dance floor and they too danced and bobbed with the throbbing crowd.

It was dark by the time they left the party and walked back through the whispering woods, both of them silent, lost in their own thoughts. Terri was hugging her arms against her chest, her cardigan slung loosely round her shoulders. An awkwardness had now settled on them as if the intimacy and laughter of the day had been an aberration, a mistake perhaps. Luc flicked a torch side to side in front of them as they padded across the dusty ground, hearing the odd rustle from the tree canopy above or from the obscure blackness of the undergrowth. Terri looked preoccupied. He noticed her flick glances into the darkness occasionally and wondered - as he often did - what she was thinking about. Oliver maybe. Maybe not. He still couldn't read her.

When they reached the clearing he offered to walk her back to the house but she refused.

'Then you should take the torch.' He held it out.

'I'll be fine.'

'Of course you will, but you might need the torch.'

She stretched her hand out for it, brushing his fingers as she took it and he noticed her start a little as if a charge of electricity had passed between them. He'd felt it too and he leaned forward, put a hand behind her head and pressed his mouth to hers greedily, his tongue exploring insistently inside her mouth. Immediately he could feel her respond, putting her arms round him, pressing her body close against his. His lips strayed down to her neck and she tipped her head back, moaning softly.

'Stay,' he murmured, stroking her hair back from her face. 'Please stay.'

But suddenly she was pushing him away, almost fighting him off and he let her go, looking at her in surprise.

'What's the matter?'

'No,' she said. 'No, I can't.' She took a step backwards, breathing heavily. She actually looked frightened and he was shocked. 'I didn't intend this. Can we go slow, Luc…please.? I'm not ready for more yet. Or maybe not at all.'

'Sure.' He released a slow, almost inaudible sigh and forced a smile. 'Sure, I can do slow. *Comme un escargot.*'

She stared at him a moment, then slipped quickly away across the clearing.

*

Balancing three mugs on the tray, Terri left the kitchen and crossed the studio. She automatically glanced towards Luc's work station as she passed. It was still empty. Luc's 'few days' in Paris had turned out to be a whole week. Long into the night, after the *fête,* she had lain awake in bed, going over the events of the day, trying to analyse what was going on between them. She had no idea. Part of her regretted not staying the night,

217

much of her was relieved that she'd had the sense to leave. That last violent encounter with Oliver, when he had tried to drunkenly make love to her, when his anger at her refusal had turned so quickly to brutality, felt as if it would always haunt her. But now, after a dreary weekend, and well into a new week, she thought the place felt absurdly empty without Luc. She was aware that their friendship had jolted a step forward but what significance that had and where it might lead she was reluctant to examine.

She silently placed a mug of coffee down on Peter's work table and he surprised her by looking round.

'Ah, Terri,' he said. 'Thank you. Nicole says the merchandising samples have arrived.'

'Yes, they have. They're in my office. Are you going to take a look?'

'Yes, I'll drop by in a few minutes.'

She moved on, dropped off a caffeine-free drink by Nicole's computer – Nicole progressed through a seemingly endless chain of special healthy diets - and took her own coffee into her office, closing the door behind her. Sitting at her desk again, feeling lethargic in limb and mind, she read a note she'd made to remind herself that the security man was returning that morning. The alarm had gone off a couple of times for no apparent reason and he had promised to sort it out. She hoped he would; Peter had been vociferously furious at having his concentration disturbed.

Her thoughts settled on Peter. Her feelings towards him had become more and more ambivalent. Over the weekend she had reached the end of Josephine's first diary and started on the second; they were still painful to read. When she was twelve years old, Peter had sent his daughter away to boarding school in England. A couple of weeks before she left, she had written:

He doesn't want me around the house. He wants to punish me. I told him I would behave better but he said he thought I needed the company of other girls. BUT I DON'T WANT TO GO.

The beginning of her stay in the school in Sussex had been recorded even more emotively:

It's freezing here and dark. The bed is hard and the girls aren't at all friendly. The food is awful. I hate it. If maman were alive she wouldn't have sent me here. I miss her so much it makes me feel sick. Papa is very cruel. Does he want me to die here?

There were similar entries and then nothing except some English clearly written by another hand:

This is the smutty diary of a French slut.

Josie hadn't written in it again until she'd returned home when she described in detail how much she hated the school and how the other girls made fun of her and bullied her because she was different. She had started to mix English with the French.

I can't believe how much Tom has grown. He can even walk a little now with aids and stuff but it's jerky and he falls over a lot. I think he's forgotten who I am. It was sort of fun spending time with him. He's a happy little thing, considering. He has a new nurse. Her name is Christine. I'm not sure about her yet. She seems lazy.

I tried to tell papa *that I hate the school but he didn't want to know. He said it would do me good but*

I don't think he cares about me anymore. Sami saw me playing pétanque *by myself yesterday and he came to offer me sweets again. But I can't say anything to him. He's nearly as devoted to* papa *as he was to* maman. *He had a funny expression on his face the other day when I was with Tom. I'm not sure whose side he's on.*

Her final entry before returning to England for the new term was an apology to the diary for not taking it with her.

I daren't be seen writing in you and there's nowhere safe to hide you.

Returning home for the next holidays, her accounts of school and of her relationship with her father were little changed. Upset by Josie's clear loneliness and isolation, Terri could feel a simmering resentment building inside her at Peter's intransigence.

There was a knock at the door of the office and Peter walked in, bringing his coffee with him. Terri dragged her mind back to the present. The samples were in a box on the floor and she unpacked them and spread them out across the table. She and Christophe had settled on a selection of postcards, prints, notebooks and mugs.

'Are you feeling all right?' Peter enquired as he watched her do it.

'Yes. Why?'

'You don't seem quite yourself.' He picked up each sample in turn, studied them, and flicked her an amused glance. 'Missing Luc I dare say.'

Terri said nothing.

'There's a mistake in the title of this painting.' He handed her one of the postcards. A minute later he added, 'The image on this mug is askew. It won't do like that.'

'No, of course not,' she replied. 'I had noticed.' It came out more crisply than she'd intended and she checked herself, reluctant to meet his eye. 'I'll get on to it.'

He frowned. 'Hurt your professional pride did I? Well, anyway, they're a good choice, I'd say. Yes, very good.' He leaned back in his chair and picked up his coffee, regarding her thoughtfully. 'I was wondering if you've seen much of Lindsey lately?'

'Lindsey? A little, now and then.'

'She's dating Thierry, you know.' He sipped at his coffee, looking at her over the rim of the mug.

'Yes, I did know actually.'

'Hm. Thought you might. I imagine fathers are always the last to hear. Is it serious then, do you know?'

'With Thierry? No, I don't know.' She paused. 'Perhaps you should ask her.'

'Ask her?' He looked astonished.

'Yes. I'm sure she'd love to talk to you but she doesn't feel she can.'

'She can see me whenever she wants.'

'Oh come on Peter, you know that's not true. You're so tied up in your work.'

'I don't think I need a lecture in how to treat my own daughter from you. You are presuming on my…my respect for you. Anyway I'm…' He looked uncomfortable. '…I'm devoted to her.'

'Then maybe you should tell her.' Terri hesitated but couldn't stop herself from adding, 'If you must know, Lindsey's besotted with Thierry but Angela insists that she

221

doesn't see him. And she's too nervous to speak to you about him in case you don't approve either and you send him away.' She paused. Peter was staring at her with an amazed expression. 'There's a lot about your daughter you don't seem to know. She can play the piano really well. She can sing too. She'd like to study music. She told me so.'

Peter stared at her, a deep frown furrowing his brow, then he got up without another word, abandoned his coffee, and walked out leaving the door wide open. Terri closed it behind him, leant against it, took a deep breath and exhaled slowly. She had not intended to do that. She didn't know what had got into her. She was interfering in matters which did not concern her. She put a hand to her head; this was crazy behaviour. It was presumptuous to think she could fight other people's battles and she was taking the whole thing too personally.

She walked back to her desk and tried to concentrate on the job in hand. The security man had not yet arrived. The first of the loaned paintings was being shipped in later that week so she hoped he wouldn't let her down. Everything needed to be in place and working. She glanced at her watch and picked up the phone.

*

Peter exchanged a few words with the newsagent, paid for his magazine, and left the shop flicking through its pages. It was a British art periodical which he had on a regular order. Even if he affected disinterest in the current art establishment and its encircling sycophants, he couldn't resist knowing what it was saying and doing. And, though she was uncertain when it would be printed, Terri had told him that an advertisement for his retrospective would appear in its pages. He began flicking

222

through the magazine in search of it. He was becoming nervously aware of the event looming over him. It could be a glorious pinnacle to his career or an insignificant flop. He tried not to care but he couldn't pretend to himself: he cared very much.

He reached the road, abandoned the magazine for a moment, cast a glance up and down and then wandered across towards the tree-shaded car park. He found his car beside the trunk of one of the huge plane trees and eased himself in. Sitting behind the wheel, he continued looking through the magazine but could find nothing. The gallery in Nice were arranging the bulk of the publicity for the exhibition; perhaps that had been a mistake and Terri would have done it better. He tossed the magazine down on the passenger seat.

He thought about Terri's barbed conversation of the day before. What had got into her lately? But it was the revelation about Lindsey which occupied his mind most – he had thought about it off and on ever since. Was he really as unapproachable as Terri had suggested? Not to his own daughter, surely? He loved Lindsey. She must know that. Though perhaps he did not give her a chance to talk as much as he should...well, ever really. Not since she was little. He blew out a rueful breath. Maybe not even then. It was a chastening thought. He drummed the steering wheel with his fingers agitatedly. How would he approach it now? He never knew what to say. Madeleine had been the only woman he'd ever found it easy to talk to – perhaps because she always seemed to know what he wanted to say before he even said it. His eyes glazed over and he remembered another daughter in another time, a whole lifetime ago, it seemed. He'd never known what to say to her either.

With his mind elsewhere, he watched a young family return to their car opposite, slowly install themselves and then drive off. A car drove into a space on the row immediately beyond. Peter watched a man get out of the driver's side then walk round to hold the door open while an elegant woman slid out of the passenger seat. Peter stared more fixedly: that was Angela. The man looked familiar too: clean-shaven, square jawed, lean and muscular, with a brushstroke of grey at each temple. Peter had seen him at the summer barbeque: an American fitness instructor, if Peter's memory served him right, talking about opening a gym in Avignon, looking for financial backers. The name escaped him though.

Closing the car door, the man moved across and pressed himself against Angela, pushing her, almost roughly, back against the side of the car. Peter saw her giggle – he could almost hear it in his head – and glance furtively round. The man leaned in and gave her a long, lingering kiss while his hands fondled her breasts then roamed down the sides of her body.

Peter watched, open-mouthed. This was the kiss of a lover. His thoughts felt both frozen and yet racing, trying to make sense of it. A host of little actions and events played across his mind and began to form a pattern. He remembered odd words or gestures; glances he had caught at parties; phone calls cut short when he entered the room or text messages, earnestly read when Angela thought his attention was elsewhere. There had been nights spent away at short notice – 'Jill has got tickets for the theatre in Avignon; we'll stay over rather than be late back' – and, yes, when he thought about it, a dreamy air of satisfaction about her the next day. He wondered when it had started, this catalogue of deception. With a deadening feeling of clarity he knew that it was not

224

recent. He had seen it all and yet not registered it until now. Angela's social circle had long been the centre of her existence; Peter lived on the periphery of her life.

He watched the kiss end and wondered at the public nature of it. This was the village where he had lived for the past fifty years. Did everyone already know that his wife had a lover? Or maybe she had had several? Unwillingly, he continued to watch them. Angela glanced around again; she appeared self-conscious suddenly and they exchanged a few words before moving apart. She said something else, leaned forward again to give the man a brief kiss and, smiling, walked away. Peter saw her get into her own car, glance back once, and drive off. The man left moments later.

Peter couldn't move. He sat, staring out but seeing nothing, his brain numbed. He expected to feel anger, almost welcomed it, but instead a slow wash of pain, embarrassment and remorse flooded over him, each jostling for the upper hand. He'd been so stupid, so deeply stupid. It was all his own fault; in recent years he knew he had neglected her. Before he'd married Angela, friends had warned him that the age gap was too great, that he would live to regret it. Of course he had ignored them but perhaps they had been right. He was an old man now and Angela, though herself middle-aged, was still a very attractive woman. Could she be blamed for wandering? Was that how it had been: a search for younger flesh, more energy, more life? The first few years of their marriage had needed work, of course they had, but they'd been close back then, had enjoyed some real passion. Looking back now he realised how much had slipped and faded away over the years without him really noticing. He had put too much of himself into his art and not enough into cherishing her as he ought. Again he thought of Lindsey and felt another pang of remorse.

He'd failed in so many aspects of his life. For years he'd tried to suppress the knowledge of it but now he felt its full force and a stealthy, enveloping cloak of regret and self-loathing swept over him. He caught sight of the art magazine on the seat and threw it roughly to the floor. The whole business seemed so pointless suddenly. Even his own retrospective was a waste of time. Terri had said she wanted to use the exhibition to interpret his life, or perhaps it was to use his life to interpret his pictures. Either way, what was his life? And some of the most important paintings of his life wouldn't even be in the exhibition. There were so many things he wished he'd done differently.

He finally gathered his thoughts and drove slowly and carefully out of the car park, taking the road home. He wondered what he should do now: confront Angela or pretend he knew nothing? Did anyone else in the house know? Maybe everyone knew, except him.

Peter drove the car up the track home, parked in front of one of the garages and switched the engine off. Again he sat while his jumbled thoughts ran pell-mell. After all this time, what could he say to Angela now? And if he overreacted, it could ruin everything. In any case who was he to start handing out recriminations? As long as she didn't make a fool of him in his own house, he thought he could turn a blind eye. After all she'd had to put up with over the years, he thought he owed her that. And he must try to show her some real affection; he was very fond of her. But if the money he had seen leaving their bank accounts was going into the pocket of her lover as he now suspected, then that would have to be addressed. There were changes to be made...in all sorts of ways.

He eased himself out of the car to find Sami standing a few metres away, watching him with a concerned expression.

'*Vous allez bien, Monsieur?*'

After all these years, he'd never been able to persuade Sami to address him less formally.

'Yes, I'm all right, Sami,' Peter replied in French. 'Could I have a word?'

Sami raised a finger to touch his cap in his habitual gesture and waited for Peter to reach him. They walked slowly up the path to the house together.

*

Terri stretched her eyes and turned the page of the diary.

Everyone loves Tom. He's always smiling and trying to do something new. I've heard papa *say several times that he's just like his mother. It hurts like crazy when he says that. He doesn't seem to see her in me but she must be there. It's hard not to like Tom though. He's fun and really affectionate. Still I sometimes wish he wasn't there. Am I wicked to think that? But I can't help it. It's just that if he weren't there,* papa *would notice me.*

Christine has it OK these days because Tom is going to a special school now. People sometimes think he's stupid because he struggles to talk properly and he drools but it's just because his muscles don't work properly. You can see in his eyes that he's really smart and sometimes he's very funny. Papa *is doing a lot more these days. He's been travelling quite a bit. Christine said he's probably looking for love. That made me laugh!*

All Josie's diary entries were in English now and her handwriting had markedly improved. Over the preceding pages, she had recounted her slow integration into the English school and she was gradually learning to stand up for herself. It was noticeable however that she never took the diary back with her; all her notes were written during her holidays.

> *I still haven't had a letter from Michael and he promised he would write during the holidays. I can't write to him if he doesn't write to me first. And if he doesn't write I'm not going to speak to him when I go back.*

Michael was a youth who worked at the stables where Josephine went riding from school once a week. For some time now her notes had been peppered with remarks about boys, complaints about her periods and frustration that her breasts weren't growing quickly enough. The girl was growing up fast.

Terri had grown to like Josie. She was passionate about what or who she liked and at times quite witty. She was prone to self-pity but by this stage likely to finish any melancholic lament with a self-deprecating jokey remark. What had made this bright, energetic girl ultimately go out and take her own life? It was the question which lurked constantly at the back of Terri's mind but which she was scared to consider too closely. For, if Celia was right and Josie didn't kill herself in the woods, then Terri was increasingly convinced that she threw herself off a London bridge nearly nine years after leaving Provence for good.

Chapter 15

Angela sat on the bench at the edge of the lawn and gently fanned herself. A fly landed on her bare arm and she brushed it off impatiently. There was an uncomfortable band of sweat around her hairline. August had arrived and with it the close, gripping heat which she so disliked. The daytime sunshine now sent the temperature soaring and the evening brought little relief; it was still sticky and humid. Despite Sami's attentions and the use of the sprinkler at night, the lawn had a parched, crisp look. Under the broad brim of her hat she watched Lindsey swing the croquet mallet and hit the red ball. It cannoned into Peter's black ball, knocking it out of the way, and Lindsey lifted her left fist in exultation.

'Yesss,' shouted Celia. 'Good shot. Two more.'

Smiling, Lindsey thumped the ball once more, this time through the next hoop.

Celia celebrated again and this time the two players exchanged a gentle high five. Angela rolled her eyes. It was Peter who had suggested the game. 'Let's have a family meal Saturday night,' he'd said and when she reminded him about the dance at the club that night he'd said, 'Sunday then. We never seem to do that any more. In fact, let's all have a game of *pétanque* beforehand. I'll ask Corinne to come in as a special and get a meal ready. Then you won't have to worry about cooking and you can join in.' When she'd hesitated he'd said, 'No. Croquet, of course. You'd prefer croquet, wouldn't you? We'll play that.'

But they could not all play. The party was an odd number because Peter had insisted on inviting not only Celia but Terri.

'But Terri isn't family,' Angela had protested. 'Is she?' she'd added for emphasis.

'No…no, but we can't very well leave her out, can we?' he'd responded.

Peter had been behaving strangely. Over the previous few days he'd been either silent and morose or unusually chatty, talking to her with a false bright air. She'd given into the suggestion – she could think of no good excuse not to – but had rejected the idea of employing Corinne just for a family meal and decided to prepare something herself. And now she'd chosen to sit the game out because she couldn't face it in this heat. But she had expected Terri to play with Lindsey – she'd seen them chatting together while they all drank cocktails – and now Terri was playing with Peter while Lindsey partnered Celia. How had that come about? Had that been his arrangement, or hers, or Celia's even? For a short while the frank conversation Angela had shared with Terri over dinner that night had dissipated some of her fears about the girl's intentions, but they were rapidly returning. Angela had the growing suspicion that this entire event was about bringing Terri into the family.

Angela watched Peter hit the black ball too close to the edge of the lawn where it slowly trickled off the grass and ran away. Terri dropped her mallet and ran after it while he looked on. Angela's gaze flicked back to Lindsey. She was laughing at something Celia had said and it looked like genuine mirth. And now she was miming some catwalk pose, nose in the air,

230

talking and waving her hands about. She looked happy and Angela knew the reason why. It had nothing to do with Celia.

'I gather Lindsey's stepping out with Thierry, one of my students,' Peter had said to Angela before the others arrived. 'She was scared to tell me in case I didn't approve but he's a good chap. I don't mind. Do you know him?'

'I know who he is but no, I don't *know* him.'

'Well, he's a damn fine painter. Yes, a good lad. I can't see any problem there, can you?'

'Really, Peter, Is that the basis on which you judge his suitability for your own daughter...' she demanded, '...that he's a good *painter*?'

He shook his head, frowning. 'No, of course not.'

'And you've already told her you approve?'

'Yes.' He hesitated. 'She said you weren't keen though and I wondered why.'

'You know why, Peter. French life might seem like some sort of Eden to you but it doesn't to me. Their culture's different. *They're* different. Lindsey doesn't see it now because she's infatuated; she's not thinking straight. *You* should be telling her that.'

'She'll be fine. Angela...' He reached out and tentatively touched her arm. '...she's not a child darling. Stop treating her like one. It's doing her no good the way you fuss over her all the time.'

'I do not fuss. But she is sensitive and vulnerable. You don't see it; you're in a world of your own. She might get hurt. Or she might spend her whole life wishing she'd made a different choice and not sure what she should do about it. So you found a special French girl, well bully for you. But let's face it your precious Madeleine didn't live long enough for you to know whether it really would have worked out or not.

231

She'll always seem perfect in your eyes, won't she? She never got the chance to show her bad side or disappoint you.'

'She didn't have a bad side,' he said, looking shocked.

'Everyone has a bad side, Peter. Stop sanctifying the woman.'

She regretted her remarks from the moment she'd said them but the words had piled out, in a rush, as if they'd been waiting to be said for so long they could wait no longer. And she'd stunned herself by the bitterness they'd betrayed. Neither of them had mentioned Madeleine's name to the other since Peter's first, awkward days of courtship. And now Angela could almost feel the woman, rising up to stand between them, conjured up again after years of being ignored. Peter was silent for a moment, the muscles of his face twitching.

'I'm sorry,' he said explosively.

Angela was glaring at him; she couldn't help herself. 'What?'

'I'm sorry,' he repeated, and looked at her as if he hoped she'd fill in what he should be sorry for. She did not oblige. 'I've made mistakes,' he eventually added. 'I mean, we used to be good together didn't we? In those early days? I didn't realise that I'd made Madeleine into…' He shook his head, then wiped the back of his hand across his mouth. 'You know…well I'm sorry. I didn't mean it to be like that. It's never been that I don't care for you. I do. Well…so there we are…'

Terri and Lindsey had walked in and he'd abruptly turned away.

So, Angela thought now, what was that all about? She tried to put it out of her mind and watched the game continue. Peter appeared cheerful; there was no sign in his behaviour of the argument which had gone before. Terri, she thought, looked subdued but it was difficult to tell with her - she ran deep, that one. Still, she was laughing now as she managed to hit Lindsey's ball and it, too, went careering off the lawn.

'Sorry,' she called out.

'No, you're not,' countered Lindsey. 'You did it on purpose.'

'I did not.'

'Bloody slope,' complained Celia, cigarette in hand. 'Who else would play croquet on the side of a hill?'

'Stop moaning and get on with it,' said Peter. 'Whose turn is it?'

'Mine,' said Lindsey, returning with her ball and placing it back on the lawn.

'That's not a metre in,' Peter protested. 'You're cheating. That must be a good five foot.'

'Don't mix your metric and imperial,' said Lindsey primly. 'You're showing your age. Anyway I don't see anything wrong with it, do you Celia? Has anyone got a measure?'

Angela stopped listening to the banter as her thoughts wandered again. Lindsey was different these days: she was less biddable, more opinionated and more likely to answer back. She was vague about her movements and parried direct questions. Angela's eyes flicked to Terri who was watching the exchange and smiling. It was ever since that woman had come into the house. It was like having the proverbial cuckoo in the nest.

*

Terri collected up the mallets and balls and put them in the croquet box. Lindsey and Celia had won the game and, though Peter wanted a return match, Angela had already gone back inside to finish preparing the meal, warning them not to be long. Celia immediately lit another cigarette and wandered off towards the *mas*. Across the lawn and still holding their mallets, Peter and Lindsey were deep in conversation. Terri decided to discreetly withdraw and made her way back to the house too.

The front door was standing open when she got there and she stepped into the relative cool of the hall. The door to the kitchen was half open too and beyond it she heard two voices. One was Angela's, raised and cross, the other was the gravelly and recognisably measured voice of Celia. Terri hesitated a moment then moved softly across to stand just out of sight behind the door jamb.

'It's no good playing the innocent with me, Celia,' Angela was saying. 'I know what you're up to and I won't let it work. And will you put that cigarette out in the house? I've told you often enough.' There was a pause. 'Oh here,' added Angela impatiently, and a piece of crockery of some kind could be heard being put down roughly on the worktop. 'Put it in there.'

'You're always accusing me of things, Angela,' said Celia calmly. 'I don't know why. I keep myself to myself most of the time. I always have. I've never wanted to trespass on your space.'

A pan lid banged. Angela was never normally this heavy-handed.

'That's a bad joke. Of course you trespass. You're here aren't you? If you'd had any decency you'd have gone back to England when I married Peter. You've done nothing but make snide remarks ever since I came here.'

234

'Why would I do that?'

'You tell me.'

'We won the croquet by the way, did I say? Lindsey's good. Very good. She's really blossomed the last few weeks…'

'Enough,' shouted Angela. There was the click of her heeled shoes on the stone floor coming closer and then she spoke again in a low, menacing voice. 'It's no good playing the dippy old lady with me. You think that you're going to install Terri as Peter's granddaughter and then your position in this house will be assured.'

'I'm sorry, I don't see how…'

'Shut up. I see through it Celia, the whole plan. When Peter dies I'll sell up and go back to England. Lindsey will have her share and we'll both be able to make a fresh start. You are not going to produce some mythical relative to take a share of the estate.'

'Is Peter going to die?' asked Celia, sounding mildly concerned. 'But you know very well, if Josephine is still alive, she is entitled to her share. And if she bore a child, the child is too. There's nothing you can do about that. What is it they used to say in those old American police series…tough cookie? Was that it?'

'Give me strength,' exploded Angela.

'Did I tell you that I sold a painting at the *fête* exhibition, by the way? I was so chuffed.'

'Josephine is dead,' Angela said between gritted teeth. 'And there is no evidence that she was pregnant. You say she told you. How amazing that you should be the only one who knew. Stop clutching at straws. I will not let you do this, Celia, I'm telling you. I will not.'

235

Angela's heels could be heard walking away again. There were bangs and clicks from the cooker.

'She kept a diary, you know,' said Celia.

Terri's heart thumped painfully. What was Celia doing? There was a heavy silence before Angela responded.

'What?'

'Josephine. She kept a diary; did it for years. I'm sure she'd have said that she was pregnant - because she was, you know. And it's the sort of thing you write in a diary, isn't it? Well, I don't know really; I've never kept one.'

'And where is this diary exactly?' The hard edge to Angela's voice had given a little. Terri thought there was a note of fear in it.

'There must be several, I suppose, unless she wrote very, very small of course.'

'You've got them haven't you?'

'Got the diaries? No dear.'

'But you know where they are?

'I couldn't say I do, no.'

'Does Peter know about them?'

'I don't know.'

'But you've told Terri about them?'

'There you go again. You're obsessed with Terri, aren't you, and all because I said her eyes looked like Madeleine's. But they do, don't they? Oh, look, here come the others. Shall I pour some wine?'

Terri, desperate not to be caught eavesdropping, slipped quickly into the sitting room and across to the rear hall. She felt a fool. She had allowed Celia to lead her on and she had willingly followed, desperate to understand why her mother had killed herself and - yes, she couldn't deny it - even grasping at some sort of family. But Angela's reasoning made

236

sense and her annoyance was easy to understand. Terri began to see what Celia's motives might be. Even so, nothing the old woman had said so far had been proved wrong.

Terri opened the door of her room and went inside. She walked into the bedroom and felt in the drawer of the chest under a pile of T-shirts. The diaries were there. Why wouldn't they be? But she was increasingly aware that she had been drawn into someone else's game and the stakes she was playing with were high.

*

Luc returned to the studio the following Monday morning. It was the beginning of August. He seemed introspective. Terri guessed that the family reunion had perhaps been tense but she decided not to ask; he would talk about it if he wanted to. He smiled, exchanged a casual greeting, chatted briefly with her when their paths crossed but made no immediate suggestion of another outing. She recognised her own disappointment but she'd asked him not to push her; she could not now complain if he took her at her word.

She was getting near the end of Josie's last diary and, keen to finish it, had been taking it to bed with her each evening. The next entry she read was from the summer holidays of nineteen seventy-four. By now, Josephine was seventeen and starting to wonder what to do with her life.

July

I suppose everyone will think it's inevitable but I think I want to go to art college. I'm not sure which one yet or even which country to study in. I could come back and study at Avignon. That's where maman *went and I know she enjoyed it. Or I could go*

237

to England and stay in London. There are several colleges there. Of course I know what papa *will say if I ask him. 'They don't teach you anything at art college any more so it doesn't make any difference where you go.' We had a row again yesterday. I said I wanted to go away for a holiday with Colin. His family have a holiday cottage in Brittany.* Papa *said I couldn't go – I'm too young. I was really cross because I'd sort of arranged it with Colin already. I told* papa *he was treating me like a child and I'm not a child anymore. He told me to stop behaving like one then, which made me even crosser. We haven't spoken since. I'm almost tempted to go anyway but he'd probably go crazy.*

Papa has employed a new bonne. *Her name is Basma. She's Algerian and only twenty. I like her. Tom does too and she's good with him. I think maybe Sami likes her too. He's been hanging around a lot lately. I thought he was a dried up stick and too old for that sort of thing! But he doesn't approve of her having a laugh with me. She told me he thought it was out of place; said she'd end up getting into trouble. I said that was nonsense – I wasn't going to get her into trouble. Anyway her English is pretty basic so I've been helping her with it.*

The summer held few entries. Josie's handwriting was now more mature, smaller and often quite cramped. As if sometimes making an effort to be more expansive, there were occasional flourishing capitals to the beginnings of sentences but they looked like half-hearted affectations and didn't fit.

Terri tried to remember her mother's handwriting but couldn't. She wasn't sure if she possessed anything which her mother had written. Back in her flat in London she had a box of her father's things. After his death, the solicitor had informed her that his house and its contents had been bequeathed to Lizzie but that he'd left Terri a substantial sum of money. It was a great deal more than she had expected. Indeed, she'd been shocked: she'd not really expected anything. Then, a few weeks before coming away to Provence, she'd received a phone call from Lizzie. She was selling up and moving away, she said, but she had a box of things which she thought Terri might want. 'Documents,' Lizzie had said, 'and personal things which don't mean anything to me. I'll burn them if you don't take them.' That box, still unopened, sat under her bed. Maybe there would be something in there which had her mother's writing on it.

She returned her attention to the diary. The entry for the Christmas holidays was full of the break-up with Colin. The Easter holidays contained endless fretting over examinations: the mocks in which she had not performed well and the examinations proper which she fully anticipated failing. Then it was summer again, nineteen seventy-five.

So I've finished with that school. I never thought I'd be sorry to leave but it's strange to know I'll never go back and there are a couple of girls I'll miss. We've promised we'll keep in touch. Does that ever happen? I've been offered a provisional place in both Avignon and London. I still don't know which one to go to.

Apparently papa *has met a girl at a house party some friends were giving in Cannes and he's silly about her. He's getting soft in the head or something. Her name's Angela and she's only just nineteen!!! It's horrible.*

The physio has taught Tom to swim. He has to have arm bands on and sometimes he gets spasms which can be dangerous so he's not allowed to go in the pool without someone there but the exercise is good for him they say. He swims most afternoons and I sometimes swim with him. He's definitely improved. I'm not sure he needs Christine any more but I think papa *likes to have someone to watch over him.*

I've seen Basma and Sami together in the garden a couple of times. They were clearly arguing the other day. Maybe they're lovers. I don't see it though.

The only other entry for the summer was several weeks later.

August

Papa *has told me he's going to marry Angela – next spring! I asked him how he could marry someone who was only a year older than me. She's very mature for her age, he said. Of course he was suggesting that I wasn't. We had a horrible row. I demanded what* maman *would have said. He said she wouldn't have wanted him to be lonely but it didn't mean he didn't still love her or miss her. Then he told me I'd like his fiancé. 'Try and be nice to her,' he said. I suppose I'll have to try but it's going to be weird.*

Anyway, that's decided it. I'm going back to college in London. I got my grades - surprisingly good. I suppose I'll find out what Angela's like at Christmas – she's coming to stay!!

So we've met. Angela is staying till New Year. I think she was nervous of meeting me too. Actually she seems quite nice. We exchanged presents. It's all really strained though. She said she wants to be friends but it's kind of strange and I can't see that happening. We don't have anything in common. She's so 'just so' and I don't think she's interested in art at all which is really quite funny. Did papa choose her because she was so different to maman? She's very pretty with golden red hair. Dazzling I suppose – to a man.

Art college is good but a lot of new stuff to get used to. New people too. It's tough starting over making friends.

The wedding, just before Easter, was recorded with little comment. Josephine was settling into college life and wrote about a man she was seeing in London but frustratingly didn't mention his name. He was a little older than she was. She was enjoying the course, she said; she spent some time with Tom. Celia had been seeing a man too.

I simply can't imagine Aunt Celia with a man. What a hoot! I asked her what he was like and could I meet him. She got very secretive. I suppose she's only thirty-six - not completely over the hill yet! Maybe she's going to marry him and leave. She doesn't seem to be so keen to stay now that papa has remarried. I'll miss her if she goes. I've found her easier to talk to these last couple of years. She said she can't relate to children; she thinks I'm more interesting now!

Then, after a gap and almost as a promise to herself, Josie wrote:

They're back from their honeymoon. Papa *seems happy and he's been really good-natured and kind to me since he got back. I'm going to try to be happy for him and make him proud of me.*

Terri was growing tired but couldn't put the book down. As unlikely as she knew it to be, she was sure now that Josie was her mother. She thought she recognised the moody nature of the girl, the exaggerated highs and lows, even the way she described people. Given how little time she had spent with her mother, perhaps it was just her desperate need to connect, but yet it all felt familiar, as if it touched a chord somewhere deep inside her. And knowing what she'd had to live through, reading her thoughts and desires and fears, Terri felt an empathy with her mother she had never felt before. Eventually she thought she might even come to understand how she could have walked out on her family all those years ago.

Somewhere, if she kept reading, she would find the proof she wanted.

June 76

I'm home. Is it home anymore? Everything seems to be different already and it's going to change even more. The house is going to be 'restyled'. I asked papa *about* maman's *studio. He said it wouldn't be touched so that's something but then he asked me not to go there. I'm really upset. He said he told Angela that he wanted it left untouched so he doesn't think it's fair if I keep going there like I used to. I told him that he was being unfair to me instead, that he'd chosen her over me. He said I was being unreasonable and childish. But that room's all I've got left of maman.*

The nurse has been dismissed. Celia says Angela didn't like Christine. Papa said she'd been skiving. He's been talking about getting someone else but it'll be difficult in the middle of summer. I said I could help Tom while I'm here but papa doesn't trust me - I can see it in his eyes. It's all because of those things I said about Tom - but that was years ago. I've changed. Papa doesn't see that I've grown up.

Saw Sami in the garden today. Guess I looked miserable. He asked about London – had I made friends there? I was shocked. He never used to talk to me like that. Then he looked at his boots and said maybe it would be better if I went away. Double shocked. What was all that about?

The next entry was nearly a week later.

Went swimming today again. It's been really hot so the water was bliss. Tom loves it too. He swims well so long as he has his arm bands on but the spasms are as bad as ever and they happen so suddenly, without warning. There are real problems with drought already in some places. We're lucky to have spring water at Le Chant.

July
Tom has got a tummy upset. He's been sick a few times and papa called the doctor. She thinks it's a virus. I've been a bit queasy too. I'm not allowed in Tom's room. He's supposed to rest.

I'm writing this in 'Raphael'. I don't care what papa said. I got another key made. It's the only place I feel is still mine. It feels safe. I have the feeling I'm being watched though. I even think I should be careful what I write.

It was the end of the diary. Terri was sick with frustration but she'd already known it would not tell the whole story. Impatient for more information, she'd glanced at the end a few days before but had willed herself to be wrong, had been sure that the preceding pages would be more enlightening. But that was it: one tantalising reference to being queasy but nothing more specific and no names. And the story of the summer was untold. There must surely be another diary. Did Josephine take it with her? Or did she leave it in the attic studio, somewhere very secret and safe from prying eyes?

Chapter 16

Holding her mobile to her ear, Terri got up and pushed the door to. Luc was hammering at the other end of the studio and it was hard to hear. The voice continued, talking at length, somewhere far away.

'Of course, if that's what you want, Mrs Biedeker,' she replied, when the voice paused. 'No, of course...Yes, I understand...Yes...Yes...Of course. But we do have excellent security meas...' The voice cut across her. Terri's face set in a resigned expression. 'Would it help if you spoke to Mr Stedding yourself?' she enquired eventually. 'No, I see. Well thank you for letting me know.'

Terri put the phone down and exhaled a long slow breath. With just eight weeks to go, the wheels appeared to be coming off all her careful plans for the retrospective. The day before she had heard that one of the paintings being shipped from Germany had gone astray.

'How can you have lost it?' she'd demanded of the man from the specialist German carrier on the telephone. 'It's a valuable painting and you assured me it would be traceable throughout its journey to get here.'

'It is not lost,' he asserted smoothly in his impeccable English. 'It is just not where we expected it to be. It is misplaced.'

He spoke as if no human hand had had any part in the problem, as if the painting had wandered off of its own accord. She wouldn't have been surprised to hear him say, 'the painting is misguided.'

'I think it might have got into the wrong consignment, that's all,' he said. 'It has been very busy here. We will track it down very shortly I am sure. I shall get back to you,' he added, and put the phone down.

There was a problem with the paintings which were being restored too. Just that morning Terri had rung up to get an approximate date for collection to be told that Stéphanie Lebrun had not been well and 'wasn't quite up-to-date with her work.' After a fraught conversation in a mixture of French and English with the woman's partner – a softly spoken woman with a harassed air - she found out that Stéphanie hadn't even started Peter's paintings yet. 'It was just a virus,' the woman said when Terri asked why she hadn't been told. 'She didn't think it would last this long. But she's better now and has just started work again. She's sure she'll have them ready in time.'

And now Mrs Biedeker, an American lady who lived in Switzerland, had changed her mind at the last moment and was refusing to let her treasured painting take part in the exhibition. To make matters worse it was one of the pictures which Peter had particularly wanted in the show. There had been a lot of robberies of famous paintings in the south of France recently, she'd said. They'd been reported on the news and she 'simply wouldn't risk it'. 'These thieves are cleverer than all your fancy security, Miss Challoner, believe me,' she'd drawled. 'I'm sorry, but that's the way it is.'

Terri blamed herself. She thought that, distracted by things which had nothing to do with the exhibition, she'd taken her eye off the ball for too long and that this was the inevitable result. Josephine had occupied too many of her waking thoughts. Nevertheless, she would have to tell Peter and he was not going to be pleased.

She got up, desultorily, and opened the office door again. It was already lunch-time. Luc had disappeared and Peter appeared to be still deeply immersed in his painting. Deciding to tell him about Mrs Biedeker another time, Terri grabbed her bag and wandered up to the house for lunch. Corinne was in the kitchen, laying the table, and looked up as Terri walked in.

'There's been a man asking for you,' she said, in French. 'An Englishman.' Her intonation was accusing, as if Terri had been keeping something from her.

'An Englishman,' Terri repeated stupidly.

'Yes. Oleeva…something. I wrote it down on the pad by the phone.' Corinne waved a finger vaguely towards the hallway. She frowned, staring into Terri's pallid face. 'Are you all right?'

'Where is he?' demanded Terri.

'He's in Ste. Marguerite. He wanted to check you were here.'

'And you said I was?'

'He said he was a friend. Why, isn't he? Did I do the wrong thing?'

Terri didn't answer but quickly looked out of the window as if Oliver might already be standing there. She took a deep breath, trying to quell her rising panic.

'When was this Corinne? How long ago?'

Corinne shrugged one uncertain shoulder, glancing towards the clock on the wall. 'Less than an hour ago. Should I have told him you weren't here?'

247

She looked so guilt-ridden, Terri reached out a hand and touched her arm.

'No, it's fine,' she said, trying to sound reassuring. 'Really.'

'*Is* he a friend?'

Terri shook her head. 'He used to be. It's OK.' She said it as much to calm herself as Corinne and left the kitchen, all thoughts of lunch gone. She needed to know where Oliver was; she needed to decide what to do.

She went to her rooms and paced up and down, stopping intermittently to stare out of the patio doors into the grounds. She'd been stupid, allowing herself to think he'd lost interest. There hadn't been a message from him in weeks and, despite sensing the ominous nature of his silence, she'd told herself that perhaps it was finally over. And there had been so many other things which had smoothly replaced him in her mind. Deep down, she supposed she'd always known that it would come to this.

She glanced outside again. He could be there already, waiting for her, standing behind some shrub or tree in the garden, the way he always had. She guessed he'd hired a car. If she went to the garages she'd know if there was a strange car parked there but she couldn't bring herself to leave. Fear clutched at her heart and dulled every rational thought. She forced herself to make a mug of tea but barely managed to drink half of it, trying to decide what to do, thinking through her options. There weren't many. It was foolish to hide away here; she couldn't stay away from him forever. A weak resolve began to form. Sooner or later she was going to have to confront him and better that it should be on her terms than on his. With a shaky hand, she threw away the remains of her tea, left her room and walked through the house and out onto the terrace.

It was a surprise that nothing looked different. The grounds were calm and inviting in the sunshine and the rolling orchards and vines still stretched out to a blue, peaceful horizon. Terri checked the parking area: there was no strange car. She retraced her steps to the terrace. Perhaps she should go into Ste. Marguerite and meet him there. No. She preferred to see him here. This - at least for the moment - was her home, her ground.

Restless, she walked down into the parterre and then across into the olive grove, toyed with going to find Luc at the *bergerie* but, having kept him at a distance, baulked now at involving him in her personal problems. This was her battle to fight. She wandered on restlessly, regularly glancing round, then changed her mind and turned back towards the house. She was half way through an imaginary confrontation in the hallway of the *mas* when a voice spoke behind her.

'Terri. So you are here, baby. I couldn't really believe it, you know?'

Terri turned slowly and saw Oliver little more than a couple of yards away. How had she not heard him? She felt winded, frozen to the spot.

'Oliver,' she heard herself say. 'What are you doing here?'

'Looking for you, baby. And I've finally found you. I couldn't get anything out of that friend of yours...what's her name? Begins with an S...Sally is it?'

Terri didn't reply.

Oliver stared at her a moment, then gave up waiting for a response.

'Well, whoever. So I went to Ferfylde's. They said they didn't know for sure where you were 'cause you'd been kind of coy about what you were going to do, but then someone mentioned they'd seen you reading some advertisement.' Oliver smiled and took a couple of steps closer. She could see the line of sweat on his upper lip, could smell the sour aftertaste of wine on his breath. His face was pale and puffy. 'Someone in the bar told me I could walk through the woods but, Christ, it's a bit hot for walking.' He reached out suddenly and grabbed her by the arm. 'You left me, baby.' He smiled but his voice was accusing, bitter. 'You shouldn't have left me.' He pulled her towards him, gave her a brief fierce kiss, and pushed her away again, still gripping her tightly by the arm. 'I thought you'd come to your senses eventually but then you ran away and left me. I think I deserved better than that Terri.'

He raised his other hand and began to stroke her cheek. Terri could feel herself shaking, a tremor which started in her feet and reverberated all the way up her legs and body. Anger fought with her fear.

'It's over,' she said, her tongue sticking to the dryness of her palate. 'Oliver? Do you hear? It's over between us. Let me go.'

'Don't be stupid, baby. Of course it's not over. We're supposed to be together. I've come to take you back. I've forgiven you.'

'*You've* forgiven *me*?' She stared at him, wide-eyed, feeling the sweat trickling down her back. 'You've got a nerve. No, Oliver. No. I'm not coming back. I've got a new life now.'

'What? Here?' He laughed mockingly, looking round. She could feel his fingers digging deeper and deeper into the flesh of her arm. 'Give me a break. This isn't your sort of place any more than mine. C'mon.' He pulled her close again and locked his lips onto hers in another aggressive kiss. She put her free hand to his shoulder and tried to push him away but he grabbed her wrist and held her all the harder, fighting easily against her convulsive efforts to free herself.

She tried to pull her knee up to catch him in the groin. It was a mistake. He was angry now and she was off balance. He pushed her hard and she thumped down on her back. Oliver was quickly on top of her, pinning her to the ground. She fought uselessly, could feel his hands tearing at her clothes, could hear herself screaming till the sound seemed to echo through her head and all she was aware of was the unequal struggle of hand and limb and the crush of his weight pressing the air out of her body. And just when she thought she could keep him at bay no longer, he'd gone. Dazed, she dragged herself up onto one elbow on the dusty ground and looked around wildly. It was Luc who had pulled Oliver up bodily and was now punching him like a man possessed. There was a brief ugly fight and Oliver was soon on the ground himself, looking bemused and holding his jaw. A trickle of blood ran from his lip.

Luc came across to help Terri to her feet. He had blood on his knuckles and a livid contusion on one cheek. She straightened her clothes, struggling to grasp what had just happened, and kept brushing herself off obsessively as if she could brush Oliver out of her mind and her life with the same motion.

'Are you OK?' said Luc.

She realised it wasn't the first time he'd asked. She nodded and tried to speak but nothing came out.

'You're sure? I'll kill him if he's hurt you.'

'I'm fine,' she managed. 'Really. Fine.'

251

Luc studied her a minute then turned away and retraced a few steps back to Oliver.

'Bugger off,' he bellowed. 'Just bugger off and don't come near Terri again. D'you hear me? Next time, you won't get up again, I swear.'

He came back, took Terri's arm and pulled her away, almost roughly. She was still shaking and felt cold, despite the heat of the sun.

Reaching the edge of the terrace, Luc stopped, cradling his bleeding hand. 'Will you be all right now? I'm going to go back and make sure he leaves. I don't think you'll be seeing any more of him.'

She looked at him doubtfully then glanced down at his hand. 'You should wash that,' she heard herself say.

'I will. Now go.'

'Thanks.'

'Forget it.' He turned and quickly moved away back towards the woods. She saw him break into a run.

*

On the Saturday morning Luc went up to the house to tell Terri that Oliver had checked out of the *chambres d'hôtes* where he'd been staying and had been seen driving away. Luc had briefed some friends in the village to keep an eye on him. It was a strange and awkward meeting. Standing in the doorway of her room, Terri thanked him again but seemed embarrassed, wouldn't look him in the eye and didn't invite him in.

'So you found my room,' she remarked, standing with her hands rammed into the pockets of her cropped trousers. 'Or did someone show you?'

'I called at the front door. Lindsey was in the kitchen. Angela's still in bed apparently.'

'She's not a morning person. She told me.' Terri's face was ashen; there was a smudge of darkness under each eye as if someone had rubbed charcoal there.

'Are you OK?'

'Yes, I'm fine…thanks.' She forced a smile. 'A bit stiff. And tired - I didn't sleep very well. How's your hand?'

He glanced down at it. It was bruised and swollen.

'A bit sore. It's OK.'

She nodded then glanced up at him, frowning. 'Did you say anything to Lindsey? Only I haven't told anyone what happened. Except Corinne.'

'Corinne?'

'She knew Oliver was here. And we get on quite well.'

'I didn't say anything to Lindsey.'

'Good. Thanks. Corinne won't talk about it. She promised me.' She produced another pinched smile. 'So it's over…for now anyway.'

'He won't bother you again. He's a coward.'

She nodded but looked unconvinced.

'Do you want to go out,' he said, 'get a coffee or something?'

'Thanks, but I can't. I'm meeting Corinne. There's a special market today with local *produits du terroir*. She thought I might be interested. I think she's got some desperate idea about teaching me to cook. Of course, she's wasting her time but…' She smiled weakly and shrugged.

'OK, well, good…I'll let you go then. I just wanted you to know he'd gone.'

'Thanks. I'm really grateful.'

The weather had closed in and it had started to rain heavily by the time Terri returned to Le Chant that evening, running across the terrace and throwing herself in through the front door. At first there appeared to be no-one home but she found Peter in the kitchen pouring himself a glass of wine. He glanced up as she came in.

'You got caught too, did you?' he said. 'I was sitting outside.'

'I was hoping to see you,' said Terri. 'It's about the exhibition. I'd intended to tell you yesterday. Is this a bad moment?'

'No, no. Everyone's out.' He reached another glass down from the cupboard and poured her some wine. 'Here.' He grabbed the bottle. 'We'll take it through to the sitting room.'

He lowered himself into one of the sofas and Terri sat on the one close by.

'*Santé.*' He raised his glass and leaned back, regarding her levelly. 'So I'm guessing there's a problem?'

'Yes. I'm afraid the 'Woman with the Braided Hair' is lost in transit. Or, as the carrier preferred to describe it: temporarily misplaced. He promised me they would find it but it's sure to be late arriving. It might make things tight.'

He grunted.

'And there's something else: the Mandini portrait. Her daughter owns it now and she's changed her mind about lending it to the retrospective. She's adamant it's not safe; there've been too many burglaries lately. Even if the 'Braided Hair' turns up in time, it leaves us one down.'

Peter nodded, lips pursed up thoughtfully. 'That's disappointing. Have you thought of a replacement?'

254

'I have a few suggestions though nothing quite so commanding. Obviously it needs to be something easily accessible at short notice.'

Terri sipped her wine and found her eyes drawn, as they always were when she sat there, up to the portrait of Madeleine. This singular portrait would have been perfect for the retrospective, but the last time they'd talked about his first wife it had ended in a row.

Peter followed her gaze and studied the painting for a few moments as if seeing it for the first time. 'No,' he said firmly. 'I know what you're thinking but I can't exhibit this.'

She eyed him warily: now he was reading her mind. But he looked surprisingly calm and she was prepared to argue the point.

'It would be ideal though,' she said slowly. 'It's a wonderful painting. Would you consider putting it up if we didn't name the sitter?'

She expected him to rage and bluster, but he was silent.

'It would provoke questions,' he said eventually, 'and Angela wouldn't like it. She…' He paused, weighing his words. '…She has felt engulfed for too long by Madeleine's shadow; it would be insensitive.'

Terri nodded but didn't reply, surprised by his reflective tone.

'You're a smart girl, Terri.'

'Why do you say that?'

'I've been wondering what you made of Celia's claims that you look like Madeleine?'

'What am I supposed to make of them? I gather she's done the same thing before.'

'Yes, yes, she has.'

255

He swept his gaze back up to the picture. She formed the impression he wanted to say something else, but nothing came.

'Celia said you had a daughter by Madeleine.' It was out of her mouth without her having consciously decided to say it. 'Her name was Josephine and she ran away. Celia said she was pregnant when she left.' Peter was already shaking his head. 'She says my age and birthday fit, that Josephine could have been my mother. I've thought it all through, over and over, and it is possible she's right.'

'Is that so?' Peter examined her face. 'Well as you've found, Celia says a lot of things. Mostly nonsense.'

'But you were the one who brought the subject up,' said Terri crossly. 'Why did you do that? And why did you ask all those questions about my mother? Tell me. Is it true? Any of it? All of it?'

He finished the last of his wine, glanced at Terri's untouched glass and refilled his own. He sat back, hugging it. For a while she thought he wasn't going to reply. When he did, he spoke quietly, as if he was scared of waking some long-sleeping ghosts.

'All right, I will tell you. Madeleine and I did have a daughter and yes, she was called Josephine.' He paused. 'In some ways, Josie was a wonderful girl: bright, quick. She had her mother's passion and spirit. But she also had my stubbornness and pride.' He smiled ruefully, glancing up. 'Yes, I know she had that from me. And she had a temper – which she must have got from me too; she certainly didn't get it from her mother. When her mother was alive she was a delightful child. It was a joy to see them together. Even so she could be...difficult.' He shook his head and sighed. 'After Madeleine died she began to steal things, she sulked, she lied. It was a nightmare. I didn't know what to do with her.'

'What did you try to do with her?' said Terri accusingly. 'She was upset.'

'Of course,' he answered crossly, 'but what was I supposed to do? No, well, maybe I should have tried harder. But I was lost too. By the time I realised there was a problem it was too late to change anything. She hated me. She didn't want to know.' His eyes glazed. 'She threw things at me, you know. My own daughter.'

'She just wanted you to notice her.'

'But I did notice her.'

'You sent her away to school. That's not noticing.'

Peter nodded slowly, staring into his wine. 'I see Celia told you everything. Yes, I did arrange for her to go to school…in England. I thought the change might do her good. And I didn't know what else to do with her. Celia came over to help out when Madeleine was ill after her last miscarriage. She was supposed to keep an eye on Josie too.' He glanced up at Terri's face. 'She might talk fine words about her niece now,' he added bitterly, 'but she didn't show too much interest in her when she was little. Too busy painting her foolish pictures.' He was silent for a moment. 'Boarding school just made Josie worse. I knew she didn't like it but I thought she'd get used to it after a bit…make friends. And she did in the end.' He nodded. 'We had a few good times together…later. Yes, she did settle down. Or at least I thought she had.' He looked up suddenly, studying Terri's face again. 'Don't you remember your mother at all?'

She shook her head.

'And your father never said anything about her? He must have.'

'No, very little. He didn't want to talk about her. I don't think they got on.'

Peter grunted.

Terri stood up suddenly. 'I've got photos though. I can show you.'

When she returned, she already had the two photographs out of the plastic wallet, feeling a strange greedy excitement building inside her.

'Did she look like this?' She thrust them at him.

Peter stared at each of the pictures in turn and handed them back, shaking his head.

'I'm not sure. That could be anyone.' He cleared his throat. 'How did she die then, your mother?'

Terri frowned but said nothing, a choking disappointment settling on her like a shroud. She slowly replaced the photographs in the wallet. 'She killed herself,' she said dully, looking up. 'She threw herself off a bridge into the Thames.'

Peter's expression froze. He said nothing, staring at her bleakly.

'You *do* think Josie was my mother. You do, don't you?'

'I don't know,' he said angrily, spots of colour quickly rising to his cheeks. 'How should I know?' He downed a gulp of wine. His hand was shaking.

'Was she pregnant?'

'I don't know. She wouldn't tell me a thing like that.'

'So why did she leave?' The volume of Terri's voice had risen several notches. 'Celia said you had a row with her. If you didn't row about her pregnancy, what did you row about?'

'We were always rowing.'

'Yes, but what made her leave and never come back?'

'I don't know. I don't know.' He was shouting now. 'For God's sake, woman, why can't you leave it alone? What do you think you're doing, coming and meddling and stirring it all up? Haven't I been through enough, damn it all? Stop it. Stop it. God Almighty.'

He downed the rest of his wine in one long gulp and as he did so Terri slowly got to her feet and moved to stand in front of him.

'I don't know what happened,' she said tersely. 'And I don't know if I have any claim to know. But Josephine was your daughter. Didn't you love her? Don't you ache to know what happened to her?' She hesitated. 'Or do you know something you're not prepared to tell me?'

She turned and walked quietly out of the room.

Chapter 17

Terri sat at the computer in her office, working through the final pages of the draft catalogue. Peter had finally agreed to her request for a fan and it stood at the end of the table, whirring incessantly, spinning side to side. Even so, her blouse stuck to her back and her scalp prickled with heat. She ran a hand through her hair, trying to release it and get the air to her skin. The rain of that Saturday night had been short-lived and the days had resumed their hot, dry routine. There had been only one brief, sharp shower since and it felt as if the heat was building, day on day. Outside, the clicking song of the *cigales* was loud and insistent. It sounded like a bomb waiting to go off.

It was now more than a week since that emotional meeting with Peter but the conversation still played across her mind, overshadowing even the confrontation with Oliver in her thoughts. Neither of them had mentioned it since - it was as if it had never happened – and they had resumed their habitual sparring relationship. In some ways, Peter was his usual self: charming, rude, impatient, sarcastic, genial. But though his mind seemed sharp enough, he had a vague air and a distant look. Terri was sure he was hiding something but was equally certain he wouldn't tell her. She was waiting for an opportunity to go back and search 'Raphael' but none presented itself. The old *mas*, basking like a lizard in the languid heat, never seemed to be empty for long enough.

She stretched her arms to free her sticky blouse and scrolled down to the next page. She had a few days off the following week but the catalogue had to be finished and sent on to Christophe before she went. It was going to be produced both in English and French and he had offered to get it translated before sending it to the printers. She read to the end, changed one word on the last page, and set the document to print. Her door was open to the studio in a vain effort to keep the air moving and she could see Luc working at the other end of the barn. He was painting today, working from sketches and a quickly executed watercolour.

She sat and watched him. On the previous Saturday he had asked her to visit Arles with him for the day. They'd explored the shops, the vibrant market and the huge Roman amphitheatre; they'd lunched in the square opposite the café terrace famously painted by Van Gogh. It had been a good day. He hadn't mentioned Oliver and neither had she. Luc was observant, witty, at times extremely thoughtful; physically, she couldn't deny the attraction. When he'd brought her back to Le Chant he'd dropped her in the car park with a quick peck on the cheek and a vague promise of another outing. She knew she was falling under his spell again but was trying to hold back. Did she still think he had a hidden agenda or was it the memory of Oliver's abuse which still haunted her? Or maybe her feelings were false anyway, clouded by emotion and gratitude for his support and help.

She pulled her eyes away and turned back to her computer.

A few minutes later she heard the main door close and then voices. Peter had returned and was talking to Luc at the end of the studio. He'd been to a hotel in town where he'd given an interview to a journalist from one of the French national papers. 'Neutral territory,' he'd remarked to Terri that morning. 'Stops them from snooping.'

The printer churned out the last sheet of the catalogue and Terri got up to clip it all together. Peter appeared in the doorway.

'How did it go?' she asked him.

'Fine. Asked some damn fool questions but that's to be expected. What she'll write is anyone's guess.'

'When is it going in?'

'No idea.'

'You should have let me come too.'

'I don't need babysitting.'

'No, but then I'd have known what was going on.'

'Well…yes.'

Terri crossed to the door and held out the manuscript. 'The catalogue's finished. I need you to read it ASAP and tell me if it's OK. If you let me know tomorrow I can send it to Christophe before I go away.'

Peter took the papers, looking at them suspiciously.

'It's all right,' said Terri, with a wry smile. 'I've been polite.'

'I should bloody well hope so,' he grunted. 'I pay you.' Then he surprised her with an exaggerated wink as he turned and left.

*

Peter poured himself a large glass of whisky, took a sip and placed it on the table by his leather armchair. He picked up the manuscript, settled himself down and pushed the reading

262

glasses up his nose. On the table he'd put a pen, ready to score through the parts he would reject, and began to read.

The first part of the catalogue was a resume of his life and work. Terri charted his early interest in art and his studies both in England and Italy. The 'commune' he'd briefly set up with his friends near Avignon sounded exciting the way she'd described it and made him smile. She touched briefly on his romance with Madeleine and used it to explain his decision to settle in Provence.

All right so far.

She wrote briefly of his personal losses – with no mention of Josephine - and of the renewed happiness he had found with Angela which had enabled him to move forward. She made an intelligent study of his artistic development through the years, giving examples, and stressed how open he was to the work of others, unafraid to learn from them. She finished by noting how much he still challenged himself as shown in his work over the last few years and that many recent paintings still had the power to move or to provoke reflection.

He frowned. It felt as if he were reading a history of someone else's life: it was rounded; it made sense. Terri seemed to understand his passion, his perfectionism, the constant drive to improve his work. He pulled off his glasses and rubbed at his eyes. God, he was tired. He took another mouthful of whisky and swung his glasses side to side, looking out of the window. But his life hadn't really been like that. Terri had made it sound so simple, so linear. Of course, that was her job and she was good at it. The piece read well - it was sensitive and informed - but it was a half-truth at best.

He perched the glasses back on his nose. The rest of the catalogue was a detailed history and description of the works on show. The final publication would contain colour

263

reproductions of the paintings but the draft had more of Terri's quick line drawings to illustrate each one, presumably to avoid confusion at the printer. He found himself smiling again. Some of the drawings were quite comical but they were descriptive and accurate. She claimed to have no artistic ability but clearly that was untrue.

So who was Terri? The question persistently nagged at him. She bothered him and she challenged him yet it was impossible not to like her. At times he felt immensely drawn to her. Was that because of a family bond? After studying her endlessly he thought he could now see the likeness to Madeleine around the eyes. Could that be? He tried to see Josephine in her too but found he could not now remember his daughter's features very well and the realisation shocked him. Certainly the photograph Terri had shown him had meant nothing.

But he did remember a day many, many years ago, when Tom was crying - and with such an anguished cry - in the nursery. He remembered going in and finding Josie leaning over the cot. No, he couldn't recall her features and yet he still remembered the quick way she'd looked round and her furtive, guilty behaviour. He tried to shake the image away but there were other memories too, awful things he had long since pushed way down, out of heart and mind, all coming back to haunt him. Why had Terri come into his life now? In any case, she was probably just another of Celia's projects, wasn't she? Or an interfering busybody.

He sipped his whisky then cradled the glass, glancing down at the spindly drawings and feeling an unfamiliar thickening of his throat. Or was she some kind of second chance: an opportunity to wipe the slate clean and make a fresh start? Surely it couldn't be that simple? And of course it wasn't. For what would she say if she found out the truth?

*

On the Friday, Luc invited Terri to dinner at his cottage. He'd offered it as a 'farewell meal' because she'd said she was going to spend her days off back in London. He wondered why she was going back now though he thought he could guess. Even so, there was a lot about Terri which he still didn't know. Every time he thought he was getting close to her, she seemed to dance away again. He'd been half-surprised that she'd even accepted the invitation.

His cottage was a rustic stone building in a clearing at the edge of the pine woods, its central door flanked on each side by a shuttered window, a skylight let into its pan-tiled roof. Luc had found he liked living there. It had none of the sophistication of his flat in London but it was comfortable enough and it gave him peace and solitude, a space in which to work. Now, in anticipation of Terri's visit, he tried to make it look welcoming. He tidied up and made sure it was clean; he bought some flowers – he couldn't remember what they were – and rammed them in a glazed earthenware jar; he bought a bottle of a local soft red wine and prepared stuffed tomatoes and herbed lamb with ratatouille.

He was in the process of checking the tomatoes in the oven when there was a brisk knock on the door and, when he pulled it open, Terri stood on the doorstep clutching a paper bag. She thrust it at him wordlessly.

'You didn't have to bring anything,' he protested.

'My grandmother's rules. Never go to someone's house without a gift.' She shrugged. 'Here. Take it. It's not much.'

265

Luc took the bag and pulled out a box of chocolate covered coffee beans.

'You remembered: my favourite. Thank you.' He leaned forward, brushing his lips against her cheek.

She turned away, glancing round the cottage. He was aware of the acuteness of her curiosity, taking it all in, his home. The old shepherd's hut had been extended and renovated long before he'd arrived. The ground floor was an open plan living space with a small kitchen to one side, two old sofas before a fireplace to the other and a dining area at the back. To the left of a door at the rear, a staircase rose against the side wall.

'Kir,' he offered. 'Or juice?'

'Juice please.'

'Apple. Is that OK?'

She nodded and stood at the edge of the kitchen and its L-shaped run of units, watching him pour it into two glasses. He handed her a glass and touched hers briefly with his own. '*Santé.*' He took a sip, watching her. She looked uneasy – no, more than that, she bristled, as if she wanted to say something but was biting it back.

'Something the matter?' he asked.

'No.'

She turned, wandering away towards the back of the room where the walls were hung with his painted canvases, looking at each one in turn. 'So will these all go in your exhibition?'

'Maybe.'

'They should. They're good. You'll need a lot of work to make an impact.'

Her voice was crisp, her manner all sharp edges. She walked back up the room and they sat on separate sofas either side of the battered wooden coffee table in front of the hearth.

266

On the floor to one side of Luc's sofa, a stack of books teetered dangerously with a bundle of newspapers hastily rammed between them and the wall.

'Are you sure you're OK?' he asked.

'Yes, fine. You?'

'Of course, yes. Why shouldn't I be?'

'No reason.'

He stared at her, brows furrowed.

'I suppose I will need a lot of work,' he answered, belatedly. 'The trouble is, I never think it's good enough.'

He cringed: now he sounded like he was fishing for compliments. But Terri was barely listening; there was clearly something bothering her. They exchanged small talk about his work, about the football club he belonged to, about her trip to the framer's that day. She was still worried about the lost painting and the pictures awaiting restoration. Maybe that was why she was preoccupied.

They moved to the table at the back of the room which he'd laid with place mats and Provençal print napkins and they dined by candlelight, augmented by the glow of a table lamp on an old cupboard against the back wall. Apart from a bland compliment from Terri on his cooking they barely spoke.

Then suddenly Terri had abandoned the lamb, laid down her cutlery and was staring at him balefully.

'Why are we doing this?' she said. 'You're married. Were you planning to tell me? Or perhaps you didn't think it was important?'

Luc glanced up at her sharply but continued eating.

'Where did you get that from?' he said coolly.

'That's not the point is it?'

Resignedly, Luc put down his cutlery and met her gaze.

267

'On the contrary. It is very much the point. Because I'm not married. So I'd like to know who told you I was.'

'Lindsey.' Doubt puckered her brow. 'Was she lying? She said Thierry overheard you referring to your wife when you were talking to one of the other students in the studio.'

Luc pulled a thin smile. 'Maybe he did but overheard conversations aren't always what they seem. I thought by now you trusted me. I really thought we'd got beyond this.'

She was still frowning, staring at him as if trying to read inside his head. Maybe he was as opaque as she was. Maybe sometimes that was a good thing.

'So it's not true?' she pressed.

'Some of it is true.' He took a mouthful of wine. 'The student Thierry referred to – Marc – was upset. I'd seen him struggling in the class, obviously not concentrating. I knew Peter would come down on him hard it he didn't snap out of it so when he went to make drinks in the kitchen I followed him in. Apparently he'd just found out his girlfriend had been cheating on him. I sympathised, said my wife had done the same thing.' He raised his eyebrows at her stunned expression and almost smiled. 'I'm not married now Terri. Thierry would have heard that too but I pushed the kitchen door closed. He shouldn't have gone telling tales.'

'So when were you married?'

He fiddled with the stem of his wine glass. 'I met someone about three months after you and I split up. Lisette her name was. She was Swiss, a journalist on a magazine. A few months later, we got married.'

'Grief, Luc, that was quick.'

'Yes, but I thought we were…' He shrugged. '…right, I suppose. Maybe it was rebound.' He flicked her a glance; her eyes wouldn't meet his. 'And I liked the idea of marriage.' He gave a wry smile. 'Perhaps it was my good Catholic upbringing.'

'What happened?'

'From the moment we put the rings on, everything went wrong. We argued and fought...' He paused, swilling the thimbleful of wine in his glass round and round. 'I found her in bed with my best friend a few months later. She said it was all my fault, that I'd become obsessed with my work and was neglecting her.'

'*Your* fault? But she could've talked to you about it, instead of jumping into bed with someone else.'

'Yes, that's more or less what I said, only not quite so politely.'

'So you divorced her?'

'*Oui, bien sûr*...despite the good Catholic upbringing. My mother understood. My father was less impressed. She was the daughter of a good friend of his, a Swiss diplomat. I suppose that should have warned me really.'

'And that's when you fell out?'

'Well, it was certainly the last straw. And the beginning of my decision to make changes in my life. After some heart searching, I had to accept that she was at least partly right.'

'Oh...' Terri looked down, picked up her cutlery and prodded disinterestedly at her food again. 'I'm sorry,' she said eventually. 'I spoke out of turn. Anyway, it's none of my business.'

'No, of course it's your business. You had a right to know. I should've said. You took me by surprise, that's all. The marriage was a stupid mistake and I don't often talk about it.'

They finished the meal in silence. Luc offered Terri more wine and, when she refused, tipped the last of it into his glass and leaned back in his chair, watching her thoughtfully.

'So…why go back to London for your holiday?' he said. 'Why not stay here?'

'If I stayed here it would be impossible not to think about work.'

'And Oliver?'

'I've heard nothing from him since he was here. I can't avoid going back there forever. Anyway, weren't you the one who said he wouldn't bother me again?'

He nodded slowly. 'Are you sure there's no other reason for the trip?'

'No. Why should there be?'

'I went up to see Celia earlier in the week.'

'Oh? Why?' Her tone was clipped, guarded.

'I was curious. You said you thought she wasn't as batty as she pretends. I thought I'd go and see for myself.'

'I see. So what did she say?'

'She said a lot of things, mostly complete nonsense, and she showed me her paintings, gave me a drink. Said she'd seen we were courting – her word – and she was *so* pleased.' He paused, finished his wine and put the glass down. 'I asked her about Madeleine and why she thought you might look like her. Apparently Madeleine had a daughter. She told you this too?'

Terri met his gaze. 'Yes.'

'She said she ran away. And that she was pregnant.'

'Ye-es. But Angela says she died.'

'And how does she say she died, this daughter?'

'Josephine. She killed herself…in the woods. She was nineteen.'

Luc's eyes narrowed. 'But Celia says you're her daughter. And you want to believe her?'

'What I want is to know why you're cross-examining me like this?'

'I've been wondering why you never told me any of this. Why have you been so secretive?'

'I'm not the only one who's secretive, am I? How come you didn't tell me you were divorced?'

He shrugged. A frosty silence settled on them.

'Do you have any reason to think Celia is right?' said Luc eventually.

She hesitated. 'Angela said that Josephine's body was never found. Doesn't that strike you as odd? And Peter virtually admitted that I might be related and told me all about Josephine.'

'Really? Peter did? What prompted that?'

'I asked him.'

'You don't actually know anything about your mother, do you? You lied to me.'

'Lied? No. Not exactly.'

'You said you knew about her. Enough, you said. And yet you've clearly convinced yourself that Josie was your mother.'

'I'm just saying it's possible.'

'Are you sure you aren't chasing shadows? You're letting yourself be sucked into Celia's strange world and it's not healthy.'

'It's easy for you to say that when you grew up with a family,' she said angrily. 'Whatever problems you had with your father, you still don't know what it's like to be a child in a vacuum, surrounded by whispering and silences. I'd like some explanation; I'd like to know who my mother was and why she did it. She left me, don't you see? She walked out and left me.'

Terri stood up suddenly, pressing her lips together and blinking tears away. She picked up her wine glass – still half full - and marched through to the kitchen. Luc followed her.

271

'So what are you going to do in London?' he demanded.

'I have some papers of my father's in my flat.' Terri left the glass by the sink and turned, chin raised. 'I thought I'd look through them.'

Luc reached into a wall cupboard and took out two brandy glasses, then picked up a bottle of cognac from the back of the unit. 'Brandy?' he offered, pulling the stopper out.

'No, thank you. And I wish you wouldn't either.'

He fixed her with a look but she stared him out. He sighed and replaced the stopper. 'So suppose you don't find anything out in London,' he said, putting the bottle back, 'suppose all your investigations are inconclusive? What then?'

'What do you mean?'

'I mean,' he said, coming to stand in front of her, 'will you let it go or will you go on trying to persuade yourself that Peter is your grandfather?'

'I'm not trying to persuade myself of anything. I didn't start this.'

'No, Celia did. But the more you look and dwell, the greater your need seems to become. As if it will answer some question in your life, bigger than anything to do with your mother.'

'That's ridiculous. That's all I want to know: was she Josephine?'

Luc shook his head. 'No. I don't think so. It's all about you. You think no-one loves you and you want to know why.'

'You've got a nerve,' she spat, and turned to walk away.

But Luc threw out a hand, took hold of her arm and pulled her towards him, covering her mouth in a rough, hungry kiss. It was over in a moment and he released her. She immediately slapped him across the face.

272

'Who the hell do you think you are?' she said, eyes dancing with anger.

Luc put a hand up to his burning cheek, breathing heavily with suppressed emotion.

'I love you,' he said simply. 'I thought you knew.' He pursed his lips up and gave a light, apologetic shrug then reached out a hand to her, palm up. 'Terri…please.'

She stared at his hand for what felt like an eternity before eventually putting her own in it. 'I'm sorry,' she said. 'I am really.' She hesitated, staring into his face. 'But I think I'm falling in love with you too. And its scares me.'

'Don't be scared,' he said, pulling her close. 'You can trust me.'

*

'I could come to London,' murmured Luc into the back of Terri's shoulder as she lay curled up in his bed the next morning, his body crooked around her. 'I'm sure Peter would let me have another couple of days off. Just in case Oliver's still around.'

Terri quivered with the tickle of his breath on her skin. She smiled softly to herself, sure that she had never felt so contented. She ran her hand slowly along Luc's forearm where it lay across her chest. He nuzzled at her neck and shifted his hand to cup the swell of her breast.

'No,' she said quietly.

'No what?'

'No, you can't come to London.'

'Why not?'

'Because I need to go alone. I have to prove it to myself. I can't let him keep me running away forever. Anyway I want to look into who my mother was and you'll try to stop me.'

He rolled away from her onto his back, put his hands behind his head and looked up at the sloping uneven ceiling. She turned over and nestled into his side, putting her head on his shoulder and resting her hand on his chest.

'Don't be like that,' she said. 'It's not that I wouldn't like you there; I would. But you'd be a distraction.'

He moved one hand to stroke the top of her head. 'I suppose I'll have to believe you.'

'Yes, you will.'

'I still don't understand why you're so sure Josie was your mother.'

Terri hesitated, then leaned herself up on one elbow, looking down at him.

'Josephine kept diaries,' she said. 'She started after her mother died and kept it up all through her teens. And I've been reading them.'

'Diaries?' Luc stared at her in amazement. 'Where did you find them?'

'In Madeleine's old studio.' She laughed at his puzzled expression. 'It's an attic room in the east wing, called 'Raphael'. It was her private space, her den. It's a fascinating place.'

'I didn't even know it was there.'

'You wouldn't. The entrance is through the linen room and it's kept locked. Peter has the key in his study and doesn't let anyone go there.'

'But he let you.'

Terri focussed her attention on the hairs on Luc's chest, curling a couple round and round with her finger. 'He doesn't know I've been there.'

Luc pursed his lips up, and shook his head. 'He'd be so mad if he knew.'

Terri avoided meeting his gaze. It was something she refused to think about: what Peter's reaction would be when he found out where she'd been and what she'd done.

'Celia told me about the studio,' she said, 'and about the diaries. I thought she was daft but everything she said was true. It was there, just as she described, and so were the diaries.'

'And what do these magical diaries say?'

'Hey, don't be so cynical. They're amazing. They chart a girl growing up, painfully, grieving and confused, and how difficult her relationship was with her father. They're harrowing, honestly.'

Luc was serious now, staring at her. 'So, have you got them?'

'Yes. I borrowed them.'

'Does Peter know about them?'

'Not as far as I know.'

'Do they give any indication of what happened to her?'

'No...not yet.'

'You haven't finished them? I still don't see why you're so sure she was your mother.'

'Everything just seems to fit. *She* seems to fit, don't you see?' Terri spoke quickly, her voice rising with excitement. She wasn't sure where this excitement had come from, only that she had to satisfy it somehow. 'If I could just be sure that Josephine was pregnant when she left here...Anyway, I'm hoping that she'll say so in the last diary. So far she's made reference to feeling sick and that's all. But she might even say who the father is and then…well…' She sighed. 'The problem is that I don't have the last diary…yet.'

'Why? Where is it?'

'I'm not sure. Probably in the attic too but I haven't been able to get back up there. It's difficult. I can't talk to Angela about it. She warned me off - she thinks I'm just a gold-digger, in league with Celia. And Peter…' She shrugged. 'So anyway I'm going to find out what I can in London and then look for it when I get back.' She glanced at the clock then leaned forward and kissed him softly on the mouth before quickly rolling off the bed sideways.

'I have to go,' she said, looking round for her clothes. 'If I miss my flight I'll never get another one today.'

'I'll ring…' Luc promised, before she left. '…every day you're away.'

Terri walked back towards the *mas* with a light step, sure that everything was falling into place at last. In love with Luc…who would have thought it?

It never once crossed her mind that it might have been wiser to keep the information about the diaries to herself.

Chapter 18

'Peter?' Angela crossed the hallway to the sitting room. It was nearly noon on the Sunday and she'd not long been up. Making herself a mug of tea in the kitchen, she'd heard his rumbling cough. Now, mug in hand, she pushed the door back, walked in and saw him sitting on the farthest sofa, two piles of papers next to him on the seat. 'Peter?' she said again. 'I thought I heard you.'

He looked up, eyes blank, his reading glasses perched on the end of his nose. 'Did you want me dear?'

She moved closer.

'Good play last night?' Peter enquired vaguely.

'Oh…yes, yes, quite good, thank you.' Angela sat elegantly on the nearby sofa, took a mouthful of tea and put the mug down on the coffee table. 'I thought this might be a good opportunity for us to talk – with Terri away.'

'To talk?' He frowned, replaced the sheet he'd been reading onto one of the piles on the seat and removed the glasses, letting them fall onto their cord. He produced a smile. 'What about?'

Angela hesitated. She'd rehearsed what she would say about Terri a million times, had been in no doubt that it had become necessary to say it, but now all the well-chosen words escaped her.

'Your hair looks pretty like that,' remarked Peter. 'You've done something different to it.'

'Yes…thank you. I…' She let it go. She didn't want to talk about her hair.

'I'm just looking again at the catalogue Terri's drafted for the exhibition.' He tapped the papers in front of him. 'It's remarkably good. Perhaps you'd like to read it too?'

'It won't mean anything to me, Peter,' Angela said briskly. 'I don't know anything about your work.'

'Well, it's not just about my work – it's also a mini biography. You are mentioned of course. Terri's written it very well actually.' He became more introspective. 'Though perhaps she's made more sense of what I've done than I deserve.'

The remark galvanised Angela's mind. 'Oh listen to yourself Peter. A few weeks ago no-one could please you, nothing matched your standards, and now this girl can do no wrong. What has she done to you?'

He gave a short, pained laugh. 'I don't know what you mean.'

'It's as if she's put a spell on you. You've become more and more obsessed with her. And you've changed - yes you have, don't shake your head at me – you've changed since she's been here.'

'I have not. Well, maybe I have a little. Yes…she's made me think.' He took a deep breath, exhaling slowly. 'It's as I said to you before, Angela. I've made mistakes. Josie…'

'What happened with Josephine was not your fault,' Angela said quickly. 'You shouldn't blame yourself.'

'It's not that black and white, Angela.' He stared lugubriously at the papers before him with a distant air, as if a long-buried scene was playing out in his mind.

278

'Peter?'

'Mm?' He raised his eyes, focussed on her face. 'Josie might have run away, you know; she might have had a child.'

'No, Peter, no. I can't believe you're letting Celia play mind games with you.'

'You didn't know Madeleine,' he said firmly. 'Terri is like her…in many ways. And the girl doesn't know anything about her mother.' He held Angela's gaze. 'It is just possible, Angela. We have to consider the possibility.'

'Why? Because there's a vague similarity about the eyes?' She stared at him, her face distorting with disbelief. 'It's all in your imagination, Peter. You just *want* to believe she's Josephine's daughter. It can't be true. You know it can't be true.'

'Well, I don't want to turn my back on her if there's a chance. Of course we could arrange a DNA test but I've been looking into it and I understand that with only one grandparent to check, the result is likely to be inconclusive.'

'Do you realise that you talk more about Terri these days than you do about your own daughter? Lindsey is being pushed out.'

'Nonsense. I was talking to Lindsey only this morning. She's thinking of going back to her music. I hadn't realised before how much it meant to her. She wants to go to music college. It'll be tough for her to get in but I'm sure she could do it if she applies herself. I promised I'd back her. Whatever it takes, hm? We want her to be happy, don't we?'

'And what about Terri?'

'What do you mean?'

'I mean what do you intend to do about her?'

'I don't intend to do anything about her…yet. I'm keeping an open mind. Maybe she'll…'

279

'You're being duped Peter,' she said across him. 'I can't believe it. And you want to be duped, that's what's so hurtful.'

'Hurtful?' He looked genuinely puzzled. 'It doesn't affect the way I feel about you, Angela, or your position in this house, or Lindsey's. But if Terri is Josie's daughter, she has rights and I have obligations. She is not responsible for…for what happened, after all.'

'I don't want you to pursue this, Peter.' Angela fixed him with her green gaze. 'She's written the catalogue; she's collected the paintings and worked out most of the exhibition for you, hasn't she? So I think you should terminate her employment now. Luc or…or…or the gallery could help you finish off what needs to be done. That's what I want you to do. If you care for me Peter…' She left the unfinished sentence hanging there, the threat unvoiced.

Peter's frown returned. 'I'm afraid I can't do that.'

'It's either her or me,' she said rashly.

'Don't push me into taking sides, Angela,' he replied, his tone and expression quickly darkening. 'Don't make me do that. I've seen you with another man. I know I've not always valued you as I should and I am truly sorry for that, but I've never cheated on you. I've had temptations, believe me, but I wouldn't do that. You are not in a position to give me an ultimatum.'

'I don't know what you're talking about. What other man? Where?'

'I don't wish to discuss the matter any further…now or in the future.' Peter replaced the glasses on his nose and picked up the top sheet of paper again.

Angela stood up, lifting her chin proudly, ready to argue. But he'd taken the ground from beneath her and she hesitated, unsure what to say. On the wall beyond, she caught sight of the portrait of Madeleine. Angrily, she turned and walked out, the tea forgotten.

*

Terri's flat in London felt dark and cramped after the brightness of the southern French sun. Travelling had played its usual trick on her mind. The light and the bleached stones of Provence, its perfumes, colours and sounds still seemed to be imprinted in her senses. London, despite its bright lights and lively bustle, felt dreary by comparison. She wished she'd not been so quick to reject Luc's offer to accompany her. But part of her wondered if the fairy tale would have continued here anyway. Perhaps their romance was born of the sunshine and the light and the fertile earth of the Luberon and would disappear to nothing in the hard-edged noise and shadow of the city. She could not yet dare to believe in it.

The apartment brought back memories of Oliver, some good times, mostly the bad, and it occurred to her that perhaps she should consider selling the place and making a fresh start - whatever happened with Luc. Sophie had told her that she'd seen Oliver a couple of times with another woman – a young actress. It was welcome news but Terri felt desperate for the girl. Even so, she still watched for him, found herself checking corners and looking behind her and only slowly allowed herself to accept that it was finally over.

Over the next few days, she was easily occupied. She caught up with a couple of old work colleagues and had dinner with Sophie and Stuart; she went shopping and did some cleaning; she paid bills and washed clothes. It was Wednesday morning before she finally retrieved the squat cardboard box containing her father's things from under her bed, dumping it on the floor in front of the sofa. Even then she looked at it distrustfully, as if it threatened her in some way. In an effort to lighten her mood, she put her favourite album on and turned the volume up.

Sitting down, she still stared at the box but did nothing. Her feelings about her father were so contradictory. Since his death she'd been surprised by how often she thought of things she'd like to ask or tell him; a chance memory had often brought her close to tears. She missed him and yet couldn't understand why because when he was alive she had rarely seen him. And yet she had carried the book on Indian painting back with her from France as if, by keeping it close, she could stop him from slipping away from her again.

'Oh come on Terri,' she muttered, 'get a grip.'

She ripped off the sticky tape sealing the box, opened the flaps back and peered inside. On the top lay a battered shoe-box containing a couple of quality biros, a fountain pen, a magnifying glass, a pocket calculator and a pair of scratched reading glasses. There were two leather-strapped watches. She remembered her father wearing the older of the two when she was a child. As a teenager she'd told him it looked old-fashioned. 'I don't care,' he'd responded briskly. 'It's a proper watch with a proper mechanism, not like the modern rubbish.' Yet the other watch was precisely the sort he'd been complaining about. Had the old one finally broken or had he given in to pressure from Lizzie to buy a new one?

She knew nothing, really, of the detail of his life over these last years. Luc hadn't been so far from the mark when he'd described them as estranged. Even his contentious article had not brought them closer together; Terri had been only distantly aware of her father's distress – a remark made on the phone, quickly passed over; cigarettes smoked nervously in quick succession the next time she saw him; a reluctance to talk about it again. If she were honest her anger at Luc had come as much from her own feeling of guilt as anything else.

She frowned, put the watches aside, and pulled out a small torch, a key fob, then a small silver charm of an artist's palette. This was her father's 'lucky charm', though why and where it came from she had no idea. Was it French? Had her mother given it to him? Highly unlikely he would have kept it then as a charm. As Terri had told Peter: her parents didn't get on. The realisation had come to her slowly over these last weeks. Looking back now, she was amazed it hadn't occurred to her years ago. It was why her father had been so withdrawn, so miserable, so bitter: he'd married a woman he couldn't love and then she'd walked out and left him with a tiny child.

In the main box she found a photograph album containing a few casual wedding photographs, and a succession of family pictures. There were two missing, presumably the ones her father had given her. Using the magnifying glass, she studied her mother's features closely but the quality was too poor to make them out. They were snaps anyway, taken by another family member or a friend. There were pictures of her childish self – a couple, small and equally unclear, with her mother - and some of her father and her paternal grandparents. The album was no help and, snapping it shut, she dropped it to the floor.

At the bottom of the box was a cardboard folder containing a sheaf of official-looking papers. She picked through them meticulously, looking for something relating to her mother: a passport, an identity card or even a birth certificate, but there was nothing. They were all her father's: certificates, licences, prescriptions and a pile of receipts and guarantees.

283

The box was now empty and Terri sat back, frustrated. There was no clue to the identity of her mother: no letters or cards, no documents which showed her handwriting or suggested that she had changed her name. But for a handful of photographs, it was as if her mother had never existed at all. And there were no relatives to ask. She vaguely remembered being told that her mother came from Gloucestershire but that might have been a story created to hide the truth, and, even if it were true, there was no trail to follow.

She made herself a mug of tea and drank it slowly, staring unfocussed at the box, her thoughts flitting over any possible lead but failing to come up with anything constructive. There was the art college connection: both her mother and Josie Stedding had apparently attended art college in London. The same one? Were they one and the same person? But Josie had never thought to put the name of the college in her diary and Terri had no idea about her mother. In any case, what college would trawl through its old records on the basis of such a far-fetched story? She had reached a dead end. Her only possible hope now – and that a tenuous one - was Josie's last diary.

She replaced everything in the box. Reaching for the photograph album, she noticed some leaflets and cuttings which had slipped to the floor beneath. They must have been tucked in the back of the album and had fallen out when she dropped it. Two were programmes for exhibitions which she herself had curated; the others were newspaper and magazine reviews of her work.

She sat back on her heels, staring at them, confounded. Her father had never asked her about her work - he'd never shown the slightest interest in it - and yet he had collected all these. Had he been to the exhibitions? He had never said.

She picked up one of the exhibition catalogues. The top corner of one of the pages had been folded down and creased, marking it. Her father used to do that. She opened it at the marked page. Beside the photograph of a painting by Holbein the Younger, her father had scrawled: 'Ask Terri.'

She stared at the writing. Ask Terri what? He never had asked her anything about it. Tears rolled silently down her cheeks.

Chapter 19

Terri returned to Le Chant du Mistral the following Sunday evening and immediately felt the chill wind of change in the house. Angela met her in the hallway as soon as she arrived, frostily informed her that there were a number of house guests staying and asked her to avoid the kitchen wherever possible. As if to emphasise the point, raised voices and laughter spilled out from the *salon*. 'If you're still seeing Luc,' Angela added crisply, 'perhaps you could spend more time at the *bergerie*. I asked Corinne to put some sandwiches in your room for tonight.'

When Terri opened the door to her rooms, the sweet scent of lavender met her; evidently Corinne had recently cleaned too. She made herself a mug of tea and had a long shower to wash the journey out of her system. Later, putting away the clothes from her case, it quickly became clear that someone had been through the drawers of the chest while she'd been away. A prickle of misgiving ran up her spine and she immediately checked throughout the room; small changes suggested the whole place had been searched. Given the conversation she had overheard between Angela and Celia, she felt sure Angela had been looking for the diaries. Fortunately, Terri had taken them with her to London as a precaution. Now, doubtful that the place would be searched again, she replaced them in one of the drawers under a pile of T-shirts.

Ironically, it was a relief the next morning to get down to the studio and the sanctuary of her office. After checking for messages, she went across to Peter who stood in front of his easel, drawing up the cartoon for a painting.

'Good trip?' Peter rested the charcoal down as she approached.

'Yes, thanks.'

He nodded. 'So-o…just four weeks on Friday then. Not long to go now.'

'No. And there's good news.' She waved a piece of paper. 'I found this on my desk, from Nicole. She took a message from the conservator: the paintings will be ready for collection by the end of the week.'

'Really? No-one ever tells me anything,' he muttered.

'No-one dares,' she retaliated automatically.

He looked up at her and they simultaneously smiled. There was a brief, awkward silence. Peter appeared about to ask something but turned away and picked up his charcoal again.

'Good to have you back,' he said gruffly to the drawing.

Terri raised her eyebrows, smiled ruefully, and went back to her office. Within the hour she had received a phone call from the art courier company telling her the lost painting had been found in a depot in Milan. At last everything was falling into place.

Terri closed the call but sat, staring into space. Her contract expired once the exhibition was up and running and she would leave. If she didn't get back into the attic soon and find that last diary, she never would.

*

Over the following days, Terri was too busy with work to have the time or energy to think about much else. She drove to Stéphanie Lebrun's studio and collected the newly restored canvases. Back in the barn she painstakingly examined each of the paintings for the exhibition, looking at the frames and the canvases, checking labels or applying new ones. The carrier fixed a date for transporting the paintings to Nice. She packed the smaller ones into the carrier's crates, ready for transit, and wrapped the larger ones. She drew up a rough guide to where each painting might hang, numbered their positions on wall maps and numbered the paintings accordingly, allowing leeway for last minute adjustments. In the week before the exhibition, it was arranged that she would go to Nice to take charge of the hanging. She sent out invitations to the Private View, made phone calls and fretted over what she'd forgotten.

In their free time, she and Luc took up where they'd left off before her trip to London and, though work was intense, still it was a quiet season. Happy with Luc, excited at the way the exhibition was shaping up, Terri gradually began to wonder if all the searching and probing about Josephine should be forgotten after all, left in the past to settle with dust again. *People who go looking for things usually find out something they don't want to know.* Maybe her grandmother was right after all. Let it lie.

By the middle of September the peak of the heat had past; the cicadas fell silent. The last of the guests left and the house was still again. Luc went away on the Friday afternoon for the weekend - he was flying up to Paris to see his mother who hadn't been well - and promised to be back by late afternoon on the Sunday so they could spend the evening together.

On the Saturday Terri idled round town, lunched at a café-bar and arrived back at Le Chant mid-afternoon to find Lindsey swimming languidly in the pool, a rare sight. Lindsey, too, had changed. When she saw Terri, she raised a hand and called out. By the time Terri reached the poolside, Lindsey had pushed herself out and was sitting on the edge, her feet still dangling in the water.

'Haven't seen you for ages,' she said accusingly.

'I've been busy.'

'I thought you'd been avoiding me.'

'Nope.' Terri kicked off her sandals, sat down and dropped her feet into the water. 'I just haven't been in the house much. Are you OK?'

'Yeah. Sure.'

They sat silently, both staring at the soft swirl of their feet in the water.

'Mama's really cross with you.'

Terri flicked her a sideways glance. 'What's she been saying?'

'Oh…you know…that you're trying to prove Madeleine's daughter didn't kill herself, that she was pregnant and you're her daughter.'

Terri frowned. 'I thought you didn't know anything about Josephine. She said she didn't want you to know.'

'Well I know now; she told me all about it while you were away. She was warning me off helping you in any way. Said you were just after father's money.'

'I'm not,' said Terri quickly, flicking her an earnest look. 'Really, I'm not.'

289

Lindsey considered Terri thoughtfully. 'Do you really think you might be Josephine's daughter?'

'No…I don't know, but it's not likely, is it?' She shrugged. 'Does it really matter?'

'Yes. You'd be sort of like a sister. OK, so more complicated than that, but still it would be cool. Mama's just over-protective of me. You shouldn't let her put you off finding out.'

'No, I suppose not.' Terri kicked her feet in the water, making light-edged drops splash up, shimmer and fall. 'Is she entertaining tonight?'

'No, she's already gone to a friend's house for a charity do of some kind. Won't be back for ages. And I'm going to a concert. Father's coming.'

'Oh? Well, have a good time.'

'You could come too.'

'Me? Thanks, but no, I don't think so. You don't see much of each other as it is.'

Lindsey grinned. 'You think we should do that father-daughter bonding thing, do you?'

'Something like that.'

'By the way, you can tell Luc that the piano's fine now.'

'Why, what was the matter with it?'

'A couple of the keys were sticking. Luc took a look at it while you were away. I haven't seen him since to thank him.'

'Fine. I'll tell him. He's away till tomorrow.' Terri got to her feet, flicking water off each foot in turn.

'Sami might know,' said Lindsey, tilting her head back to look up at her.

'Know what?'

'About Josephine. I was just thinking: he's been here, like, forever. He might know something…if she ran away, I mean.

290

But maybe mother's right after all...' Lindsey pulled her feet out of the water and stood up, facing Terri. 'I mean, after she killed her brother she probably went into meltdown or something, you know, couldn't face what she'd done.'

'Whoa. Wait a minute. Who told you she killed her brother?'

'Mama did.'

'That's not true. She didn't tell me that. No-one's said that.'

'I thought you knew. Apparently she'd always been jealous of Tom because he was the centre of everyone's attention. She'd had tantrums about it off and on for years. When everyone got back to the house on the day he drowned, Josie was in the pool with him. She was raving. The police were called. The next thing, she'd disappeared.'

Terri stared at Lindsey blankly. She felt as though her mind would explode; she couldn't take it in.

'It's not true,' she said dumbly. 'She said that because she knew you'd tell me.'

Lindsey slowly shook her head.

'No Terri. I'm sorry, but it's true. I don't think mama thinks it should be talked about – because of father, you know? But I told Thierry about it and apparently his grandmother remembered it happening. It caused a huge stir in the village at the time - with the police involved and everything. Everyone knew it was the daughter who'd done it.' Lindsey put her hand on Terri's arm. 'I'm sorry. I thought you knew,' she repeated. 'But it doesn't affect you, does it?'

*

It doesn't affect you. No, it doesn't affect me, thought Terri. Why should it? And yet it wasn't that simple. As the weeks had gone by, she had convinced herself that Josie was her mother; it was what she had wanted to believe. And after all those nights reading the girl's diaries, she thought she knew her. It had been a help to feel some empathy with the girl, to understand why she was the way she was, even perhaps why she had become the mother she was. But murder...? That was a step too far and Terri couldn't go there. And it didn't fit surely? Or maybe she just didn't want to accept it. At the back of her mind was a creeping fear she refused to acknowledge, that her mother was a murderer, and that she had inevitably inherited the stain: they shared the same blood. Whatever the truth was, she told herself, she should forget about it, put it away from her, walk away. It didn't need to concern her.

But she couldn't. The issues circled and drummed repeatedly through her head, and the temptation to resolve the matter one way or the other was overwhelming. Now she knew that the house was going to be empty all evening, there was a fleeting chance - probably her last - of finding Josie's final diary. So half an hour after she was sure Lindsey and Peter had left the house, clutching the stolen key from Peter's desk, Terri let herself into the attic room once again.

The low evening sun filled the room with a soft, rosy light; it was stuffy and hot. It was all so familiar and yet she didn't know where to start. But if the last diary was here it couldn't be far away; perhaps she'd already looked straight at it without realising. She crossed to the work station, pulled open the drawer in which she'd found the first three and searched it again. No, it wasn't there.

She worked her way through all the other drawers with no success, straightened up and surveyed the room. Perhaps it was on one of the bookshelves after all. She ran her eyes over the spines, systematically, top to bottom. A couple of the books were proud of the others - she automatically pushed them back – but there was no diary. The sunlight was now sickly and spent and she flicked the top light on making the dirty bulb shed an insipid light over the room. She tried the record cabinet without success. This was foolish; Josie must have taken it with her. Closing the cupboard door, she noticed the dust on the top of the cabinet had been disturbed.

The books had been shifted and the record cabinet had been handled. Someone else had been in the attic since her last visit. Suppose whoever it was had already found the diary and taken it away? But, for no rational reason, Terri didn't believe it; she felt sure the book was still there. She stood in the middle of the room, eyes wandering over every surface. At length her gaze fell on the writing box on the long low cupboard by the sofa and her pulse quickened. 'A writing box,' she murmured to herself, already moving towards it. 'Isn't that where people put precious things?'

The box was beautifully crafted, veneered with figured walnut and inlaid in geometric patterns with satinwood. The corners and lock were finished with brass. In each end a brass handle lay, at rest, flush into the wood. And the key was in the lock. Terri turned it and lifted down the lid to reveal a worn green leather writing surface with, at the back, a narrow box section containing two brass-topped inkwells and a ridged pen holder. An old fountain pen lay in one of the grooves. She pulled on a tiny leather flap which lifted the writing slope to reveal a shallow compartment containing fine writing paper, yellowed with age. There was no diary.

And yet the depth of the box was clearly much greater than that of the compartment, so somewhere there had to be

293

another, hidden, section. She lifted out the inkwells and the pen holder and began pushing and pulling everything at random until something suddenly clicked and a drawer, the full length of the box, slid out. Inside it lay a soft exercise book with 1976 scribbled on the cover. Terri's breath caught in her chest; she could hardly believe it. Gingerly she lifted it out and opened the first page. The handwriting was unquestionably Josephine's.

Without stopping to examine it further, she put the box back together, locked the room up and ran down the stairs to put the diary in her room. Then she slipped out into the night and down through the shadowy garden to take the keys back to the studio. She was just in time. Returning up the stone steps and on into the olive grove, she heard the unmistakeable sound of a car returning up the lane from the road, the grind of tyre on gravel carrying loudly in the still night air as it came to a halt in the car park.

*

Angela stepped out of the door into the sunshine and, holding a mug of tea, picked her way carefully across the terrace to where Peter sat by the pergola, a pot of coffee on the table, a Sunday newspaper in his hand. He looked up as she drew near and looked at her over the top of his glasses.

'Angela…my dear. I didn't realise you were up.'

'I couldn't sleep.' Angela eased herself into one of the chairs nearby. 'It was a sticky night, didn't you think?'

'Hm? Well, yes, perhaps it was. I fell asleep reading a book. Don't know what time that was.' Peter picked up the cup at his elbow and drained the last of the coffee from it. He immediately lifted the coffee pot from the table and poured himself another. He glanced across at Angela, hesitated a moment, then immersed himself in the newspaper again.

'Peter?'

'Hm?'

'I've been thinking about what you said.'

Peter rested the newspaper down and looked at her enquiringly.

'You know: about...well...cheating.' Angela glanced around the terrace as if someone might be listening. 'Look, I'm sorry Peter. I mean it: really sorry. Of course, you're right. I have been seeing another man. It was wrong of me. But I never meant to hurt you. I...well, I didn't think you'd ever know. It wasn't serious and I thought it would all blow over with no harm done. I was...actually I'm not sure why I did it. I think I was frightened of growing old. I wanted to prove that I still had it...you know...one last fling?' She self-consciously stroked her hand down the soft jersey cotton of her dress where it stretched over her thighs. 'I *am* sorry,' she repeated.

Peter nodded slowly. 'You look as beautiful as you ever did,' he said. 'Quite beautiful.' He forced a grim smile. 'It's me that's getting old.'

'Nonsense darling, you're mature,' said Angela melodically, 'like a good wine.'

Peter smiled more broadly. 'Thank you for that, my dear.' He examined her face for a moment. 'We've both made mistakes, haven't we?'

Angela reached across and rested her hand on his knee. He put his own over the top and squeezed it as their eyes met. At that moment, Terri emerged from the house, her bag slung over her shoulder. Angela quickly withdrew her hand.

'Ah, Terri, good morning,' said Peter. 'Have a coffee?'

'Morning Peter, Angela. Sorry to disturb you.' Terri stopped nearby. 'No, I'm fine, thank you. I've just had some tea.'

'As you wish, though they're hardly the same drink.' Peter watched her over his glasses. 'Are you all right?'

'Yes...fine. I overslept. I'm feeling...odd.' She glanced at Angela who was staring at her. 'I thought I'd go for a walk, work it off, you know.'

He grunted. 'Well, don't go too far and get lost. It's too late to break anyone else in now before the exhibition.'

Terri offered a pinched smile and walked away. Angela watched her go and sipped her tea.

'Going to see Luc again, no doubt,' she said.

'He's away.'

'Oh? That's odd. I saw her coming back into the house late yesterday evening.'

'So? Does that have some significance?' Peter said impatiently.

'No, I suppose not.'

'She doesn't look quite herself though, does she?'

'Doesn't she?' Angela looked towards Terri's receding figure again, frowning, then turned back to Peter. 'So tell me about the concert,' she said, picking up her tea and smiling.

*

Terri walked briskly, paying little heed to where she went. She wanted to get away from the house and to breathe fresh air. The night before she had stayed up late, reading the diary, unable to settle until she'd finished it. Even then, she couldn't sleep. Josie's last entries had been completely unexpected. She'd assumed the diary would give her some closure but

296

she'd been wrong and when she'd finally drifted off to sleep it had been a fitful rest, disturbed by vivid dreams. Now it was a relief to be up again and outside and she pushed herself to climb up through the woods, happy to sweat her confused thoughts out of her system.

When she finally stopped she was high up, in a clearing, with the whole valley stretched out below her. It looked like paradise from up here. Turning to the right she could see the house, its grounds and the swimming pool, the water glinting now in the sunshine. All so innocent – a world away from the tortured story she had read the night before. She turned away and sat down on a huge stone nearby, pulled a small bottle of water out of her bag and took a long drink.

She sat for ages, odd sentences from the diary going through her head. A bank of cloud began forming in the west and a brisk breeze tugged at her hair. She didn't notice. The book was in her bag and a couple of times she glanced down to where it lay on the ground beside her. It was a can of worms she wished she'd never opened. She sank into a weary reverie and lost track of time, Josephine walking through her half-sleeping dreams. Then the wind rose in earnest and she was roused by its anguished howl through the trees. She started back down the hill, changed her mind and detoured left, making for the *bergerie*. Luc would not be home yet but he never locked the door, had said he didn't see the point. There would be something to eat in his cottage and she could wait for him there. She dearly wanted to tell him what she'd found out and talk it through.

The clearing was silent, the cottage still. Terri knocked briefly then let herself in. Inside it was cool and offered a pleasing respite from the wind outside. She walked into the tiny kitchen and smiled indulgently. Luc's breakfast things from the Friday morning were still in the sink where he'd left them with a couple of flies circling over the top. He wasn't as domesticated as he pretended. A quick search of the kitchen revealed half a sliced loaf and some Emmental cheese. She made herself a sandwich and a mug of tea and took them over to the sofa, killing time flicking through some well-thumbed art magazines.

Afterwards, cradling the mug of tea, she toured the room again, studying Luc's paintings. A light flashed on the answering machine on the cupboard against the rear wall. Terri looked at it, ignored it and moved across to study the painting on the other side of the dining table. But she glanced back at the machine then wandered back to face it. Luc said that, as a 'last base back-up', he often told people to leave a message on his landline if it was important because the mobile signal in the area was so patchy. Terri reached out a finger, let it hover over the button a moment, then pressed it. There were two new messages.

A deep male voice spoke in French, exhorting Luc to get in touch to arrange a meeting about his paintings. The next message was from his friend Eric about a game of football. The third message had already been played and was from a woman, recorded on the Thursday, speaking in English:

'*Bonjour Luc.*' The woman laughed. 'It's Grace here. I've left two messages and a text already on your mobile but you haven't replied so I wondered if you were so buried in the sticks that your phone doesn't work. Or maybe you can't afford it any more? Are you *really* leading the life of a hermit down there?' Another laugh. 'Look, you remember our discussion about a story on your Peter Stedding? I've discussed it higher up and there's real interest. The timing of it would be so good now with his retrospective coming up and you've put yourself in a great position for the inside track. I've emailed some thoughts I've had about the piece. Whatever, you need to get back to me soon. Timing is everything as you should know. I'll be available to take a meeting this weekend if you could get your cute little arse over here to London. Call me.'

'Wha-at?' said Terri, incredulous.

She pressed play again and listened to it a second time, then stood staring at the machine. She backed away and turned, took a deep breath and blew it out slowly, thinking rapidly. This Grace was Grace Meachin, section editor of the newspaper Luc had been working for when he'd done his most famous exposés.

Luc's laptop was on the table and Terri quickly dumped the mug and booted it up. She already knew his password from searching the internet with him a couple of times. A few minutes later she found the email from Grace. It had been read but there had been no reply. Terri urgently searched through Luc's documents. He wrote at the computer so if there was a story brewing, it would surely be here. She scanned quickly down the list and a document entitled *Painting in the Shadows* caught her eye. She opened it, willing it to be nothing, a personal reflection on his own artistic career maybe.

She was fooling herself. It was a comprehensive series of notes on Peter's life and, though much of it was commonplace, some of it had come directly from Terri, including the disappearance of Josephine and the speculation about her fate. He had even noted down, virtually verbatim, accounts she'd told him from Josie's diaries. He had a stunning memory, she'd give him that. Or maybe he'd been secretly taking notes all along. She felt punched, winded.

Everything started to fall into place: his constant questions; the way he'd gone to see Celia; the disturbance in the attic; even the searching of her own room – after all, he'd been at the house 'fixing the piano' while she was away so that must have been him too. All he'd ever wanted from her was information for his article. There had been no romance: he'd just casually used her…again.

Terri meticulously closed the computer down and replaced it where it had been. A chill calm settled on her. She glanced at her watch, took her mug back to the kitchen and made herself more tea. She sat again on the sofa, glancing through the magazines. The wind continued to wail outside; rain began to patter against the window. It was after six when she heard Luc's car drive up the track into the clearing and stop. She heard the car door slam and then the front door open as he rushed in out of the rain.

'Terri,' he exclaimed. 'What a great surprise. I didn't expect you to be here.'

'No, I'm sure you didn't,' she said evenly, getting up.

She ignored him and walked across to the kitchen where she rinsed out her mug and set it aside. He came up behind her, putting his arms around her but she pushed him roughly away and turned.

'Hey, what's the matter?' he said.

'Where have you been Luc?'

'What?' He frowned and gave a short laugh. 'Is this some sort of joke? You know where I've been: to Paris to see my mother.'

'You're sure?'

'Of course I'm sure. What's this about?'

'It's about not telling me any more lies, that's what it's about. You see, I know.'

'You know what?' His eyes narrowed.

'Don't pretend any more Luc. You're good at cover stories aren't you? All those questions you ask – and so innocent, everyone's friend.'

'What are you talking about?'

'And me,' she went on, her voice rising. 'I wasn't much of a challenge, was I? I come across as all tough but you knew perfectly well that it was all an act. I was just ripe for someone's shoulder to cry on, wasn't I? And I suppose I've no-one to blame but myself: I knew what you were like right from the beginning and still I fell for it. So well done you. Congratulations.'

Terri walked back to the sofa, retrieved her bag and slung it on her shoulder. She felt the comforting shape of the diary inside it; to think she'd nearly shown it to him. She crossed to the door but Luc moved quickly and grabbed her by the arm.

'What do you mean?' he said, '*What I'm like*? What am I supposed to have done?'

'You're hurting me.' She tried to pull away from his grip and failed, stopped fighting and stared into his face. 'You should clear the messages on your machine more often if you're going to play the spy. I heard them.' Terri affected a light, childish voice: '*Bonjour Luc,*' she mimicked. 'It's Grace here.'

Luc nodded. 'Ye-es, Grace. So what? Anyway what were you doing going through my messages?'

'I came here because I couldn't wait to see you; I wanted to talk to you. Then I saw you had a new message so I listened to it. I thought it might be urgent. Then I listened to the other messages, yes. What a coincidence that you should go away the same weekend she suggests for a meeting. And I found your computer notes on Peter. You haven't got the whole story

301

but lack of facts never stopped you from writing a sensational article, did it?'

She could feel a mounting hysteria; she hoped it wasn't audible in her voice. She wanted to be strong here, desperately clinging on to the last crumbs of her dignity. She waited for a response but Luc glared at her, not offering one. He released her arm and she rubbed at the place where his fingers had been.

'It seems you have a very low opinion of me.' His voice when he did speak was low, controlled, bristling with anger. 'It's clearly pointless to try to explain. You've appointed yourself as judge and jury. And you appear to be very pleased to have found out that I'm the terrible person you thought I was at the start. Does it make you feel better in some way? Superior perhaps? Does it?'

Terri flinched back as if he had physically threatened her though he'd barely moved. He glared at her another moment, then turned and moved away into the back of the cottage and up the stairs. Terri immediately let herself out and began to run across the clearing into the woods. A minute later she was crying, weeping uncontrollably, and had to stop to steady herself against a tree, the rain running down her face mingling with her tears. How could she have been so stupid?

Chapter 20

Peter took the piece of cheese the stallholder offered him and chewed it appreciatively, rolling it around his tongue. Rather salty but creamy and good, yes, very good. He nodded and asked the man to cut him a small slab. He was at the Saturday morning market in Ste. Marguerite and the narrow streets were sticky and noisy with people. Pocketing his change, he noticed Terri at the adjacent stall. She was watching him with a strange expression on her face and produced a wan smile when she realised she'd been seen. She eased her way round a couple of people to get to him.

'So is this a cheese you can recommend?' she asked lightly, glancing at the paper bag he'd just been given.

'Indeed, it's excellent. Here...' He delved into the bag, broke off a piece of the cheese and offered it to her.

'Yes, very good,' she said. 'But...whoa...very salty.'

'Yes, isn't it? My doctors would disapprove. Coffee? That would wash it down.'

'Er...thank you, yes, OK.'

'Good.'

He took her to his favourite café and they sat on the terrace, watching the people passing by. Terri ordered a *café crème*; Peter asked for a large, black coffee and two chocolate brioches.

Terri was silent, her gaze wandering aimlessly around the terrace and out over the street. He noticed a slight tic in her lower eyelid. She had been working hard all week. What she still found to do he didn't know. The paintings had all been taken to the gallery; the invitations had long gone; the catalogue was being printed. Surely everything was organised? He'd become increasingly aware of her tension as she bustled up and down the studio, getting drinks, wandering in and out of his office, speaking to Nicole, stalking outside with her mobile phone stuck to her ear, speaking rapidly. She was in overdrive, it seemed to him, and she looked pale and drawn.

'Is there a problem?' he'd asked her eventually on the Friday morning. 'Why all the activity?'

'I'm sorry?'

'You haven't stopped all week. I thought the exhibition was all organised.'

'There are lots of loose ends to sort out and things to check up on. We don't want any unpleasant surprises, do we?'

'Certainly not.' He'd been obliged to stop himself from smiling then. He'd been getting rather nervous himself but watching Terri almost made him feel calm.

Now she sat stirring the spoon round and round in her coffee – which was odd because she took no sugar – and looking very serious.

'Do you have a job lined up?' he asked.

'Possibly. There's a post at the National in London. They're interviewing next month.'

'Need a reference?'

She smiled, properly this time, and her face briefly lit up.

'Thank you. I will. Though I think the exhibition will be my strongest reference…or not.'

304

Peter took a mouthful of his hot, sweet coffee and swallowed with satisfaction.

'I think it will be good,' he said. 'You can only do so much, then you have to let it go, let it out into the world, like…like…'

'Like a child,' offered Terri.

He frowned, studying her face in case she'd intended some significance to the remark, but she looked embarrassed as if she regretted saying it.

'I was thinking: like a painting,' he said. 'It's always tempting to think that you can make a picture perfect by keeping on working at it. But it's not true. You get so far and then you start to lose the original idea, the creative force, if you will. And it'll never be perfect, whatever you do. Nothing is, is it?' He picked up the plate on which the two chocolate brioches lay and held it in front of her. 'Brioche? You should. You're looking thin. Have you been eating?'

Terri took one of the pastries, flicking him an accusing look.

'You sound like my grandmother,' she said.

Peter didn't respond. He took the other brioche and pulled it into two pieces before eating it with relish. He watched Terri eat her own slowly, without apparent appetite.

'Have you and Luc had an argument?' he asked eventually.

Terri looked up at him with a frosty glare.

'I know it's none of my business,' he said, 'but I couldn't help notice that you're barely talking to each other. I'm not the best person to hand out advice, but I've learnt a lot…recently…and I know that it's important to keep talking.'

'Sometimes talking is what gets you into trouble in the first place,' she replied bitterly.

He got the impression that she was working herself up to saying something to him and he felt a frisson of unease. Perhaps she had found out something about her mother. He was curious, certainly, but he flinched from knowing yet. All was calm and well and he didn't want the boat rocked now. He was scared of what she might say and what chain of events it might set in motion. It would be a conversation best held another time – after the exhibition was up and running.

He forced a smile. 'So-o, you're off to Nice on Monday,' he said quickly.

'Yes.'

'Don't let Christophe tell you how they should be hung. You do it your way.'

'I will.'

'When will you be back? You are coming back before the Private View?'

'Yes, of course, but it depends how long it takes.' She played with the teaspoon in her saucer and added, 'How long is a piece of string?'

'Sometimes very long indeed,' he said, without thinking. He finished his coffee, slipped some money in the saucer on top of the bill and stood up.

'Thank you for your company,' he said. 'I'm afraid I really must be going.' And he moved away briskly, without looking back.

*

For Terri, impatient now to get on with hanging the exhibition, the weekend dragged. She wanted to set it up, attend the opening night and then leave. Le Chant du Mistral held

306

nothing for her any more and the last week could not come and go soon enough.

She had hoped to get an opportunity to return the diaries to the attic but Angela had caught what she described as 'the summer flu' and was spending the days drifting around the house in a silk wrap, looking forlorn, coughing and dabbing her nose with tissues. And Peter had spent much of the weekend down in the studio, effectively guarding the key, so returning to the attic was impossible. Guilt haunted her: she should have told him about Luc's article. She'd been on the point of doing so several times but never seemed to find the right moment or the right words.

On the Sunday, with time to kill and too much time to think, she went for a walk, grabbed some lunch, then retreated to her room again and tried to read; she watched television without concentrating. For the umpteenth time she wondered what Luc would write. How would he approach it? He had always been quick to defend Peter. Had that all been part of his act or did he truly like the man and would that be reflected in the article? At least she hadn't shown him the diaries but she did wonder what he would have made of the final one. She missed being able to talk things through with him for there was no-one else in whom she could confide.

Restless, she got up, retrieved the last diary from the drawer in her bedroom and read it through again, hoping something would finally slot into place. There were barely half a dozen entries.

August
I still keep feeling sick but I daren't tell anyone. It's
not just in the mornings though, so someone's bound
to notice. It must be what I was dreading. I think I've

missed a second period now. And he said it couldn't
happen the first time. Stupid of me to believe him but
it was only once. How can that be fair? If it is I don't
know what I'll do. Papa *will be so angry.*

At least Tom is better. He's still weak but now I
can play board games with him.

Of course, Tom had been ill at the end of the previous diary: a
virus, they thought. Now Josie recounted the cleaning of the
pool and noted that by the middle of the month Tom was
stronger and was allowed to go swimming again.

The weather is so hot. We go in the pool a lot. I even
persuaded Basma to borrow one of my costumes and
join us the other day. She seemed a bit embarrassed
but she can swim OK. She's a bit of a mystery really,
won't talk about herself or her past. Says she's made
a new start for a new country. Not sure what she
means. Papa *and Angela went away for a couple of*
nights or she wouldn't have dared come in. Maybe
he's starting to trust me again. I thought Sami was off
for the day too but he suddenly appeared, watching
us, glaring. I don't think he approved of Basma being
in the pool – or maybe it was Tom. Basma said Sami
thinks it would have been better if Tom hadn't lived.
He thinks he has no life and no future and causes so
much trouble and anguish. I was shocked but
remembered I used to think something similar myself.

Terri quickly turned the page. Her stomach began to knot up
inside, just as it had the first time she'd read these last entries.

I think I'm going to go mad here. I thought it was
going to work out but everything is horrible and

308

getting worse. I feel like a stranger here and Angela told me that Tom is going to be sent to a special boarding school in the autumn. 'So he can get help and be with other children like himself,' she said. But I'm sure he'll hate that. Papa's doing the same thing to him that he did to me. Tom hasn't been told yet so I'm not allowed to say anything. I feel like a traitor – especially when he's so happy here and in the pool.

Aunt Celia has been kind to me in her own strange way. One minute she ignores you then she says something which shows she's been paying attention all along. She told me her romance is over. No explanation. She looks unhappy and I feel sorry for her. She offered me money – 'just in case.' When I asked in case of what, she didn't answer. She must have guessed I'm pregnant. Maybe I should talk to her but can I can trust her not to tell anyone else?

Terri moved on to the last entry. The handwriting was uneven, scribbled in a hurry with a distraught hand.

This is going to be the last time I write to you. I'm relieved you're still here. This room is the only constant, the only thing I can rely on.

The worst possible thing had happened. Tom has died. I still can't believe it. He drowned in the pool but I don't know how. There was no-one around and I was supposed to be keeping an eye on him but I wasn't there. I had a secret appointment with the doctor. I'd done my own pregnancy test and it was positive but I wanted to be sure.

I'd asked Basma to watch over Tom. She's so good with him and I wasn't going to be long. Oh God, what have I done? When I got back to Le Chant I found Tom floating face down in the pool. There was no-one else there. He was dead. He didn't have his arm bands on. I jumped into the water but it was too late to do anything. It was so horrible. I shouted for help and eventually Sami came and found me in the pool holding Tom's poor head. When he asked me what happened I didn't know what to say. I didn't want to say where I'd been and I didn't want to accuse Basma. Now everyone blames me.

It's been awful ever since. The policeman questioned me for ages. He kept trying to get me to say I'd done it intentionally. He said he'd heard that Tom and I didn't get on. I wanted to shout no, it's not true, but what's the point - everyone knows how I used to feel about him. I told him I'd hadn't gone swimming with Tom because I didn't feel well so I went to the toilet in the pool room and it had happened while I was there. I know I shouldn't lie but I wanted to speak to Basma before I said anything else. Why wasn't Tom wearing his arm bands, he asked me. I said I thought he was. What else could I say? The policeman said they'd speak to me again. I'm sure he knew I was lying. He said there were other enquiries they want to make. Then papa *sent me to my room and told me to stay there. When I tried to find Basma, Angela told me* papa *had sacked her. Apparently her papers weren't in order and she was here illegally so with the police around, my father had no choice. She's already gone. Angela's the only one who's been kind to me.*

I have no idea where Basma has gone. I don't know what to do. It can't be her fault. Why should she hurt him? Or did she make a mistake? But the fault's mine. I shouldn't have left him.

I sneaked out yesterday and went to the studio. I tried to explain to papa *but he was so furious with me he wouldn't let me talk. He said he didn't know me anymore, that I was no daughter of his. We ended up shouting at each other, worse than ever before. I threw a couple of books at him and he slapped me hard. I fell over and my face is cut and bruised.*

I can't stand it anymore. It's the middle of the night – the only time I could risk doing this. It's my best chance of getting out and...No, I shan't say what I'm going to do. I'm leaving the book behind. Maybe papa *will find it and read it one day when I'm gone. Then perhaps he'll believe I'm innocent. We'll never meet again.*

Terri finished the entry and stared at the page, her eyes glazing over. It was harrowing but offered no real information: Terri was no wiser about the father of Josie's child and neither was it clear how Tom had died. Was Josie to be believed or was she just covering her back by leaving this account behind? Could she conceivably have let her brother drown so that he didn't have to go away to school? She didn't seem that unbalanced and Terri found it hard to believe. But if not Josie, was Basma to blame after all?

She closed the book and put it aside, got up restlessly and put the kettle on, tossing a teabag in a mug while the issues ran round and round in her head.

If Josie was telling the truth, Basma was clearly the key to what happened, but she was long gone. Thirty-five years gone. Did she go back to Algeria? Or did she find work somewhere else in Provence despite having no papers? There seemed to be little chance of finding her now. She supposed Lindsey was right: Sami might know. What had been his relationship with Basma exactly? But no, not Sami. After all surely it was no coincidence that Sami had been the first person to turn up when Josie was cradling Tom's dead body in her arms? And he had 'appeared' by the pool when Josie and Basma had been swimming with Tom that previous time when he wasn't supposed to be there. He was the man who had lamented the fact that the boy had survived so long, causing 'trouble and anguish'. So had Sami played some part in Tom's death? Maybe he persuaded Basma to do something terrible. *If* Josie was telling the truth. Terri sighed. The argument had come full circle; she needed to find Basma.

The kettle boiled and she poured water into the mug.

'You obviously can't ask Sami where to find Basma,' she muttered to herself, 'even if he knows.'

She stared unseeingly at the water as it darkened.

'But I'll bet Celia knows where she went,' she said suddenly. 'She seems to know just about everything else.' Terri rolled her eyes, pushing a weary hand through her hair. She didn't relish another cat and mouse conversation with Celia, but Basma was her only chance of finding out what happened. At least Celia would be unlikely to tell anyone else what she was doing.

She abandoned the stewing tea, slipped her feet into some sandals and went outside.

*

Terri found Celia sitting on the circular wooden seat fixed round the trunk of a cherry tree in the orchard. The sun was high but the tree offered generous shade and a light breeze blew up the hill from the valley below. Celia's pram was parked immediately behind the tree, a garish painting balanced on its top. Inconsequentially Terri noticed a couple of flies stuck in its oily surface. An empty plastic food box lay on the seat beside Celia who was staring down over the trees to the spread of the Durance valley, sucking vigorously on the velvet flesh of a peach. She looked up at Terri's approach, removed the peach from her mouth and produced a broad smile.

'Terri dear. What an unexpected pleasure. Have a seat.' She looked down at the half-eaten peach, appeared to consider whether it was too late to offer it to her new companion, then apologised for having finished all the food.

'It's OK, thanks.' Terri perched on the other side of the food box. 'I've had lunch.'

'Oh good.' Celia studied her a moment. 'You're off to Nice tomorrow I gather.'

'Yes. It'll be a relief to get the thing underway.'

Celia nodded, put the peach back to her mouth and sucked off the remaining flesh. She dropped the stone in the box and glanced at Terri expectantly.

'Celia, do you remember the *bonne* who used to work here, years ago. Her name was Basma.'

'Basma,' repeated Celia. 'That's an interesting question. The name seems a little familiar. Remind me why I should remember her?'

'She was working here when Tom died.'

Celia nodded slowly. Terri got the impression she had remembered all along. 'Ah yes, that Basma. Small girl; pretty. Good with Tom.'

313

'Yes. Do you know where she went when she left here?'

Celia grinned, eyebrows raised. 'That's a very long time ago, Terri. I'm flattered you think I'd remember. What makes you think I'd even know?'

'You seem to know everything else that's gone on here.'

'I'm afraid not. I wish I did.'

Terri examined her companion's face. It was the first time she'd heard Celia talk in an apparently earnest way – no sing-song flippancy or hedging answer. Or was this just a different game?

'Is finding Basma important?' Celia asked casually.

'I think so. Do you have any idea where she went?'

'You've found the last diary.' Celia stated it as fact, her gaze fixed down the valley.

'The last one? I don't know what you mean.'

Celia turned her head and rested accusing eyes on her companion.

'Oh come on, girl. We both know there were three diaries in 'Raphael'. But they don't finish the story. There had to be another one. And unless you've read the last one you wouldn't know that Basma was still here when Tom died. I'd be curious to know where you found it. I looked everywhere.'

Terri refused to commit herself.

'What do *you* remember of that day Celia, the day Tom died?'

Celia pulled her gaze away and sighed. She pulled a face.

'Not enough. If you knew in advance that something momentous and terrible would happen you'd make an effort to imprint it all in your mind, wouldn't you, every detail. But of course you don't know. And perhaps that's just as well.'

'But who was here, at Le Chant?'

'Well, let me see… I'd gone to an exhibition in Avignon. Angela was out, gone shopping, I think – Aix probably; she was always shopping back then. Peter spoiled her foolishly. He was in the studio working. He didn't need siestas then the way he does now. He used to get straight back to work after lunch.'

'He was *here*?'

'If you can call Peter 'here' when he's working,' said Celia drily. 'You know what he's like.'

'And Sami?'

'Sami?' Celia frowned and turned to look at Terri again. 'I don't know where Sami was. Why? What did Josie say in her diary?'

'I didn't say I'd found another diary,' said Terri coolly. 'I just wondered. Do you have any idea how I could track Basma down? Did she stay in France?'

'So it *is* important. Well, I'd have to think about it. Of course Sami might know.' Celia looked at Terri meaningfully, eyebrows raised again. 'But I'm guessing you don't want to ask him.'

'I don't intend to talk to anyone else about it.'

Celia nodded. 'I know people who know people. I'll ask a few questions…careful questions.' She put a smug finger up to touch the side of her nose. 'That's how you find things out in this world, my dear. It beats the internet every time.' She leaned her head back against the tree trunk and closed her eyes. 'But first I'm going to have a doze. I'm knackered.'

Terri got up and turned away. Out of the corner of her eye she saw a movement and looked round sharply. Sami was maybe ten metres away, idly raking at the rotten fallen cherries on the ground. He was moving away from her with his slow, silent tread, the collection of the old cherry stones an

315

apparently haphazard affair. How had neither of them noticed him there? She determinedly walked past him, gave him a greeting to which he touched his cap, and moved on, wondering just how much he had heard.

Chapter 21

Peter checked the lie of his cravat in the bedroom mirror one more time, accepted that he wasn't likely to improve it and moved away. He glanced at his watch. He'd looked at it some five minutes earlier but had barely registered the time. He crossed to the chest of drawers, picked up the copy of the catalogue Terri had given him and flicked through it once more. The thick, glossy paper felt satisfying to his touch; the effect was sophisticated and smart. The Opening View of his retrospective started in four and a half hours. It was *his* retrospective, maybe the ultimate glory of his career. He thought he should feel excited and proud; at this moment he just felt nervous and couldn't settle. Terri had asked if he would prefer to spend the Thursday night in Nice so that he'd be fresh for the show but he'd thought he'd go mad, stuck in a hotel room with nothing to do except worry about how the exhibition would go, so he'd declined. It was only around two and a half hours to Nice, three if the traffic were really bad. Better by far to drive to get there with not much time to spare. Even so, nerves had made him get ready too early. He strode to the window and looked out to the garden.

Peter's bedroom looked sideways out over the kitchen garden and the garages towards the winding lane through the trees. Beyond was the further blue line of the Luberon hills. It

317

was a pleasant aspect but one of the least impressive views from any of the rooms. It mattered little to Peter; he rarely spent time looking out of his window. Now his eyes vaguely scanned the ground outside while his mind returned again to the exhibition. The previous week had felt very long with Terri away in Nice, knowing that she was hanging his exhibition, not taking charge of it himself. Of course he could have insisted on being present but he'd recognised that it would be a mistake. Terri knew what she was doing. Even Christophe, he reluctantly accepted, probably did. Indeed, they would hang the exhibition better without his interference.

He heard a wardrobe door close and his mind turned to Angela who was in her bedroom next door getting ready.

'What time do we need to get there?' she'd said. 'Would you like me to drive?'

'You're coming?' In his surprise he thought he'd sounded rather stupid.

'Of course I'm coming,' she'd responded indignantly. 'This is a special event isn't it? I've lived with this exhibition for God knows how many months, Peter. I've got to *see* it. Anyway, I want to.' She'd smiled then and kissed him and he was pleased. They would never get back to the early days of their marriage – who ever did? – but he thought they had started moving in the right direction.

Would the man with whom she'd had the affair come to the exhibition? Not to the opening preview surely? But though invitations had been sent out to the great and good in the art world, there was nothing exclusive about the event. It was not policed in that way. He wondered if she still ever saw him. Of course she had apologised – she'd sounded sincere - and the implication had been that the affair was over. He wanted to put it out of his mind but it had proved harder than he'd expected.

When he saw her talking on her mobile he found himself trying to listen in; when she went out 'with friends' he was unable to stop himself from wondering if she would be seeing the man again; when she came home from a trip out he would look her over for any sign of intimacy with another. It was embarrassing and he felt foolish: a man of his age behaving in this way, but he had found that jealousy – or perhaps the fear of betrayal – was no respecter of age. Indeed, if anything, he thought getting older simply made it worse; he felt more vulnerable now.

Peter watched Sami walk into the kitchen garden with a spade and begin to turn over an area of ground, digging in the remains of some crop or other. He'd been behaving a little oddly this week, Sami. He seemed…preoccupied. Peter smiled to himself. That was a strange thing to think about Sami – he who never normally said ten words when five would do. But Peter thought he had seen so much of Sami over the years that he knew his mood, just by looking at him. He hoped the man was not sickening for something. Perhaps he should ask him. The idea came as a novelty and he let it roll around in his mind for a couple of minutes and decided that perhaps he would, when occasion allowed.

Peter glanced at his watch again. It was nearly time to go. Lindsey had said she'd make her own way. He supposed she might go with Thierry. Terri had already left; she wanted to check on everything before it started. And Luc? He was unsure what Luc was doing though there had clearly been no *rapprochement* between them. Still, it really was none of his business. Luc could fend for himself; Terri too, he didn't doubt.

He turned away from the window, picked up his waistcoat from the back of the chair and went next door to Angela's room, knocked on the door and walked in. She was sitting at her dressing table, brushing her hair, and turned to look at him as he entered.

'Are you really wearing that?' she asked.

*

Terri made another slow tour of the exhibition, exchanged remarks or information with anyone who approached her, watched people's reactions and listened in to conversations, trying to gauge the success or otherwise of the event. The turnout was wonderful - the gallery was crammed – and a loud babble of conversation filled the air. There were numerous critics chatting, taking notes, cracking jokes, though what they would say in the days that followed would be quite another matter. She knew from experience that compliments and good-natured banter at a preview did not always translate into good reviews.

She looked across the room to where her employer stood, talking loudly and flamboyantly to a freelance arts journalist, a woman in a tight dress and toe-squashing high heels. Peter was wearing red trousers, a grey silk shirt and a red cravat. His waistcoat was a swirling paisley in both red and grey. He leaned forward conspiratorially, said something then straightened up, added the punch-line, and appeared to laugh at his own joke. He was putting on the performance of his life and Terri found herself smiling. How she had come to like the man over these last few weeks and how unexpected that was. Peter was such a contradiction. In public he hid behind this act, behind the outrageous remarks and the equally attention-seeking clothes. He was infuriating and pompous; he was weak and sometimes cruel; but she had seen glimpses of his humanity and of a surprisingly big heart.

But then she frowned, thinking of that last conversation with Celia in the orchard. Terri had been under the impression that Peter had been away from Le Chant when Tom died. Ever since, she'd been trying not to give the revelation any significance but still the information bothered her.

A tall, dapper man came up to her and drew her attention away. Speaking English with a pronounced French accent, he complimented her on the exhibition and asked questions about her experience and her French language skills. He informed her that his name was Bernard Simon and he was the director of a large Parisian public gallery.

Angela interrupted them. 'Terri, dear, haven't you been busy?' She came alongside and put a proprietorial arm around her shoulder. In these last few days she'd been more like her old charming and affable self. Now she looked stunning in a pastel violet silk dress. She turned to the man and added, confidentially, 'She's worked so hard.'

Terri introduced *Monsieur* Simon but he made his apologies and moved away and she watched him go regretfully, scenting a lost job opportunity.

'So it's your last weekend with us,' Angela said, sipping her white wine. 'We'll be sorry to see you go.'

'It'll be strange to go. I hope I haven't caused too much trouble.'

'Of course not, darling. I'm sorry if we've had some misunderstandings. Nothing too serious though, hm? Now I have to tell you: Peter and I thought we'd have a little leaving party for you tomorrow night – you know, to see you on your way.'

'Really, that's not...'

'But we insist. It'll be a buffet…casual, you know? Family and a few close friends. Of course we'll be sure to invite Luc too.'

Angela patted Terri on the arm as if she'd just awarded her a consolation prize and slid away, still smiling. Terri watched her go but her thoughts inevitably turned towards Luc. She'd watched for him from the start of the evening and he'd arrived late. Since then they'd both moved in different areas of the gallery. Despite wanting to ignore him, she found herself surveying the sea of bodies, trying to locate him, checking to see to whom he was speaking. She toyed with trying to talk to him. In three days' time she would be on a plane and away from here for good, unlikely to see him again. She should ask him some questions, give him the chance to explain himself. Perhaps she should try to talk him out of writing the story? Or maybe, she thought, she was just desperate enough to want him to dupe her again? 'You really are pathetic,' she muttered to herself.

Even so, she glanced around and caught sight of him at the near edge of the linking room and began to nudge her way through the crowd towards him. But a collector who'd loaned one of the works approached her, keen to say how much he'd enjoyed the exhibition and by the time the conversation had finished, Luc was out of sight. Terri continued on her way to the next room and saw him nearby, in deep conversation with an older woman, heavy with make-up and, to judge from the way she kept touching him, somebody he knew well. Terri backed off, was asked a question by someone to her right and turned to answer. Then Peter appeared at her side and put his large hand on her shoulder.

'Excellent work, Terri,' he said gruffly. 'Excellent.' He reached down to take her hand and bent to kiss it. A flash lit

322

the air as two different people took photographs of them. Peter grinned at her. 'Bloody press,' he said, without rancour. 'Good picture for the rags tomorrow though.' He smiled. 'So...' He raised his eyebrows speculatively. '...we were thinking of having a little party tomorrow night – to see you off in style. What do you think? Could you cope with that?'

'Of course. Thank you. Angela has already mentioned it to me actually.'

'Has she, has she?' Peter automatically glanced round to where his wife was chatting animatedly to a man nearby. He returned his eyes to Terri's face. 'Well, there you are then. I believe Angela's going to invite Luc too. You don't mind, do you? No...well that's good.'

Terri glanced across to where Luc was still talking to the made-up woman. On a second inspection, she thought the woman looked familiar.

'Peter?' She touched his arm as he began to walk away. 'Do you know the woman Luc is talking to?'

'Mm?' Peter gazed across the room. 'Oh, that's Grace Meachin. He used to work with her at the paper.' He dropped his voice a notch. 'I hope she gives us a damn good review.' He moved away.

Terri stared across at Grace Meachin. The clearly intense nature of the conversation now made sense. Someone pushed into her line of vision and she turned away. The Parisian gallery director came back to speak to her. He asked her to email a résumé to him; he promised he'd send her details of a vacancy which would be coming up in the new year. She smiled and said all the right things as if someone else were speaking for her. He left and she wandered away aimlessly. She should have been excited but felt completely flat, devoid of emotion.

'You must be Terri?' said a voice behind her. Terri turned to find herself face to face with Grace Meachin.

'Yes, I am.' She studied the woman's features dispassionately: the make-up seemed to overlay a pinched complexion; the smile looked strained.

'I'm Grace Meachin,' the woman said and mentioned the newspaper as if she expected Terri to be impressed. 'Luc used to work for me.'

Terri nodded but said nothing. Grace cast an eye round the exhibition then fixed a shrewd gaze back on Terri.

'It's good,' she said simply. 'I'm impressed. When I heard he'd employed you to do this I laughed. Not because of you, of course.' She put an overly familiar hand on Terri's arm. 'But because of him. He had such a reputation. I didn't think you'd last a month. But here it is and it's a great show.' Grace nodded and puckered her lips up in an amused way. 'You've tamed the beast, it seems. He was almost civil to me.'

'He's been a pleasure to work with,' said Terri.

'Really? You surprise me. And perhaps it's you that's had such an effect on Luc too? There was a time when he wouldn't have dreamt of turning down the kind of opportunity I've been offering him. Now all he wants to do is paint…and presumably be poor.' She scoffed. 'I can't imagine he's going to be the next Peter Stedding. I mean…really…'

'Actually he paints very well,' said Terri. 'But he turned you down, you say?'

'Yes…twice now. I suppose he must mean it.'

Terri smiled. 'Well I don't think that had anything to do with me.' She bit back an insolent remark, reluctant to jeopardise Peter's reviews.

Grace stared at Terri for a moment with undisguised curiosity and a knowing smile.

'But I got the distinct impression from the way he spoke about you that you were rather close.'

'Did you? Well, Peter's studio is quite an intimate working environment; inevitably you get to know your colleagues well. Anyway, I'm glad you enjoyed the exhibition. Please excuse me.'

'Terri?' Grace put her hand on Terri's arm again.

'What?'

'Do you have a job to go to?'

'Possibly.'

'It's a very insecure profession, isn't it?' Grace smiled. 'I wondered if we could have a chat some time?'

'And that would be about?'

Grace glanced round and dropped her voice. 'It occurred to me that an insight into the workings of a professional artist's studio could make an interesting article. Peter's especially.' She brandished the catalogue. 'I see that you can write. It could be a lucrative assignment.'

'I see. I'm afraid you're wasting your time. I'm not interested. Excuse me.'

People were starting to leave and Terri moved away, searching everywhere for Luc. It was important that she speak to him; she had to apologise, seriously apologise. She negotiated more compliments and enquires and managed to check all three rooms of the exhibition. There was no sign of Luc anywhere. She found Lindsey and Thierry together near the doors and asked them if they'd seen him.

'He's gone,' said Lindsey. 'I saw him slip out a few minutes ago.'

*

325

The clearing in the woods was deserted when Terri walked there late the next morning. The door of the *bergerie* was closed and there were no lights; she knocked but got no answer and turned away. She should have come earlier but it had been nearly three by the time she'd got to bed that morning and she'd overslept. Now she'd missed him and her carefully rehearsed apology would have to wait. Would he come to her leaving party that night? She doubted it. Maybe he'd gone away, determined not to see her again before she left. With her suspicions, distrust and allegations she'd ruined everything. She couldn't blame Luc; she'd been an idiot.

There was a clear blue sky; it was pleasant and warm but Terri was in no mood to linger and she returned to her room. There were things to sort out; she should start packing. Fleetingly, she considered calling at the *pigeonnier*. She had neither seen nor heard from Peter's sister since seeking her out under the cherry tree, and Celia hadn't come to the exhibition preview, apparently unwell and unable to face the journey. 'Food poisoning,' Peter had declared roundly. 'Hardly surprising; she eats some very strange things.' But, increasingly, Terri thought chasing after Basma was a fruitless exercise anyway. With hindsight, she wished she had not been so quick to involve Celia.

Barely ten minutes later she was pushing note pads into a bag when she heard a light rapping on the patio doors and, quickly looking up, saw Celia standing outside, gesticulating at the lock and quickly glancing around behind her. Terri let her in and pushed the door to, automatically looking out herself across the terraced gardens.

'Are you all right?' said Terri.

'Yes, yes, dear. A bit weak is all. Something disagreed with me. A bad mushroom perhaps. I pick them in the woods, you know. I don't suppose you've got any brandy have you? No? Well, not to worry.'

'Tea?'

Celia gave a pained expression and shook her head.

'I've found out where Basma is,' she said in a stage whisper, glancing towards the patio doors before continuing. 'She's working as a housekeeper at a hotel in St. Rémy-de-Provence. She's married now. Finishes work around three-thirty usually. I can tell you how to find it.' She grinned broadly. 'This cloak and dagger stuff is exciting isn't it? Have you got a map?' She surveyed the room. 'Have you really been living like this for six months dear? It's so *spartan*.'

*

The hotel stood on the outskirts of St. Rémy de Provence, a cream-painted rendered building set back off the road in large leafy gardens. A broad gateway in the walled perimeter gave access to a car park, dotted with olive trees. Terri drew the car to a halt and glanced at her watch: it was twenty past three. She turned off the engine and glanced around. Though not exactly deserted – there were a handful of cars parked – the place was uncomfortably quiet. Sure that her very presence looked suspicious, she thought she stood out like an adult in a children's playground. She fingered the ring in the pocket of her jacket, checking it was still there, got out of the car and made her way across to reception.

The girl behind the desk, olive-skinned with short, dark hair, dragged her eyes from a computer screen and smiled a welcome. Terri explained that she was looking for a Basma Chabanas whom she believed worked at the hotel.

'Is she working today?' Terri asked.

The girl studied her a moment, frowning, then tapped at her keyboard, glancing up at the screen. She turned back to Terri.

'Yes, she's working. Is there a problem?'

'No. No problem. I was simply hoping to speak to her when she finishes. Will that be soon?'

'Yes...probably. They should be back with the keys before long.' The girl still regarded her suspiciously. 'Please take a seat.'

Terri said she preferred to wait outside. She couldn't imagine making her approach under the watchful gaze of the receptionist, and Basma was sure to pass that way - it was the nearest way through to both the road and the car park. She slipped out into the sunshine and perched on a low stone wall which gave her a view through the glass doors of the entrance straight into reception.

Each minute felt like an hour. Terri kept glancing at her watch. She had to be back at Le Chant for the party at seven-thirty and it was a good hour's drive from St. Rémy. Three-thirty came and went. Three forty-five. Three fifty-five. Perhaps Basma had used another exit after all. But she hadn't returned the keys to reception so hopefully she was changing out of her work clothes ready to go home. Terri decided to give it another ten minutes; she got up and began pacing up and down. A couple approached the door, suitcase in tow, and went into register. They were still at the desk when Terri saw two women cross the entrance hall. One of them stepped behind the desk and exchanged a few words with the receptionist before they both walked outside. The taller, broader woman was fair with dyed blonde hair. The smaller woman was slight, her dark hair peppered with grey, her skin the colour of pale cinnamon. Terri took a couple of steps towards them.

'Basma Chabanas?' she said uncertainly, her gaze settling on the smaller of the two women.

'*Oui*,' Basma had large, soft eyes and a nervous smile, quickly replaced by watchful mistrust. The lines on her face suggested that she often frowned. 'What do you want?' she asked in French.

'Could I have a word?'

The blonde woman quickly said her farewells and left, walking away towards the car park.

'I don't know you do I?' Basma pulled the strap of her bag higher onto her shoulder as if about to leave.

Terri hesitated. She had one chance here to persuade Basma to talk to her.

'No, you don't know me. I've been working at Le Chant du Mistral, curating an exhibition for Peter Stedding. In the course of my research, I found out that you were friendly with his daughter, Josie, and I want to know more about her. I wondered if you would be prepared to talk to me about your time there?'

Terri felt as though she were holding her breath. It had sounded so much better when she'd rehearsed the words in the car on the way. And now an expression of fear had indeed formed on Basma's care-worn features; she was already backing off.

'I promise I won't pass on anything you don't want me to,' Terri added hastily. 'Look…' She fumbled in her pocket and withdrew the ring. It was a gold hoop, asymmetrically set with aquamarines, which Celia had prised from her finger, insisting that Terri took it with her. All those years ago, in the grounds of Peter's estate, Basma had apparently admired the ring and Celia had joked that she would leave it to her in her will. It would be a gesture of faith, she'd said, for she had always got on well with the girl. Now Terri held it out for Basma to see. '…Celia told me to bring this to prove I meant no harm. She said she promised she would leave it to you in her will. Do you remember the ring?' She held it out on the flat of her hand within Basma's reach.

Basma glanced at it and nodded warily. 'Did *Monsieur* Stedding send you?'

'No. This was my idea, honestly. It's a long story but I'll explain if you'll let me.'

Basma's dark eyes flicked behind Terri as if someone else might be hiding there.

'I'm alone,' said Terri. 'Completely alone. I promise. Could I buy you a drink somewhere? A coffee? Something cold? Then I could explain to you what I want to know and why. If you don't believe me, you don't have to say anything. I'll go and that's the end of it.'

She waited. Basma was staring at her, expressionless. Eventually, she nodded.

'There is a café over there,' she said, and led the way with short brisk steps.

The café-bar was set back off the road with a terrace of tables in front. Basma chose a table on the edge of the terrace, pushed in beside a trough of box hedging, and they both sat, neither speaking until the order had been taken. Terri was aware of Basma suspiciously scrutinising her face. The waiter returned with an espresso for Basma and a Perrier for Terri and they both watched his receding figure.

'Where are you from?' asked Basma.

'England.'

Terri poured the fizzing water over the ice in her glass and replaced the bottle on the table. She raised her head and met Basma's gaze.

330

'Six months ago,' she began, 'I came to Le Chant du Mistral to work as a curator for an exhibition by Peter Stedding. I'd never been to Provence before. As far as I was concerned it was just a job – and a way to get away from a man who was causing me trouble. But Celia said I bore a surprising resemblance to Peter's first wife. She implied that there might be a connection between me and the family.

'I thought it was an absurd idea. But my own mother died young and she was always a mystery to me so I tried to find out more. I already knew that Peter's first wife had died in childbirth. It was only a matter of time before I then heard about how his son Tom had accidentally drowned and his elder sister had killed herself soon afterwards...or perhaps run away. Apparently she was pregnant at the time.' Terri paused. Basma was looking down now, vigorously stirring sugar into her coffee. 'I may have been the child she was carrying,' Terri added.

Basma said nothing.

'Anyway, it seems a lot of people don't think Tom's death was an accident at all; they think Josephine killed her brother. So I wondered what you knew about it. It's important to me. You see, in her diary, Josie says that she wasn't there when the accident happened.'

Basma looked up sharply, eyes wide. 'She kept a diary? What else does she say?'

'She says she went to see a doctor in Ste. Marguerite and when she got back Tom was alone. He was dead in the pool.'

'She said I killed him?'

'No,' said Terri quickly. 'No. She said she was sure you wouldn't have hurt him.'

'She said that? In her diary? Have you got it here?'

331

Terri shook her head. Still uncertain where she stood in this conversation; she wasn't prepared to hand over a diary she wasn't supposed to have to a woman she didn't know.

Basma's eyes narrowed. 'Are you recording this conversation?' she demanded suddenly.

'No, certainly not.'

'Prove it.'

Terri emptied out her pockets. She stood up, turned round and showed Basma the inside of the cotton jacket which she had thrown over the back of her chair. The woman looked satisfied.

'Who else has seen this diary?' she asked.

'No-one. I haven't shown it to anyone. Look, I just want to know what happened. Josie says she left you to look after the boy while she went to the doctor. What happened after she'd gone? Was there someone else there?'

'I did not hurt him,' said Basma emphatically. 'But it's a long time ago. I've been many places since then, done many things. I'm not sure what happened now.'

'Really? I'd have thought it was a day you'd always remember. Tom liked you and Celia said you were good with him. I thought maybe you liked him too.'

The aggression faded from Basma's face to be replaced by an expression of profound sadness. She sat back in her chair and stared towards the chalky outlines of the Alpilles hills as if trying to come to a decision. Terri said nothing, and waited.

'You think Josie was your mother?'

'Yes. It's possible.'

Basma studied her again, perhaps assessing her features for a likeness.

'And what will you do when you find out what happened?' she asked.

Terri shrugged. 'I don't know. Nothing. It's for me. I just want to know.'

'Perhaps it would be better if you don't know. For if you know you have to carry the knowledge with you…forever.'

'Josie didn't want to tell anyone that she'd left Tom with you because she didn't want to get you into trouble. So she was blamed.' Terri leaned forward, passionate suddenly, angry. 'My mother killed herself when I was a child. I want to know *why*. I want to know what happened.'

Basma continued to consider her thoughtfully.

'It's true,' she said slowly. 'I did like Tom. He was a good boy. And I liked Josie too, though she was more serious…she was an emotional girl. But you have to understand: I am Algerian. I did my work. I kept out of trouble. It was very important for me that I didn't attract trouble.' She paused, chin raised defiantly. 'I came here illegally, you see. No papers. I have them now, but not then. I had no position. No-one would believe me. It was a very difficult situation.'

'Yes, I can see that.'

'Can you?' Basma shook her head, smiling ruefully. 'I doubt it. How would you understand? It's not always easy now. Then it was much harder.' She drank her coffee, finishing it in one gulp. Again she looked poised to go.

'Maybe you're right,' said Terri. 'How could I understand? So tell me what it was like. Help me to understand.'

Basma watched her, unblinking. 'Sami is still there?'

'Sami? Yes. Why?'

'Does he know you're here?'

'No. Only Celia knows.'

'So he doesn't know about the diary?'

Terri shook her head. 'No. I didn't tell him. Are you scared of Sami? Was he there, that afternoon?'

'Sami is always there. And he's been at the house for many, many years. *Monsieur* Stedding is very good to him.'

'Wasn't he good to you?'

'I hadn't been there that long when the boy died.'

'I don't see what you mean.'

Basma leaned forward suddenly, rested her elbows on the table and pushed her face close towards Terri's.

'Do you really want to know what happened?' she asked fiercely. 'Because I do know. But no-one wants to know the truth. And who will believe me anyway?'

'I will.'

Basma stared at her, clearly trying to gauge if she meant what she said. Then she began to talk in a quiet, urgent voice, and the words tumbled out as if she'd been waiting for this chance to speak for years.

Chapter 22

Terri drove the long winding lane up to Le Chant du Mistral and parked her car next to Angela's BMW. It was already after seven o'clock - much later than she had expected to be. All the way back Basma's story had run through her mind, over and over and over. Getting out of the car, she tried to clear her head and focus on the evening ahead instead. Walking up the path from the car park, she was aware of the diary in her bag. Now it felt like an incendiary device, waiting to burst into flames. Had Celia realised what Terri would find out if she found the diaries and followed up the leads? What strange game was she playing? It would have been so good to talk to Luc; she badly needed his input into her confused thoughts but that was out of the question now. Even if he was prepared to speak to her, there was no time; the party would be starting in a few minutes.

Terri crossed the courtyard. The meeting with Basma had left her jumpy and she regularly glanced round, checking to see if anyone was watching her. Letting herself in through the front door, she stepped as quickly and lightly as she could across the hall and through the sitting room to the rear hall. Once in her room, she locked the door with hands that shook, then leant back against it.

She knew she should do something about what she had just learned. But what? And was Basma to be trusted? In a

335

sudden change of heart at the end of their meeting, she'd said Terri could do what she liked with the information, that it was time that the truth came out. She would not cover it up any more. But was it the truth?

Terri straightened up and began to peel off her clothes. She needed to wash and dress; she needed to compose her thoughts and paint on a smile.

*

Peter unlocked the door to the studio and let himself in. The falling sun shed a warm pink glow through the room. He loved this melting light – if it had a smell it would be musky – and the place was empty, as he preferred. Even so, it was going to be strange without Terri squirrelled away in her makeshift office. He wandered across to the door of her room. All her things had gone and it was a storeroom again. It had a forlorn air, he thought, like an empty ballroom when the dance is over. He was going to miss her enthusiasm and her drive – and, yes, even the verbal sparring. Stubborn, forthright and tenacious, she had shaken him up, breathed new life into him.

He walked into his study and glanced at the clock on the shelf. There was no need to rush; he was dressed and ready. He poured himself a whisky, his mind still on Terri. It was unthinkable that she should be his granddaughter and yet he'd become increasingly convinced that it was so. He had certainly heard stranger stories. But if Terri's mother was Josie, his daughter was dead and the thought wrenched at him deep inside. How he wished now that he had never pushed her away. It had been an act of self-preservation, a way of coping with his own sense of guilt. He'd been cowardly and cruel.

He knocked back the whisky and took Maddy's jewellery box from the cupboard. There was still time to make some reparation. He extracted the small padded box containing the sapphire earrings, put it in the pocket of his trousers and put the rest away. Locking the studio door and retracing his steps back to the house, he found himself whistling.

*

Terri walked through and paused inside the drawing room door. Someone was playing ragtime piano while guests stood around in small groups, clutching drinks. A buzz of conversation punctuated by occasional laughter competed with the music. She could see Angela, stunning in a sheath of pale blue satin, chatting nearby to an elderly couple.

'Terri darling,' said Angela, smiling a welcome and moving across to join her. 'Don't you look pretty? I was beginning to get worried about you. Is everything all right?'

Terri forced a smile. 'Yes, fine. I'm sorry I'm late. I completely misjudged the time.'

'Not to worry. Not everyone has arrived yet.' Angela leaned close and dropped her voice. 'I'm afraid Luc isn't here. Peter says he hopes to come along later. I'm so sorry.' She straightened up and gave an expansive smile to the room. 'But you know most of these people don't you? We'd intended something smaller but it's difficult to leave people out, you know? Anyway, everyone's waiting to see you. Oh, Hugh and June have just arrived. Do excuse me.'

Terri stood, looking round blankly. She recognised a few faces and some of them had been at the preview the night before though she barely remembered their names. Fortunately there was no sign of Celia but Lindsey was standing with

Thierry by the patio doors. At the top of the room, Corinne, wearing her customary black dress and white apron, was moving back and forth between the kitchen and the dining room, carrying plates of food.

'Terri, you haven't got a drink.' Peter's booming voice cut through the chatter and he descended on her, pushing a glass into her hand. 'Don't look at it so suspiciously. It's a Manhattan. Haven't you had one before? Try it. Everyone's talking about the exhibition. Such a success. Have you seen the reviews today?'

'I'm afraid not.'

'No? I'm shocked. I thought that would've been the first thing you'd have done.' Peter stared at her as if only now seeing her properly. 'Are you feeling well? You're pale.'

'Yes, of course. I'm fine, just a little tired.'

'Reaction,' said Peter stoutly. 'Hardly surprising. Well, believe me, the reviews are excellent.'

'Good, I'm glad. You deserve them.'

'We all deserve them.' He raised his glass to her. 'Congratulations my dear.'

Terri raised her own glass to touch his. 'And to you.'

'I'm afraid Luc's not here. I was hoping you'd both…you know.' Peter cleared his throat and left the thought unfinished. A stocky man with a grey moustache approached and patted Peter on the back. 'Nigel, how are you?' Peter turned and flashed Terri a smile. 'Excuse me, dear. Nigel's an old friend. I'll go and get those reviews for you when I get a moment.' He moved away. 'Yes, Nigel, thank you. Glad you enjoyed it.'

The next couple of hours passed in a daze. Terri spent time with Lindsey and Thierry, chatted to people she didn't know and ate food she didn't want. She was complimented on the exhibition and accepted the congratulations by rote. Angela, drink in hand, sang a couple of songs; Peter persuaded Lindsey to play the piano. He retrieved the reviews and Terri dutifully read them but struggled to take them in. Then he was standing at the head of the room, clapping his hands and calling for quiet.

'Thank you everybody. I won't keep you long. But, as you all know, this little party tonight is a farewell affair for Terri.'

People moved back leaving a broad semi-circle of space in front of him and several hands pushed Terri forward until she was standing on the edge of it. Behind Peter, she saw Celia walk into the room and look in her direction. Terri quickly pulled her eyes away.

'Don't be shy, Terri,' said Peter. 'You weren't that shy in the studio as I recall when you were telling me how I should re-organise myself.' There was a sprinkling of laughter. Terri tried a smile. 'Don't worry, I won't embarrass you for long.' He paused and embraced his audience with a roaming gaze. 'It's hard to believe that it's only six months since Terri came into our lives. She's managed to not only change my working habits – something which no-one would have thought possible…' (More laughter) '…but she has entered our affections too and become, if I might make so bold, one of the family.'

Peter turned towards the archway and nodded. Corinne walked towards him pushing a trolley bearing glasses filled with champagne. Peter turned back to his audience.

'I'd like you each to take a glass of champagne for the toast.' He waited while the glasses were distributed. The buzz of chatter in the room slowly subsided and was replaced with an expectant silence. 'The retrospective is excellent,' Peter went on. 'Thanks must go to Terri who has done me proud, but sadly she must move on. Someone else's gain will be our loss.

But we would like, Terri, to drink to your future health and happiness and what we are sure will be your continued success. Though we hope that your success won't be so great that you forget where we are.' He hesitated. 'Indeed there is actually a strong possibility that Terri *is* a member of the family and I couldn't be happier about it.' He looked at her directly. 'I'm sure I speak for Angela and Lindsey if I say that you will always be welcome here.' Peter lifted his glass. 'To Terri,' he bellowed.

Her name was echoed round the room and everyone drank the toast.

'Terri?' Peter produced a small blue padded box and held it out to her on his upturned palm. 'Please accept this small gift as a token of my appreciation. These belonged to Madeleine. It seems appropriate that you should have them.'

Terri frowned and glanced around uncertainly. Celia had moved to her left. A short distance to her right, Angela was staring, open-mouthed, an expression of horrified amazement on her face.

'Really Peter, it's not necessary,' said Terri.

'For once in your life, don't argue.' Peter thrust his hand further towards her. 'For God's sake, just take it.'

Terri relinquished her champagne flute to Celia's grasp, reluctantly picked up the box and lifted back the sprung lid. Inside, resting on a padded cushion was a pair of stunning diamond and sapphire earrings. She pulled one out and watched the stones dance with light as they fell over her fingers.

'They're beautiful.' She lifted her eyes to Peter's face. He was smiling but she felt dead inside.

'I remember Madeleine wearing those,' proclaimed Celia. 'She loved them. She'll be so glad they've come to you.'

'Indeed,' Peter grunted. 'Well, time we got the coffee going, hm?'

He moved away towards the kitchen. People began to cluster round, wanting to see Peter's gift. There were murmurs of astonishment at the generosity of it, puzzled questions about the reference to Madeleine and then whisperings about 'some long lost granddaughter'.

'Silly old fool,' Terri heard Angela mutter at her shoulder. 'Stupid, bloody silly old fool,' she said more loudly as her temper grew. 'What *does* he think he's playing at?'

Her anger was palpable. The veneer of hospitable charm had slipped away and the green eyes now fixed on Terri held pure hatred. Terri had a sudden memory of the dinner they had shared, out under the pergola, when Angela's easy conversation had smoothly given way to insinuation, accusation and barely veiled warning, before just as smoothly reversing again. This woman wore a different mask for every occasion; she was clearly able to change them at will.

Angela turned on her heel, pushing her way through the circle of people towards the kitchen. A couple of minutes later raised angry voices could be heard from behind the half-open door.

The interest in the earrings quickly subsided and people began to shuffle away, embarrassed, talking loudly to cover the row. Lindsey exchanged a few words with Terri and said she was leaving with Thierry. Corinne, with a fixed expression, emerged through the door with a trolley of coffee things. Terri quickly closed the jewellery box and pushed it into her clutch bag. Celia thrust Terri's champagne flute back at her.

'Drink up,' she said. 'You can't waste good bubbly.'

Terri took it and immediately put it down on a side table nearby.

'I don't want it,' she said crisply.

'Now, now. What's got into you?'

'You should know,' snapped Terri. She couldn't tolerate Celia's whimsy when the woman had been manipulating her into this intolerable position all along.

The kitchen door banged and there was silence. The conversation started up again and an atmosphere of fake bonhomie filled the room. Peter walked in, looking strained, took a cup of coffee and engaged in loud but flat conversation. Celia began telling Terri about a painting she'd started on the Thursday but hadn't been able to finish because of the weather. She rambled on, wondering when the light conditions would be the same again. Terri excused herself and walked away.

People had started to leave; Peter was sitting on a sofa, looking suddenly very weary. A few people made their excuses; others just slipped away. Terri went across to him.

'Are you all right?' she asked.

He raised bleary eyes. 'Mm? Yes, champion m'dear. Champion. Did you have a good party?'

'Yes, thank you. And thank you for the earrings. They're lovely but you shouldn't have done that.'

'I wanted to.'

'Angela didn't like it.'

'No. No, she didn't. I hoped she'd understand.' He frowned, then sighed heavily. 'God I'm tired. I should go to bed.' He made a weak effort to get up and she automatically put out a hand to help him. He waved her away impatiently and struggled to his feet. 'I'm not decrepit yet,' he said brusquely.

The *salon* had rapidly emptied; footsteps and subdued voices could be heard from the terrace. Celia, a fresh glass of champagne in one hand, a cigarette in the other, was standing just outside the open patio doors, staring up at the sky.

'Is the sky more of an ultramarine or an indigo, do you think?' she could be heard enquiring of no-one in particular.

Terri walked with Peter through to the hall. Corinne had already set the dishwasher going and gone home. After the bustle of the party the house had a melancholic air. Terri watched Peter slowly climb the stairs to his room, then turned away and walked into the sitting room. The front of the room was thick with darkness but the table lamp was still lit on the cupboard at the back and in the circle of light it shed, Terri noticed something wrong with the portrait. She moved closer. The canvas had been repeatedly ripped across Madeleine's face, leaving sections of it hanging down in strips.

'Oh my God,' she said, stretching her fingers up to push the canvas back in a completely futile gesture. 'No...it can't be...what's happened?'

'Yes, *such* a shame,' said a voice behind her.

Terri spun round but struggled to see into the gloom. A dark shape rose up from the wing-backed chair and walked into the ring of light. Terri already knew who it was, though Angela's distinctive voice now had a slurred edge. She'd clearly drunk a great deal and still had a balloon glass in her left hand containing a finger of brandy. In the dim light her eyes glinted darkly. It was clear her anger had little abated.

'But I suppose we'll manage to find something...' Angela hesitated and gestured vaguely with her right hand which held a sharp little kitchen knife. '...fresher, to replace it. Did I hear Peter going to bed, by the way?'

'Did you do this?' Terri pointed at the canvas with a shaking hand. 'What the hell were you thinking of?'

'Don't you dare speak to me like that, Terri *Challoner*. You're not family, whatever the stupid man says. Not now, not ever, not if I have anything to do with it.' Angela's eyes narrowed. 'I knew all along that you were in some conspiracy with that crone. And now you've got the old fool giving you Madeleine's jewellery. What's next? A new car perhaps, a down payment on a flat? Lindsey pushed out and forgotten because *you've got Madeleine's eyes.*' She scoffed.

'I didn't ask for presents…or anything else. That's not what it's been about and you know it. I just wanted to know if Josephine was my mother.'

'Darling, you can drop the act now. This is me, remember?' Angela took a sip of brandy. 'You know, I really thought Peter had begun to lose interest in this fantasy but then we get that nauseating performance…and in front of everyone too.' She regarded Terri disdainfully. 'There's no proof that Josephine was pregnant, you know. That's just Celia's bit of fiction.'

'But she *was* pregnant,' said Terri, increasingly angry. 'She said so in her last diary.'

'Oh please. There are no diaries, Terri.'

'Yes there are. There are four and I've read them all.'

'You found them?' Angela was frowning now. 'Where?'

'In the attic.'

Angela studied Terri's face, then laughed shortly.

'You're bluffing. I searched everywhere up there for those diaries. They weren't there.'

'They were. I found them weeks ago. Though it took me a while to find the last one. It was hidden in the writing box.'

344

A flicker of doubt ran across Angela's eyes. She raised her chin in a show of defiance. 'Show me this diary then.'

Terri shook her head. 'I'm keeping it in a safe place.'

'Are you trying to blackmail me?' Angela pointed the knife dangerously close to Terri's face, her eyes blazing. 'You are, aren't you? Well, it won't work. You're a parasite.'

'No,' said Terri in a quiet, steely voice. 'It's you. You're a cheat and a liar.' She met Angela's gaze and stared her out.

Angela looked disconcerted, momentarily uncertain. She let the hand drop and turned away, glancing back at Terri uneasily. 'What is it you want exactly? Tell me. I can see you're not going to go until you get something out of this.'

'What I *wanted* was to find out the truth about Josie and Tom. And now I have.' Terri snorted, scornfully. 'And what a sordid story it is. Even so, I'd half decided to let it go. I thought, why make Peter hurt again after all this time? But I can't let it go. And no, Angela, I won't.'

'Peter? Everyone always worries about Peter, don't they? Poor Peter this and poor Peter that. What about me? No-one thinks how hard it was on me, always playing second fiddle to that.' She pointed the knife towards the shredded portrait. 'Little Miss Perfect there. And not only do I have to live in her shadow but I inherit her insolent daughter and a spastic boy as well.'

'Is that why you let Josephine take the blame for Tom's accident: to get rid of both of them in one go?'

'I don't know what you're talking about.'

'Yes you do. You'd arranged to meet one of Peter's students in the pool house. I'm guessing you'd found out somehow that Josie had an appointment at the doctor's so you thought you'd be safe. Then you saw Basma bring Tom to the pool instead and you had to get her out of the way. But if you'd

345

told her to take the boy and go, Tom would have made a fuss, so you said you'd watch over him and you sent Basma away. Or maybe you saw a perfect opportunity to get rid of him permanently and it wasn't an accident at all.'

'You're making this up,' said Angela. 'I wasn't even at the house when Tom went swimming. I only got back after it happened.'

Terri ignored her. 'When Tom asked for his arm bands, you told him to manage without them. *You're too big a boy to use those now,* you said.'

'You can't possibly know what happened,' said Angela, looking scared. 'It won't say in the diary; Josephine wasn't there.'

'No, exactly, because Josephine wasn't there. But Basma was - and she heard what you said to Tom. She hung around, didn't she?'

Angela's expression froze, then she laughed, ostentatiously downed the last of the brandy and put the glass on the sideboard. 'Basma was a liar, a thief and an illegal immigrant. I sent her packing.'

'Well, she's legal now - and ready to talk. She was never a thief or a liar, she simply didn't want to leave Tom with you - she'd seen the way you treated him. So you got cross and told her to disappear, permanently, or you'd tell the authorities about her. You couldn't risk her saying who you'd been meeting. Later, you'd tell Josie that it was Peter who'd sent her away. And then you let Tom drown while you made out with your lover, just a stone's throw away. Tell me, was it easy to ignore his distress while he thrashed around in the water, struggling to breathe?'

'No,' pleaded Angela. 'No, you're twisting everything. I didn't do it intentionally. I would have helped him if I'd realised there was a problem. By the time I got dressed he was already dead. I never meant that to happen.'

'But you didn't give him his arm bands on purpose. He had to have them to protect him from his spasms.'

'No, no,' she almost shouted. 'I didn't think it would matter. I didn't like handling him. He was…all hands and silly grins…and he dribbled. I didn't like to touch him. And he could swim surprisingly well. I didn't know about the spasms. I didn't.'

'You knew. Everyone knew. And you abandoned him. When Josie came back from her appointment with the doctor, she found Tom dead in the water and no-one else around. What sort of woman are you to leave a boy to die while you cheat on your husband, then let the boy's sister take the blame?'

'The sort who is treated as second best behind a dead woman who can do no wrong.' Angela pointed angrily at the painting again. 'I was just looking for a little tenderness,' she said pathetically. 'I mean is that so bad? I was unhappy. I was young and lonely. I didn't mean anything by it.' Her voice hardened again. 'Don't you dare lecture me.'

'You had tenderness,' said a man's voice.

Terri swung round to see Peter standing in the doorway behind them. He stepped further into the room and let his gaze wander over the scene, then settle on the damaged portrait beyond the two women.

'Peter darling…'Angela stepped quickly across to join him. '…what are you doing here?'

'I came down to get a book and I wondered what was going on. What have you got in your hand?'

Angela looked down at the knife. 'Oh, this, I…' She put it down hastily on the side table and looped a hand through his

347

arm. 'Peter, darling. I'm so sorry I got cross earlier. I'd had too much to drink.'

He shook her off. 'I've been standing outside the door, Angela,' he said coldly.

'Darling, what's the matter? Oh, it's the picture isn't it? I'm so sorry. Really I am. But we can get it restored can't we? They can do wonderful things now. I don't know what got into me. I…I had a brainstorm, that's what it was. I've been under a lot of pressure recently.'

Peter's lip curled contemptuously. 'It's no good, Angela. I heard everything. I can't believe you allowed me to think Josie killed Tom. The hell it's been all these years, thinking she'd done it, blaming her but blaming myself more for letting her become so unstable. What must she have…?' He broke off and ran a distracted hand across his forehead, closing his eyes for a moment. He opened them again, fixing Angela with his pale gaze. 'And you've got the nerve to suggest I neglected you. We'd hardly been married six months when Tom died and I'd done everything I could to make you happy in those early days. You lacked for nothing. And you repay me by having an affair with one of my own students? And while my precious son was drowning? For Christ's sake Angela. Terri was right: what sort of woman are you? God knows I've blamed myself for not making you happy these last years, but not then.' He shook his head. 'So it's been all the way through has it? I don't suppose Lindsey's even mine, is she?'

'No, Peter, it wasn't like that…really…'

Peter turned to Terri.

'Terri, please leave us.'

She nodded. Peter put a hand briefly to her shoulder as she passed him.

'How can you treat her like that Peter?' she heard Angela say, plaintively, as she walked out into the hall. 'She's fooling you.'

*

Terri closed the door behind her and stood, dazed. She heard the voices in the sitting room rise in anger and quickly walked away, reluctant to hear any more. Wandering into the kitchen, she removed the stopper from an opened bottle of red wine, poured herself a glass, and meandered through to the drawing room. It was empty. The lights were still on but Celia had gone, leaving the patio doors wide open. The room smelt of expensive perfumes, wine and coffee; odd cups and glasses still lay abandoned in places, some half full. Terri flicked the lights off, paused a moment to let her eyes adapt to the gloom, then picked her way down the room and walked out of the patio doors onto the terrace. The moon was new – an elegant crescent hanging in a clear dark blue sky. Ultramarine or indigo, she remembered Celia asking. Who cared?

Her attention was caught by a flicker of light on the other side of the terrace. Someone sitting on one of the wicker seats under the pergola had just lit a cigarette. In the soft light shed from the sitting room window, there was something very familiar about the person's shape and manner. Terri walked slowly across the terrace.

'I thought you'd given up smoking,' she remarked mildly as she drew near.

'I have,' said Luc, looking up at her.

'May I join you?'

'*Je t'en prie.*'

Terri eased herself onto a seat next to him and put the glass of wine on the table.

'I thought you didn't like drinking too much,' he said.

'I don't.'

They sat in silence.

'I've been wanting to talk to you so much,' said Terri eventually.

'About what?'

'Oh…lots of things. Why are you sitting here?'

'Because I was hoping to see you.'

'I don't know why. After all the things I said, I didn't think you'd ever speak to me again.' She paused, searching to meet his eyes. 'I'm sorry Luc. I should have trusted you. I didn't even give you a chance to explain.'

He drew on the cigarette and exhaled slowly. 'I could have tried harder. And the truth is…' He paused, flicking her an apologetic glance. '…I was tempted by Grace's offer. More tempted than I was prepared to admit to myself. That's why I reacted so violently to your accusation. I was embarrassed. All those notes… I told myself it was just for my interest, for how the story might shape. And it would have made a great story. It's hard to break old habits.'

He looked at the cigarette reproachfully then threw the butt onto the ground and trod it down.

'Grace told me how you rejected her offer,' said Terri.

'Did she?' He grinned. 'She's used to getting her own way. She was cross; that gave me some pleasure.' The smile faded. 'I saw you with Angela.'

He nodded towards the sitting room window. With the curtains open and the table lamp on at the back of the room, the figures inside were clearly visible. Peter stood, rooted to the spot, while Angela either paced up and down, or stood

350

facing him. Terri took a drink of wine then put the glass down on the table.

'I couldn't hear the words but I didn't like the look of Angela,' said Luc. 'Was she threatening you?'

'Not really…though she did have a knife.'

'*Merde*, I didn't see that or I'd have come in. What was that all about?'

'She'd just trashed the portrait with it. I was too pumped up to be scared.' She sighed. 'I think it would have been better if I'd never come here. They were happy before.' She shrugged. 'Or at least not unhappy. Look at them now.'

Luc reached across, picked up her glass and took a drink.

'What are you blaming yourself for?' he enquired.

Terri took the glass off him and drank another mouthful of wine. She handed the glass back.

'I opened Pandora's Box,' she said lugubriously. 'I persuaded myself I had a right to know, that it was all about my mother.' She paused. 'I found Josie's last diary.' She told him the whole story about Basma and Angela and how Peter had overheard it all. 'I don't know if I would ever have said anything if Angela hadn't challenged me like that.'

She took the glass again and had another sip of wine.

'It would have come out some time. Peter had a right to know.'

'Yes, but did he want to know? Sami didn't think so.' She automatically glanced towards the garden. 'Basma said Sami was so protective of Peter. He thought Peter was happier not knowing what his wife was up to. But to let Josephine be blamed like that?' She frowned, put the glass down and tipped her head back to look up at the stars.

'Peter probably wouldn't have believed Sami even if he'd told him.'

'I suppose not,' she said vaguely. 'You know, I reckon Van Gogh would have loved a night like this.'

'Mm.' He paused. 'I wasn't completely honest about the weekend I was away.'

She forgot the stars and looked back at him, frowning. 'What do you mean?'

'I did go to see *maman* in Paris. But then I went on to London. I know someone who works at one of the art colleges. I persuaded her to make some enquiries and find out where Josie went. And she did; and she knows a teacher from that college too. But I'm not sure you'll want to know what I found out.'

'Why not?'

'I'm afraid you're not Josephine's daughter.'

It was like having a bucket of cold water thrown over her: sudden, shocking, taking her breath away. She took a moment to let it sink in, then leaned forward. 'How can you be so sure?'

'Because the teacher now at that college was a student in the same year as Josie: her name's Kate Nayland. I spoke to her. Your mother was a year older and went to a different college but bunches of art students used to hang out in the same places and she knew her quite well. Anyway, Kate was friendly with Josie and was still in touch with her until a few years ago. Apparently, she lives in Australia now. She lost that first baby she was carrying but she's had a family since then.'

Terri was silent, trying to process this new information. She felt a twisting pain inside, hard to identify, harder still to understand, then a hollowed out feeling of emptiness.

'You're disappointed?' said Luc.

'I don't know. Yes. Yes, I am.' She nodded, frowning. 'Yes. I felt I sort of knew Josie and I thought…well, you

352

know…' She shrugged, sat back, offered a weak smile. 'But I'm glad she's still alive.'

'Are you going to drink that?' Luc indicated the wine glass on the table. Terri shook her head and he picked it up and finished the last mouthful.

'So this Kate…' said Terri. 'She was a friend of my mother's then?'

'At one time. She said they'd drifted apart. I sensed maybe a falling out. But I explained how you wanted to learn more about her and she said she'd be happy to talk to you…if you'd like that. Apparently your mother was a loner and a bit of a troubled woman. Her family wanted to emigrate to Australia when she was a teenager and she didn't want to go. There was a big row and she left home. The family carried on with the emigration. I'm not sure she saw them again. She struggled to come to terms with it. Anyway, I can give you Kate's number. She can tell you more.'

'Right…thanks.'

'You don't sound that pleased. Won't it be good to at least know?'

'Yes, yes. It's just…' She fiddled with a leaf that had fallen on the table. 'I'm absurdly nervous. Isn't that daft? I'm maybe scared of what I'll find out. But no, it's good. I'll give her a call some time. Thank you.'

The terrace was plunged into sudden darkness as the light in the sitting room was put out.

'I think it's time for bed,' said Luc.

'I need a cup of tea.'

Luc laughed, shaking his head. 'Of course you do. OK, I'll make you some tea. Just to show how much I care.'

Chapter 23

Peter was taken ill in the night. By the time Terri returned from the *bergerie* around one o'clock the next afternoon, he had been taken to hospital. She found Corinne in the kitchen, come in specially to clear up the debris from the party and, glad to have someone to tell, the *bonne* quickly passed on the little she knew. Apparently Peter had felt sick and had suffered chest and arm pains. Reluctantly he had finally called the doctor who had arranged for him to be admitted. Angela was gone too; she had already packed her bags and had left to stay with a friend.

'They're separating,' Corinne said. 'Angela will come back some time to get the rest of her things.'

'How do you know?'

'Celia was here.' Corinne rolled her eyes. '*Monsieur* Stedding spoke to her before he left.'

'Is he going to be all right?' said Terri.

Corinne shrugged and pulled a face. 'Who knows? He abuses himself. This was waiting to happen.'

'Does Lindsey know?'

'Yes. Celia contacted her. She was going to the hospital, I think.' Corinne gave Terri a penetrating look. 'So tell me what went on here last night. That picture in the sitting room is in a terrible state.'

'Yes, I know. I'll take it down to the studio.' Terri was unwilling to elaborate. 'I've been with Luc,' she added. 'I don't know everything that went on.' She wandered back out of the kitchen, only too aware of Corinne's dark, sceptical eyes on her back.

In the sitting room the portrait of Madeleine, a sad testament to the passions of the night before, still hung on the wall. Terri lifted it carefully from its place and examined the tears. It was badly damaged but she thought a good conservator might be able to do something with it. She left it propped up against the wall, went through to her rooms to change, then hung around the house, unsure what to do and unable to settle. Should she go to the hospital? Would they even let her see Peter? But Lindsey was there with him so Terri thought she'd feel like an interloper. He'd want family around him at this time and she had no such claim now.

She took the portrait down to the studio, left it in her old office and returned to the house. Corinne was ready to go home.

'There's food in the fridge left over from last night if anyone wants it,' she said. 'Are you still leaving tomorrow?'

'Possibly. I'm not sure.'

Corinne insisted on hugging her and air-kissing both cheeks. 'In case you go,' she said. 'And stay in touch, yes?'

Terri was left alone. She tried to finish her packing, putting things in bags, endlessly rearranging them, her thoughts elsewhere. Regardless of Corinne's opinion of the state of Peter's health, she felt culpable: he was ill because she had brought this situation about. If he didn't recover she thought she would never forgive herself. She wished she could stay. At least she'd like to be around long enough to be sure that he was going to be all right. And of course she thought of

Luc; she had arranged to see him again for what was supposed to be her final evening at Le Chant.

As it turned out, she didn't have too long to wait. Just after five, there was the sound of the front door opening and closing, then voices. Sure that one of them was Peter's, Terri hesitated, then went to investigate. He had discharged himself from hospital and arranged his own transport home. She was in time to see him disappearing up the stairs to his bedroom, pale and a little more stooped than usual. Lindsey, who had accompanied him back from the hospital, went into the kitchen to make him a drink and Terri followed her.

'How is he?' she pressed.

Lindsey sighed as she filled the kettle. 'He's my father. How do you think he is? I've no idea. He says he feels better. He's had some tests and they've taken blood samples to do more. So far they haven't found anything wrong with him except his blood pressure's up. But, God knows, that's not unusual. They've given him some tablets and he's booked in for some scan or other – on Tuesday. But he insisted he was well enough to come home. '*I'm not going to spend the night here.*' So he signed himself out. Now he's supposed to rest. Huh. Fat chance of that. And he was given a load of advice about his diet and drinking. He won't pay any attention to that either.' She fixed Terri with a resigned look. 'Can you imagine him drinking decaffeinated coffee and no whisky?'

Terri shook her head.

'Neither can I.' The kettle boiled and Lindsey made a pot of tea. 'I told him to go to bed. He wasn't keen. The trouble is he gets bored. Maybe you should come up to see him. Perhaps he'll listen to you.'

'Me? No way.'

356

'He might. At least your company might help distract him a bit. Please?'

'If you don't think I'll make him worse?'

'Nah. You can give me a break. I've had him all day.'

Peter was lying on top of his bed, propped up with pillows, wearing a red satin dressing gown tied loosely at the waist. With the remote pointed accusingly at the television screen, he was flicking channels peevishly. His head turned as Lindsey appeared bearing a tray with a cup of tea and some crackers.

'Tea. Good. I don't know what they call it in that place but it certainly isn't tea. Thank you Lindsey.' He stared at the tray as she put it down on the bedside cabinet and his nose wrinkled in disgust. 'Crackers?'

'The doctor said you should avoid anything heavy.'

Peter grunted. Then he saw Terri, hovering uncertainly in the doorway.

'Terri. Come in, come in. Sit down.'

Lindsey slipped out and Terri moved forward. There was a small padded chair against the wall and she brought it over to place by the bed.

'So you're feeling better?' she said.

'I'm fine. Should never have rung the doctor. He fussed.'

She nodded. He was abnormally pale but there was still a familiar glint in his eye which was faintly reassuring.

'If you'd like to be left alone…' she began.

'Nonsense. I've got things I want to talk about with you. Don't you dare leave me.'

'I don't think this is the best time to talk.'

'If you think I'll rest without saying what I want to say, you're wrong. And you're supposed to be leaving tomorrow. That's one of the things I want to talk about.'

'Peter, I think I should tell you…'

'Ssh. I'd like you to stay on a bit longer. Would you do that? *Can* you do that?'

'Yes, I'd like to but…'

'Good. I think we all need to draw breath. And I'd like you around for a while. Also, there's a proposition I wanted to put to you.' He stopped suddenly, as if the talking had exhausted him.

'Peter, I must tell you: Josie was not my mother.'

Terri wanted to tell him before he started making plans for her but it came out too abruptly and she searched his face anxiously, concerned what effect it would have on him. He was frowning at her.

'How do you know?'

She hesitated. Was this the time to be telling him this? But really, she had no choice.

'Luc has found someone – a woman called Kate - who knew both my mother and Josephine in London. They were definitely two different people.' She paused, giving him time to assimilate this. 'But Kate saw Josie after she ran away from here. And later on, apparently, Josie moved to Australia and, as far as Kate knows, she's still there and she's got a family.'

'She's alive?'

'Yes. They'd been exchanging Christmas cards until three years ago. Josie moved house. There was a mix-up with addresses and they lost touch. But, if you want, sometime, I could help you track her down.'

Peter's expression had frozen.

'Are you all right Peter?'

'Yes, yes, I'm all right. I'm fine.' He nodded repeatedly, staring into the distance. 'I can't believe it. That's wonderful. But she…she probably wouldn't speak to me. I mean, why would she? After all I said…' His gaze shifted to Terri's face, eyes puckered with concern. 'She'd probably not want me near her.'

'You could write her a letter first. Tell her how you feel about everything. Then it'd be up to her to decide.'

'Yes, yes, I could do that. Good idea. Apologise…try to say…mm. Yes. Yes, that would be the way to do it.' He tried a smile. 'Australia eh? Well, well, Australia. Who'd have thought it? But I'm glad. I can't tell you how glad.'

'I think you should rest now.' She stood up and turned to go.

'You haven't heard my proposition.'

Terri turned back, surprised. She'd thought the proposition was something to do with her being 'family'.

'I was wondering what you'd think about writing a book about me.' He raised a quizzical eyebrow. 'Of course I realise I'm not Rembrandt or Reynolds so you'd be compromising yourself somewhat.' He screwed up his face and sucked his teeth. 'There have been a couple of books written about me – all absolute drivel, of course. You might make a better fist of it…considering. Edited highlights only of course. What do you think?'

She smiled. 'It'd be a challenge.'

'Yes, wouldn't it? I thought that. For both of us. But I'm getting old. Now is the time, I think.'

'We could probably work something out…if you don't argue too much.'

Peter grunted and Terri walked to the door.

'By the way, Terri?'

She stopped and looked round.

'I daresay you've heard that Angela has gone. I'm going to make sure she's set up. She's Lindsey's mother…you understand? But I haven't told Lindsey what happened and I insist no-one else does either.' He sat forward suddenly, his face white and pinched. 'Oh my God, the portrait's still there in the sitting room…'

'No, it's not. I've taken it down to the studio.'

He leaned back and took a long breath, exhaling slowly. 'Lindsey may not be my biological daughter. I don't know and I don't care. She can live with her mother or she can stay here or live with Thierry. She can do whatever she likes. But as far as she is concerned, we have parted amicably because we've grown apart.'

'I understand. I've said nothing.'

'Good.' He looked drained now. A spot of unnatural colour had formed on each cheek. He turned his head away and closed his eyes. A moment later she saw his breathing slow and he twitched a little in his sleep. His colour settled.

Terri slipped out and went downstairs. At some point she would have to admit to exploring Madeleine's studio, to finding Josie's diaries and to hiding the portrait of Tom, but now wasn't the time. She wished he hadn't been so quick to discharge himself from hospital.

*

In the kitchen, Terri found Celia, sitting at the table with a plate of party leftovers: quiche, tapenade and toast, chicken, *saucisson sec* and assorted salads.

'Lindsey said Peter's home,' said Celia. 'How is he?'

'He's sleeping now but he looks exhausted. I hope he's going to be all right.'

'Don't worry. He's done this before you know - got worked up and had a turn. Tough as old boots is Peter. A bit

360

of rest; he'll rally.' Celia picked up a piece of the sausage and bit into it. 'Angela's gone, you know.'

'Yes.'

'And we have to pretend that it's all a friendly arrangement for Lindsey's benefit. Though since it happened rather suddenly I imagine our Lindsey will think that a little suspicious, don't you?'

'I'm sure Peter has made it sound plausible. Or maybe she'll believe what she wants to believe.'

'We all do.' Celia finished the sausage. 'Have you eaten dear?'

'I'm having dinner with Luc later.'

'Well, aren't you the lucky one. Still, have one of these little tarts.' Celia examined them. 'They're courgette and goat's cheese, I think.'

Terri took one and sat down at the table.

'It'll do Lindsey good to have you around for a bit,' said Celia. 'Peter too. He pretends he doesn't need anybody but of course he's useless by himself.'

'How did you know that I was going to stay on?'

'I didn't. Seemed likely though. Family needs to stick together at a time like this.'

'I'm not family, Celia. I've found out. Josie wasn't my mother. I've just told Peter.'

'Really? Oh well never mind.' Celia looked unmoved. 'Family is as family does. Does this chicken wing smell funny to you?'

She held it out to Terri who sniffed at it, pulled a face and drew back, nodding.

'Why did you think I was related in the first place?' she asked.

Celia picked up a baby tomato and popped it in her mouth. She chewed for a minute and swallowed.

'I tried to track Josephine down after she'd gone. I even went to London in hopes of finding her. The RA exhibition was on too so that was convenient. Anyway I couldn't find her – any friends I could find were keeping mum. So I came home but I kept buying newspapers, French, British, just in case. I *knew* Josie wouldn't have killed herself.'

'But Angela said she left a suicide note.'

'She simply left a note saying she couldn't stand it here any longer. She didn't say she was going to end it all. Angela told the story she wanted to believe. Anyway Josie was artistic so I paid attention to the art press. Then it occurred to me a few years ago that her child might work in the art world too, given the family it came from. One day I saw your photograph with an article about you and I was struck by the eyes.'

'But Celia, I'm not...'

'But you've got her eyes dear. And you were the right age.'

'Co-incidence,' said Terri flatly.

'Yes. Isn't that funny? Life is full of them though isn't it? But then Peter had his accident and I thought it was a great opportunity.'

'But how could you be sure I'd come? Or that Peter wouldn't give the job to someone else?'

'I couldn't. But I asked around – I still know a few people in London – and I knew you were at the end of a contract. And as for Peter.' Celia grinned. 'I manipulated him a little bit. He wasn't feeling too well, poor dear, and he's no good with computers and printers at the best of times. I offered to do it for him but I only sent out a couple of adverts, you see. Then I went through the applications with him, told him I'd already set aside the ones who couldn't start immediately. I didn't push too hard – you know how stubborn he can be – but fortunately he remembered that exhibition you'd curated so he offered it to you. He insisted on dictating the letter. Then it was up to fate. If you were meant to come, you would.' She picked up a gherkin and studied it dispassionately. 'I'm a great believer in fate.'

'Well, you were right about Josephine: she didn't kill herself.' Terri explained where she was.

Celia stopped eating and looked up.

'Australia? Well, I never thought of that.' She smiled. 'Good for her.' She picked up the last piece of sausage on her plate and waved it vaguely at Terri. 'Still, I'm sorry you're not *exactly* related. You'll have to adopt us.' She shrugged and bit into the meat. 'If you think you could cope with us,' she added, a couple of minutes later.

*

Terri wandered back to her room and slowly unpacked her case. She came across the Indian art book and ran a finger over the smooth, glossy surface of the dust jacket, then sat down and slowly turned the pages once more. Hunting scenes and animals, deities, family gatherings, portraits - a huge range of vivid, colourful images. She remembered her father showing her the pictures when she was still too young to read the complex text, explaining the symbolism to her, dwelling on the portraits, describing how the best portrait painters always capture the character of their subjects. He'd done it with other books too. Was that how she'd first developed an interest in portraiture? Probably. She lingered over an eighteenth century portrait, the man's finely drawn face in profile and keenly

363

expressive. Her father's passion for his work and for art in general had been the centre of his existence. Consciously or unconsciously, he had passed it on to her. She couldn't deny it; it was in her blood.

How she missed him. There were so many things she'd like to tell him. Silly things mostly, like…how the wind in the trees really did sometimes sound like a song; or what amazing aniseed bread they made here; or…how Provence was just like all the paintings she'd ever seen, only more so somehow: more intense, more concentrated, an assault on every sense. Because it was only since finding his note on the catalogue in London that she'd realised he might have wanted to know what she thought about anything. And she'd have told him about Peter too, the grandfather who wasn't, and Luc… What would she have told him about Luc? She wasn't sure yet.

All that time she'd spent blaming her father for her mother leaving, and then resenting him for not caring that she'd gone. What a waste. Of course, he'd made it difficult - he was hardly without blame - but she thought she could have made an effort when she'd grown up, tried to get to know him better. She should have got past it years ago. So many missed opportunities; so many regrets.

Her thoughts flicked back to Peter, then to Celia. Not *exactly* related. After all that angst and self-examination, no-one seemed to care that she wasn't a blood relative after all. The Stedding family was a confusion of love and heartache, discord and silence, feuds and devotion, and yet they managed somehow. They'd even get over Angela eventually. And Luc's family wasn't much better. Terri used to think it was only her family that was abnormal, fractured; it had made her insular and defensive. She'd been a fool and it had taken her long enough to work it out. No-one's family was perfect. It was a matter of muddling your way through it, loving where you could, letting the bad things go.

So maybe Kate Nayland would tell her something about her mother which she could relate to, or maybe not. She was going to try not to care so much. Maybe it was time to start concentrating on the here and now and stop letting the past colour her present.

She closed the book but continued to hold it, still, thinking. Eventually she put it down. It was time to go and meet Luc - but not before she'd slipped upstairs to check on Peter.

Note

The Ste. Marguérite des Pins of my story does not exist: it is a composite of a number of small towns and villages I have visited over the years in Provence. But I hope it captures the atmosphere of this truly special region, its colours and its perfumes, its architecture and its staggeringly beautiful views of forests, olive groves and vineyards. If you visit the area yourself, you will not be able to identify the street or café, but still I hope this story will help to make you feel as if you know it.

Acknowledgements

I should like to express my heartfelt gratitude to family and friends for all their support through the writing of this book. A particular thanks go to two kind and patient friends, both coincidentally called Jane, who took the trouble to read an early draft and offer their opinions.

Thanks also go to Design for Writers for the wonderful cover design, and for their untiring patience with my endless questions.

Last but not least, I should like to thank my husband, Dave, whose belief in my writing and my stories is fortunately greater than my own, and who keeps me going when the doubts shout too loudly.

Deep Water, Thin Ice

Kathy Shuker

When her husband - a flamboyant conductor - kills himself, Alex is mortified that she failed to see it coming. Confused, guilt-ridden and grieving, she runs away to Hillen Hall, an old house by the sea in Devon, abandoning her classical singing career and distancing herself from everyone but her sister Erica.

Hillen Hall, inherited by Simon from his mother and once a fine manor house, is now creaking and unloved. When Theo Hellyon, Simon's cousin, turns up at her door offering to help with its renovation, Alex is perplexed and intrigued, previously unaware that Simon even had a cousin. And Theo is charming and attentive and reminds her strikingly of Simon so, despite Erica's warnings, it is impossible not to want him in her life.

But the old hall has a tortured history which Alex cannot even begin to suspect and Theo is not remotely what he seems. So how long will it be before Alex realises she's making a fatal mistake?

Some reader reviews:

'...*hard to put down*'

'...*sorry to get to the last page*'

'...*fine attention to detail brings the characters & their surroundings to life*'

'...*an intriguing and engaging plot...I loved every minute of it*'

Available now

Lightning Source UK Ltd.
Milton Keynes UK
UKOW01f2230280917
310070UK00006B/287/P